PRAISE I

If You A

"A gracefully crafted tribute to searching for the right answer—and to finally realizing that sometimes it doesn't exist. *If You Ask Me* is a heart-mending tale about the importance of being our authentic selves, and the joys to be found in embracing our vulnerability. Equal parts funny and moving, Violet's messy, hopeful journey and her beautiful romance will resonate with everyone who struggles with the unexpected twists and turns of life. Libby Hubscher is a master at creating compelling, relatable characters and heartwarming, emotional stories. I cannot wait for her next book!"

—*New York Times* bestselling author Ali Hazelwood

"I gasped, I ground my teeth, and I cheered along with Violet as she gathered the smashed pieces of her life and used them to build something better than before."

—National bestselling author Jesse Q. Sutanto

"Full of southern charm and self-discovery. Libby Hubscher brings a light touch to heavy emotions in this witty novel about starting over in life and in love."

—*New York Times* bestselling author Virginia Kantra

"A funny, feminist, feel-good novel about making mistakes, asking for advice, and writing your own happy ending. I laughed and I cried—this novel is an absolute joy!"

—Freya Sampson, author of *The Lost Ticket*

PRAISE FOR

Meet Me in Paradise

"A beautifully moving mix of self-discovery, sister bonds, and slow-burning romance that's 100 percent pure pleasure!"
—*USA Today* bestselling author Priscilla Oliveras

"*Meet Me in Paradise* is such a compelling read! By turns heartwarming and heartbreaking. Libby Hubscher truly takes us on a journey as Marin learns to find happiness on her own terms. Her adventures are brought so vividly to life that I want to start a #ProjectParadise of my own!"
—*USA Today* bestselling author Jen DeLuca

"*Meet Me in Paradise* is a stunning tale of love, loss, and the capacity for wonder. Marin's adventure will touch anyone who has ever felt adrift in a sea of responsibility and decided to swim toward the shore. Hubscher expertly crafts a delicious blend of humor, whimsy, and raw emotion that left me laughing, crying, and unable to put it down."
—Denise Williams, author of *How to Fail at Flirting*

"Both a romantic escape and an ode to sisterhood, *Meet Me in Paradise* made me swoon, laugh, and then sneaked up on me and made me cry. Marin and Sadie are the beating heart of this story—I adored them in all their wild, wonderful messiness. A radiantly hopeful book."
—*New York Times* bestselling author Rachel Lynn Solomon

"*Meet Me in Paradise* will sweep you off your feet. Marin's leap into the unknown is full of love, romance, and adventure, and I felt like I was right there with her on the pristine beaches of Saba as she climbs mountains, dives for pearls, and learns how to open herself up to the possibilities of love."

—Sonya Lalli, author of *Serena Singh Flips the Script*

"Hubscher's debut novel is the perfect book for anyone longing for family, travel, and romance. Prepare for some tears mixed with the happy-ever-afters." —*Library Journal*

"A poignant, emotionally authentic story of sisterly bonds and unexpected love. . . . This is sure to tug at readers' heartstrings."

—*Publishers Weekly* (starred review)

"Debuting author Hubscher gently weaves in the more somber story lines, so readers aren't blindsided yet will still feel the full emotional impact. The romance blooms beautifully, and while there are several complex and endearing secondary characters, this is primarily Marin's story told mostly through her own captivating narrative. Tissues should be on hand."

—*Booklist*

"Not simply a breezy romantic comedy, *Meet Me in Paradise* captures the duality of life's highs and lows. This romantic comedy offers tropical vacation mishaps, a burgeoning romance, and an undercurrent of heartbreak." —Shelf Awareness

Hubscher, Libby, author.
Play for me

2023
33305257523732
ca   06/20/23

Play for Me

Libby Hubscher

Berkley Romance
New York

BERKLEY ROMANCE
Published by Berkley
An imprint of Penguin Random House LLC
penguinrandomhouse.com

Copyright © 2023 by Elizabeth Hubscher
Readers Guide copyright © 2023 by Elizabeth Hubscher
Excerpt by Libby Hubscher copyright © 2023 by Elizabeth Hubscher
Penguin Random House supports copyright. Copyright fuels creativity, encourages
diverse voices, promotes free speech, and creates a vibrant culture. Thank you for buying an
authorized edition of this book and for complying with copyright laws by not reproducing,
scanning, or distributing any part of it in any form without permission. You are supporting
writers and allowing Penguin Random House to continue to publish books for every reader.

BERKLEY and the BERKLEY and B colophon are registered trademarks
of Penguin Random House LLC.

Library of Congress Cataloging-in-Publication Data

Names: Hubscher, Libby, author.
Title: Play for me / Libby Hubscher.
Description: First edition. | New York: Berkley Romance, 2023.
Identifiers: LCCN 2022051570 | ISBN 9780593547229 (trade paperback) |
ISBN 9780593547236 (ebook)
Classification: LCC PS3608.U2524 P53 2023 | DDC 813/.6—dc23
LC record available at https://lccn.loc.gov/2022051570

First Edition: June 2023

Printed in the United States of America
1st Printing

Book design by Laura K. Corless

This is a work of fiction. Names, characters, places, and incidents either are the product of
the author's imagination or are used fictitiously, and any resemblance to actual persons,
living or dead, business establishments, events, or locales is entirely coincidental.

To anyone who is having the worst day of their life—
here's hoping it leads you to something better than
you could have ever imagined, or at least
a very fun roommate situation

And to Kate, the best friend and high school roommate
a person could ask for

Other than my dad, I love three things more than life itself: baseball, the fine city of Boston, and cannoli from Vitales . . . not necessarily in that order. Anybody who tries to take them away from me will have to pry them out of my cold dead hands.

—Sophie Doyle, head trainer of the Boston Red Sox
and first woman trainer in the MLB

Dein Schicksal ist die Musik, die du in deinem Herzen hörst; Sie haben keine andere Wahl, als mitzuspielen. Und wenn es aufhört, ist es vorbei.

Your destiny is the music you hear in your heart; you have no choice but to play along. And when it stops, it's over.

—Jonas Voss, pianist, Berliner Philharmoniker

Chapter 1

I lost everything I loved in the span of twenty-four hours. Well, nearly everything, since Dad was still safely tucked away in Sommerset Meadows, but that's a different story. Heartbreak comes in all forms.

For me, baseball went first.

My home in Boston and cannoli from Vitales in the North End quickly followed.

I was eating my feelings in the form of a chocolate chip cannoli when a man holding a sheet cake paused to look me over, and upon recognizing me, he promptly spit in my face. He was wearing an autographed Big Papi jersey and an expression that can only be described as murderous. They say hell hath no fury like a woman scorned . . . well, a woman scorned has nothing on a Red Sox fan who just stumbled upon the trainer responsible for ruining the team's World Series run stuffing her face with pastry.

"That's for benching Iwasaki!" he hollered. "You cost us the series!"

The rabid fan couldn't have known that only two hours

earlier I'd been forced to resign in front of a room full of middle-aged men in ill-fitting polo shirts. He wouldn't have seen me sitting on the T next to a cardboard box full of my things, willing myself not to cry. And he definitely had no earthly notion that I'd arrived home to find the rest of my worldly possessions packed away in a matching luggage set my boyfriend, Patrick, had originally bought for me to use on our trip to Zurich in January. As the team doctor, he hadn't taken kindly to me calling his medical judgment into question. He'd carved me out of our shared brownstone and his life with speed and surgical precision.

I didn't fault any of them for being angry, even this guy. I was a Red Sox fan, after all, one who grew up watching every home game while my dad worked as a custodian in Fenway; the agony of defeat had rocked me to my core more than once. But I wasn't at my best, and my cheek was damp with spittle, which is probably why I exploded out of my chair, knocked the cake box out of the man's hand, and smashed my half-eaten cannoli into his face.

"I'd do it again!" I yelled. Cake splattered on the floor around us. It was completely out of character—the aggression, I mean, not the thing that had brought me to that moment; still, I meant what I said. At only twenty-two, Iwasaki was already the kind of pitcher that comes along once every hundred years. He'd had an ulnar collateral ligament sprain that the medical team had been treating with stem cells and plasma injections, but his body wasn't ready. I could see it in his face, the way he grimaced and guarded his arm when no one else was looking. Just hours before the game, he'd been drenched with sweat after throwing a couple of easy pitches.

"How bad is it?" I'd asked him.

He'd shaken his head. "Not bad," he'd said. "Just nerves." As if the league's best pitcher had ever been that nervous a day in his life. I gave him a look. "I'm good," he lied.

What ensued was a series of fights with what felt like everyone in the organization from Patrick to the GM, but in the end Iwasaki went back on the injured list, and I went on a list too—one that started with "black" and ended with "balled."

"It'll be fine," I'd assured everyone. "Morano is one hundred percent and he's looking great."

The backup pitcher, Morano, was solid. The pitching coach agreed, and everyone conceded; no problem, I thought. I am an optimist.

Morano choked. Epically.

The Phillies hadn't just beaten us; they'd humiliated us in Fenway Park.

The man who'd been on the receiving end of my cannoli was screaming, a strangled animal sound. Espresso cups stilled. Around us, the bakery patrons fell silent. There were no shouting spectators here egging us on. A woman with a small child cowered, shielding the toddler with her body. The worker behind the counter who had winked at me when he handed over my food now picked up a phone to make a call. I retreated, accidentally placing my shoe directly in the middle of a chunk of cake. I slipped on the mass of buttercream and nearly fell. Frantically, my arms windmilled, and I grabbed for anything to keep myself upright. I caught the man's shirt; a button popped off and thwacked against my forehead.

I looked up. The man's screaming ceased. He reached up and wiped the cream from his face. A glop of frosting landed in my hair—pale white against my deep red waves. I had a sudden, sickening realization that there was no team behind me, ready to get in the mix, and there never would be again. I was on my own, and my life in baseball—and at my favorite bakery—was over.

There's no bullpen in the North End, no dugout to cool off in, and since, as I learned later, the delectable flaky pastry scratched the man's cornea, I spent the better part of the afternoon in a holding cell in the Boston district A-1 police station.

I was braiding my hair and trying to figure out how I was going to tell my dad about my fall from grace when my best friend, Astrid, appeared, looking like a cross between a blonde bombshell with a foul mouth and a glorious angel. She was wearing oversized black sunglasses, ripped high-waisted jeans, and a tube top with puffed sleeves that revealed her pale midriff. She might have been the only person over the age of thirty who could pull a look like that off. Astrid was warm and disarming, and at the sight of her, relief pooled in me and that feeling of utter loneliness dissipated.

She tossed her blonde waves over her shoulder and removed her sunglasses.

"Sophie, in all of our years of friendship, I never once envisioned having to bail you out of jail," she said, tucking the glasses into her purse. "I feel like we've reached a whole new level of closeness."

"Thank you for coming." I smiled; I couldn't help it.

A cop unlocked the door and gestured for me to get out with a quick jerk of her head.

"It better be a good story," Astrid said, folding me in her long arms. "Was it a pervert? I love it when a perv gets what's coming to him."

I grimaced. "I *was* defending my honor. Sort of." I eyed the room. From the glares I was getting, the police were also Red Sox fans. It was Dunkin' Donuts with a side of dirty looks in there. "I didn't mean to hurt him."

"Let's get you out of here," Astrid said. "I know everyone loves Iwasaki, but geez." She raised her voice. "It's just a game."

"Astrid, shhh. Don't antagonize them." She slung one arm around my shoulders and together we speed-walked toward the exit.

"So, where to?" Astrid asked once we were outside beneath the old blue station sign, standing in the shadow of the brick behemoth. "Home?"

"About that . . . Patrick's pretty mad." I glanced up at the brick building. The architect must've had a mandate to put in as few windows as possible.

Astrid's eyes narrowed. "How mad?"

"'I can't be with someone who would question me at work. It's over' mad. At least that's what he wrote in his note."

"Wait, you haven't talked to him? He left a note?"

"It was taped to my suitcase."

"You've been together for what . . . four years? I know you said things had kind of cooled off a bit, but that's beyond cold. Okay, well . . . I never liked him anyway. His nurse was an extra with me on *ShadowWorld* back in March and she said he's a dick to all the office staff."

"You're just telling me this now?"

"Yeah, game night's been wicked awkward."

Astrid was trying to cheer me up, so I obliged her, but the laugh I managed to conjure was paper-thin. My stomach swirled. I wasn't sure whether I was going to burst into tears or throw up, but some kind of dramatic emotion was threatening to surface.

"Could I stay with you for a bit?" I asked.

"I would love to be your roommate again, Soph, but I'm headed to Toronto in two days for that film I told you about. Since I'll be gone for a while, I sublet the place to a family of four. You should see the baby. Cheeks for days. Anyway, you can crash until they arrive on Thursday, but after that, you'll have to figure something else out."

"Okay, no problem. Two days is fine. It's great, actually. I'm sure I can figure out something. How hard could it be to find a new place and a new job, right? I mean, this is Boston, the land of opportunity."

Astrid wrinkled her nose. "Especially now that you've been fired and charged with assault."

"I don't think I was actually charged. It's all kind of a blur."

"I think I know exactly what this situation calls for," Astrid said.

I peeked up at her. "You do?"

"Yup, I do. I'm going to feed you and get you really drunk."

"Seriously? I don't think that's the best idea."

"Good thing I'm in charge now, because you need to drown your sorrows, and I do my most optimal thinking when I'm hammered."

I opened my mouth to argue, but Astrid's legs were longer than mine, and she was already several steps ahead of me. "Let's go, Cannoli Kid," she called over her shoulder. "I promise you, by the time I leave for Toronto, we'll have this sorted out."

Astrid's ideas for sorting things out were generally questionable, even in the best of times. But lobster rolls from Neptune Oyster and unlimited Sam Adams Porch Rocker in Astrid's rooftop garden with a view of the Charles River felt like an inspired choice, even if she'd claimed to have selected lobster rolls because they were soft, in case my temper flared again. It was a beautiful evening: we couldn't see the stars, but the lights of our beloved city twinkled and the air turned cooler. The beer and the buttery lobster smoothed out the rough edges of my horrible day.

Astrid leaned forward in her lounge chair. "What about another team?" she said. "The Lowell Spinners, maybe?"

I shook my head. "The Spinners have Ricky Phillips as their trainer and he's fantastic. Besides, there's no point deluding myself; I'm tainted goods right now. A job in pro baseball isn't going to happen. At least not until everyone forgets about this—*if* they forget—or some kind of miracle takes place."

"It's such bullshit," Astrid said, slamming her beer down. "You said if he pitched he probably would have blown out his elbow completely. You were just doing your job. It's not your fault Morano had a bad night. Did they fire *him*?"

"I see the point you're trying to make and I love you for it, but I'm sure Morano's getting his fair share of abuse right now. And it happens. The pressure he was under was immense. Everyone forgets that, at the end of the day, athletes are people too." I pulled at the label on my bottle.

"I know! Morano is *definitely* a person. A fine person. I enjoyed watching him wind up for every terrible pitch he threw last night," Astrid said, mischief twinkling in her gaze. "How about this? Maybe you could come to Toronto with me. I could be your sugar mommy."

I squinted at Astrid and took a long draw from my beer. "You are an angel, but you're not really my type."

She tossed her hair over her shoulder and batted her eyelashes. "I thought I was everyone's type."

"You're too beautiful."

"That's fair."

We opened new bottles and clinked them together, then fell into the kind of comfortable silence that only longtime friends can have.

"Besides, I can't leave Dad without a visitor for that long. But I do think you're onto something. It might be nice to get out of the city for a bit," I said. "A girl can only be spit on so many times before she needs a change of scene . . . and a new bakery. And by so many, I mean one. Once was one time too many. Plus, I'm pretty sure I'm banned from Vitales until the end of time. And the idea of running into Patrick at Trader Joe's is not appealing."

Astrid grabbed another lobster roll and took a bite.

"I've got it," she said, her mouth still half-full. I waited for her to swallow. "Where's the perfect place to hide away and reinvent yourself?"

"Is that supposed to mean something to me?"

Astrid narrowed her eyes.

I held my hands up. "Okay. I don't know, Vegas?"

"That's ridiculous. Vegas is where you go to see a Britney Spears concert and somehow wake up married and broke. No. The place you go to hide is New Hampshire."

"How many beers have you had?" I asked. "You go to New Hampshire to hike and buy stuff without sales tax. It's not exactly transformative."

"Not true. And also, not enough beers. But that's beside the point." She pulled out another bottle and used the side of the farmhouse table to thwack the cap off in one smooth and slightly vicious motion. "Remember how I got into some trouble junior year?"

"Yeah?" How could I forget? Astrid's parents went through a brutal divorce when she was sixteen, and her coping strategy had been her mother's painkillers and a pretty bad shoplifting habit, culminating in an actual chase through Faneuil Hall, of all places. Her parents had shipped her off to boarding school in New Hampshire for the rest of high school. At the time, I'd been devastated and braced myself for what were sure to be the loneliest two years of my life. About a month after she'd left, Dad let me borrow his car to meet her in Concord at Bread & Chocolate, and sitting across from her, I could see that she was happier and more herself than she'd been in a long time. So I was thankful, and content to count down the days until we could be roommates at college together.

While I'd been lost in memory, Astrid had fiddled with her phone. She thrust it in front of my face.

I squinted at the bright screen until the words *The Monadnock School* and a mountain scene came into focus. "The boarding school you went to? I'm not following."

"I donate a boatload of money every year to the theater department, so I get all the emails. I remember seeing one recently that said they had a position open for a trainer for the school year that's already underway."

"Isn't it an arts school?"

"They have sports teams. They're just not very good."

"'Not very good'? What does that mean?"

"They suck, okay, but that's not important. This is your answer."

"I feel like I'm missing something. How does a training job at a school in New Hampshire solve my problems?"

"Boarding school," Astrid corrected.

"And?"

"And everyone on staff at a boarding school gets housing, smart-ass." Astrid leaned back in the chair she was sitting in, a smug smile spreading across her face.

It took a few more beers before I was convinced. Astrid waxed poetic about how much she'd loved it there. The nature, the community, the fresh mountain air, the hours of therapy with the school's psychologist. It had changed her life, she said. She'd gotten clean, made a handful of lifelong friendships, and fostered her love of the arts, which had led her to her career. A really good career. The kind of career that got you a rooftop garden with the view we were currently enjoying. Acting was what Astrid was put on this earth to do. Kind of like me and working for the Red Sox.

God, Astrid was compelling. No wonder people loved seeing her on-screen. The way she spoke about the school, I started to wonder whether it might change my off-course life too. Also, truth be told, the beers were going down a little too easily, and since I'm not a big drinker to begin with, they were hitting pretty hard.

"I'm a distinguished alumna," Astrid said. Energized by the drinks, she had started dancing around her roof and was doing something that looked like a cross between a runway pose and an arabesque. "With me as a reference, you'd be a shoo-in."

"Okay," I replied, trying not to slur.

"Really?"

I nodded. "I'll do it. How do I apply?"

"I can just email them from my phone. They'll probably want your CV or something later."

I thought maybe that should wait until morning, but Astrid was already pecking away.

"I told you I could solve the problem!" she said, triumphant.

"I never doubted you for a minute."

I woke in the morning, sore from sleeping on a small love seat and sticky hot from the sun blazing over the edge of the rooftop, forcing me to to shield my eyes. The evening had been exactly what I needed to feel better about the state of things, save for the severe hangover I was going to have to nurse.

Across from me, Astrid was splayed out on a sectional, her hair fanned out around her like a halo, a single pool of drool at the corner of her mouth. My stomach grumbled.

"Hey, Astrid," I whispered. "Want a bagel sandwich? I can go get us Dunkin's."

She sat up. "Best roommate ever," she said. "I need an iced coffee. Extra cream, extra sugar. And I want bacon on my sandwich."

Her phone pinged and she looked at the screen. "Guess what, buttercup," she said, stifling a yawn. "The job is yours if you want it."

Did I want it? I didn't know. In the car, I pulled up the school's website on my phone. A glance at the athletic program page was enough to make me question what on earth I'd been thinking letting Astrid even plant this seed. But by the time I'd finished my breakfast, I was pretty sure I was going to take it despite my ambivalence. Things usually worked themselves out—maybe I could turn their lackluster athletic program into something special or take the opportunity to do some cool research that would put me back in the big leagues. Plus, there weren't any other viable options, unless I wanted to crash on the recliner in Dad's room at Sommerset Meadows. There was nothing left for me here. At least not now, not until I could stage some sort of comeback. I'd figure it out. I always did. In the meantime, fresh mountain air and a free apartment couldn't hurt, *and*—you gotta love a good silver lining—I was already packed.

Chapter 2

After I met with the head of school, a woman called Tabitha Worthington who was constantly moving during our entire ten-minute interaction, I followed a map she'd given me to my housing. The faculty apartment was on the third floor of a historic brick building called Sondheim. Music filled the stairwell: a strange cacophony of drums, string instruments, and the normal laughing and shouting one would expect when a bunch of high school students were in close proximity to each other. It was strangely soothing, I thought, akin to the normal soundtrack of a full training room post-practice.

I lugged my suitcases up the stairs, thankful that I'd always insisted on doing the same grueling workouts I put the team through *and* that I wasn't someone who owned a lot of stuff. As promised, the large oak door marked *3A* was unlocked, and I stumbled inside with my bags.

"Hello?" I called. The woman from the email, Mandy, had let me know that I would be sharing the apartment with other faculty members, but my new roommates didn't appear to be around. I did a slow turn to take in the room. The windows, which looked original, were massive, and light flooded the space. I let it wash over my face. On the drive up, I'd been convinced that this was quite possibly the stupidest idea of all time, but maybe Astrid hadn't been off base after all. Not only did I have housing, but it was *sun-drenched* housing. I could get used to this. I took my shoes off and placed them by the door next to a set of sneakers that were several sizes larger than mine. Beneath my feet, the hardwood floors were worn smooth. The white walls were trimmed in the same deep oak as the door. There was a smattering of books on a coffee table, and I dropped onto a somewhat worn leather sofa to take a look. You can tell a lot about a person by what they read. Take my dad, for example—he's a Grisham man. Smart, but not pretentious. Interesting. Passionate about sports. I flipped through a tattered copy of *Zen and the Art of Motorcycle Maintenance*, a legal thriller, and a book called *Red, White & Royal Blue* that looked intriguing and like something Astrid would love. Near the window, a giant Christmas cactus was overtaking a plant stand. Other than wanting a few personal touches, the apartment was warm and inviting. In the city, I would've never been able to afford something like this, and I started to think maybe my luck was changing.

I took my chances finding my room. I didn't want to start off by invading my new apartment-mates' personal space, but, fortunately for me, two of the bedroom doors were ajar. A quick glance into one room gave the impression a laundry bomb had exploded, and the other room featured a neatly made bed and enough computer equipment to start an electronics store. On the other side of the apartment, I found a single bathroom with two stalls, two sinks, and a single shower. Opposite the bathroom, facing the quad, were two closed doors, which I guessed must be the other two bedrooms. I figured the corner bedroom was probably occupied since it seemed to be the larger of the two options. I pushed the other bedroom door open tentatively and, finding it empty, stepped inside.

The room was small. *Closet* small. That was fine by me; I liked cozy and didn't need much space. I was what some people call petite, and less-nice people called shrimpy. There was a twin bed with a metal frame and a bare mattress, a slim chest of drawers, and the best and perhaps most curious part of all, a piano that looked older than the building taking up an entire wall. I ran my hand over the wooden lid that covered the keys. My fingers slid across the smooth surface and came away clean; it had been dusted recently. When I was little, I'd always wanted a piano, but we'd never had the money. Astrid's family had a monstrous baby grand that we'd sometimes played "Heart and Soul" on until her father emerged from his office, crimson faced and reeking of bourbon, to yell at us. I lifted the cover, found the spot for my hands, and began to play. I smiled. *There's a piano in my room*, I'd tell Dad at my next visit. Maybe I could even learn to play a real song—"Danny Boy," maybe, he loved that one—for him on the Steinway in the activity room at Sommerset Meadows.

"What do you think you're doing?" A man's voice with a mild British accent cut through the music.

I swiveled around to face the person who had interrupted my impromptu concert. I don't know what I'd been expecting, but this guy wasn't it. First was the fact that I'd assumed my roommates were going to be women. That was on me. When Astrid had gone to Monadnock, the dorms had been separated by gender, but now that we were well into the twenty-first century, it made sense that schools were more inclusive and had started offering some all-gender housing. Still, it wasn't totally ridiculous that I'd envisioned a warm welcome, not an icy accusation from someone tall and glaring and not at all happy to see me. Judging from the angle at which I had to crane my neck to look at him, he was solidly over six feet. I gave myself a moment to collect my thoughts and take him in: lean frame, lightly tan skin, and blond hair shorn close to his scalp. His face was angular—the cheekbones, the bladelike line of his jaw—but a faint sprinkle of freckles over the bridge of his nose softened the sharpness.

One thing I'd learned during my time with the Red Sox is the harder and more blustery the man, the more smushy he usually is inside. And given the harshness of this guy's tone toward a person he'd never met, I wagered I was actually dealing with a giant softy.

"Hi," I said, rising from my seat, "I'm Sophie." I stuck out my hand for him to shake, but he scoffed and reached down to replace the key cover. The scent of Irish Spring soap filled my nostrils.

"Don't touch this again," he said. His voice was deep, and his accent would have been particularly alluring if it hadn't been delivering such unpleasant words.

"Oh, sorry. It seemed fine, I didn't—is it broken or something?" I asked.

"No, and I'd like to keep it that way."

"Okay," I said slowly. "Sure. In that case, maybe we can move it somewhere safer? My room is a bit cramped for a piano, especially if I'm not allowed to touch it."

"This is a highly sensitive instrument, one can't just—" He paused and shook his head. "Sorry, did you just say *your room*?"

I nodded. "I'm your new roommate, Sophie Doyle. I took the athletic trainer job."

Instead of letting his expression soften, he eyed me like something stuck to his shoe. Hmm, a worthy adversary. I kept eye contact. I waited for him to break down and either say "welcome" or try to scrape me off with a stick, but he didn't speak. Both his hands were occupied with a slow, frustrated sweep back over his head. I seized the opportunity to reach down and lift the key cover. Then, I fixed a sweet smile on my face and pressed one key, hard. *Da, da, da, duh.*

"Listen, Sophie Doyle, I think it's best if you go," he said, narrowing his eyes at me. He tried to commandeer the key cover, but I gripped it hard.

"I'm not the one in the wrong room."

"Storage closet."

"Has anyone ever told you that you're rude," I said.

"I could say the same of you."

"The last man who spoke to me like that got a cannoli in the eye," I said, my voice rising.

"Jonas? What's going on?" someone called from the hallway. A man I assumed was roommate number two appeared in the doorway, followed by another.

"You must be Sophie," the one now leaning against the doorway said. He had rich brown skin and a mop of glossy black curls. "I'm Revi Malek. I teach Algebra II and calculus. Nice to meet you." From the disheveled hair and the sweatpants and wrinkled T-shirt he was wearing, I guessed his room was the messy one.

"Sophie! Glad to meet you," said the other man. He had an expressive face with a hint of summer tan, a broad smile, and short hair that had been bleached to a deep shade of auburn. "Andrew Chen. You can call me Andy if you want. I run the science department here."

"I'm happy to meet you," I said, stepping past the ill-tempered Jonas to shake their hands. I meant it. I liked them immediately. Revi looked like the human equivalent of an adorable puppy, and Andy seemed like the grown-up version of the kid who rode his BMX bike in empty swimming pools and was secretly on honor roll.

"Nobody told me about this," Jonas said.

"You really should've come to last week's dorm parent meeting, bro."

"If you'd heard the bloody woodwinds that day, you'd have understood why I had to hold a last-minute evening session before their performance. Besides, you guys promised to fill me in on anything big."

"Yeah, we weren't sure how you'd take this particular roommate news, so we figured we'd surprise you," Revi said.

"You mean because she's a woman?" he asked.

I narrowed my eyes at him.

Andy laughed. "No, man. Why would that bother you?" Andy and Revi exchanged a look. "It's because you're a mis-anthrope."

"No, I'm not."

"You are, but we love you anyway." Revi crossed his arms. "Anyway, Jonas, Sophie here needs to stay in the piano room. None of the other faculty housing is available."

"What about Hammerstein Hall? There's that first-floor apartment—the one Ms. Thorn left?"

"There was a leak, and now it has a mold situation and a bathroom that has to be completely replaced."

"She could be flatmates with Rebecca."

"In a single? There's not even room for two beds in there. Face it, this is it, dude."

Jonas heaved a sigh.

"*We're* glad to have you," Andy said, sounding very parental.

I eyed them, these guys who I was going to be living with for the foreseeable future: Revi, nodding along; Andy, smiling brightly; and Jonas, staring at the floor.

"You'll hardly know I'm here," I said.

At that, Jonas looked straight at me. His gaze practically bored a hole into my skull. "Somehow I find that very hard to believe."

"C'mon, man, give her a break," Revi said. "Not everyone can handle your particular brand of gruffness."

"Actually, I'm from Boston, so there's not much I can't handle, including all brands of gruffness." My mind flashed back to the scene in Vitales, which I had *not* handled well. Thank goodness the fan had decided not to press charges.

"Good to know," Revi said, giving me a congenial pat on the shoulder. "Still, we're all going to make sure you're happy here. Even you, Jonas. Like it or not, Sophie is our new roommate and our colleague, so let's play nice."

"Fine," Jonas acquiesced. Then he turned his attention back to me. "But do us both a favor, then, Doyle. Keep your hands to yourself." He gestured at the piano with a tilt of his head, then he shoved his hands in his pockets, spun on his heel, and left the room.

A few minutes later he returned—to apologize, I figured, since that's what a decent person would do. But no. He was wielding a sheet of poster board. I watched in stunned silence as he brandished a thumbtack and affixed the poster board to the wall of my new room above the piano, just out of my reach. In large letters, inked in Sharpie, it read: *Do Not Touch*. We eyed each other for a moment, heat sizzling between us, before he stalked off.

. . .

Dinner was served in the dining hall, a room that was more grand ballroom than cafeteria, promptly at six. The four of us went together. Andy and Revi walked beside me, pointing out the various buildings on the way: the library that resembled an ornate Victorian mansion with a Sistine Chapel–esque ceiling that I just had to see, the science and math building that connected to the music building by way of an underground tunnel mostly used by people avoiding the harsh winters . . . or students wanting to make out between classes.

While they oriented me, Jonas trailed behind us. Once or twice during our trek, I glanced over my shoulder at him. I knew he didn't want me there, but I didn't mind. It wasn't the first time that I'd been unwelcome—I was a woman in major-league baseball. I'd navigated that situation just fine, until recently. I was confident that I'd win him over eventually; I just needed a plan.

"Once a week we have formal dinner, where we all dress up and there is assigned seating," Andy told me as he pulled open a heavy door that led to the dining hall. "But Saturdays are always casual. Lots of students go downtown and get pizza and stuff."

The meal was a whirlwind of trips to the buffet for eggplant parmesan, green salad, hot crusty garlic bread, and tiramisu in little glass cups.

"So, Sophie, Tabitha said you worked for a professional sports team before you came here. What brought you to Monadnock?" Revi asked halfway through dessert. "We're not exactly well-known for our sports programs."

I swallowed hard and shrugged. "I was ready for a change. My best friend, Astrid, went here for high school—"

"Wait, are you talking about Astrid Tyler?"

I nodded.

"That's wild!" Revi said. "You know how some schools have trophy cases with pictures of the hockey or soccer players who went pro? Well, we have a picture of Astrid when she won that Emmy. She's like our goddess of theater arts."

"Seriously?" I couldn't wait to tell Astrid that she'd been referred to as Monadnock's theater arts deity. She would get a good laugh out of that, though she probably wouldn't be as jazzed about the Emmy picture. She'd gotten stuck wearing a purple lamé number that had been so tight she'd had to waddle across the stage to claim her award.

"Oh yeah. The wall of fame in the music building is wild too. Multiple gold-record-holding recording artists, a bunch of first chairs at international symphonies—"

"Daphne Lenore went here," Andy interjected.

"Who's that?"

"She's like the next Hans Zimmer."

"—but no athletes," Revi finished.

"Yet," I said.

"Oh, your optimism is adorable, Sophie," Andy said. "But I coach the field hockey team, so believe me when I tell you we have about as much chance of having a famous athlete here as I have of winning the Powerball. For a long time, we didn't even have enough kids to field teams, but years back they changed it so that if you play on a team, you don't have to take gym."

"They're all just getting out of gym class?" I asked, trying not to let my disappointment show.

"Maybe not all of them. But even if they are into sports and have some athletic ability, it's not their priority."

"As it should be," Jonas said. It was the first time he'd spoken the entire meal.

"They're great kids," Revi added. "They make up for their lack of athleticism with charisma."

"I'll take charisma," I said.

"I'll bet," Jonas grumbled.

"What do you think of the food?" Andy asked. He stretched back and rubbed his belly contentedly.

"It's incredible," I said. "Is it always this good?" The food at my high school had been nearly inedible.

"Pretty much," Revi said, scraping his tiramisu cup. "Anyone want a coffee?"

Andy and I both wanted decaf. Revi started to rise, but Jonas stood abruptly.

"No worries, mate. I'll get them," he said.

When he was out of earshot, I leaned forward. "So, dish. What's Jonas's deal?"

Revi shrugged. "Some sort of secret wound? Sordid past? We don't really know. This is only his second year here, and the first year, he was barely in the apartment. He teaches most of the music curriculum—theory, composition—and he runs the orchestra. They're really good. And the kids absolutely love him. He's a decent guy, despite the evidence to the contrary he provided this afternoon."

"He's pretty touchy about that piano. Why doesn't he keep it in his room?"

"Another mystery."

"So he's not going to be coming into my room to play, or—"

Andy swiped a finger around the rim of his tiramisu cup. "Doubt it. We've never heard him play it."

"Weird," I said. "It's fine. I'm only here temporarily anyway."

I looked up, my mind wandering through the possibilities of Jonas and why he'd been so against me living in the apartment, but there were too many variables and not enough information. In the distance, Jonas was making his way across the dining hall. He carried three coffee mugs in one hand and one in the other. I watched, mesmerized, as he wove gracefully around the tables and careless students rising to get their own second helpings. He seemed to react automatically, the way an athlete does. If not for his cold, unfriendly attitude and the fact that I'd crossed an invisible line I hadn't even known existed, I might've found him handsome. But he was just a man who did not like me—*Join the club*, I wanted to tell him. People who detest me: Jonas Voss and ninety-nine percent of the population of Boston.

I consoled myself with the knowledge that I was very good at fixing things. I would treat Jonas like an athlete's injury, inflamed and cranky, except in this case, the discomfort said injury was causing was mine. Whatever hidden issue Jonas had going on was the key to winning him over, I wagered. So I'd rely on my training. You almost always had to do tests before you knew what was wrong. Movements, pain, a history of how the injury had come about, imaging—all of these things helped make a diagnosis and a plan for recovery. This was no different. With time and effort, I'd break through. I always did.

He handed out the coffees, saving mine for last.

I eyed it. "Is this safe for me to drink?" I quipped. I'd been trying to be funny, testing his sense of humor.

It failed. Wordlessly, he switched our mugs.

I pressed harder. "But it's so simple. All I have to do is divine from what I know of you: Are you the sort of man who would put the poison into his own goblet or his enemy's?"

Jonas's brow furrowed.

Revi burst into laughter. "Did you just *Princess Bride* him? You did. She did. I love it."

Andy nodded his head, his eyes crinkling with amusement. "That's freaking fantastic. Cheers, Sophie, you just won dinner." Andy held his coffee cup out and the three of us toasted. Jonas abstained. "The brilliant conductor has been bested by our newest roommate."

"Oh, this is going to be fun," Revi said.

Jonas lifted his mug and took a long sip. He made eye contact with me for a second. His eyes were warm hazel with streaks of a deep green like the wall at Fenway, and despite the tension between us, I felt a strange sensation, somewhere between homesickness and coming home. He set his coffee down, and the corner of his mouth quirked. It was such a subtle movement, I bet most people wouldn't have noticed. He'd been looking at his cup, made sure he placed it down just so, but I'd still been watching him. I wanted to see the familiar green in his irises again, but instead, I caught that little promise where his lips met.

Maybe not a completely lost cause, I thought. Andy and Revi were fabulous and warm, and Jonas? Well, I was going to figure out a way to identify whatever was making him so miserable, and I was going to make him like me in the process.

Chapter 3

In the morning, I got up at sunrise and went for a long run around the campus grounds while everyone was still asleep. It really was a beautiful place. Sure, there was no Charles River, but Astrid had told me about a hidden lake on campus, and there were mountains in the distance and trees everywhere I looked. I was struck by the quiet. In the city, there was always some sort of noise. Traffic or people, all hours. Yesterday when I arrived this place had been practically musical with all the kids' voices and instruments. Now the only sounds I heard were birds, my steady breathing, and the rhythm of my footfalls. The campus stretched on for what felt like miles. There was the dining hall; the chapel on the hill that was used for school meetings and seminars; the ornate library that was just as the guys had described it, exquisite with intricate woodwork—I couldn't wait to see the inside (and I would soon, apparently, because the faculty took turns doing evening duty there each week)—but it took me a while before I found what I was searching for. The athletic fields. At first glance, I was relieved. When Astrid had said that the teams were bad, I'd

been envisioning one of those Disney movie scenarios where
the coach shows up and there's a team of ragtag kids on a field
with no grass. They had grass. It was green and lush and had
its own irrigation system. There were tennis courts, a football
field with bleachers, two soccer fields, and, at the very end, a
baseball field. The woods started at the edge of the sports
complex and stretched on into the distance. Astrid hadn't been
kidding about the nature and the fresh mountain air. I was
pretty sure I could make out a chairlift on one of the hills . . .
as well as the telltale signs of an actual ski slope and an honest-
to-god ski jump. What was this place?

I stopped at a water fountain next to the football bleachers to
quench my thirst and then jogged over to the baseball field. I had
this stupid idea to run the bases. But when I got there, I realized
I wasn't alone. A boy stood on the pitcher's mound. He was clad
in a pair of jeans and a sweatshirt with the hood up, so I couldn't
see his face. But he had the kind of awkward lankiness of a teenager and didn't seem to have a glove or anything. He wound
up—not bad—and threw. My eyes struggled to keep up with the
ball; before I could track it, I heard the loud metal clang of it
hitting the fence. He jogged over to where it had landed in the
dirt, dusted it off, and returned to the mound. I narrowed my
eyes. He wound up again and let it fly, and I swear on my last
cannoli, that fastball must've been well over 90 miles per hour.

"Hey!" I called, loping toward the kid. "That was awesome. Do you play for Monadnock?" Andy and Revi had been
quite clear that the athletic program was no one's priority, and
it showed. And Astrid had said the teams sucked . . . with conviction. In my estimation, few high school kids could even hit
a ball at that speed, let alone throw one.

The kid turned in my direction for an instant and then
bolted into the woods.

"Wait," I yelled. "You're really good."

But he was gone.

I didn't chase after the kid. His legs were way longer than mine, and even though my knowledge of teenagers essentially was limited to the fact that I was one once, I wagered that sprinting after him (even if I had no hope of catching up) might send us both deeper into the woods, where we'd both get lost and/or eaten by a fisher cat. Astrid had warned me about those. It'd been a rough week, and I wasn't about to top it off by becoming a cautionary tale in which a scrappy, disgraced city girl from Boston gets consumed by a creature in the woods on her second day in New Hampshire. Also, if I were going to be eaten, I'd prefer it be by a Sasquatch or something powerful and cool instead of a vicious oversized cat.

I headed back to the football bleachers and ran stairs. A part of me hoped that the kid might think I'd left and would reappear. As I motored up two steps at a time, my quads burning with lactic acid, I crafted a plan to ambush—no, *reestablish communication*. Dad would have called it a sign from God, seeing a player with an arm like that, so young and talented . . . and who the heck was I to walk away from that kind of miracle? But also, truth be told, I was dying to talk baseball without the fear of salivary retribution.

My optimism and persistence kept me powering up the stairs for far longer than my normal workout, but in the end my poor low blood sugar tolerance won out, and I gave up and headed back to the apartment. Sweat-drenched and ravenous, I was in desperate need of a shower and a breakfast buffet. This seemed like the kind of place with a make-your-own-waffle bar featuring all the toppings.

Back in the apartment, I made my way straight to the bathroom, locked the door, stripped out of my clothes, and stepped beneath the stream of water. I'd been trying not to think about Boston and Patrick and everything that had happened—no good could come of that—but the shower was a stark, or should I say scalding, reminder. Patrick had one of those digital systems that had colored lights and spray heads at every angle. I never could figure it out and was always afraid I would break it. Whatever happened to a basic shower? This one was just that, except for the fact that I couldn't quite get the temperature right. A tiny turn of the knob and the water changed from burning hot to ice-cold. There was no in-between. I muttered obscenities to myself as I attempted futilely to strike a balance. A slight chill seemed better than a second-degree burn, so I took a deep breath and sudsed my mottled, goose-bumped skin as fast as I could. Then I squeezed some shampoo into my hand and initiated what probably could've made a Guinness record for world's fastest wash and shampoo job under the frigid stream. "Oh my goodness," I said, while I scrubbed my scalp. "Holy shit, that's cold." Some shampoo got in my eyes, so I squeezed them shut, quickly rinsed the soap off, turned off the water, and practically flung myself out of the shower. I'd planned to grab my towel and wrap myself in its fuzzy warmth, but instead I plowed directly into a shirtless form. Firm, broad chest, an arm in front of him maybe? It happened so fast it was hard to say, but there had definitely been some sort of contact of my, uh, *bare skin* and someone else's hand. I squeezed my eyes shut, the sound of my racing pulse like a bass beat in my ears. A toothbrush clattered to the floor.

Please don't be Jonas.

I forced my stinging eyes open. Oh, it was Jonas all right.

All six foot three of him, in only a pair of warmup pants. I had to give it to him—he was fit. So fit that I found myself unable to look away. Or maybe it was the shock of the situation and not his physique that rendered me stunned, staring, searching for words while my cheeks flamed.

"Bloody hell, Doyle," he grumbled, pulling out his earbuds.

"What are you doing in here?" I asked, grabbing for my towel.

Between simultaneously trying to cover myself and being distracted by abs that would probably be characterized as mesmerizing by someone who hadn't worked with professional athletes and also hadn't been on the receiving end of his you-touched-my-piano wrath, I misjudged the distance between me and the towel hook and missed a couple of times. Jonas, to his credit, kept his gaze locked high on the wall behind me. But then he extended an arm slowly in my direction. I swallowed hard. A moment later, he dangled my towel in front of me, while he studied the ceiling. I grabbed the towel from him and secured it around myself.

"What's wrong with you, Voss? Didn't you hear the water running?"

Jonas readjusted the trajectory of his gaze to my forehead. "Mussorgsky's *Pictures at an Exhibition*," he said, as if it explained everything.

I stooped and picked up his toothbrush. "Is that supposed to mean something to me?"

"I guess not, Sporty Spice. Let's say it's not intended to be listened to at a low volume and leave it at that." He eyed the toothbrush like I'd extracted it from the toilet.

"Okay, but I locked the door." I jammed the end of the towel a bit deeper into my cleavage.

He cleared his throat. "Lock doesn't work."

"No one ever thought to fix it?"

He shrugged. "It wasn't really an issue before."

"It's not an issue for me," I said trying to keep my cool. "You're the one making a big deal out of it."

"You slammed into my hand," he said.

"So?"

He paused, his face unreadable. "My hands are important to me," he mumbled.

I let out a breath. "If I could handle a morning run next to woods full of fisher cats this morning," I said, "I think you'll survive bumping into me." I put the toothbrush, rather aggressively, into his large and apparently fragile hand.

Jonas's face flushed crimson, but he recovered his cool demeanor and raised his eyebrows. "Wow. Your animal encounter sounds very dramatic, Doyle."

"It could've been. Those giant cats can tear a human apart."

The corner of Jonas's mouth twitched. He ran a thumb over the rogue anatomy that seemed to respond to me without his consent, and I couldn't help but track the movement with my gaze. He had a nice mouth, I had to give him that; what came out of that nice mouth was a very different story.

"Fisher cats?" He picked up his phone from the sink and fiddled with it for a moment. "You mean these overgrown ferrets?" He held the phone in front of my face, putting what looked like a cross between a teddy bear and an otter below a newspaper article titled "Fisher Cats: New Hampshire's Shy Weasel" directly in my line of view. I pushed the phone down. "Fine. You made your point. My friend Astrid, the one who went here and helped me get this job, warned me that they roamed around here and attacked people."

"Sounds like we both have a grievance with this Astrid," he teased.

"Are you this rude to everyone, or do you just save your special manners for me?"

"Sure you wouldn't rather live in Hammerstein?" he said. "I hear everyone who resides there is just *delightful.*"

I turned in the doorway and flashed a huge grin. "No thanks. Against all odds, Jonas Voss, I actually prefer you to black mold. Nice abs, by the way; you might want to add some push-ups to your routine though."

Jonas threw his toothbrush into the trash can, but didn't say a word. I skipped back to my room to get dressed.

A minute later there was a knock on my door. I snatched the closest article of clothing in front of my chest. Jonas was more persistent than I'd expected, and Hammerstein Hall was starting to look a little tempting.

"Changing!" I yelled.

"Cool," Revi called back. "We're just heading to breakfast. Want us to wait?"

"Yes, please. Two minutes," I answered, yanking a shirt over my head. I pulled on a clean pair of jeans and wrestled my sopping hair into a high ponytail. I flung the door open.

"Tell me you have a waffle bar," I said.

"Of course we have a waffle bar. What are we, North Lakes Academy?" Andy said, shaking his head.

"Whipped cream, strawberries, chocolate chips."

"Check, check, check."

"What about fisher cats?"

"The weasel things?" Revi said. "Nah, we just tell the students about them to keep them from sneaking in the woods to get into trouble."

Suddenly Astrid's warning made complete sense. *Not bad, faculty*, I thought. Young Astrid would've been up to no good in those woods on day one without a deep fear of fanged furry creatures. I shook off the embarrassment I felt about touting my bravery to Jonas and focused on more important things. Waffles and baseball.

Even teenage pitching prodigies had to eat, right?

Andy and Revi rushed out into the hallway while I stooped next to the door and laced up my shoes. I could hear them hollering about chow time to the dawdling students and the ones who'd overslept. I rose, ready to join in the fray. It was sort of like getting the team amped up for game time, and I knew how to do that. Jonas reached in front of me and blocked my way with his long arm. I moved to duck under it, which would've been easy based on our height differential. Except that he'd removed a sweatshirt from the coat tree in the corner and now my view was obstructed.

"I'm hungry," I said, clutching my hollow midsection.

He leaned down toward me. I twisted my neck just as he stopped inches from my cheek. When he spoke, his breath was warm on my skin.

"Sorry about bursting in on you in the bathroom," he said in a low voice. "It won't happen again." He strode off, leaving me standing in the doorway of our apartment, dumbfounded.

King grump Jonas Voss, with his precious piano, moody gruffness, and general disdain for me, had apologized. My skin was still tingling where those words had touched the pulse point on my neck. My lips curled into a smile. Sometimes being an optimist blew up in one's face, and sometimes, it just made you right.

When I arrived at the dining hall minutes later, Jonas was already several forkfuls deep into the largest plate of waffles I have ever seen, replete with mounds of whipped cream, piles of strawberries, and hundreds of chocolate chips. And the waffle bar was closed.

Chapter 4

Astrid called after breakfast. "So, how is it? Tell me everything."

I groaned.

"Sounds like someone hit the waffle buffet a little too hard."

"I wish," I said. I had, in fact, been relegated to the omelet bar, which was pretty great as far as breakfast fare went, but an omelet is *not* a waffle.

"How's your apartment? Do you have a good view of the quad?"

I glanced toward the common room window, where Jonas was camped out in an armchair, frowning down at something in a notebook. "It's, uh, interesting."

"You're not giving me anything to work with, Soph! I have ten minutes before I have to be in the makeup trailer, and I need to know that I didn't lead you down some sort of path toward disastrous misadventure. At least tell me about your roommate. Is she nice?"

"My roommates are dudes," I whispered. "Three dudes."

"Are they hot?"

"Does it matter?"

"What kind of question is that? Of course it matters. You're single and ready to mingle."

"I am not ready to mingle. Besides, one of them hates me."

"Is *he* hot?"

"Astrid, focus."

"Okay, we're going to put a pin in the fact that you didn't answer my question about your roommates and that you are, apparently, under some sort of post-Patrick vow of celibacy. I just find it implausible that this guy hates you. Who *doesn't* like you?"

I resisted the urge to spout, "Ninety percent of Boston!"

"You're so likable . . ." *Aww, Astrid, such a sweetie.* ". . . when you aren't maiming someone with a cannoli and getting arrested, of course."

"Thanks for that, pal."

"What'd you do to him? Cream horn attack?"

"I touched his piano," I mumbled, glancing over for an instant to see if Jonas had heard. We caught each other's gaze for a moment and he immediately returned to scribbling.

Astrid snorted. "His *piano*? Is that a code? Is *that* why you've sworn off sex?"

"You'd like that, wouldn't you, pervert," I retorted lightly.

Jonas cleared his throat.

I slid down in my seat and lowered my voice. "I meant the literal musical instrument. The kind with black and white keys. Honestly, maybe it wasn't that. I don't even know. The other guys, Andy and Revi, seem really nice, so that's good. And you know me—I'm not giving up yet."

"That's my girl. You know, my first roommate at Monadnock hated me too. Cornelia Caldwell—her father was a senator from South Carolina. She used to lock the door from the inside so I couldn't get in when I went out after curfew. I'm ninety-nine percent sure she threw away all of my favorite snacks and one hundred percent sure she put a spider in my bed."

"Wait, are you talking about Neely? You were in her wedding last spring."

"Exactly. We worked out our differences, and I'm sure you and your new roommate will too."

"You told me you guys made out."

"Now, there's an idea. It's a great tension breaker."

"I don't need a tension breaker. I need a recipe."

"I'll be right there, Maggie . . . Sorry, Soph, a what?"

"My mom's recipe."

The line went silent while I let the realization wash over Astrid. "Apple cake," she said, with a reverence that Astrid almost never displayed. But my mother's apple cake was award-winning, mouthwatering Irish magic on a plate. And given the sheer volume of spiced apples Jonas had devoured on waffle number six, I was willing to bet he would not be able to resist it.

"Apple cake," I confirmed.

"You are not playing around."

"I play to win," I said at a volume that Jonas would have probably described as a forte, because he actually hurled a pillow in my direction and grumbled, "Oi, some people are trying to work here!"

I smiled aggressively, fixed the pillow, and then headed back toward my bedroom. In a whisper, I told Astrid, "And when I've won him over and he's realized that I am the best roommate of all time and he doesn't deserve to be in my proximity, I'm going to lean over and get right up in his face and say, 'How do you like them apples?'"

Astrid laughed. "Okay, Good Will Hunting. God, I love you. I wish I could be your roommate."

"I love you, too. I also wish we were roomies again, but then you wouldn't be doing your movie, and I can't be the thing that keeps you from your destiny. How's the filming going, anyway?"

"Well, my costar is an arrogant nightmare with bone structure that I'd kill for."

"So you're definitely sleeping with him."

"My costar is a woman, Soph. And just give me time." She laughed wickedly. "The script is great, though. I'm excited to finally get to do something a bit darker and show my range. The director's brilliant . . . I don't know, I just have a really good feeling about this."

"I am so proud of you. I can't wait to see it. I'll have to tell Dad . . . he loves bragging to everyone at Sommerset Meadows that he knows a famous movie star."

"How is Gerry? Did he take it okay when you told him about what happened?"

I waited for a moment before answering. "I might not have told him the full story."

"Sophie!"

"I just don't want to worry him—or, worse, let him down. Me getting that job was basically the most exciting thing that ever happened to us . . . his words, not mine. He's had such a rough time and already lost so much; I didn't want to ruin anything else for him, you know?"

Astrid sighed. "You didn't ruin anything for your dad. You can't control biology, isn't that what you always say? Besides, wouldn't it be better if he heard it from you? What are the odds that he doesn't find out another way and then he's facing the bad news plus the fact that his daughter kept it from him?"

"I told him that I'd decided to step away from the Red Sox for now. That's not exactly untrue."

"I guess . . . in the same way that being shoved out of a moving train and deciding to disembark are the same exact thing."

"Okay, so I left out the part where it wasn't my choice and that it was permanent, but—"

"You forgot about the bakery incident."

"Harsh. You never know, if I can accomplish something here that makes me stand out, they might let me come back. At least, that's my plan. Then me leaving out the specifics of my departure won't matter."

"Maybe they will," Astrid said. "Even so, I still think you should be honest with your dad. You both deserve that."

Astrid was being gentle, but she was right. I had to tell him the whole story. I knew that. Plus, I hated keeping things from my dad, since us keeping things from each other was part of the reason the Parkinson's had gotten so advanced before he sought treatment. I was just going to need to put on my big-girl pants and tell him the truth. Next week when I drove down, since this was one of those difficult conversations that needed to happen in person.

"If you need a pep talk, you know I'm here for you. But take it from someone who has let her parents down plenty— it'll be okay. Shoot, time's up, Soph. Talk soon?"

"Always."

I set my phone down and glared at the piano before I shimmied past it toward the bed. I had a notebook in my bag, and I figured if I thought about it long enough I could remember the ingredients in Mom's famous apple cake. It'd been so long since I made one, but if I could remember maybe I'd make an extra to bring to Dad on the weekend. Sugar, flour, apples obviously . . . what else? I tapped the pen to my forehead while I tried to call up the times I'd assisted Mom when I was younger. It was our Father's Day tradition. There were the Granny Smith apples on the counter. A single cup measurer. The orange baking soda box. Irish butter. Egg. I could hear her warm laugh when I cracked it too hard and got the liquid whites everywhere. It was all so vivid in my mind until I tried to picture her face and my memory refused to cooperate. My heart squeezed.

"Sophie!" Andy called through the door. "We're going to get an Ultimate Frisbee game going with some of the kids on the quad. Wanna join?"

I dropped the notebook and headed toward the door. "You know it," I said, grinning at Andy, who was trying, and not succeeding, to twirl a disc on his finger. I pulled on a sweatshirt and followed him toward the door.

"Jonas, you in?" he said.

Jonas glanced up from his work and squinted at us. He made a grunting noise and then returned to his mad scribbling.

"I don't know why you bother," Revi said to Andy once we were in the hallway. "You know he doesn't like to get his hands dirty."

"What's that?" I asked.

"It's nothing," Andy said. "Jonas is just very protective of his hands."

My mind leapt back to him and me alone in the bathroom, his intense reaction to me accidentally bumping into him. That moment of skin-to-skin contact. I gulped. "What's that about, anyway?"

Revi shrugged. "The neuroticism of musicians?"

Andy said nothing. He wound up and flung the Frisbee,

sending it sailing across the green expanse of the quad. Revi chased after it and that was the end of that. Was Jonas neurotic? I wasn't sure about that. Moody, rude, yes. But maybe it wasn't about his hands or anything else . . . it was me. Would he have played if I hadn't been there? I'd just left a place where it felt like everyone hated my guts, and I wasn't completely convinced that I wanted to be living with someone who shared that sentiment. Revi tossed the Frisbee to a lanky teen who bungled the catch in the end zone. I snatched it before it hit the ground and hurled it toward a student who was waiting on the other end of the quad. She managed to snag it out of the air before toppling onto her back.

"Nice one, Sophie," Revi shouted.

I glanced up at the third-floor window for a moment, wondering if Jonas had seen my perfect throw. It was a good thing he'd opted not to play with us. I would've destroyed him.

Chapter 5

Mondays were for practices. In the fall season, Monadnock had two varsity soccer teams, a field hockey team, and cross-country. They'd tried to have football, but never had enough players for a team. Practices started at two forty-five, so I got to the training room hours early to get all of the tape and other supplies organized the way I liked them. The space was in the back of the gymnasium, adjacent to an indoor rock-climbing wall that was practically begging for me to scramble up. I unlocked the heavy wood door to the training room and stepped inside. I would be responsible for the players' health and safety—treating injuries, conducting rehab programs— the same kinds of things I'd done for the Red Sox. Before practices, I'd do the pretreatments, taping whoever needed it, and then I'd head over to the fields to watch practice. My weekends from now on would be spent prepping for and observing home games and traveling to tournaments.

The training room was a large space, especially for a school that didn't prioritize sports. Even though it was not what I'd gotten used to at the Red Sox, most of the basic elements were there, albeit fewer in number and older. I took a quick inventory of the space. There was an ultrasound machine, a professional e-stim machine, ice maker, large whirlpool, two padded tables for treatment, a variety of colorful resistance banding tied around a large post in the center of the room. I could work with this.

I cleaned the treatment tables and checked the ice machine to make sure it was putting out plenty of ice. Then I sat down at the desk and got started on reviewing the stack of files there. My predecessor was supposed to give me an in-person orientation, but she'd gone into labor a few days early, so I was on my own. Fortunately, she had left detailed notes on all of the students currently being treated for minor injuries or ongoing issues, organized by team. The cross-country runners were plagued by shin splints and iliotibial band tightness. I was going to need to make a rehab and prevention plan for that—maybe even do a running mechanics clinic, since I postulated that there were some overstriders in there. One girl on the field hockey team had a grade 2 MCL tear and was on crutches. Among the soccer players, there were two cases of patellar tendinitis, three sprained ankles, and a recovering concussion. I'd definitely be filling up the giant steel whirlpool with an ice bath each day.

I was contemplating a nap on one of the tables when the door opened. A petite girl stood holding an instrument case in front of her.

"Oh," she said, looking surprised to find me at the desk.

"Come in," I said. "Were you looking for Ms. Winters?" I asked. "I'm Sophie. I'm her replacement while she's out on maternity leave."

The girl stepped forward, still hesitant. She tucked a few spirals of black hair behind her ear.

"Are you on one of the teams?" I pressed gently. "You're here for treatment?"

She shook her head. "I'm not on a team. Sorry, Ms. Winters used to let us come in anytime to get things."

"You're not on a team?"

"I play viola. We have a big competition coming up, lots of practice, and my arm's been a little sore. I just wanted to grab some ice—would that be okay?"

"Sure." I walked toward the ice machine and then filled up a small bag for her, flattening it. "If you come here, I can put it on for you."

She came over and gently set her viola down. Then she extended her arm. I took a look at her forearm, turning her hand over gingerly in my hands. "Where's most of your pain?" I asked.

"Here," she indicated, pointing to her elbow.

I palpated the spot and she winced. There was definitely some swelling there. "This looks like lateral epicondylitis. You've probably heard of it before—tennis elbow? How have you been managing the pain?"

"Ibuprofen." She shrugged. "It's not that bad."

"Okay, make sure you keep to the dosing on the bottle. Ice can help with pain and calm down some of that inflammation, but it's not a long-term solution." I took the Saran Wrap and secured the ice pack around her arm. "What you really need is rest."

She laughed, picking up her viola. "You're only saying that because you haven't heard my rendition of Chromatic Fantasia and Fugue in D Minor. If you had, you wouldn't be telling me to practice less."

"Maybe start with a day or two off from music? You don't want it to get worse."

"Better for my elbow to get worse than my playing."

· · ·

The athletes came in soon after she left. They were a nice group of kids. Undisciplined, inflexible (I'd need to work on that), generally in need of better conditioning, but nice. I drove a golf cart loaded with big Gatorade coolers filled with ice water and my kit down to the fields and parked it in the center between the soccer pitches, where I could keep an eye on all of the athletes. I spent two hours watching the teams practice. Occasionally, I let my attention drift over to the base-ball field at the edge of the woods, but the early-morning pitcher wasn't there.

It was a beautiful afternoon, sun-soaked with a bite in the air. It made me want to go apple picking. Miraculously, no one got injured, and while it left little for me to do, it was a relief to have an uneventful first day. The cross-country team mo-tored by—my hunch about the overstriding turned out to be spot-on—and a girl from the field hockey team asked for some tape to fix her stick handle.

"Finley, hustle up! We're going to scrimmage," Andy yelled. I squinted. He darted around a player, giving a ball a thwack, and she took chase.

I turned my attention to the soccer field. Some of the play-ers were decent, but generally, I understood now why Astrid had said they sucked. That hadn't been an overstatement. But I was here now. I knew I was good at my job. I couldn't make them better, but I could make them stronger, faster, more flex-ible, more responsive, and healthier. That was something.

When practice was over, Andy came bounding over and hopped in beside me. "Hey, roomie!"

"I never pictured you as a field hockey player," I said.

"As you New Englanders say, it's wicked fun. Besides, no

one else wanted to do it and there's a couple of kids on the team who really need the outlet, so I volunteered."

"You're one of the good ones," I said.

"In that case, mind giving this good one a lift back to the gym?" he asked.

"They wore you out, huh?" I said, stifling a laugh.

"They're faster than last season. So, about that ride— what's the verdict?"

"For my favorite roommate?" I said, grinning, "No problem." I extracted a pouch of Big League Chew from my pocket and held it out to him. He raised an eyebrow but took a large pinch.

"I won't tell Revi you called me your favorite," Andy said, and then popped the gum into his mouth. "He's very sensitive. I love that about him."

I took my own sizable helping and then tucked the pouch back into my vest. "Good to know. But he's also my favorite roommate. I'm like a mom with two kids who she loves the same."

"If Revi and I are the kids—forgetting that we're all the same age—what does that make Jonas?" he teased.

"A rude cousin?"

Andy bumped me with his shoulder. "Don't let Jonas get you down. When he first got here, he barely spoke to me and Revi for a month. He didn't seem psyched to live with us either at first and even mentioned moving out. Full disclosure— we thought he was a real tool. But it didn't last. He's got his own problems, but he's not a bad guy. Once you get past that crusty exterior, he's a good friend and a loyal one. Nobody is more dedicated to their students than he is, and he's super generous. Don't tell him I told you, but he gives free lessons to kids from town and he pays for a couple of students who can't afford their tuition. He also cleans the apartment. Anyway, I don't think his dislike for this situation has that much to do with you."

I mulled over Andy's confession about Jonas, turning the key to start the cart. "It's okay," I told Andy. "He might not like me now, but I'll win him over eventually."

"I support your optimism, but I'm not sure I'd bet on it. You two are just diametrically opposed—he doesn't think Monadnock should even have a sports program. You'll notice none of the orchestra kids are on the teams. Jonas may be the only game you can't win."

"We'll see about that," I said, turning the cart toward the exit. "You might want to grab on to something."

I jammed down the cart's accelerator, and Andy clamped a hand over his hat. "My god," he hollered over the wail of the engine, "what they say about Massachusetts drivers is true! You're a wild woman."

I grinned at him. The cool, fresh air on my face and the feeling of being in control were a rush. The cart tore up the hill toward the science and math building.

"Mind stopping here, Sophie?" Andy asked.

"Had enough of my driving?" I teased.

"Nah, Revi had some grading to do and I thought I'd pick him up."

"Do you want me to wait? He can sit on the back."

Andy fixed his backward hat. "Nope, we'll walk. You good with all those water coolers?"

"I'm good. Hefting them around is part of my physical fitness program," I said with a laugh. "Anyway, I dumped them out at the field, so they're light now. Say hi to Revi."

"See you at dinner?"

"You got it."

"It's chicken cordon bleu tonight with mashed potatoes and caramelized brussels sprouts," he said. "I recommend wearing something with an elastic waistband."

"Thanks for the tip," I said, and then motored off.

I tossed my duffel bag next to my shoes beside the apartment door. There was just enough time before dinner to shower and get changed. I needed something to indicate that the bathroom was occupied to ensure Jonas and I didn't have another naked run-in. After digging around in the drawer in the kitchen, I found a Sharpie, a piece of printer paper, and some tape. I scrawled *Shower in use* on it and then headed toward the bathroom.

Jonas was crouched down by the bathroom door, blocking my way. Of course he was.

I cleared my throat, but he didn't move. He didn't even acknowledge my presence. I was about to muscle past him when I noticed the earbuds in his ears. Okay, so maybe he hadn't been ignoring my passive-aggressive throat clearing. He just hadn't heard me. I tapped him on the shoulder, and he dropped something as his head whipped around.

"I really need a shower. Do you mind?" I asked, as nicely as I could.

He picked up the object he'd dropped, a screwdriver, and stepped out of the way.

"By all means," he said. "Probably for the best if you got that grime from the athletic fields off of you before you contaminate the entire apartment."

"Don't forget about the sweat," I said, stepping toward him. "So much sweat and dirt from those filthy fields, all over me."

He fumbled with the screwdriver.

"I'd rather not hear about your desperate need for stronger antiperspirant and a bar of soap," he volleyed back, lifting his eyes to meet my gaze. Something unfamiliar flashed in his expression.

I spun and faced the door. Then I ripped off a piece of tape and fixed my sign to it. "Bathroom's closed. Got it? That means no barging in."

"You don't have to tell me twice, Doyle."

I washed as quickly as I could, put on my very best elastic-waist pants, and waited in the living room for Andy and Revi to arrive for dinner. I let my eyes drift closed for a moment, before I was awoken by a loud "Let's feast!"

Revi was standing in the apartment entryway, leaning on Andy and grinning. "Come on, Sleeping Beauty! It's French cuisine night. Jonas, man, let's go."

Jonas appeared in his bedroom doorway. It looked as if we'd both had the same idea of how to pass the time while we were waiting for dinner. He stretched his arms up and the bottom of his Henley rose, revealing a patch of skin above the waist of his chinos. For an instant, I was back in that bathroom, steam swirling around, staring at him. I forced myself to look away and bounded out of my seat. We both eyed the shoe shelf by the door at the same time and made a mad dash for it. I wasn't getting stuck behind him again. With my luck, he'd eat all the chicken before I made it to the dining hall. I slid on one shoe and hopped into the other one in the hallway.

"Vive la France," I said, thrusting my fist into the air.

Revi threw an arm around my shoulder. "So, Soph, how was the first day? Were the other kids nice to you?"

"It was a solid first day. No emergencies. That's a good thing. The only excitement was a random visit from a viola player with a bad case of tennis elbow who stopped by for some ice."

"Tennis elbow without tennis? Is that a thing?" Revi asked.

"Yup. It's just called that because it's common in tennis players. But it's a repetitive motion injury. Sweet girl must be practicing an awful lot."

"Wait, was it Riley?" Jonas asked. "Is she okay?"

I hadn't noticed he'd caught up with me. His brow was creased with what looked like genuine concern.

"She's one of your students?" I asked.

"Yeah, she's a sophomore. Phenomenally gifted."

"She's fine," I assured him. "I encouraged her to take a break, but she was not hearing it. Maybe you could talk to her about that?"

"I'll have a chat with her, but I doubt she'll change anything. The Salzburg International Mozart Competition is coming up. Now would be a difficult time to take a break," Jonas said.

"I tend to think that a person's health is more important than playing an instrument well for a contest."

"I hear what you're saying, but that contest could make or break her career."

"She's fifteen. I'm sure there will be other chances," I said, glancing up at him.

The muscles in his jaw twitched. "You should stick with sports," he muttered. Then he picked up his pace, until I couldn't keep up with his long stride.

Maybe cake wasn't going to cut it after all. It was as if everything I said seemed to offend Jonas. But my conviction about listening to your body and taking care of it ran deeper than I could ever explain to anyone. Really, only my dad and Astrid understood, and even we never talked about it.

Back when I'd gotten the Red Sox job, I'd insisted on taking Dad out to a fancy dinner at Giovanni's, where they had a wine list and real tablecloths, to celebrate, wanting to share that joy, to bask in his pride. And I had, until I noticed the tremor. It was in the fingers of his right hand, a motion like he was rolling a pill between them. He followed my gaze and then slid his hand out of sight beneath the tablecloth. We didn't talk about it; we weren't really talkers. Maybe that was part of why I loved baseball so much; it gave us a common language. We never discussed Mom, her heavy absence, or the mortgage payments we were often short on, but we could ramble for hours about designated hitters and the elegance of the left-handed submarine pitcher.

Dad would've been a talented scout if things had turned out differently. He could spot a pitcher and know in mere moments if that kid had something. I had an eye too—for pitching and for signs of Parkinson's, it seemed. So even though he'd tucked his hand away and we hadn't spoken of it, I knew, and when it got worse, and he refused to go to a doctor, I didn't push even though I knew I should have. Even when he started shuffling and accidentally set our kitchen on fire, he insisted that nothing was wrong in the same breath he told me he wanted to move into Sommerset Meadows, where Barry the hot dog man was living after a stroke. I'd gone along with it, helping him pack and decorating his room with pale yellow curtains and an afghan I'd knitted. Meanwhile, I carried the guilt that if I'd only spoken up sooner, maybe he could have started treatment earlier and we could've slowed down his progression. Now he couldn't do his basic tasks without help from the staff. Injuries were simpler. Rest, ice, compression, elevation—that usually did the trick, though some recent studies had suggested gentle movement might be better than rest. Iwasaki and Riley would heal with time and appropriate treatment; Dad wouldn't. It wasn't about a game or a competition or pride. It was about the future.

I was pretty sure that was something there was no point in explaining to the implacable Jonas Voss.

"You're awfully quiet there, Sophie," Andy said. "Everything okay?"

"Everything's great," I said. "I'm just fantasizing about mashed potatoes."

Chapter 6

Thanks to the strange New England boarding school schedule, in which classes finished at eleven thirty on Wednesdays and Saturdays (sorry, kids) to allow time to travel to sporting events and performances, and the fact that only cross-country was at home, I found myself with a few hours free on Wednesday afternoon. I'd been informed that this week, formal dinner was on Thursday, which meant that I needed to buy something dressy to wear. Back when Astrid had attended Monadnock, formal dinner dress code for girls and women staff members had meant a dress or a skirt, but now the rules were not gendered and consisted of a list of appropriate clothing. Jacket and tie with pants or a skirt or a dress. I wasn't really inclined to wear a suit or a dress, which is why I didn't own one, but I figured wearing a specific article of clothing once a week was a small price to pay for a free all-I-could-eat gourmet meal.

After I finished the last post-meet ice treatment, wiped out the whirlpools, and closed the training room, I headed down the hill into town. I was glad that I'd grabbed a Monadnock

School fleece before I'd left. Despite the golden wash of late-autumn sun, the air had a wintry bite to it. Revi and Andy had told me that there were a few cute shops within walking distance, including an indoor farmer's market with local produce, cheese, and candles; a used bookstore; and a boutique. If I wanted more selection, there were some designer outlets, but they were a twenty-minute drive. I stopped by the boutique first.

I've never been very good with fashion, but, lucky for me, I had a friend with phenomenal taste. I put in my earbuds and dialed Astrid.

"Sophie!" she said. "I'm so glad you called. I was just thinking about you."

"How are you?" I asked.

"Freezing! I thought Boston was cold. Turns out she's got nothing on Toronto. I'm wearing layers, Sophie."

"Oh, that is desperate!" I said, chuckling. "Is there flannel involved?"

"Long underwear. I'm not even kidding. Whoever offers me some of those little pocket-warming things, I'm marrying. It snowed here today, and I did not pack properly."

"Speaking of not packing properly, I'm a bit unprepared for the formal dinner situation. I was hoping maybe you could help me pick something?"

"I would love to!"

"Thank goodness. I'm at a boutique in town."

"Turn on your FaceTime and we'll do a survey," she said.

I glanced sheepishly at the shopkeeper. "My shopping companion's in Canada," I confessed as I swept the camera around the room.

"Let me know if you want me to start a fitting room for you," she said, unfazed.

"Grab that plum-colored one. Is it long sleeved? You'll want sleeves or a cardigan. Oh, what's that charcoal gray?" Astrid said.

"You really think charcoal would look good with my coloring?"

"You're right. It would look better on me."

"Everything would look better on you."

"Ridiculous. Grab the green one."

I headed into the dressing room and promised to send Astrid pictures of each outfit. The plum was a soft, flannelly material that was understated and didn't look like it was trying too hard, yet flattered my athletic figure. I snapped a quick picture in the mirror and texted Astrid. She sent back a heart-eye emoji and "hubba-hubba" text. I tried a navy blue plaid number that the woman working there had told me would look amazing, but Astrid and I both agreed that even though it was very pretty, it made me look like a cartoon lumberjack's bride. The green was a peasant-style maxi dress with subtle puffed sleeves and a fitted bodice. It brought out the gold flecks in my eyes and made me feel pretty but like myself. I twirled in front of the mirror before I took a quick picture for Astrid. I changed back into my regular clothes just in time to answer her call.

"Tell me you are buying the green one. That one is fire. I bet your moody roommate won't be able to resist you in that. Next thing you know, he'll be making you waffles instead of eating them all himself."

"Give me a break," I said, willing the corners of my mouth down. "I'm not looking for a romance, just a tenuous truce."

"Still planning on making him cake?"

"Hang on a second, Astrid."

I plopped the dresses down on the counter and got out my

credit card. I thanked the woman, who handed me my receipt and a bag with the two dresses, and then I left the shop. "Sorry about that. I hate talking when someone is helping me in a store. It feels so rude. Anyway, to answer your question, my next stop is grabbing some apples from the farmer's market. Jonas has some rehearsal this afternoon, so I should have time to make it before he gets home if I hurry."

We made a plan to talk later in the week so I could let her know how my cake baking and dress wearing went. I found the indoor market and made my way inside. Pumpkins and gourds lined the front of the shop; one wall was stacked high with wooden crates turned sideways and full of every shape of fresh bread. I found the produce near the front of the store—cylindrical bins with all sorts of local greens and several kinds of apples. I picked the dullest-looking ones. My mother always told me that the shiniest apples are the ones that taste the worst. Of course, she'd likened it to people, but I'd gotten the message and held on to it all these years. I couldn't say the same for the recipe though. Despite racking my brain, I couldn't remember it, and none of the recipes I found on the internet seemed right. I dialed Dad. Wednesday afternoons he played bingo, but there was a chance I could still catch him. He was the kind of person who treasured things and curated our memories, and Mom's recipe was one he would've kept.

"Hey, Sunshine," he said when he answered. "How're things?"

"Good. Hey, do you remember the recipe for Mom's apple cake?" I asked.

He paused for a moment. "I remember the taste, but she was the baker in the family, so I'm not sure I ever knew it. What's the occasion?"

"I need to win over one of my roommates."

"Must be pretty bad if you're making a cake. Though it's hard to imagine someone not taking a liking to you."

"It's a mystery. Maybe he's just a miserable little man, I don't know."

"Man? How's Patrick feel about that?"

I squeezed my eyes shut. I'd told Dad that after the drama with Iwasaki and the series, I needed a break from the Red Sox. I had left out the part about the breakup, and the fact that the hiatus wasn't temporary *or* my choice. I sucked in a deep breath.

"I'm not sure he'd care," I said.

"Oh. Things not working out so well between you two? Let me guess—he didn't understand you wanting to work at a boarding school for the off-season. You took the loss hard; we all did. I can get you needing a change of scene . . . he should too. You know what I'm going to say, don't you, Sunny?"

I did not, but I'd been having anxiety dreams about confessing everything to him, in which my teeth tumbled out of my mouth along with the words "I got fired and arrested and Patrick and the team management sent me packing." In the dream, I had to carry my teeth in a suitcase all over Boston looking for a place to take me in, like some kind of gummy pariah. I shuddered. Things had been going south for a while before the boarding school news. I probably shouldn't have moved in with Patrick; I never really felt at home there. And he said we were supposed to support each other, but it seems like he meant I should just go along with him.

"Never let anyone, especially someone who is supposed to love you, dull your light. If you want to work at a boarding school and help some future pro athletes, that's your right. If he doesn't like it, then he can take a long walk off a short pier."

I smiled. Some things didn't change, but then I remembered

where Dad was and where I was—some things change more than we can imagine, and not for the better.

"You're the best, Dad, you know that? Speaking of pro, wait till I tell you about the kid I saw pitch up here. You'd be blown away."

"What are we talking about here?"

"He has one of the smoothest arm actions I've ever seen. I'm pretty sure I clocked him throwing fastballs in the high nineties."

"I want to see this whiz kid. If you've got some video, bring it with you this weekend. You're still coming, right?"

I had planned on driving down, donning my big-girl pants, and telling him everything . . . but work had gotten in the way. "Sorry, Dad, I wanted to, but I've got a tournament in Maine all weekend."

"Okay, well, at least I'll see you at Thanksgiving?"

"You know it."

"Now, that's something to be thankful for. Bingo's starting, kiddo. I'm handing you over to Maureen so she can give you the details."

Maureen was my favorite staff member at Sommerset Meadows. Dad had taken an immediate shine to her, which was one of the reasons I hadn't objected to him moving there. After she gave me the times for Thanksgiving, I asked her how he was doing.

"He's doing all right, hon. He misses you."

Without the recipe, I decided to attempt the cake another day. I grabbed a loaf of bread and some local goat cheese that had been mixed with blackberries and crusted in pistachios that looked too delicious to resist. Then I lugged my purchases back to the apartment. About halfway up the hill, I regretted not driving. The lovely reusable bag that the market had provided for my groceries dug into my hand, and the apples were heavier than they looked. I managed to make it to the music building before I had to set everything down and give my hands a break.

The stone stairs were cold, but it felt good to sit down and take a short rest. I dug around in the grocery bag for the bread and ripped off a hunk of the baguette. The yeasty scent was undeniably welcoming. I pressed the soft inside between my fingertips, shaping it into a ball, and popped it into my mouth. It tasted like home. While I sat, I surveyed my surroundings. The trees had already begun to lose their leaves; the fiery and rich jewel-hued leaves that tourists drove up to see littered the paths. Behind me, a door opened, and a gush of warm air carried out the sound of piano, violins, and woodwinds. The melody was beautiful and mournful. It was the kind of song that compelled you to listen through until the end. The door shut and I couldn't hear the music anymore. I brushed the crumbs from my lap and headed inside.

Chapter 7

The strings hit me first, starting as a flutter and then transforming into a full vibration in my chest. I followed the sound down the hallway, wondering if one of the players was the girl with spiral curls and tendinitis.

Despite the ancient-looking stone exterior, the interior of the music building was decidedly modern. The orchestra room was a multifaceted sphere with small windows of tinted glass here and there. Everyone in the room was seated, except for Jonas and the violin soloist. Jonas stood in the center, a conductor's baton in his right hand. He was completely entranced by the music; he fixed each orchestra section in his sights at just the right moment, spurring them along, commanding them with his movements. I'd never seen him like that. In fact, the only expressions I'd seen him wear were annoyance and some sort of evil amusement. His muscles flexed and relaxed in time with the music with intensity and moments of calm peace. He was in complete control.

Not what I came here to see, I reminded myself. I leaned in to get a better view of the violinist. It took a couple of different attempts to get the right angle. A few feet away from Jonas, the violinist stood, swaying as their right arm swept back and forth in a graceful arc. I studied the mechanics, the long arcing arm, the twist of the torso, the fluid precision—there was something familiar about it. The music stopped, and the rest of the orchestra broke into thunderous applause. The soloist took a small bow and turned to face the students who had been behind him. I blinked. The violinist was the pitcher I'd seen the other day at the fields.

"Oi. Rehearsals are closed."

I'd been so busy staring I hadn't noticed Jonas leave his station in the center of the sphere. He was standing in the doorway, glaring at me like I'd walked in on him in the bathroom.

"He's amazing," I said, still entranced.

Jonas's face softened. He approached the window. "Can't argue with that. Tyson's one of a kind. At twelve, he played with Yo-Yo Ma. He won the Wieniawski-Lipinski and Tchaikovsky young musicians competitions' first prize, twice. But his musicality, his emotion—I've never seen anything like it in someone his age."

"What was that song? I felt it in my soul," I said. My cheeks flushed as soon as the words left my mouth. "That probably sounded incredibly trite," I confessed. "I don't even like classical music."

"Not really. The point of the music is to make the listener feel something. Wait, you don't like classical music? That's total bollocks. If you don't like the great composers, what *do* you like then?"

"The Dropkick Murphys—specifically 'Tessie,' the theme song of the Boston Red Sox. Now that is a song. They play it at the games, and everyone goes crazy. It's like having this feeling of community and excitement and being home all at once. It's the best feeling in the world." I missed it. I sucked in a breath and shook off the sadness. "Still, the way Tyson plays the violin . . . unlike anything I've ever heard. Imagine being that good and being a baseball star. His family must be so proud."

Jonas's brow furrowed. "Baseball?"

"Yeah, I saw Tyson pitching the other day when I was out on a run. He's incredible. A hundred-year arm. Natural, fluid, fast. He has a fastball that I doubt most minor league players could get a piece of."

Jonas shook his head.

"What?" I asked.

Jonas returned to the orchestra room door and leaned in. "Tyson. When you're finished, I need a word."

A few students came out first; one I recognized as the girl with the tendinitis. "How's the elbow?" I asked her.

"All good, Coach," she said, though I noticed she was carrying her instrument case in the other hand.

"Ice tonight. And rest, okay?"

"I'll ice, but I need to practice," she said.

"You already had an excellent practice today, Riley," Jonas said, his voice surprisingly gentle. "Remember what we talked about before rehearsal? It's important to take care of yourself."

She nodded. "Okay. I'll take a break."

Tyson stopped near her. He was a lanky boy, built a bit like a violin bow, tall and elegant.

"Hi, Tyson," she said, smiling shyly. "You were great today."

"Thanks, Riley."

She gave a little wave and Tyson turned his attention to Jonas. "Was there a problem with the Paganini, Mr. Voss?"

Jonas rubbed his forehead. "No. The Caprice was breathtaking. Don't change a thing. But Ms. Doyle here tells me that you were at the baseball field again."

I took a step back.

"I only threw a couple of pitches," he stammered. "For fun. I didn't throw hard."

"It's okay, Tyson. You're not in trouble. But your parents have been clear about this. No baseball."

"I know. I'm sorry."

"I don't want to be the bad guy here, but I have to agree with your parents. Baseball puts your career as a musician in jeopardy. What if you get injured? You have a rare gift, and that must be protected."

"I get it," Tyson said. His shoulders sank. "Won't happen again."

"Glad to hear it. Wonderful work today." He patted him gently on the shoulder, and I found myself meanly wondering if that was for the sake of his precious hands or Tyson's rare gift.

When Tyson was out of earshot, I picked up my grocery bags. "You can't be serious about the no-baseball thing, right?"

"Why wouldn't I be?"

"He's just a kid. Shouldn't he be allowed to do what he enjoys?"

"Sure—just not a sport that could destroy his violin career when it's only beginning."

"He's a teenager. He doesn't have a career."

"With all due respect, I wouldn't come into the training room and tell you how to tape an ankle, so I'd appreciate it if you wouldn't try to push my musicians into endangering their entire futures for a bit of sporty fun and a few minutes of high school glory."

"People make careers out of baseball too, you know," I said.

"A fact that never ceases to amaze me." He reached over and picked up the grocery bags.

"I can carry those," I said. "I wouldn't want to be responsible if you were to get a boo-boo."

Jonas raised an eyebrow. "A boo-boo, Doyle? What are you, five?"

He plucked an apple out of the bag, rubbed it on the hem of his shirt, and took a giant bite as he set off in the direction of our apartment.

Chapter 8

I left the dorm later that evening to head to the library for study hall duty and was pleased to see several of the cross-country guys in the common area trying the new stretches I'd given them. It almost made up for the frustration I felt in not being able to make Mom's cake and my guilt over not being able to spend the upcoming weekend with Dad. I reminded myself that I had a lot to be grateful for. Dad and I missed one another, but we were still there for each other. We'd be to-gether on Thanksgiving, eating stuffing and pie and telling stories. He was so good at stories. I'd lost the Red Sox and my apartment, but I had a warm place to live, a new job that I was enjoying, and two roommates who were already becoming friends. That left only the third roommate. The anti-athletics, no-piano-touching, poster-board-wielding, bathroom-invading, waffle-eating roommate. He was the only downside to my new living situation.

I needed to stop focusing on him and spend my energy finding ways to help the sports program at Monadnock get stronger and somehow show the Red Sox that forcing me out had been a mistake. Between my training duties, comeback planning, and prepping for the anatomy and physiology unit that Rebecca Brown, the biology teacher, had asked me to help teach, it would be easy to steer clear of him.

The campus at night was beautiful, with winding paths lit by old-fashioned lampposts. Even so, I could still make out what felt like a million stars above me, all those tiny pinpricks of light in the inky black sky. That was one thing rural New Hampshire had on Boston. The stars weren't visible in the city. I'd always loved the lights of Boston, but this splendor was different. It gave me a strange sense of just how small we all are.

The library was as glorious as Andy had said. The ceilings were high and covered with intricate paintings that truly did resemble the Sistine Chapel ceiling—not that I'd been there. Long, glossy wood tables were lit by brass lamps with green glass shades. It was like stepping back in time to someplace very special.

"Sorry. We need to get by." I turned to face Jonas and several students packed together in the entryway. Clouds of breath billowed around them. My face flamed as I stepped aside. Jonas let the kids go ahead of him, and they scrambled to find their preferred study spots.

During study hall, the faculty on duty were required to circulate periodically and sit at the front desk in case anyone wanted to check something out or needed help finding a resource. Jonas sat in a chair and I dropped into the seat next to him, my cheeks still hot with embarrassment. The desk was small, and Jonas's lanky frame took over most of it.

"I stood in the doorway my first time in here too, you know," he whispered to me. "It's pretty spectacular."

I swiveled in my chair to face him. "Are you being nice to me?"

"*No*," he said, almost playfully. His eyes gleamed. In a low voice he added, "I'm just trying to do something to stanch the heat radiating from your red face. I'd rather not have to take off my sweater."

"Whatever you say," I replied, eyeing him suspiciously. Maybe Revi and Andy were right and he wasn't a completely lost cause.

He put in his earbuds again—this was becoming a common theme—and turned his attention to a notebook. The pages were lined with rows of staves, and he was busily scribbling what I assumed were notes. I found the process, the way his hand swept across the page scattering symbols in its wake, mesmerizing; I didn't even notice when a student approached the counter.

"Ahem."

"Oh, hi." I looked up to face the pitcher-slash-violinist. "Tyson, right?"

"You're the new trainer . . . Coach Doyle."

"That's me." I collected a stack of books from him.

"I want to check these out, please."

I scanned each of the titles. *Nine Innings* by Daniel Okrent, *Red Smith on Baseball* by Red Smith, and *The Duke of Havana* by Steve Fainaru and Ray Sanchez.

"No music books for you?" I asked. "Seems like you're pretty interested in baseball."

He nodded.

"Me too. You know, before I worked here, I used to train a professional team."

"Seriously? Which one?"

"One hundred percent. It rhymes with 'head box,'" I said, voice low. "You've got amazing raw talent. If you wanted, you could have a real future in the sport."

Tyson shrugged, casting a furtive glance at Jonas, who was in his own world, composing. "You heard Mr. Voss. I can't. I wish I could, but violin comes first."

"It still could. Lots of people do more than one thing."

"Not me."

He took the books from me and walked away without a backward glance.

"Was that Tyson? Did he need something?" Jonas asked, brow furrowed.

I shook my head. "He was just checking out some books."

His expression was still troubled, so I changed the subject. "What are you working on? Are you writing a song?"

"It's an arrangement," he said. "I'm taking a piece of music written by someone else and rewriting it for piano."

"Are you going to play it? Or the kids?"

"Not me," he said, voice gone flat. "I don't play."

"You don't? I guess I just assumed that the piano you have such strong feelings about was one that you *played*."

"You know the saying 'when you assume, you make an ass out of you and me'? Seems apt." He closed the notebook and the conversation. "I'm going to go make sure that none of the students are fraternizing in the stacks."

"They do that?"

"You really don't know anything about teenagers, do you, Doyle?"

"Of course I know about teenagers. I was one."

"A boring one, apparently." There was no trace of venom in his tone; in fact, as he passed by me, I was fairly certain I detected the faintest suggestion of a smile at the corner of his lips. Was Jonas Voss teasing me? He was a curmudgeon, but also an enigma, and I wanted to untangle him. Why didn't he play the piano in my room when he so clearly loved it? Loved it enough to torment me and to pass his evening writing music to be played on one. There had been a sadness in his eyes when he'd admitted he didn't play, a droop in his shoulders. He reminded me of an athlete being told they were going on the injured list. They say they're fine, but you can see the physical signs of pain no matter how they deny it. Like Iwasaki. Sometimes it was obvious, other times subtle. I'd trained myself not to miss those signs after what had happened with Dad.

Maureen's message had been circling my thoughts all day. *He misses you.* When I'd committed to the move, I'd told myself I'd go down every Sunday, but at the first chance, I'd put up an obstacle. Dad'd assumed I was busy, and while that was partially true, I would always find time for him—if I was honest with myself, I had to admit that I was avoiding him because I still couldn't muster up the courage to confess the truth about what had happened during the World Series. We'd kept things from each other before, like when he'd started seeing the signs of his Parkinson's disease and he hadn't told me, but this was different. I was holding out hope that the team management would realize their mistake and ask me to come back, so I kept my confession locked away and tolerated sharing my tiny room with the piano that was "too sensitive" to move. I'd been through a lot in my life; I could handle some temporary discomfort.

After the game, Astrid had put me on a full media lockdown. She'd had some hacker she'd shadowed for a role block certain sites and keywords from my phone and laptop. *It's for your own good, Sophie*, she'd said. Astrid knew the highs and lows of celebrity life. People were always gossiping about her, posting pictures that should've been private, publicizing wild accusations about her diet, her sexual orientation, secret pregnancies. They loved and hated her acting, calling her a genius or a hack, depending on the day. The internet makes the commenters anonymous and dehumanizes the subject—a perfect recipe for bold and brazen commentary and vitriol. The man in the bakery was nothing compared to the trolls who had been coming for me. She knew the damage being exposed to the court of public opinion could cause. But her tech friend hadn't blocked those things here. When I was younger, my mom used to recite the Emily Dickinson poem "'Hope' is the thing with feathers," and I'd grown up believing that I was some kind of little bird, meant to chirp songs merrily and believe that things would be okay. I opened the internet browser and searched. Five minutes of scrolling the search results plucked the feathers out. By the time Jonas got back from his lap of the library, I was neck-deep in feathers and trying to keep myself together.

They'll forget, Astrid had told me.

Baseball fans never forget.

I don't know how Sophie Doyle could ever show her face in Boston ever again, famous New England sportswriter Ricky Evans had written.

There was an interview with Iwasaki dated one week ago. They'd asked him how the arm was feeling. *Solid*, he'd said. *I'm already thinking about spring training. How do you feel about being kept from the series? I'm a player, so I always want to play. Right now, I'm focused on the future. And what about Sophie Doyle*, they asked. *Would you ever work with her again? I'm not going to talk about Sophie Doyle.*

I sighed. Did he blame me too?

"Doing a little light reading?"

I squeezed my eyes shut.

"Everything all right over there?" Jonas asked.

"I'm going to the stacks," I said, willing him not to respond.

"Hey, Doyle. I—"

"Not now, Jonas. I'm not up for whatever it is that you want to say to me." I brushed past his chair. Paused. Looked around.

Wordlessly, he pointed in the opposite direction. I reversed course and headed toward the stacks. Maybe it was foolish of me, but I'd comforted myself through this whole horrible experience with the knowledge that I'd done the right thing. I was willing to accept the consequences if it meant protecting an athlete and his career. I had thought that I was helping Iwasaki. But even he didn't seem to think so. I'd foolishly told myself that if I just kept it together, kept my head down, and worked hard, I could find a way back. But every word I'd just read seemed to make that notion more and more implausible. I found a space between the tall shelves where no one was around and took several slow breaths. I thought of the technique that I'd taught some of my athletes who struggled with stress and severe performance anxiety; I'd read about it somewhere, though I couldn't remember where now. Think of one thing you see, one thing you smell, one thing you hear, one thing you can touch. I pressed my fingers against the spine of an old book and closed my eyes.

Something brushed against my fingertips, and my eyes snapped open.

"Jesus!" I said, startled.

"Sorry," Jonas said. "I wanted to make sure that you were okay. You didn't look well back there."

I glanced up at him. His face was earnest. There was no trace of mocking or disdain or annoyance. His normally hardened features were soft, his eyes gentle, questioning. "I'm okay. I just have some stuff on my mind."

"Something about why you came to Monadnock?"

I shrugged. "I should be in Boston—my dad's there. A while back, he moved into an assisted living facility just outside the city. He has Parkinson's and I worry. It's hard to be away from him. But Boston's not an option for me at the moment."

He stood silent, then gave a dip of his chin.

"You don't want to know why?" I asked, surprised that he hadn't taken the opportunity to pry into my downfall.

"Why would I?" he asked, shoving his hands in his pockets.

Of course. He didn't care.

He softened his voice. "The way I see it, most of us are running from something. Your reasons are your business."

"Sorry," I said, "I don't get you. You've made it clear you don't want me to be here. Since the moment you saw me in the apartment, you've been unbearable. Now you're being kind?"

He shrugged. "You seemed upset. Why would I mess with someone who's struggling? I'm not a totally heartless bastard, Doyle."

I took a step toward him. My eyes narrowed as I stared at him. "Are you sure? You ate *every single* waffle. That seems somewhere in the vicinity of 'heartless bastard.'"

He stared back at me. I hadn't expected the eye contact or the heat that seemed to emanate from his gaze. "I like waffles." His voice was smooth and sweet like syrup.

I drew a breath in through my nose. A strange tide of nervous energy had risen in me and settled into my stomach.

One thing I could see. The maple-and-moss depths of his irises. One thing I could smell. The faintest aroma of Irish

Spring soap. One thing I could hear. My own heart thrumming loudly in my ears. One thing I could touch. I gulped.

"Just so I'm clear, then. You like waffles . . . but not me."

"Right," he said, looking at me intently. "Exactly. I don't like you."

He stood motionless for a moment; his words hung in the air between us, and then he turned and left me standing alone in the stacks.

Chapter 9

It sounds like you had a 'moment' with your testy room-mate," Astrid said. "I'm going to try really hard not to laugh about the fact that I called him testy." She snorted.

"You're sick. Tell me you're not making a joke about his nuts."

"What's wrong with a nut joke? They are funny by their very nature. But I digress . . . you had a moment. The swirling stomach, the proximity in the stacks. You weren't really talk-ing about waffles at all, were you?"

"Please—that's ludicrous," I shot back.

"Is it, though? I always found Grouchy to be the hottest Smurf."

"Astrid, for the love of everything holy, can you focus? A waffle is just a waffle. A piano is a piano. Nothing more, noth-ing less. And there was not a moment. It's just hard to wrap my head around. He's been giving me a hard time since the moment we met and then out of nowhere he's *nice*? You have to admit, that's weird, right? This guy is giving me whiplash."

"Fine. I hear you. And I promise to behave. I'm not even

going to say anything about him giving you a *hard* time. Even if I *really* want to. Is it possible that all this time when he's been grumbling at you, he's been flirting?"

"Impossible." Right?

"I'm saying possible. Maybe the accent's throwing you off. But I can't give you a definitive ruling without more information. What were you talking about before the non-moment?"

"About Dad." I sighed.

"What do you mean?" Astrid said, her tone shifting to serious. "Is he okay?"

"I think so. I don't really know, because I'm here and he's there and I'm a shitty daughter who's too busy with an away game and avoiding uncomfortable conversations to go see him this weekend."

"Soph, I can tell you're upset, so what's really going on?"

"I let everyone down. There was this article and Iwasaki said——"

"What article?"

"I saw an article at the library."

"You searched yourself on the internet? Sophie! I told you nothing good ever comes from that. Trust me."

"He said he didn't want to talk about me."

"That doesn't mean anything. They can choose what to include or exclude to make things look a certain way. If you really want to know what Iwasaki thinks, you should ask him. You were friendly, right?"

I frowned. She was right. Except I just couldn't bring myself to do it. "They were my family—the team. And even though I was sure he shouldn't play that night, I can't help but think, what if I hadn't stepped in? Would they have won? Would he have been okay? I mean, that's possible. Patrick said he was fine. Maybe I should've trusted him. At the time, I was confident that I was making the best choice, yet I can't help feeling like I let him down somehow, just like I did with Dad."

When Astrid spoke, her voice was strained. "I know how much you care about those guys and how much you love your dad. But you are not responsible for everything that's happened. Should you have shoved a cannoli in some guy's eye in response to being fired and accosted? Maybe not. But I know you did your best to protect Iwasaki. That's all you could do. And it was your job. Look, I think this is going to be okay. I really believe that; I'm not just bullshitting you. And I know you feel like you've lost so much, but even if it isn't okay . . . you will always have me, you got it?"

I sniffed and wiped the tears that had pooled. "I know. I just want to fix things."

"I get that. But promise me that you won't tie yourself into knots trying to mend things that you have no control over."

"You're such a momma bear. Your fans wouldn't believe it."

Astrid laughed.

"So you told the grouchy roommate about your dad? That's pretty personal . . . especially for you. I remember when you and Patrick first got together you didn't even let him see your apartment for six months."

Why *had* I told Jonas about Dad? I didn't want to explain to Astrid that I had the sense that he would understand having something pressing on him. Or that those hazel eyes of his had melted my defenses just enough for me to ask him to compare his feelings for a breakfast food item to his feelings for me. *I don't like you*, he'd said. And why had that been so hard to hear?

"He was the only one there."

"Who was the only one there?" Revi asked, hanging his jacket up on the coat tree.

"My roommates are home," I told Astrid. "The nice ones."

"Oh, are you talking to Astrid?" Andy said.

I nodded and put her on speaker. "Want to say hi, guys?"

"Do we want to say hi to your friend who is also Monadnock's most famous alumna?" Revi asked. "Is that even a question?" They dropped down to flank me on the couch. "Hi, Astrid. I loved you in *Moon Gazers*. You were robbed by the Academy."

"Hi, Revi and Andy! It's great to meet you. Soph's told me good things about you both. And I fully agree with you about the Academy. That was my best work—the whole scene is very political. You give a woman a happy ending and oops, it's not art anymore. Can I be frank, though? Tell me, please, what is the deal with your other roommate? Am I going to have to have him taken care of?"

Andy looked at Revi and then at me. He mouthed, *She couldn't do that, right?* I shook my head.

Revi said, "He's harmless. Honestly, he's a good guy—no one is more invested in these kids. And he has some redeeming qualities."

Like the smell of his soap and his deep, expressive eyes. The way the corner of his mouth curled up involuntarily when he was messing with me. Maybe Astrid was right . . . I'd had a moment. Just me, though, because Jonas definitely had not.

"He fixes all the stuff that breaks in the apartment. We asked maintenance to repair the broken lock on our bathroom door, and they kept putting it off. So out of nowhere, he just goes ahead and buys a new lock and installs it himself. Plus, he keeps the apartment clean and insists on treating whenever we eat out," Revi said.

"Okay, I'll take your word for it. For now. Since we're friends, I'll tell you this: Sophie's family to me and I don't abide anyone mistreating her. Capisce?"

"On that note, we should go," I said. "I need to get ready for formal dinner."

"Oh, yes! I forgot about your new dinner dresses. Have you decided which one you're wearing first, plum or green?"

"Does it matter? I'll just throw one on."

"It matters," Astrid said. "Guys, can you help my fashion-clueless friend pick her dress?"

Andy's face shone. "I've been waiting my whole life for that very request."

Revi and Andy waited on the couch, still chatting comfortably with Astrid as if they'd known her for years, while I retreated to my tiny bedroom to change my clothes. I tried on the plum-colored dress first. I ran a brush through my hair until it was smooth and glistening and then returned to the living room, where my audience waited.

"Option one," I declared, and did a little spin.

"I'm sold," Revi said.

"You look gorgeous, Sophie," Andy added. "That color looks amazing with your red hair."

"You really think so?"

"Andy takes fashion very seriously," Revi said. "He'll be the first one to tell you that you look great, and the first one to tell you to go change."

"Show them the green one," Astrid demanded.

"Okay, boss."

Moments later I emerged, not sure if I felt silly or like a goddess. I was certain about the color. Maybe it was the Irish in me, but I'd always favored green. Andy and Revi were laughing hysterically about something—probably something

Astrid had said. I twisted my hands together, waiting for them to notice me.

"Wow, Sophie. You are such a stealthy stunner. No offense, but the sweatshirt / track pants combo you've been sporting since you got here doesn't do you justice," Andy said.

Revi added, "I like the sweats. Besides, Sophie's dressing for herself, not the rest of the world. But this green one is my favorite." A mischievous twitch in the corner of his mouth left me uneasy. "What do *you* think, Jonas?"

I closed my eyes. In the quiet of the room, Jonas's footfalls as he approached were practically thunderous. *It's just an outfit. He's just a roommate.*

Is there anything more vulnerable than wearing a dress and being appraised by a man with whom you maybe had a moment in the stacks? I resisted the urge to bite my nails.

"We're waiting," Andy said, and I opened my eyes for an instant to glare at him.

Jonas said nothing. He stood a few feet away from me, staring wordlessly. My skin went from mildly warm to broiling with humiliation. He couldn't even manage a "nice dress" or "looks good"? Instead, he rubbed the back of his neck, like he was trying to find words to describe the hideousness of my appearance but coming up empty. He gave an abrupt dip of his chin and then walked away.

Revi's entire body cringed. Astrid's voice rattled through the speaker. "Tell me the connection went bad and he didn't just say nothing. Not even a peep? I will literally get on a plane tonight and come down there and—"

I snatched the phone out of Andy's hand. "Okay, we've got to go to dinner now. Love you, Astrid. Bye!" I rattled off and then hung up.

"Sorry, Sophie," Andy said, as he rose to go get into his

formal dinner clothes. "For what it's worth, you look absolutely lovely."

Revi gave me a hug. "Maybe he was speechless."

"It's fine," I said. "Why would I care what Jonas Voss thinks when I have you guys? Hurry and get changed. I'm ravenous."

I went to my room to get out my wool coat—the only warm thing I owned that was fancy enough to wear with a dress—and a pair of tall leather boots. Why *would* I care what Jonas Voss thought about anything? I slicked on some mascara and a bit of lip gloss. As far as I was concerned, he didn't get to have an opinion about me. I'd gotten enough opinions for a lifetime after reading those posts on the internet. And then there was Patrick, who had always had some lackluster observation he just needed to make about me. My hair was a bit frizzy. The salmon I'd made was dry.

When I emerged, the guys were all waiting in the living room, clad in their dressy outfits. Revi hadn't been kidding. Andy's suit was a deep mauve plaid that looked like it could've been on a runway at fashion week. Unsurprisingly, Revi wore the standard prep school attire of wrinkled chinos and a blue blazer with a Monadnock-maroon striped tie. Next to them, Jonas was clad in a simple fitted black suit. He looked infuriatingly attractive. I thought I'd have to avoid eye contact, but lucky for me he was focused on fashioning a Windsor knot.

"Let's jam," Andy said.

After a frigid walk to the dining hall, we all found our table assignments and split up. At each table of eight, there were two faculty, so of course—because the universe has a weird sense of humor—I ended up at the same table with Jonas.

Chapter 10

A ndy hopped onto the golf cart at the end of practice two
weeks later, grinning wider than usual. It was a perfect
New England afternoon. I pulled the hood of my fleece-lined
Monadnock jacket up against the late-fall nip in the air.

"TGIF!" he announced.

"You're in a good mood," I said. "Feeling optimistic about
your chances for a win tomorrow?"

He laughed. "Seriously, Soph? After stretching was over,
half my team spent the entirety of practice putting on a dramatic rendition of the second act of *Hamilton*. The performance was fire, but let's not delude ourselves. Miss Maria
Reynolds tripped herself with her own stick. We're going to
get obliterated tomorrow."

"At least you'll do it with dramatic flair?" I said with a
wince.

"And in perfect harmony." He grinned.

I steered the cart off the grass and onto a sidewalk. "So,
roomie . . . what are you up to tonight?" Andy asked.

Since I'd come to Monadnock three weeks ago, I'd kept a

Friday night ritual of working out and then settling in for a quiet evening in preparation for a weekend jam-packed with events. "I have a thrilling evening of deadlifting planned, followed by a date with Ben and Jerry and the movie *Million Dollar Arm*."

"I take issue with this plan."

I glanced over at him while I whipped the golf cart around the corner. "Like what?"

Andy grabbed on to the golf cart's metal frame. "Good god, this thing needs some seat belts!"

I released the accelerator a tad.

"Thank you," Andy said. "Where was I? My life flashed before my eyes and I forgot what I was talking about."

"You have issues with my Friday night plans?"

"Oh yeah. Your evening sounds like some sort of post-breakup mope. You're not doing that."

"I'm not?"

Andy shook his head. "Nope. You're leaving Ben and Jerry at home and coming out with your other two favorite guys."

"Larry Bird and Big Papi?" I opened my eyes wide in faux amazement. "My dream is finally coming true."

"Meanie. Maybe you and Jonas are a perfect match after all."

"Wait, what? Who said that?"

"You know Revi, he's a romantic at heart." Andy smiled at the admission. "He didn't mean anything by it."

I thought about this for a second. The notion of me and Jonas—I shook my head—was ridiculous. Sure, he was handsome, and our verbal sparring sometimes had a slight undercurrent to it that a part of me was starting to enjoy, but that was it.

Andy continued, "You're coming out with me and Revi. A

bunch of us are off duty and we're heading down to Pumpelly's Pub for a night of drinking and debauchery. You haven't done anything fun since you got here. All you do is work and work out."

"Games are fun," I said. "Okay, maybe not when we're getting annihilated."

"Are we ever *not* getting crushed? Besides, watching games is your job, Sophie. This is for fun. Friends listening to music and talking while drinking Sam Adams. And eating cake."

"You are very convincing, you know that?"

"Was it the cake?"

"You had me at Sam Adams."

Later that evening, I stepped into the living room wearing a black off-the-shoulder cashmere sweater that Astrid had gifted me last Christmas along with a pair of jeans and suede boots.

"What do you think?" I asked the guys.

Revi grinned. "Perfection," he said.

"And you didn't even need our help. I'm so proud," Andy added, linking his arm through mine.

Jonas emerged from his bedroom, clad in a charcoal gray half-zip sweater and a pair of dark jeans. I hadn't realized he was coming with us. I also hadn't realized that I would feel something when he walked into a room. That was only natural—finding Jonas hot was like finding a panda adorable. There's no point fighting a simple fact. It didn't mean anything. I recalled Andy's comment from earlier about Revi's romantic musing about me and Jonas and quickly pushed it out of my mind.

"Let's go," Andy said. "Rebecca and Cynthia texted me that they're there and already got us a round."

"Have you met them both, Sophie?" Revi asked.

"Hang on, I forgot something in my room," Jonas said.

I watched Jonas disappear into his room and turned back to Revi only to find him examining me with a funny expression on his face. "Uh, yeah, I've met them. Rebecca asked me to help out with a few lessons for her bio students, and I've talked to Cynthia when I've gone to the soccer team's away games. They're both really nice."

Jonas reappeared with a flannel coat over his sweater. Revi laughed. "Sophie has bare shoulders and she isn't wearing a coat. It's not even winter," he teased.

Jonas threw an arm around Revi's shoulder. "Listen, mate, when I'm toasty on the walk home and you're shivering, don't think I'll take pity on you."

Andy, who was putting on a green bomber-style jacket, looked up. "Don't look at me—I'm from Southern California, friends," he said good-naturedly.

"You blokes tease, but I had your presents in my coat pocket," Jonas said. "I gather you probably didn't want to miss out on a gift."

He pulled out two identical boxes wrapped neatly in newsprint. "Can we open them now?" Revi asked.

"It's your anniversary," Jonas said, smiling. "Open them whenever you want."

I looked from Andy to Revi, who were grinning adorably at each other. I'd assumed they were together but were just being low-key about it, since neither of them had mentioned it to me. But seeing them with anniversary gifts—from Jonas, no less—made it clear that this was serious. They tore off the wrapping and opened the identical boxes. Andy's jaw dropped and he threw his arms around Jonas, knocking him back a couple of steps.

"You're crushing the plane tickets," Jonas groaned.

"This is too much," Andy said.

"No, it's not. It's the exact right amount for my favorite roommates. You guys didn't have Thanksgiving plans, right?"

"These are precious," Revi announced. He accepted the envelope that Jonas had procured from his jacket. "I'm putting all of this somewhere safe and then we are going to go buy you a drink"—he glanced at Andy—"a lot of drinks."

I was dying to know what kind of present Jonas had bought Revi and Andy. He didn't strike me as a gift-giving kind of guy, let alone an anniversary gift kind of guy. But I didn't want to ask. We were too deep in this game for me to give him the satisfaction of knowing I was curious. I led the way to the exit.

Pumpelly's was a small pub, cozy and dimly lit. There were a pool table and darts in the back, and the mahogany bar was polished to a high shine. A local indie-rock band was playing on a small stage in front of some high-top tables. Cynthia and Rebecca were standing at one table guarding a bunch of full pint glasses. We all exchanged hugs when we arrived.

"You look gorgeous," Cynthia said. "I don't think I've ever seen you in anything other than athletic wear."

"You sit too far from her at formal dinner. She wore the cutest dress yesterday," Rebecca said.

"Thank you," I said.

"Who do you sit with?" Cynthia asked.

"We sit together," Jonas volunteered, claiming a pint. "Should we toast the fellas?"

We all turned to face Andy and Revi. Andy had his arm around Revi, who was resting his head on Andy's shoulder.

Jonas held up his glass. "A year ago, I was at the end of

something big in my life, and you two were at the beginning of this wonderful thing you have together. We were in totally different places, but we all ended up in the same apartment. And even though I was a knobhead with a bloody chip on his shoulder and you probably would've rather had an apartment to yourself, you made room for me, not just in the space but as a friend. I am just as lucky to call you my mates as you are to have each other. So, Revi and Andy, this year, I wish you both fewer troubles and more blessings. All the love in the world. And nothing but happiness."

I watched Jonas while he spoke with such sincerity, as he raised the glass to his lips and took a sip. Goose bumps prickled my arms beneath my sweater.

"You look confused," Cynthia said, touching her fingers to my wrinkled brow.

"I think she looks thirsty," Rebecca volunteered.

"I have a beer," I said.

"Not that kind of thirsty," Rebecca said, and laughed. I wrinkled my nose. "What? You think you're the first faculty to find Jonas Voss hot? Join the club. He is a tall, fine drink of tea."

I took a big gulp of beer and stole a glance at Jonas. Okay, he was *kind* of a tall, fine drink of something. But I wasn't thirsty, I was bemused. Ninety-nine percent of the time, the most appropriate adjective for Jonas was "cranky" . . . and here he was giving anniversary gifts and moving toasts? At the moment, he was watching the keyboard player and nodding along to the music. Next to me, Cynthia and Rebecca had moved on and were now talking about some modern dance performance that was happening on Sunday. Several of the girls on the soccer team were accomplished dancers and had asked if they could miss the game to get in an extra rehearsal.

"Are you going to let them skip the game?" I asked.

Cynthia shook her head. "I understand that dance is their priority. But I made it clear that they needed to honor all their commitments."

"How'd that go?" Rebecca asked.

"They rescheduled the rehearsal for later in the evening. They're going to be so tired for the performance," she said. "Are you going to watch, Sophie? I know our games can be a little painful to witness. But the modern dance troupe is incredible. Our goalie choreographed the first piece with the captain of the boys' team."

"Sure," I said. "I'd love to see it."

"What about you, Jonas?" Rebecca asked. "Are you coming to the fall dance performance?"

Jonas turned. "Yeah, I'll be there. One of the numbers has an original violin duet written by one of the seniors in the orchestra. He'll be away on a college interview, so he asked if I would fill in for him and play with Tyson. Who's ready for another round?"

"Me," Rebecca said, with certainty. "It's been a week."

"Becks, guess what Jonas gave us for our anniversary," Andy said when Jonas was out of earshot. "A trip to Disney for Thanksgiving."

"Seriously?" I sputtered. I set my drink down. I'd heard the part about Thanksgiving and plane tickets, but hadn't put it all together.

Andy nodded. "There were MagicBands in the boxes. Both of us want to see our family, but India's too long of a trip for Revi to do over Thanksgiving break, and my parents and sisters are on a cruise in the Riviera, so we were just going to stay here. We freaking love Disney—well, I've only been to Disneyland, so this will be my first time in Orlando, but Revi tells me it's awesome."

"That's wild!" Rebecca said. "He's so generous. I had no idea. I don't mind him since I've gotten to know him, but I know some staff think he's kind of a dick since he sort of—"

"Acts like one?" I volunteered.

"Sometimes, yeah," Rebecca said, grimacing.

"We were really nervous when he moved in," Revi confessed. "He was so sullen and quiet. And not everyone is accepting, you know? Then we told him we were a couple and he said he'd move out, so both of us immediately figured—"

Andy interjected, "It wasn't like that. He must've seen our faces, because he immediately explained. It turned out that was because the other couples on campus are all married and get their own apartments. He was super supportive of our relationship; he just didn't want to cramp our style. He thought maybe we didn't want him as a roommate."

"Well, I'm glad it all worked out," Rebecca said. "Sounds like you'll both be having an awesome time over break. What are your plans, Sophie?"

"I'm heading down to Boston to spend time with my dad. It's just the two of us. I'm going to make his favorite pie since the place where he lives does all the catering."

"Sounds fancy," Rebecca said.

"Not really, uh, it's an assisted living facility. My dad has pretty bad Parkinson's, so he didn't, well, he's not able to live alone."

Rebecca put her hand on my arm, nodding. "I bet he'll be glad to see you, and your pie."

"How about you, Rebecca? All ready for Thanksgiving break?" Revi asked.

"Beyond ready," she said. "I'm not even doing anything exciting, just dinner with the family and watching football, but it will be glorious to be in a teenager-free zone for a few days. I don't know what's going on this semester, but the kids have been really pushing boundaries."

"They're under a lot of pressure," Jonas said, arriving with a fresh set of full pints. "This is the first year where they all have to carry a full five-credit academic course load in addition to their creative specializations. It's a lot. Some of the orchestra kids have mentioned how stressed they are."

"That's a good point," Revi said. "I've noticed the same. Maybe we should plan some fun breaks for them after the vacation?"

"We've started doing ten minutes of meditation in my theory and composition courses," Jonas said. "It seems to be helping."

"No shop talk!" Andy announced, swiping a beer from Jonas. "Who wants to play pool?"

"Smashing. I'm in," Jonas said.

I couldn't help myself—I scoffed.

Jonas locked his eyes on mine. I tried to break the eye contact, but the farthest I seemed to be able to redirect my gaze was to his mouth, which was curled into a smirk and was causing a strange tingling sensation on the skin of my neck. "Something to say, Doyle?"

I shook my head. "No. I'm just surprised. I thought you would never deign to play sports."

"I'll make an exception," he said, leaning very close to me. I could smell the faint aroma of his soap, woodsy and clean. "For billiards . . . and beating you."

Lightning sizzled down my spine. "*Please*. Are you even good?" I asked, trying to control my heart rate.

"Oh, I'm *very* good." His voice was low, nearly a whisper. If he hadn't been so near, I might not have heard him. I caught the inside of my lip between my teeth for an instant. Then I downed the rest of my beer.

I took a deep breath and collected myself. "Want to make a bet?" I said, eyes narrowed.

An hour later, Andy, Revi, Cynthia, and Rebecca had all been knocked out of the tournament and I was four games down to Jonas and well on my way to being drunk. This is what happens when an overly proud, ultracompetitive person takes on the man who has been pressing her buttons—all of her buttons—for weeks. She refuses to accept defeat and she drinks too much in the process. The drinking didn't do much for my playing, and now I was stuck in a vicious cycle of my own making.

"Time for more Sam Adams," I announced, nearly banging the light over the table with my cue.

"Are you sure, Doyle?" Jonas asked. "Wouldn't you rather have a piece of Andy and Revi's cake? It's a giant whoopie pie." He made it sound so good. *Focus, Sophie*, I told myself.

"A bet is a bet," I said, taking Jonas's beer from his grip and accidentally sloshing it on my hand. "Whoever misses a shot has to drink. I'm a woman of my word."

"We don't have to keep playing," he said. "It was only a bit of fun, and everyone else has left."

I leaned toward where he was bent down to prepare for an easy diagonal shot into the corner pocket. "You want me to give up, right? You'd probably love that. Just like you'd love it if I moved out of the apartment. Isn't that what you want?"

He stopped lining up his shot. "Not particularly." He reached out and put his hands on the pint glass I was holding. His hands were warm against mine; drops of condensation mingled between our fingertips. As he slowly withdrew the beer, his eyes met mine. I watched as he proceeded to drain the contents.

"I don't think you have a clue what I want, Doyle." He set the empty beer glass on the edge of the table and promptly scratched on the eight ball.

"Looks like I lost the bet," he said.

"You did that on purpose."

"I guess we'll never know. Look, you're clearly pissed."

"You're right, I am pissed. I wanted to beat you fair and square. A pity win is not a win . . . it's worse than losing."

"Okay then. But in this case, 'pissed' means 'drunk.' If I were a barman, I'd have cut you off two pints ago. Let's go. I'll walk you home."

"What about everybody else?" I asked, swaying just a little. "I want to stay with them."

We surveyed the bar. Bored with our competitive antics, everyone else had abandoned us. The band had finished somewhere during our third game, and the atmosphere had shifted to more club-like, with a DJ playing dance party music. Cynthia was grinding against a lumberjack with a man bun and Rebecca was dancing with a group of people I didn't recognize. Andy and Revi were taking a break from the dance floor to feed each other cake.

"Looks like it's just you and me, Doyle. Everyone else is in for the long haul."

Jonas told the guys that we were heading back to campus, and then we stepped out into the night. Despite the warmth from the alcohol in my system, I shivered. Jonas had been smart to wear a jacket. The temperature had dropped significantly since we'd arrived and now frost was starting to form on the windows. Unsteadily, I started down the street.

"Wrong way, Magellan," Jonas said, gently grasping my arm to steer me back on the sidewalk. "Campus is in the other direction."

"You know, I'm tired. I think I'm going to take a little break on this bench for a minute." I dropped down onto the cold metal.

"Oh, bloody hell." He stooped down in front of me. "C'mon, I'll give you a piggyback so we can make it back before we both succumb to hypothermia."

I leaned forward and flung my arms around his neck. "Jonas Voss, are you being a gentleman right now?"

He laughed. I hadn't realized he was capable of laughter, but he had a nice laugh, rich and warm and melodic. I liked it. I wanted to hear it again.

Jonas straightened and started up the hill. "Don't get used to it."

Chapter 11

Thanksgiving break started the following Wednesday after morning classes ended. The dining hall served gourmet bagged lunches for students to eat while traveling—sandwiches with fresh baked bread and chicken salad with grapes, walnuts, and fresh dill. Homemade sweet potato chips. Soft cranberry-oatmeal cookies with white chocolate chips. Revi, Andy, Jonas, and I ate in the sun on the quad and watched as luxury vehicles flooded the campus and the students departed in a strange, sweatshirt-clad exodus.

Andy and Revi were headed to Disney, where they were going to eat their turkey feast in the Beast's castle. They were already wearing T-shirts—Donald Duck for Andy and classic Mickey for Revi.

"Will you guys wear the ears?" I asked.

"Of course," Andy said. "You can't go to Disney and not wear the ears. It's like cartoon blasphemy. Rev, did you get our FastPasses set up? I really want to make sure we get on the Seven Dwarfs Mine Train as soon as we get there."

"What am I, an amateur?" Revi asked, feigning hurt.

"Is that one of those spinning rides?" I asked.

Revi and Andy both swiveled around to look at me. "It's a roller coaster, Boston. Wait a minute. Have you not been to Disney?"

"Nope." I took a bite out of my sandwich.

"Seriously?"

"Never. Is it that hard to believe? I bet lots of people haven't been."

"Even Jonas has been, Sophie," Revi said.

I turned to look at Jonas, who was having some sort of singular experience with the cookie he was eating. There was a crumb at the corner of his mouth, and for a fraction of an instant, I had the urge to reach out and wipe it away. He stopped eating.

"No way," I said.

"Way. How do you think I managed to get them into the Beast's castle for dinner? Never mind." He took a slow bite of his cookie. I watched his jaw work, his Adam's apple dip as he swallowed, and his tongue make its way around his lips as he located and took care of the crumb I'd been eyeing. Then I remembered that this was a man who would only be at Disney if he were playing the role of villain, not someone I should be mesmerized by, and that Revi and Andy were watching. Oh boy were they watching. The expressions on their faces made me feel more self-conscious than if I had been wearing nothing but a pair of glittering Minnie Mouse ears and my underwear in the middle of the quad.

"So is your lack of Disney experience because you don't like it or a tragic tale of missing out?" Revi asked.

"I missed a lot of things. We didn't really have the money or the time. When I was little, both my parents worked constantly and then when I got older I was usually working too, and then my mom got sick. I also missed prom. I do love *Mulan* though," I confessed. I knew the story wasn't exactly aligned with the original tale, but I still loved the idea of a daughter risking everything to protect her father and her country. The scene where the emperor and all of the people bow to her never failed to bring me to tears. "I guess I just never had the opportunity."

Revi glanced at his watch. "We should go," he said. "I know how you hate cutting it close for flights. Next time, Sophie, you're coming with us."

Andy stood up and brushed crumbs and grass from his jeans. "Be good while we're gone. No burning down the apartment in your War of the Roses."

"Don't worry," I assured them. "I won't even be here, remember?"

"That's right. Hope you have a wonderful time, Sophie. Give your papa our love."

I folded my knees in and clasped my arms around them. "I will. Enjoy your roller coasters. And send me pictures. I need to see what the Disney experience is all about." I smiled.

Jonas and I sat in silence as Andy and Revi picked up their rolling carry-ons, which they'd left beside the dorm, and headed toward the parking lot. I tipped my face to the sun. The breeze was cool against my skin, but it felt so good to be out in the fresh air.

"How long are you planning to stay in Boston?" Jonas asked.

I shrugged. "Until the weekend, maybe? My friend Astrid sublet her apartment, so I have to stay in a hotel now. Why? Have some hot date planned and don't want to risk the bloody roommate interrupting?"

Jonas snorted. "No. I just wanted to know how long I would have this place to myself."

"You're predictable, I'll give you that, Jonas." I stood and collected the remnants of my lunch. "Here, give me your trash," I said. "I'll throw it out." I extended my hands and Jonas put his crushed lunch bag into them. His fingers grazed my palm in a touch that rocked me through with sensations. It felt like one of those tantalizing, memorable, earth-shaking moments, the ones you play on a reel in your head long after they're over. Grand slams. A perfect game. The last cannoli. I cleared my throat. This was Jonas, I reminded myself. What I was feeling was not attraction but some strange combination of anxiety, animosity, and loathing. Those kinds of things could get the heart racing, surely. "I should probably start making the pie I promised to bring. I need to be up early to miss the traffic."

"You're leaving in the morning?" he asked lightly. "However will I manage without you around to hog all the hot water and trounce about in your athletic wear?" The corner of his mouth quirked up. Was this good-natured sarcasm?

I fixed a smug grin on my face and batted my eyelashes. "Somehow, I think you'll survive, Voss."

I balled up the trash in my hands and pitched a slider into the metal trash can next to the lamppost.

Chapter 12

In the morning, I tucked the pie I'd made for Sommerset-giving, Dad's favorite maple pumpkin, carefully into a small cardboard box and surveyed the kitchen. I extracted the second pie I'd made from the fridge, placing it carefully on the clean counter. I'd only intended to make one, but then it occurred to me that Jonas had no plans. He wasn't taking a trip to an amusement park or visiting family—I supposed a few days wasn't long enough to fly to the UK—and even though he was nearly intolerable and moody, at least to me, the idea of him sitting alone without friends and family and pie was just too sad. I pulled out a paper napkin and scrawled a quick note on it—*Hope you enjoy this pie as much as the endless supply of hot water for showering. Happy Thanksgiving!*—then collected my bag, Dad's pie, and my car keys and left the apartment.

The Subaru was parked in the faculty lot behind Sondheim Hall. When I'd gotten hired by the Red Sox, everyone had expected me to get a new car. What they didn't know was that assisted living facilities, like the one Dad lived at, were expensive. And some of the services that would help him the most weren't covered by insurance. We'd sold the house, but the market hadn't been great. My car, an Outback from the 1990s with an emergency brake that was nonfunctional, still worked okay, especially considering that I didn't need to drive much in Boston—that's what the T was for. I settled into the driver's seat, buckling up and turning the engine over. The car made a wheezy noise. I cranked it again and it wouldn't start. *Perfect*, I thought, but at least I'd figured it out now, leaving myself enough time to devise an alternative plan to get to Boston well in time for the festivities. I got out, popped the hood, and took a look. I knew how to change a tire and how to check the oil—Dad had made sure of that—but those skills were about the extent of my car knowledge. Everything looked normal.

I sank back into the driver's seat and pulled out my phone. I wasn't getting Uber or Lyft up here, and even if I could, the trip would cost a fortune. There was a small bus station in town. Maybe I could walk over there and catch one. But it was Thanksgiving. The odds of me getting a ticket were slim.

"I thought you were leaving. You know, missing the traffic and all."

I looked up to find Jonas squinting down at me. "My car won't start."

He made a face that almost looked sympathetic. "You know, for an honorary leprechaun, you're pretty unlucky, Doyle."

"Helpful," I grumbled. "Actually, you *could* be helpful. You aren't going anywhere, right? Can I borrow your car?"

He shook his head.

"Please, Jonas. I know you hate me, but this is beyond our petty differences. I really need to be there for my dad."

His expression softened. "Sorry. No. You can't borrow my car."

I tried to stay cool and focused on the screen of my phone. My signal wasn't good here, and the bus schedule was still loading. I resisted the urge to fling the phone in his general direction. *That won't do you any good*, I told myself.

"I'll drive you, though."

I looked up. "Wait. Did you—"

"I'll take you to Boston. Give me a few minutes to gather my things."

I opened my mouth to speak, but nothing came out. I thought about pinching my arm very hard in case this was a dream. It felt a bit like a dream, which would also explain why the sight of Jonas eating a cookie yesterday had been so erotic.

"It's the blue one over there."

I turned and scanned the parking lot. There were only a few cars left. Two other Subarus, one silver and one green, which felt a bit like a New England mountain prep school cliché; an antique MG that Revi was restoring; an ancient Land Rover painted a dull green; and a royal blue Tesla.

I waited next to the car, trying not to admire its metallic sheen or wonder exactly what driving this kind of car said about Jonas. He cared about the environment? He thought he was hot shit? I knew the price tag because Patrick had once talked about how dumb one of his fellow surgeons was for dropping over a hundred thousand dollars on one. *If you're going to drop that kind of cash, get a Lamborghini*, he'd said. *At least then people know you're driving a luxury vehicle, not going to soccer practice and your Greenpeace meeting.*

Jonas arrived, slightly winded, and laid my bag and his in the trunk. I settled into the passenger seat.

"So, you drive a Tesla," I said.

"Electric vehicles are better for the planet."

"Do you have a trust fund?" I teased.

"My previous profession paid well."

"Do you miss it?"

"Every day."

He was a straight shooter, I had to give him that. I couldn't blame him for missing the money—I did too—though I hadn't exactly been expecting the disclosure. My Monadnock salary didn't come close to what I'd made working for the Red Sox, but I'd been smart and not bought a new car, so I had savings to help supplement the shortfall. Actually, the one upside of working at a boarding school is that other than the new dresses and baking supplies, I'd barely spent a cent since I'd arrived. Some of my paycheck went toward paying off my student loans, and the rest could go into the account that was reserved for Sommerset Meadows.

"What did you do before?"

Jonas's hands tightened around the steering wheel.

I shouldn't have asked that, I thought, and was about to say so when he answered. "I was a concert pianist. Mostly in Europe."

"I knew it," I said. "That's why you were so mad about me trying to play the piano in my bedroom."

"My mom gave it to me." He stopped to check traffic and then eased the car onto the main road.

"Is she why you don't play anymore?" I asked. It would be understandable. When I lost my mom, I didn't have the desire to do anything I'd done before. Everything felt sideways and wrong. All those things that reminded me of her—baking, feeding the ducks in the Boston Public Garden, photography— were simply too painful.

"No. My decision to stop playing had nothing to do with

her. I'm sure she wasn't pleased about it—not that she would've said—in her mind, my life is my decision, and she was always supportive. I suppose that's to be expected from a parent who is a psychologist."

I tried to contain my laughter, but failed miserably.

"You find that funny?"

I swiped away a tear. "Sorry," I wheezed. "I just find it ironic that *you're* the product of a psychologist."

"Are you implying that I need psychological help, Doyle? Interesting take from someone in a health profession. I'm surprised by you," he said, feigning dismay.

"Don't get me wrong; I find mental health important, not funny. I find you funny though. As for thinking you need therapy, it's not really my area of expertise," I said. "You don't seem to have the easiest time meeting new people."

"That's fair, but you have to admit, that debacle wasn't entirely my fault. Revi and Andy kept the whole new roommate thing a secret, and you didn't exactly make the best first impression by assaulting my ears with whatever you were trying to play."

"Assaulting your ears! You're so dramatic. I can't even imagine how you'd characterize the time I bumped into you in the bathroom."

A flush rose on Jonas's neck. "No comment."

Chapter 13

We arrived at Sommerset Meadows almost exactly at noon. I checked my reflection in the visor mirror, smoothed my hair down, and unbuckled my seat belt. My stomach fluttered with excitement about seeing my dad after several weeks and nerves about the conversation we needed to have. But I was armed with the pie and a Monadnock sweatshirt. Jonas hadn't budged from the driver's seat, and I eyed him.

"Have a nice time," he said.

"Oh, are you driving back? I can get a bus tomorrow, that's fine."

"I thought I'd stick around the city, find something to do, since there's nothing going on on campus right now."

"I don't think there's going to be much to do today," I said. "I don't want you to feel like you have to stay in town to wait for me. I definitely wanted to see him tomorrow too, especially since I haven't spent much time with him lately. It seems like every weekend since I started at Monadnock there's a tournament or kids who need some kind of treatment on Sundays."

Clearly neither of us had considered the practicality of the situation. I'd been too shocked by his surprise display of humanity that the logistics of what exactly he'd do once we got there hadn't crossed my mind. He pressed his head back into the headrest.

"If there's nothing to do in Boston, I guess I'll just head back to campus. I can come back for you. Just call me and let me know when you think you'll be ready to go back," he said.

"You don't have to do that."

"It's not like I have anything better to do."

I pictured Jonas sitting alone in the apartment on campus while everyone else was with family or having fun. For some very inopportune reason, an old Irish folktale my mom used to read me popped into my head. *There's always room for one more.* "You could come to Thanksgiving here, if you want."

"I wouldn't want to crash your holiday."

I shook my head. "It makes the residents really happy to have visitors. There were quite a few who didn't have anyone last year. It was kind of sad. I promise you no one would mind."

He turned to me. "Even you?"

Something about the expression in his eyes, the soft, low, questioning tone of his voice, sent a ripple through me.

I smiled. "Of course not. You got me here. The least we can do is feed you."

He acquiesced with a half smile, unbuckled his seat belt, and climbed out. "You can carry the pie," I said.

We headed inside, stopping to sign in at the front desk. Carla, the activities director, gave me a big squeeze when she saw me. "Sophie! He's been talking about you coming all week. It's so good to see you! And you brought that doctor boyfriend of yours finally!" She leaned to the side to eye Jonas and winked.

"Oh, um, no," I said. "This is my roommate. He was nice enough to drive me down here when my car wouldn't start."

"Ah. Gotcha. Well, everyone here loves Sophie, so you're our new hero," she said, and then enveloped Jonas in a hug neither of us had been expecting. He looked like a deer in the headlights over her shoulder, and I had to stifle a laugh. "Gerry's in the common room. Head on over. After we eat, there's going to be Thanksgiving-themed bingo and a movie."

The common room was a large open space with comfortable couches, a flat-screen television, some tables and chairs that were used for cards and other games, and a wall of bookshelves loaded with large-print books. Dad spent a lot of time there with his friends, telling stories and playing cribbage. I found him in a chair sitting at a table with his longtime friend Dennis, who was a former Boston firefighter. I snuck up behind Dad and gave him a big squeeze.

"Hi, Dad," I said, and planted a kiss on his cheek. He normally had a bit of scruff, but he was clean shaven today. He was wearing a nice pullover sweater and a pair of chinos. He'd dressed up. "You look nice."

He pressed a hand to the table and rose. "Aren't you a sight for sore eyes? It's good to see you, Sunny." He hugged me hard.

Dennis extended a hand to Jonas. "I'm Dennis Golding. You must be Patrick, the good doctor."

Dad released me. "No, Dennis. I told you, the doctor was dulling her light. This must be her new fella."

"No, Dad. This is my roommate Jonas."

"Nice to meet you, Mr. Doyle," Jonas said.

Jonas reached out and shook Dad's hand. If he noticed the tremor, he didn't show it. "He's got a good handshake," Dad said. "You sure you don't play baseball?"

"Jonas hates baseball," I said.

"Who said I hate baseball? I don't recall saying that."

"You're a Brit?" Dad said, sniffing.

"My mom is. My dad's German. I grew up near London, but then lived in Berlin from the time I was fourteen."

"What brought you to the States?" Dad asked.

"I actually came to work with a young violinist I met in Germany. He'd just won first prize at the Wieniawski-Lipinski and Tchaikovsky young musicians competitions and was attending an arts school in New Hampshire. Turned out that they needed an orchestra instructor just when I was looking for a new opportunity." Was he talking about Tyson?

"Are you a violinist? There was a great violinist who played in the MLB. Called him The Fiddler. What was his name? Oh right"—his fingers shifted, as if he were about to snap them—"Eddie Basinski. Dodgers shortstop back in the forties."

"I can play violin, but not well. I was a concert pianist with a symphony in Europe for a few years."

"That's something. I haven't had much experience with that. A little too highbrow for me—no offense. Now the sound of 'Tessie' at Fenway, that's the one. Gave me chills, every single time. Or 'Sweet Caroline,' that's another good one."

I squeezed Dad's hand. "Me too. I miss that."

"You'll hear it soon enough, Sunny. I know that loss got you down and you needed a break, but I'm sure if you wanted to rejoin the team, they'd welcome you with open arms. Come spring training you'll be back to what you love, and you'll be in good spirits again. Those boys will be riding the laundry cart nonstop and that smile of yours will return in full force."

I swallowed my shame. I'd promised Astrid that I was going to tell him the whole truth, but instead I'd been avoiding the conversation. Mostly I had been trying to figure out how to get the team to want me back so the exact scenario my dad had just described would come to fruition. Across from me, Jonas's brow furrowed. This wasn't the time. Today was supposed to be a celebration.

"I'd love to watch another game with you, Dad."

"Who're you kidding, Sunny, you'd be too busy working to watch with your old man. But maybe Jonas here could come along. We could introduce him to the gloriousness that is Red Sox baseball."

"I'd like that," Jonas said.

We all sat down. Dad's eyes narrowed. "You said you teach orchestra?" Dad asked Jonas. "Sunny mentioned having a bit of an issue—"

"I brought you a pie," I interjected awkwardly.

Jonas's brow furrowed. "An issue?"

"And a sweatshirt. Look, it has the crest!"

"Isn't my girl the sweetest thing?" Dad said.

Dennis smiled. "You got a real winner. Come on, you two, Gerry was just telling me about the time he caught one of Wade Mack's foul balls in the back of the noggin."

I remembered that game. The night had been unseasonably warm. I'd been wearing cutoff shorts and a tank top and was eating an ice cream cone when Mack, who was a phenomenal hitter, caught a piece of that pitch and sent the ball pummeling toward where my dad was working. The ball had struck him in the back of his Red Sox hat. I could still feel the panicked pace of my heart, the cold drop of ice cream on my leg. But then he popped up holding the ball in his hat and took a dramatic bow, letting everyone know that he was okay.

"I looked like Geena Davis's character—what was her name . . . Dottie something—in *A League of Their Own*," Dad said. "The crowd went wild. That's not even the best part. When the game ended, he comes out of the locker room and climbs up in the stands and finds me. I'm cleaning up, and he comes over. Says he wants to make sure that I'm okay."

I nodded. "He signed the ball, and then he offered to take us both out to dinner. I was twelve and he was basically my idol, so it went from the worst moment of my life earlier when I thought this guy was hurt to the best night of my life."

Dad laughs. "We went to Marinello's. He told us to order whatever we wanted."

"I had the best chicken parm of all time. And cannoli—so many good ones."

"Chocolate chip!" Dad and I said at the same time.

"You're not into baseball, so it probably doesn't sound amazing to you, but—"

"No," Jonas said, "it sounds like an ace adventure. I met Lang Lang once by chance in the duty-free store at Bern Airport after a music festival. It was life changing."

"Lang Lang?" Dad and Dennis wore identical puzzled expressions.

"He's a brilliant concert pianist from China. He's the piano version of Wade Mack . . . or Geena Davis."

"Ah, got it. A real legend."

Carla poked her head into the common room. "Who's ready for a feast?" she said.

We all made our way into the dining room, which had been decorated with mums and pumpkins, and found seats at the tables. "Looks like the apple cake was a hit," Dad said. I snorted. Not so much.

"I'll go get you your food, Dad. What do you want?"

Despite his medications, he wasn't able to hold a plate, and sometimes was a bit unsteady on his feet. He rattled off a list, and I went off to get his food for him. Dennis used a walker, so Jonas offered to get him his food too, and Dennis beamed.

"What service! And they say the youths these days aren't all right. One of everything," he said.

"That was nice of you," I told Jonas as we went through the buffet line.

"Do you think me a hooligan or something? I'll have you know I have excellent manners."

"I guess you reserve them for people other than me."

"What can I say, Doyle? You seem to bring out my baser tendencies."

"What's that supposed to mean?" I asked, dropping a healthy portion of stuffing on my plate.

He leaned over. When he spoke, his voice was low and gruff in my ear. "You drive me absolutely mad."

I lost grip of my plate and nearly sent mashed potatoes and cranberry sauce flying. I managed to recover the plate, but not my ability to speak in that moment. I was sure he'd meant it as an insult. It wasn't news to me that I annoyed Jonas, that my very presence made him act petulant and downright prickish, but the tone of his voice, his breath warm on my neck, the tingling sensation on my skin, made me wonder if there wasn't an undercurrent of another meaning there. No. That notion was absolutely ludicrous. He just took pleasure in messing with me. I quickly took a slice of turkey, poured some gravy on it, and sped back to the table.

"So fill me in," Dad said. "Your roommate is the apple cake guy, right?"

"In the flesh."

"He went from a horrible grump who supposedly hates you to coming home with you? Your mother's baking is powerful."

"I didn't—"

"Horrible grump?" Jonas said. He'd overheard. I buried my face in my hands.

"Must've been someone else," Dad covered. "You seem like a first-class guy."

"I get low blood sugar," Jonas said. "I'm afraid from time to time I am what you might call 'hangry.' Perhaps your daughter was referring to that. We didn't get off on the right foot, so to speak. I caught her banging on my mother's piano. I would be quite keen to try apple cake though. I love cake and I love apples."

He handed Dennis his plate and then sat down. I gave him a look, but he ignored me, and instead cut a piece of turkey and took a bite.

"Did you do that, Sophie?" Dad asked.

"I wasn't banging on it. I was trying to play."

Jonas scoffed. "I didn't even play like that when I was a toddler."

"Well, not all of us can be prodigies, Voss."

"We have a piano here, but no one ever uses it," Dennis said. "You should play! No one's touched it since Evangeline passed away. These days for music we're stuck listening to Bold Oldies 104.7 on the radio."

"Absolute crap," Dad said. "The other day, they played the Spice Girls. Since when is that old?"

"I liked that one," said Dennis. "But nothing's better than live music."

"'Danny Boy.' That's what I'd like to hear," Dad said. "Do you know it?"

Jonas shifted in his seat.

"We probably have some sheet music. My Esmerelda always kept some in the compartment under our bench back at home. This one's probably the same." Dennis stood up and started shuffling toward the piano.

"Actually," Jonas said, "I can't play. I don't anymore."

"Oh, come on. It doesn't have to be anything fancy," Dennis said.

"No, I'd be rubbish. I couldn't interrupt everyone's meal."

"He probably doesn't play for free," a short woman with purple-tinged white hair said. She'd been sitting near us, but this was the first time she'd spoken.

Jonas pushed his food around on his plate.

"The mashed potatoes are better than last year," I said, trying to shift the subject.

"It sure would be nice," Dad said, "to have some live music."

Jonas wiped his mouth carefully with his napkin. "I'm very sorry, Mr. Doyle." He really did look apologetic; that familiar sadness in his eyes had returned. "My answer is no."

Chapter 14

I don't get you," I said. We were perched on stools at a bar in the back of a pub I'd never been to on Tremont Street in the South End, far enough away from Fenway that I didn't have to face the memories. I just hoped I wouldn't be recognized. It had been weeks—these things blew over, didn't they? "You were being so kind to my dad and Dennis and then someone brings up the piano and you morph into a complete jerk again. How hard would it have been to spend five minutes playing a song for a couple of old people?"

"I told you, I don't play anymore," he said. He called the bartender over. "Two whiskeys, neat, please," he said. He waited for the bartender to slide the lowball over, and then he took a long pull of the liquid before he spoke. "It's complicated."

"You said you played. You were a concert pianist. Was that not true?"

He shook his head. "I was the pianist for the Berlin Philharmonic for three years. I also played with other orchestras for several years before that." He looked down at his glass and swirled it round before taking another slow draw. "Then I stopped."

"Why?"

Jonas gestured toward the whiskey. I'd never been much of a whiskey drinker; however, under the circumstances, it only seemed right to join him. I threw back a giant gulp and tried not to wince as it burned its way down my throat.

"Because I couldn't do it anymore."

"I don't understand. What does that mean? The pressure got to be too much? Or the lifestyle?"

He set his glass down hard on the bar top, then turned to look at me. "I mean I couldn't physically do it anymore." His shoulders sagged. "I started to notice some errors when I was practicing. Pieces that had once been easy, I couldn't get right. And then one night, there I was in the middle of a concert—Chopin's Etudes. I'd played the one piece, Opus 25, number 11, hundreds of times. It's a challenging piece, of course, but . . ." His thumb traced the rim of the glass. "Pianists make errors, finger slips happen, and we just play through it and the audience is none the wiser. But this wasn't a single note. It was a string of misplayed notes. I finished the piece, but I was utterly humiliated."

I put my hand on his forearm. "They probably didn't realize. I don't think I would notice if a mistake was made in a piece of music."

Jonas shook his head. "They heard it. I'm sure of it. There was this pause before the applause, as if everyone was just processing what had happened. The silence was absolutely crushing."

The dim lighting hanging over the bar cast Jonas's angular face into shadows. He looked broken by the memory.

"I'm sorry. That sounds . . ."—*devastating*—"horrible."

He shrugged. "It wasn't great. Funny thing, that wasn't even the worst part." He turned the glass with his thumbs. "I was still living with my father then. I'd been apartment hunting in Berlin and hadn't moved out yet. I don't know why. When I got home, I thought he might ask what had happened or if I was all right or had a plan, but he didn't say a word. And I don't mean he never mentioned it. I mean, he didn't speak a single word to me that night and after. He ignored me until it became too uncomfortable for both of us and I left."

"Your dad gave you the silent treatment." I let that sink in while I signaled to the bartender for two more whiskeys. It seemed the only proper response to such a revelation. No wonder Jonas had trouble being a good roommate. His dad was an asshole.

"I'd embarrassed him with my mistake. It was better if I wasn't around."

"Where was your mom?"

"Back in England. I lived with him in Germany after they divorced, except when I was touring."

"Oh."

"She probably would've been mortified too. She'd always been so supportive of my music career. And anyway, we weren't close."

"Oh." I shook my head.

"It's fine. Just not the way I'd envisioned my career ending. Utter disaster."

"No one's perfect, though, Jonas. Even concert pianists."

"At the level I was at during that time, people were expecting magnificence, not mistakes." I could tell by the tenor of his voice that he was being sincere.

"You stopped playing because of one bad night?"

Jonas took a slow breath. I watched his chest expand and

collapse before he spoke. "I probably could have come back if it had been a single incident. Truthfully, I lost the ability to play certain complex pieces that require a very high level of dexterity and agility in the right hand. My ring finger simply won't cooperate. I saw several orthopedists. No one could figure out what was causing it."

"Sounds sort of like the yips in baseball."

"The what?"

"It's when the thing that was automatic becomes impossible, and it happens sometimes to high-level athletes." *Musicians, too?* I wondered. I stared at Jonas's hands. They dwarfed the lowball glass. His fingers were long and tapered; I could imagine them gliding across the keys.

He shrugged. "Maybe. I honestly couldn't say. All I know is that, ultimately, I couldn't do the job I was hired to do," he said, "so I left the philharmonic and tried to focus on other things."

"Teaching." Jonas had spent most of this conversation examining the contents of his glass, but he looked up when I said this. The light came back into his eyes.

He nodded. "And conducting, composing. All activities that don't require perfectly functional fingers."

"Is that why you've been so intense about Tyson not playing sports and given me such a hard time in the apartment? You made it pretty clear that you wish the sports program and I were not at Monadnock."

"Believe it or not, I'm not actually keen to get rid of you or the entire athletic program. I know I can be, uh, a bit difficult at times. Most days, I feel like the mistakes in my past are following me around. It's hard to be positive when you feel like that . . . and then you're the opposite. You're upbeat and into sports. You get under my skin." I could understand that. I knew what it was like to be reminded of my own mistakes. "I care about Tyson and his future. I know all too well what it's like to lose the one thing that defines you. I had a purpose, a gift, and I don't mean that to sound cocky; it was the thing I felt I was put on this planet to do. And I worked hard to be great—so hard, so many hours. Then suddenly one day it was gone. He's just a teenager. He doesn't know what life would be like for him if he's messing around sometime and injures his hand and can never play again like he can now. I don't want him to be filled with regret. I know you think I'm being a controlling prick, but I'm just trying to protect him." He lowered his head and gripped his glass of whiskey. "From this," he muttered.

Maybe it was because I was two whiskeys in at this point. Perhaps it was a faint memory of that single moment of chemistry we'd had in the stacks where I'd wanted to touch him. Or it might've been the sensation of those fingers tracing my palm accidentally yesterday on the quad. But I reached out and gently took his right hand from the glass.

His brow furrowed. "Doyle," he croaked, "what are you—"

"Orthopedists don't know everything," I said, turning his hand gently over in the dim bar light. "They are the construction workers of medicine. Give them an injury that can't be repaired with a power tool and they'll give you a shrug and send you to me."

I ran my fingers up the length of his ring finger. "This muscle is called the extensor digitorum. It functions to extend your finger." I couldn't be sure, but I thought I heard him suck in a breath. I shifted my contact point, pausing just long enough to recognize the warm, pleasant sensation of his skin against mine. "Here, the palmar and dorsal interossei are what make your finger flex and move back and forth, toward and away from your middle finger. Your finger has four joints. Ligaments, tendons. Each has a specific job."

I expected Jonas to withdraw his hand, but he didn't. "What are you saying?"

"I can help you."

He shook his head. "Not that I doubt your abilities, but I was told by several experts that it was a lost cause."

"Experts said that about Danny Fernando's pitching career too after he cut off half his index finger in a woodworking incident and had to have it reattached surgically." Unconsciously, I traced a slow path across the topography of his hand. "I helped bring him back. I've assisted other baseball players in their recovery from analogous issues. I can help you too, if you let me. Or, you know, there's always the alternative."

When Jonas's eyes met mine, the hazel of his irises seemed to flame with heat. "What's that?"

"Do nothing and spend the rest of your life alternating between wondering what might have been and being a horrible curmudgeon." I dropped his hand.

"Oi. Careful!" he yelped.

"If you're not going to use them, why are you so intent on protecting them? Like that time I bumped into you in the shower and you freaked out."

Was that the alcohol getting to him too, or had his cheeks flushed?

"I deeply regret listening to my music so loudly and barging in on you that day," he said. There was something in the way he looked at me when he spoke that made me think that even though it'd been an accident, maybe there was a part of him that didn't regret it. "But I don't recall 'freaking out.' I think you're exaggerating."

I sat up a little straighter. "You said, and I quote"—I deepened my voice and put on my worst British accent—"'My hands are important to me.'" I dissolved into laughter. Jonas's lips curled into a slight smile.

He held his hands up in surrender. "All right, you got me. I'm not admitting I said that, but . . . it could be worse. There was this one guy, Glenn Gould, bloody brilliant pianist, wildly eccentric—he wore gloves and wouldn't shake hands."

"You're not going to take it that far, are you?"

He shook his head and took a sip of his whiskey.

"Then let me help you."

"Why would you want to help me, Doyle? I've been a tosser to you since you moved in."

I shrugged. "Then there'll be no doubt that I'm a better person than you."

"Very funny. I'm aware that you would love nothing more than to beat me in a contest, especially after your stunning defeat at billiards. But it's a serious question."

"Are you trying to psychoanalyze me? Did your mom teach you this?"

He eyed me while he sipped his drink.

"I guess if we really wanted to analyze this, it probably has something to do with the fact that I can't help my dad, so I want to use my energy on helping with something I *can* do. Does that make sense?"

"Strangely, it does. But what if you can't fix it?"

"Lucky for you, I'm an optimist. Let's start tomorrow."

A large man in a Patriots jersey bellied up to the bar. "Danny, another round of Guinness for me and the boys," he shouted to the bartender. He wrangled the pint glasses, sloshing beer onto my sweater as he swung around.

"Watch yourself, mate," Jonas said. "You're soaking the lady."

The man looked down at me, his alcohol-slackened features tightening as he eyed me. I recognized the moment he placed me, and I spun on my stool, flung down some cash on the bar, and grabbed Jonas's sleeve.

"We need to go."

"Hey!" the man shouted. "Everyone look! It's the Red Sox bitch. I should've dumped these beers over your head."

Jonas rose out of his seat and locked an icy glare on the belligerent bar-goer. "Oi! Anybody ever tell you you've got a foul mouth, brother?" he said, voice taut and blue-flame hot. Everything about his expression was unfamiliar—the tense muscles of his jaw, the fire flashing in his eyes. If this was what Jonas looked like when he was mad, then I'd never seen him angry.

"What'd you say to me?" the man snarled.

No, no. This was not going well. The last time I'd been in Boston, the nice fellows down at the police station had made it quite clear to me, even though the fan had dropped the charges thanks to Astrid's powers of persuasion and a selection of signed photos, that another fight would have serious consequences. And while I'd teased Jonas for being precious about his hands, I was certain that a brawl wasn't going to help him get back his concert pianist career. Plus, even though Jonas was fit—his chiseled abs were a testament to that—he was tall and lanky, whereas this guy looked like a retired linebacker with his own crew of offensive linemen.

"If you think my mouth's bad, wait until you experience my steel-toed boot up—"

"You wish, you half-witted—"

The man wound up with his beer-filled glass, and instinctively I reached up and grabbed a fistful of Jonas's shirt, then I yanked him down toward me, just as the man hurled a pint glass where Jonas's head had been moments earlier. In my urgency, I'd pulled a bit too forcefully. Jonas's lips grazed my mouth and for an instant both of us froze with only a whisper between our lips. I expected him to recoil; instead he eliminated the space between us, sliding his fingers into my hair, pressing his lips to mine. He tasted like whiskey and want, and what the heck was happening. My entire body crackled with electricity; I dug my fingers into the back of his shirt, clinging to him in this moment of madness. Everything else seemed to melt away, leaving only the sensation of his mouth on mine, his hands holding me—a couple of whistles brought me back into the room and our precarious situation. The kiss had only lasted a few seconds, but when we parted, I was breathless and my lips felt bee-stung. Jonas looked at me, his expression unreadable. I cast a furtive glance behind us toward the exit.

"Doyle," he whispered, his voice ragged in my ear.

"We have to go right now," I said. I led him through the crowd by the cuff of his shirt.

On the street, we faced each other, condensation thick between us in the chill night air. After we'd both made sure that the men who physically resembled a bunch of retired Patriots players hadn't followed, Jonas turned to me. "What in god's name was that?" he asked.

"Think of it as mouth-to-mouth. Because I just saved your life in there."

He ran his hands over his hair. "I didn't mean the kiss. Why were they calling you the Red Sox—"

"Oh, that?" My beer-drenched sweater was wet against my skin, and I shivered. I tried to wring the moisture out of it and failed.

"Yeah, that."

"Let's just say I'm not well-liked around here."

"You told me that you worked for the Red Sox—did something happen at work? Is that why that disrespectful wanker called you a—"

"Bitch?" I looked up at Jonas in the streetlight. There was a faint remnant of my lipstick beside his mouth. "I did what I thought was right to protect an injured player. The fans, team management, and team doctor didn't agree. If that makes me a bitch, so be it. After I fought to keep Iwasaki from pitching and they lost the World Series, I guess I have to accept my fate."

Jonas leaned over and settled his corduroy jacket over my shoulders. "I'm sorry he called you that."

"Yeah, I noticed. You were really mad. I thought you were about to throw down."

"Good thing you, ah . . ." He cleared his throat. ". . . stopped me."

I slid my arms into his jacket, thankful for the warmth of the fleece lining. Jonas pushed at a crushed to-go cup with his shoe and then stooped to pick it up and drop it into a nearby trash can.

I pulled the coat tighter around me. "Yeah well, that's the first and last time I *stop* you. Next time you try to defend someone's honor, you're on your own."

"Understood." Jonas rubbed his hands together and blew into them to warm them from the cold.

"So . . ." I began, "given that you've had, what, a whiskey and a half, and there's probably black ice, should you maybe stay in town tonight?" Jonas looked up from his hand-warming attempts. "We can hang out with Dad in the morning and then head home to start your recovery program."

He cocked his head to the side. A playful smile spread

across his face. "Is this your way of telling me you don't want me to go, Doyle?"

I rolled my eyes before turning away to hide the heat that was on full display on my cheeks. My lips still tingled from the memory of his kiss. "I bet you'd just love that," I scoffed.

"Maybe I would," he said, his voice deep and quiet. "You'll never know."

W eeks ago, I'd booked a room at a mid-priced hotel in the South End. On the street, I figured I'd pay for an extra room for Jonas since he'd driven me down and then almost gotten into a brawl defending my honor. It was the least I could do.

We stood at a high front desk counter with a large mirror and modern art behind it. I looked ridiculous in his giant jacket, and he must've seen the lipstick residue the kiss had left on him, because he was making quick work of wiping his mouth with the cuff of his Henley. A woman wearing a maroon uniform shirt emerged from a back room.

"Can I help you?" she asked.

"Yes, thanks," I said. "I have a reservation under Doyle. I need to add another room."

The woman pecked away at a computer keyboard. I did not like the way she was shaking her head. "I had you booked in a double on the sixth floor. That's the only room that's available, unfortunately. It's the holiday—gets booked up wicked fast. Do you still want it?"

I turned to look at Jonas to gauge how much horror was in his expression before I could respond. He said nothing, and his face was surprisingly blank, so I nodded and slid my credit card across the counter. She pushed two key cards and my credit card back. "Room six-twenty-two. Ice maker's broken, so if you need ice, you'll have to go to five or seven."

"We won't need ice," Jonas said. "Have a nice night." He picked up my overnight bag and headed toward the elevator.

We rode the elevator up in silence. "Sorry about the room," I said as we walked through the parted doors into a hallway that reminded me vaguely of *The Shining*. "I should've tried to change the reservation while we were on the road."

"No worries." He paused in front of room 622. "We hadn't discussed whether I was staying. Besides, I can put in earbuds to drown out your snoring. At least it's a double."

I laughed as I pushed open the door and flipped on the light. "You're telling me. After this evening's excitement I don't think I could handle an only-one-bed situation."

"What was that you were saying again, Doyle?" Jonas said, letting my overnight bag drop to the floor with a thud.

I looked at the brightly lit room. It was clean and neat, with a small desk, several lamps, and a single king-sized bed in the center of the room. "For fuck's sake," I said. "First my car, then the near brawl, and now this. I'm cursed."

Jonas headed into the bathroom, leaving the door slightly ajar so that I could see him peeling his Henley off and revealing a tapered back rippling with muscles. "Better call the front desk and get a rollaway," he called, snapping me out of my moment of physical admiration. "There's no way in bloody hell that I'm sleeping on the floor."

"And I have to take the rollaway?"

He stuck his head out through the door opening, revealing just enough of his upper chest for me to ponder if he'd actually taken my advice that day about adding push-ups to his regimen. "Well, you're a Lilliputian leprechaun and I'm a very tall guy. I'm not contorting myself on a child-sized cot while you sleep in some sort of Da Vinci—esque pose in the middle of that massive bed."

Fair point. Though being called a leprechaun made me wish I had another cannoli on hand. I shrugged off his jacket and flung it at him, just as he slammed the bathroom door shut.

Fortunately for both of us, the very understanding woman at the front desk did have a rollaway available, and she felt so bad about the predicament and the nonfunctional ice maker that she sent up a tray of chocolate-covered strawberries with the cot. While Jonas used up what I estimated to be the entire hotel's worth of hot water, I started in on the chocolate-covered strawberries. The berries themselves were gigantic and coated in dark chocolate and white chocolate so artfully that they looked like they were clad in cocoa tuxedos. *Just one for now*, I told myself. There were four, more than enough for both of us. I relished the sweet-tart combination, nibbling every last morsel of chocolate and berry until all that remained was the stem. I set it carefully down on the tray. The rollaway was still sitting where the hotel staffer had left it, just inside the door, so I pushed it over near the window and opened it up. I thought Jonas had been exaggerating when he had called it a child's cot, but in fact his description was quite apt. There was no way he would have fit on the thing.

Still, for good measure I called out, "Your cot has arrived!" Then I stuffed an entire chocolate-covered strawberry into my mouth. The water cut off. In the new quiet, I could make out the subtle sound of Jonas unfurling a towel. I had a deeply unsettling image of him drying off his drenched skin and then leaning in for a repeat of the kiss we'd shared at the bar, only instead of my sweater being damp from a drunk's beer, it was wet from his freshly showered skin. My mouth went dry. I needed to think about something, anything else, anything other than the warm current that was coursing through my body right now. Flaws. Yes, his flaws, of which there were many to choose from. Arrogance. Bossiness. Inability to have a good time. Waffle gluttony. So what if he got Dennis's food for him at the buffet and defended me when a sloppy drunk Neanderthal called me names. Or left my body shimmering with desire after a simple, accidental kiss that had only lasted a moment. Thank goodness for this tiny cot. Otherwise, it would be easy to get the wrong idea.

I eyed the strawberries again. These were the kind of decadent treat lovers fed each other in bed. Wrong idea city. I'd fully intended to leave the last two for him, but instead, I snatched them both up. I devoured one, and then, when the bathroom door finally swung open and he stepped out clad only in a towel and surrounded by a wall of steam like some kind of Norse god, I shoved the other in my mouth.

"What's that you've got there, Doyle?"

"Nothing," I tried to utter, my words jumbled by my mouthful of food.

He stepped closer and my body braced itself. I looked around the room, everywhere, anywhere else, because even though I was a woman who had been in a very dry relationship for a while before I was cast off with a note and a packed luggage set and frankly that kiss in the bar and the sight of Jonas half-undressed had awakened something primal within me, I was smart. Our living situation was complicated enough without adding an ill-advised holiday hookup to the mix.

"Oi! Were those chocolate-covered strawberries?" He picked up a leafy stem like a lawyer presenting evidence and then let it fall back to the tray. "I love chocolate-covered strawberries."

"Well, I love waffles, and as they say, payback is a bitch. They were delicious, by the way. Or, to put it in language you would understand, positively scrummy." I thought I'd won this round, though I couldn't be sure whom I was battling, Jonas or my own desire. What I hadn't counted on was him striding over in his towel, running a thumb across the platter in slow motion, and sucking the chocolate off of it while maintaining eye contact that was so intense it converted my frozen core to liquid and brought it to a boil. I swallowed. At that particular moment and in my particular mindset, he was the thing that was scrummy, and it was absolutely fine, convenient even, that there was likely no hot water left, because what I needed more than anything was a cold shower.

Jonas arched a brow, mischief gleaming in his eyes. "What's wrong? Didn't think you'd be able to resist me if you had to witness me eating a sweet, succulent chocolate-coated strawberry? Had to eat the lot of them so you wouldn't be tempted?"

"Get real," I said, lifting my chin.

"I don't know. You seemed pretty *interested* in watching me eat my cranberry-oatmeal biscuit at lunch yesterday."

Oh my god. He'd caught me on the quad. I had thought only Andy and Revi had noticed. If the cot had been made, I would've crawled under the covers and self-combusted from humiliation.

Jonas leaned over the tray until he was so close that I could feel his breath on my skin. "You know, Doyle, sometimes being around you is absolute bloody torture," he said.

"Believe me," I said, trying my best to manifest the sensation of the freezing cold water snapping me out of whatever lunacy was driving this sudden attraction to Jonas, "the feeling is completely mutual."

. . .

A few minutes later, I emerged from the shower and found the cot neatly made up with flawless, taut hospital corners. Climbing between the sheets, I cast a glance at Jonas. His eyes were closed, his face neutral, his perfect lips—the ones that had kissed me earlier—parted slightly. He'd made the bed for me? *Who are you and what have you done with my grumpy roommate?* I wondered. I switched the light off.

"Good night," I whispered into the darkness, mostly to myself.

I lay my head on the too-soft hotel pillow and pulled the covers up to my neck, vowing not to think anymore about Jonas or his perfect lips or how he'd kissed me like the world was ending.

The room was quiet for a beat.

"Good night, Doyle."

Chapter 15

I woke up early and dressed quickly in the weak dawn light that filtered through a slit in the curtains. Jonas was still asleep, both hands nestled beneath his head. My back hurt. I pulled the curtains together to darken the room and headed downstairs for the complimentary breakfast. If the strawberries last night had been any indication, I had high hopes for the breakfast bar. Bingo. Belgian waffle station. I assembled two plates, piling them high with eggs and bacon and sliced fruit. Then I made myself the perfect waffle, full and crisp and golden. I was grateful to Jonas for driving me down here and for standing up to that jerk at the bar, and I was going to see what I could do to help him get his career back, but otherwise nothing had really changed between us. We still probably wouldn't be able to get along, and that, coupled with the cot-induced back spasm, meant he wasn't getting a waffle from me.

I let myself into the room, miraculously managing not to spill the tray of food in the process. The lights were on and Jonas was sitting at the desk staring at his phone.

"I brought sustenance," I said.

"Brilliant, I'm famished." He reached for the waffle but I gave him a look and he pulled his hand back. I set a plate of eggs and bacon in front of him.

"Eat up," I said. "I want to do some basic mobility tests on your hand before we meet up with Dad."

"Want a coffee?" he asked.

He brewed two cups of coffee using the coffee maker on the dresser, then handed me a cup and a fistful of tiny creamer cups and sugar packets. To his credit, Jonas ate the food with enthusiasm, even though the bacon was rubbery and the eggs were a little undercooked for my liking. We ate in silence and then cleared the trash away.

"Okay," I said, "I'm going to ask you to do certain things with your hands. The point of this is to see if there are any noticeable differences between your left and right sides or any obvious issues in the way your joints move. Ready?"

"Not really," he said. "But don't let that stop you. You certainly didn't last night."

I narrowed my eyes at him, hoping that the heat in my cheeks would come off as fury instead of mortification.

"Show me your hands," I said.

He put them out on the table in front of me. I was still for a moment, overcome with images of those large, skilled hands sliding into my hair, wrapping themselves around my waist, until I reminded myself firmly that I was a professional. It wasn't unusual to work with an athlete who was attractive. The key was to focus on the task and nothing else.

I had Jonas go through all of the movements with both hands: flexion, extension, pronation. I had him tap a set of piano keys that I drew on a sheet of paper I'd taken from the office next to the lobby. Jonas sighed loudly and deemed the activity "ridiculous," but he complied. While he did these things, I watched his movements carefully, searching for anomalies. His ring finger was slightly curled in toward his palm and less responsive. I tested his hand strength. I had him squeeze mine, resist the different movements. His left hand was slightly stronger, but that was to be expected, since Jonas was left-handed and his right hand had been giving him problems for over a year.

"Anything?" he asked.

"Nothing obvious. But that doesn't mean anything."

"I told you that it was a lost cause." He drew his hand away.

"You're not getting out of this that easily." I checked my watch. The day before I had promised Dad we'd stop by with coffees and French crullers from Dunkin'. Jonas and I got our things together and headed over to Sommerset.

Dad was sitting in the common room playing a game of cribbage with Maureen when we arrived bearing food. Jonas held out the drink tray.

"Morning, Gerry. Three coffees and a hazelnut latte," he said, setting the drinks down on the table. Dad procured a doughnut and took a bite.

"Heaven," he declared.

"Those are not on your meal plan," Maureen said.

"It's a holiday!"

"Since when is Black Friday a holiday?" Maureen asked.

"You know this game?" my dad asked Jonas.

"Can't say that I do. I'm more of a poker man myself."

"It's easy," Dad said. "I'll teach you. Don't play Sophie though—she's a mercenary. I haven't beaten her in years."

Jonas cast a glance over at me, a mischievous smile forming on his face. "So what you're saying is she cheats."

"Hey!" I said.

"Jury's still out," Dad said, his eyes twinkling. "She doesn't like losing, that's for sure."

Jonas laughed. "You're not kidding. She's relentless—we played billiards last week, and let's just say it's a miracle that I emerged unscathed."

"Sounds about right." Dad chuckled.

It was nice to see Dad in such good spirits. He turned his attention to teaching Jonas the rules, and a fraction of the heavy weight I'd been carrying lifted.

By the time we finished our coffees, my dad had practically nominated Jonas as his new best friend. This was a development I found deeply unsettling. What had happened to his pep talk about not letting anyone dim my light? Jonas made flipping my personal light switch an art form. And then there was that kiss in the bar and him walking around our hotel room in just a towel, licking chocolate off his thumb and being all tantalizing, which had flipped my switch in other ways and made delicious electricity course through every nerve ending. Still, I appreciated the distraction. Jonas had saved me from having to confess to Dad the full details of what had really happened with my non-optional departure from the Sox and the cannoli incident. I wrapped Dad in my arms and held him tight before we left.

"Don't be a stranger," Dad said.

"Never," I told him, and planted a big kiss on his cheek. "I'll call you tonight."

"I was talking to Jonas."

"Dad!"

He turned to Jonas. "See, told you she hates to lose," he said, and then laughed. "Best girl in the world."

"Your dad is amazing," Jonas said as we made our way through the parking lot. I waited for him to make a comment about that being a shocking revelation, given his opinion of me, but he did not. I supposed we were in some kind of strange demilitarized zone in a nursing home parking lot.

"Yeah. He's the best. I miss him a lot."

"It must be hard to be so far away from him. Is that why you're going back to Boston?"

I settled into the passenger seat and buckled my seat belt, unsure how to answer.

"Are you really only at Monadnock until spring training, like he said?" Jonas checked the mirrors and then moved the car out of the parking lot. I hadn't realized Jonas had been listening.

"The old trainer will be back from maternity leave by then, probably," I said, tucking my hair behind my ears. "I won't be needed anymore. Good news for you—you'll have your piano room back."

"Seems a bit moot to regain a piano room if I can't use it. If you're going back to the Red Sox in a few months, that doesn't give you much time to fix my hand."

"It's just a plan. Maybe there's a chance I might get myself back into baseball, but it would take a major miracle in the next couple of months. The truth is, my dad knows that I'm the one who kept Iwasaki on the injured list and that after the loss I left the Red Sox, but I kind of made it seem like my leaving was voluntary. He still thinks I could just go get my job back if I wanted to. I know I shouldn't have gone along with it when he said that . . . I intended to tell him the whole story—in fact, Astrid made me promise I would—but there was never a time that felt right to unload everything on him. I guess I just couldn't tell my dad that I was forced out."

"Why? He seems like he'd support you no matter what. You're really lucky." There was an unspoken heaviness to Jonas's words. I thought back to what he'd told me about his last performance and how deep being ignored during an already painful time would cut.

"He would, he's great—I know that. It's just complicated. He worked at Fenway his whole life as a custodian. He used to bring me to work for the home games. He knew more about the game than the coaches did; he could pick a prodigy out of a field full of hopefuls and spot a problem with a pitcher before anyone else knew. I think he always wanted to be a pitching coach or a scout but never got the chance." I thought back to those games that constituted my favorite childhood memories, along with the smell of my mother's baking and her brushing my hair each night while we watched *Jeopardy!* Fenway felt like home as much as our living room, except that it was more special somehow, something rare, like the end of a rainbow. Dad hadn't reached it, but I had. "While my dad swept popcorn and picked up crushed cups to make the stadium clean and safe for everyone, I ate my fill of hot dogs gifted by his friend Mario and stuffed myself with cotton candy and Cracker Jack the Pernassus twins would sneak me. I loved Cracker Jack— okay, I still love it. Lots of times I tagged along after Dad helping him, but mostly I watched the games. From the nosebleeds, the players were just these tiny figures, but to me, they were huge, legends, gleaming in their white uniforms against the Green Monster. It was some sort of mythical thing . . . and I don't mean just the wall, which is legendary for keeping so many would-be home runs from making it, but the whole experience—the cheering fans, the crack of the bat, the blinding lights of the night games." I kept the most important part to myself. Mostly I loved it because it was time that only Dad and I shared. He made it magical; our proximity made it magical. And I missed that magic so much that my chest ached.

I glanced over at Jonas. "You wouldn't get it," I said.

"Actually, it's the opposite. The way you talk about baseball reminds me of how I felt about the symphony and the piano. It's like my own personal brand of magic. When things were good, when I played well, I felt a kind of peace that was untouchable. The audience was spellbound. And my parents were happy. They were proud."

I nodded. So maybe he did get it.

"When my mentor took me with him to join the Red Sox athletic training team and I told Dad about the job, he was over the moon." That day I'd thought if I smiled any harder my face might shatter. How much happiness can our fragile forms contain? I've seen how easily bodies break. Ligaments tear, tendons rupture, bones fracture. And my happiness had broken apart too. I'd made him proud once, and now, the truth of what had happened, all of it, would probably break his heart.

Jonas said, "So you followed his dream—"

"It was my dream too—"

"And now you don't want to disappoint him."

"I know, it's shitty to lie."

"Sometimes we go along with something that isn't true because it seems better that way . . . for everyone involved. I don't think that makes you a bad person. It means you care. Doesn't it?"

"Or maybe we lie to make ourselves feel better. Either way, keeping things from my dad makes me feel like a garbage human."

"Tell me something honest then."

I sighed, not wanting to play this strange version of truth or dare in a Tesla with my roommate/enemy. "Fine."

"Do you really think you can help me play again?"

I turned to look at him. He was staring at the traffic ahead of us on the highway. The muscles of his jaw flexed involuntarily and gave him away. For someone who purported to not care about anything, he struggled to seem disinterested in my response.

"I will try my very best. As my dad mentioned—I like to win and I don't quit. But most of it is up to you. Are you going to be a good patient?"

"Probably not."

"Why doesn't that surprise me? Let me rephrase. Will you work hard?"

He turned to me, letting his rich hazel eyes fix on mine for a fleeting moment before he returned his attention to the road. "I will work harder than you can fathom, Doyle," he deadpanned.

Why did those words send a thrill up my spine?

I coughed. "I'll believe it when I see it," I said. I grabbed his jacket from the back seat and pulled it over myself like a blanket, then let my head rest against the window. Jonas turned on some classical music on the stereo, and I pretended not to listen.

Chapter 16

Without students, the campus was both peaceful and incredibly lonely. I hadn't wanted to stay longer in Boston—the trip had been emotionally draining and harder than I'd anticipated—but being back in an empty building didn't do much for my mood. The moment we'd stepped back in our apartment, the common ground I'd thought we found had disappeared. Jonas returned to his normal sullen state and disappeared into his bedroom. Then Astrid's outgoing message said she was off shooting in some remote location where cell service was poor. Andy and Revi came through with pictures, one of them with their hands in the air, mouths agape, in a hollowed-out log that was plunging over a waterfall, and another of them posing with Chewbacca. They were wearing the ears with expressions of undeniable glee on their faces. I went for a run.

When I got back, I went straight to Jonas's door and knocked. He opened it, yawning and rubbing his eyes. "What now, Doyle?"

I tried to ignore the fact that he was shirtless and clad only in a pair of flannel pajama pants. "What are you doing for the rest of break?" I asked.

"I had planned on sleeping, but I guess that is out the window," he said. He wrinkled his nose. "Are you *sweating*?"

I ignored his comment and forged ahead. "I was thinking. We have all this free time. We should make the best of it and work on your rehab program."

He pondered this for a moment and then acquiesced. "All right. What did you have in mind?"

"It's a three-part plan. One, nutrition. Two, research. Three, physical therapy. Get dressed; we're going to town."

I'd expected some sort of protest, but instead, Jonas grabbed a sweatshirt and pulled it over his head. "Let's go."

"You're wearing pajamas?"

"It's part of *my* plan. One, chicken finger grinders. Two, go back to bed while *you* research. Three, fine, physical therapy or whatever."

"I was thinking more along the lines of vegetables from the farmer's market and some nice fish," I said, hopefully.

"Chicken. Finger. Grinders," he grumbled.

I gave in, even though it seemed like a poor choice compared to the antioxidant-rich meal I'd been planning. I didn't see the merits of a chicken finger grinder—until I'd taken my first bite. The place that served them was an unassuming delicatessen called The Grind, which was situated in an old Victorian house that needed some work but made up for its state of disrepair with charm. They roasted their own coffee and served homemade bagels, doughnuts, pizza, and grinders. The chairs were mismatched and the booths were wooden and frankly a little uncomfortable, but the food was out of this world. The sub roll was the perfect combination of crusty on the outside and soft on the inside and the tenders were piping hot and flavorful. Jonas ate two sandwiches while I relished mine.

"What's the verdict?" he asked.

"Delicious."

"Told you. This place is usually jammed with students on the weekends; it's nice to come here when it's quiet."

I took in our surroundings. It was late afternoon—too early for dinner unless you were an aged early bird or had kids with an early bedtime—so the restaurant was relatively empty, with only a few tables occupied. An older couple was sharing a meatball sub next to the window. The woman had frothy white hair and would hold out a forkful of food for her husband after every bite she took. I stared at her hands, which showed the normal unsteadiness of age, and then turned my attention back to Jonas, who was draining his root beer.

"I've considered your counteroffer," I said. "I think you should help with the research."

Jonas pushed his straw around in his ice. "I'm no good at research."

"I don't buy that. Are you just being lazy, or do you have a real excuse?" Or was he avoiding me after everything that had transpired in Boston?

He was silent for several seconds. "What if it's too depressing?"

"I'll find the resources and read them—you can just fetch them for me. The library is pretty big."

"You want me to be your *errand boy*?" He raised an eyebrow.

"If the pajama pants fit."

"That's silly, Doyle. Our library isn't large enough to warrant someone fetching books for you. Who's lazy now? I thought you fancied yourself an athlete."

"Our library won't have what I need. We're going to Dartmouth. One of my friends from college works in the biomedical sciences library, and he said that we can do our research there."

"Friend, eh? Like a boyfriend?"

"Not a boyfriend. And before you make some sort of comment about not being surprised that I don't have a boyfriend, I'll have you know, I was dating someone before I came here."

"I know. You told the kids at dinner and then Carla mentioned him at Thanksgiving."

I took a gulp of my Cherry Coke. I'd walked into that one. "Well, we broke up."

He frowned. "I don't find it beyond the realm of possibility that someone would date you, you know. You have positive qualities."

I thought about asking him to elaborate on these qualities, but I didn't think that would take us in a productive direction.

"Patrick was a surgeon," I said.

"Oh, so he's the power-tool-wielding handyman you were referring to? What happened there—you realized he was a wanker?"

I took a deep breath. Even before the suitcases in the hall, things between me and Patrick hadn't been all that great, but it wasn't always like that between us. There was a time when we drank each other in, floated through moments together blissfully smitten, and then at some point, the air just started to leak out of our happy bubble. At the end, I felt like a deflated balloon, small and shriveled and discarded. I didn't relish the idea of reliving it. Definitely not with Jonas.

"He also thinks I'm the Red Sox bitch, if that makes sense. Never question the team doctor's decision-making, especially if you live with him."

"Sounds pretty serious." He tied his straw wrapper into a knot and yanked.

I shrugged. "I guess not, in retrospect. He didn't seem to have too much trouble throwing me out. What about you? Did you have someone special in your life, or just piano groupies?"

Jonas flushed.

I put my hand on his arm. "Wait, are piano groupies a thing?" I asked. "I was joking."

He glanced down at where I was lightly gripping his forearm, not even thinking, and I retracted my hand.

"My life didn't leave much room for relationships."

"That's not fair," I said. "I told you my story. Not much room for relationships, that's it? That's all you're going to give me?"

He sighed audibly. I'm fairly certain that the older couple at the window heard him.

"I was in a serious relationship once, when I was in my early twenties," he said. "Her name was Mei." The expression on his face was a strange combination of regret and longing, and something inside me twisted. "She was a zitherist from Shanghai. As you said, it simply didn't work out."

I tipped my head, urging him to go on.

"I thought it was hard because we were apart so much. She played mostly with symphonies and opera companies in China and only came to Berlin maybe once a year, when she was touring. From the beginning, it was always a struggle where we were oscillating between wanting to really make a go of it and breaking apart. It wasn't until later that I realized that if we were meant to be together, we could've made it work. I wanted to, but wanting something on your own isn't enough. There's no point in loving someone who can't truly return your feelings. She taught me that." He straightened up, shrugged.

"But it's fine; the music demands a certain level of angst, and she gave me plenty of it. All the critics said the music I played in that time after things ended between us was the most beautiful; that was before my hand, of course."

"I don't understand that. Why does great music require your suffering? Sports don't. Not always. How is music any different than sports? Both take discipline, practice, one person or many digging deep to overcome the odds . . . but at the end of the day, the brilliant players, they were the ones who did it because it was the thing that made them feel alive, lit them up with joy from the inside. You could tell the difference between them and the ones who were grinding it out."

"They're not the same." His eyes locked on mine, and I swallowed hard. "One is life. The other is just a game." He rose and picked up our trays, turning his back to me. "We should head out. If we're going to Dartmouth, I need to put on real pants."

Chapter 17

I found my friend James working at the front desk at the Dartmouth biomedical sciences library. He grinned when he saw me and came jogging out to sweep me up into a bear hug.

"Great to see you, Sophie," he said. "It's been way too long."

"Thanks for having us," I said, smiling back. James was that big-brother type of guy who just made you feel good. I'd known him since we were kids running around Southie together. "Uh, this is my colleague, Jonas."

Jonas gave me a look, then stepped forward to shake James's hand. "Nice to meet you."

"Likewise," James said. "A friend of Sophie's is a friend of mine. I reserved you a study room. Let me know if you need any help finding anything."

Jonas and I headed to our private study room. As we walked, he leaned over and whispered in my ear, "Friends, huh?"

I twisted my neck to glare at him.

"Aren't you getting a bit ahead of yourself?" he said.

I pulled open the door to the study room and let it close behind us. "Are you forgetting that I'm doing this to *help* you?"

He held up his hands. "Point taken," he said.

"Play nice," I told him.

We sat down beside each other at a table and got to work. Jonas had brought some grading with him to occupy his time while I researched. He took out the papers while I booted up my computer. Our thighs touched, making my skin tingle.

I had to remind myself to focus. I was curious about the contracted state of his fourth finger. Without imaging studies, it was hard to say whether the problem was structural. I needed medical textbooks and clinical journals in orthopedics and neurology to get more information about all of the potential differential diagnoses. If I didn't get to the root of the problem, whatever I tried would be of little help to Jonas; inappropriately targeted efforts could even make it worse. I worked on my laptop, searching the library catalogue and scribbling down call numbers on scraps of paper. For his part, Jonas didn't complain. He found all the hard copies of what I needed and brought them to me. When he wasn't playing errand boy or grading papers, he put in his earbuds and worked on his arrangement in his notebook.

It took me two hours before I had a breakthrough. I touched his arm to get his attention. "Can you get me this?" I asked.

He eyed the piece of paper. "*Merritt's Neurology*? What do you need a neurology textbook for?"

"I'll tell you after I find what I'm looking for."

Wordlessly, he left the study room. I watched him navigate the open area where a number of students and staff worked at tables. One table seemed to take particular note of him. In fact, they were having trouble keeping their eyes on their studies and off of him. A sensation that was so absolutely ludicrous that I could only chalk it up to being emotionally off-balance after the visit to Boston bubbled up in my chest. I did not like the way they looked at him. Not at all. I pushed it out of my mind. I'd never been a jealous person, not even when Patrick would tell me about the patients who'd propositioned him. I certainly wasn't about to be bothered by some twenty-two-year-olds who found my annoying roommate hot. But I was *bothered*.

Jonas returned and deposited the massive textbook in front of me. I flipped through the index rapidly, until I located the term I was looking for—"dystonia"—and then found the section. I scanned the pages, searching for the evidence that would substantiate my suspicions. I turned back to my laptop, entering search terms until I identified some relevant recent articles and case studies. They all confirmed my hypothesis. Jonas was likely suffering from something called musician's or focal dystonia. It wasn't even all that uncommon, except that professional musicians were often reticent and didn't want to advertise issues that would sabotage their careers, so they avoided seeking medical help. Sometimes they even practiced more, worsening the condition. And ruin careers it did.

I took a break from my reading and glanced over at Jonas. He'd finished grading and was entranced in the music he was listening to on his earbuds, opening his eyes only momentarily to jot something down in his notebook occasionally before returning to his dreamlike state. We weren't friends, not really. In fact, I had no idea what we were. But I was sure that I didn't want his career to be ruined. I knew the unique pain of having reached the pinnacle of your profession and landed the perfect job—the one you've worked, studied, trained for, the one that made all the sacrifices worth it—only to have it slip through your fingers.

He looked up at me. "I'm not sure that you're fully committed to the plan, Doyle. You don't seem focused to me."

I turned my attention to the research paper on the screen in front of me and frowned. "Ridiculous."

"Or was that a physical exam you were giving me just now?"

"In your dreams, Voss." I stood up.

"Hey, I was joking there. No need to run off."

"I need to make a phone call."

I found an alcove outside the library to make the phone call. Dr. Vurgun, Dad's neurologist at Mass General, was one of those amazing physicians who gave out their number to patients' families. I dialed.

"Hi, Dr. Vurgun, it's Sophie Doyle, Gerry's daughter. I'm so sorry to bother you."

"Oh, hello, Sophie. Is Gerry okay?" she asked, her voice tinged with concern.

"He's fine, as far as I know. He seemed good on Thanksgiving." I could hear the worry in my own voice. *Is he?* I wondered, and the strange sensation of guilt bubbled up again. "I just had a question and you're the only neurologist I know. Have you ever treated someone with musician's dystonia? I have a . . . patient. I'm not very familiar with the condition."

"Oh." She was quiet for a moment. "Is it a hand dystonia? Or—"

"Hand."

"How progressed is it?"

"Seems to be only the fourth finger of the right hand. No improvement with rest. Slight strength differential."

"I have treated a few musicians. It's not really my specialty.

In general, very few physicians are well equipped to treat them. If you think about it, they're athletes. Practicing for hours a day. Repetitive stress. Inflammation. Over-practiced gross and fine movements. Honestly, this is a part of medicine that is years behind. Dystonias are not wholly predictable as far as course. There seems to be a family component, so we see them more often among patients who have a first-degree relative with some kind of dystonia. In general, the prognosis is not great. Of course, there are exceptions . . . I know in some cases there have been good results with retraining, so it's not entirely hopeless. I can send you some names of people who know more than I to reach out to."

"I'd really appreciate that. I'm sorry to bother you."

"Actually, I'm glad you called, Sophie. Your dad canceled his last checkup and hasn't rescheduled yet. Do you think you could see about getting him back in? It's really important that we keep track of his disease and make sure he's not progressing or having any problems."

I hadn't realized he hadn't gone.

"The medications are still working now, and that's great. But at some point, they may need to be adjusted, or we may need to consider other options."

"I know. I'll make sure he reschedules; I'll bring him myself if I need to. We're so glad to have you as his doctor."

"Of course. Take care, Sophie."

I leaned against the brick wall and let my eyes close. Jonas's situation was worse than I'd imagined. And Dad? Why hadn't he gone to the doctor? Was he hiding something again? I'd left my jacket inside, and the frigid air left me shivering. I dug into the conversation, searching for positives to cling to. *Good results with retraining. Medication is working.* I repeated them to myself as I headed back into the warmth of the library and the study room where Jonas was waiting.

"What's the verdict?" he said when I returned.

"Huh?"

"Look, you asked me to get you a huge neurology textbook but won't tell me why. Is that research for me, or were you looking up something for your dad?" The last part he said gently, as if he recognized that I might need to talk.

"I think I know what's wrong with your hand."

"Can you fix it?"

I lifted my shoulders a fraction of an inch and let them fall. "It may be musician's dystonia. It's not orthopedic, it's neurological; that's why the orthopedists couldn't address it. I still believe I might be able to help, but the outlook isn't great."

Jonas deflated before my eyes. I'd never seen him look like that. He was always full of bravado or brooding, but now, his six-foot-plus frame folded in on itself. He shook his head. "I keep thinking that if I'd known it would end so soon, I would've done things differently. I can't believe this."

"It isn't over," I said, my voice firm. I put my hand on his shoulder. "I told you, I never give up on anything. I'm not about to start with you, even if you are a pain in the ass."

"You walked away from the Red Sox," he said quietly, ignoring my attempt at a playful jab. "You knew you were right making the call you did. You could have fought back and convinced them to keep you."

"I just know when it's time to fold so I can stay in the game. I needed a place to live and regroup for a bit, so I came to Monadnock. That doesn't mean it's over for me and pro baseball. I won't let it be. I worked my whole life for that job, and nothing is going to take it away from me. Understand?"

He nodded. I knew he got it.

"The piano is your Red Sox. I will do whatever it takes to help you get it back."

Jonas stared at me. "You mean that?"

"Believe me," I said, meeting his eyes, "I'm in this."

Chapter 18

Despite all the evidence that Jonas's hand problem might be impossible to fix, I'd promised we were going to beat the odds. I needed a win, and I sure as heck wasn't planning to lose in front of Jonas. I did what any desperate and determined person would do and stayed up all Saturday night crafting a detailed plan to overcome his complex condition. The first step involved improving his physical health and reducing stress through jogging and yoga.

On Sunday, I rose with the sun and pulled on a pair of running tights, a sports bra, and a long-sleeved compression shirt like I was preparing for battle. The mornings were getting colder these days and soon the quad would be blanketed in snow or, more likely, muddy slush and ice. Since I'd made it my personal mission to have Jonas playing again by spring training, there was no time to waste.

I knocked on his door, but he didn't answer. The previous evening, we'd agreed to run at seven a.m.—was he already giving up? Not on my watch. I slowly turned the knob and opened the door a crack.

"Jonas? It's time for our workout."

He groaned. "Go away, Doyle."

I pushed the door all the way open. "You wanted me to help you. This is me helping." I stalked across the room and yanked the covers off of him.

"You call this helping! This is abuse."

"You're a giant baby."

"And you're a pervert intent on seeing me in my drawers, apparently."

I glanced down. In truth, I'd been so singularly focused on our plan that I hadn't noticed, but now . . . I *noticed*. Jonas's upper half was bare, and his long legs, corded with lean muscle, were exposed; the rest of him was covered only by a pair of gray boxer briefs that left little to the imagination. Oh. *Oh.* He rolled away from me. I turned around, my face blazing.

"I'll, ah, just let you get dressed," I said, heading toward the door. "You have running shoes, right?"

"How about you worry about your own footwear," he said.

I swiveled around to glare at him and caught another full view of him standing and stretching, his muscles taut and tantalizing. A wave of attraction coursed through me and I made a beeline to the common area. *Okay*, I told myself as I paced the living room, *so he's hot. I can acknowledge that. But he's mind-bendingly irritating, and that cancels out the hotness.*

If the sight of Jonas in his underwear was surprising, so was his physical prowess. For someone who moped around most of the time and found sports useless, he was surprisingly fit. He kept pace with me even when I got annoyed and shifted into another gear to motor up the massive hill on campus. We stood at the top, chests heaving, our exhalations forming clouds around us. Jonas folded over to catch his breath, and I took the opportunity to dash off toward the sports complex at a full sprint. The cold air and lactic acid burned my lungs, but it was worth it for the satisfaction of knowing Jonas had to chase me.

We did a short session of hot yoga in the rehab room, working on connecting the body and mind. I'd expected Jonas to complain about yoga. But he got into it. I'd step over and adjust his positioning from time to time, pressing my fingertips into his damp skin. I tried to ignore the sensation on my skin, the voice whispering in my ear, *This is dangerous.*

Workouts finished, we got down to the real effort. He sat with his arm on the treatment table while I assembled my supplies.

"This is the first time I've been in here," he said. He gestured to things and asked what they were used for and if we'd use them for his therapy.

"No," I said. "Today, the goal is to release the trigger points in your arm. You've been compensating for this issue for a long time, and it's led to issues with the muscles in your hand and forearm. Think of it as a chain reaction. We're going to undo that."

"How are you going to do that . . . massage?" There was a gleam in his eyes when he asked this. I regarded him critically for a moment before I set my kit down.

"Dry needling."

"*Needling?*" His eyes widened. "Jesus, that looks like one of those torture kits. You know, on second thought, my job here is very rewarding. I'm quite fond of the kids."

I grasped his wrist and guided his arm back to the table. "Jonas, you have to trust me."

He eyed my face, appraising it, like he was trying to decide if I really was worthy of his trust. I pulled on a pair of gloves and took out one of the thin monofilament needles. "This shouldn't hurt," I assured him. "Basically, I'm going to insert this filament into the muscle, and it should help the muscle release some of the pain points that may be related to your hand. It's not a fix. Just one piece of the puzzle. You ready?"

He nodded. But his body was full of tension. Under the table his knees bounced. I scooted my stool closer, our legs brushed, and his legs stilled. I gently laid my hand on his forearm.

"I won't hurt you." Beneath my touch he relaxed, just a fraction.

I proceeded carefully, slowly. "Remember to breathe, Jonas," I said.

He met my gaze. "I find it hard to do that around you."

The comment and the rasp in his voice when he said it left me unsettled, with so many questions and a strange stomach-flipping sensation, but this was careful work that required complete focus. I looked at my kit and took a deep breath. I pushed the thoughts down, quieted the physical reaction, slowed my heart rate, and steadied my hands.

When we were finished, I massaged his hand gently, taking it through a set of movements. His skin was warm, a perfect blend of soft and calloused. I could sense the history of what his hands were capable of in the hills and valleys of his knuckles, the swirl of his fingerprints, the lines of his palms. The strange feeling in my core returned.

"So—" Jonas stopped to clear his throat. "Do you have a plan to get back into baseball?"

I glanced up from my work. "Kind of. I was thinking that a few strategic publications in key sports medicine journals and maybe helping support the training of a rising star could help."

"Who's this rising star?"

"A young pitcher."

"How'd you find someone around here? We're practically in the middle of nowhere, and our baseball team is abysmal. It's like the *Bad News Bears*, honestly."

I placed his hand gently on the table and then went to the sink to wash the massage cream off.

"Wait. No. Tell me you don't mean Tyson."

"He doesn't have to play on the team. I just thought I could work with him."

"I thought we were on the same page with this. I told you why it's important that he doesn't play baseball. You really don't care, do you? All of this is just about you and getting your job back." He rose.

"I'm thinking about what he wants. I think he deserves to choose who he wants to be. If it's a violinist, then so be it. I'm not trying to make him a baseball player. He *is* one. He's not sneaking out of the dorm to practice violin or checking out music books in secret from the library. He's reading about base-ball, he's practicing baseball—on his own. He could hurt him-self that way, you know. At least if I help him, I can teach him how to protect his shoulder and his elbow. He's better off with me training him than going it alone."

"He shouldn't be going at all. I was under the impression you understood that. You said you did. But it seems like you're more focused on what you need and what you think is right than what's best for the people who are around you."

"Just because I might benefit from something doesn't mean that my motives are bad."

"Is that why you're helping me? You think you'll get a pub-lication out of it? Didn't you say what I had was like what some baseball players get? Is that your angle?"

I had compared his problems to the yips, that much was

true, but I wasn't using him. I shook my head. "No. That's not what I'm doing at all. I just want to help."

He took a step toward me. I thought he was angry, but now that I'd seen him truly mad in the bar in Boston, I knew he wasn't. His tone when he spoke was almost plaintive. "Why? Why would you want to help me?"

"Because you're my roommate. We're friends."

His face hadn't been so close to mine since the kiss in the bar. The air between us was charged with electricity. The memories of his hands on me, in my hair, grazing my ribs, my hips, his lips on mine, the heat that boiled beneath the surface, came flooding back. My shallow breaths came rapidly.

"Doyle," he said slowly, as if he had to drag the words from his mouth, "we are *not* friends."

I took a step back. I hadn't expected his words to smart, but still I was surprised by them and how much they stung. *How stupid*, I thought, *of course we're not friends.* Friends don't eat all the waffles and exchange constant verbal barbs and make the other person take the cot.

I cleared my throat quietly. "That's enough for today," I said.

We trudged home in silence, white-hot animosity seething between us. Andy and Revi popped up from their spots on the couch while we kicked off our shoes way more aggressively than was warranted.

"We brought souvenirs!" they chorused. We didn't stop. We both headed toward our bedrooms and slammed the doors.

I took a couple of deep breaths and then emerged. "Sorry," I told the boys. "I'm so glad you're back. Tell me about Disney! Was it magical?"

"So magical. Come sit on the couch and watch my video of the fireworks," Andy said.

"First, what the heck was that about?" Revi asked.

"We tried to get along."

They pulled me down on the couch between them. "What does that mean?" Revi asked. "Did you guys hook up?"

"No!" I yelped. But my flaming cheeks were practically screaming, *We kissed! I was jealous in a library. I checked him out in his underwear. He said we weren't friends and hurt my feelings.*

They scrutinized me. Andy pressed the back of his hand to my forehead.

"I want to see the fireworks," I said.

"Seems to me we already saw the fireworks," said Revi.

"You are so bad," Andy said.

I rested my head on his shoulder. "I missed you guys. How was Mulan? Did you see her?"

"We got an autograph for you. Look." Andy pulled out a set of glittery silver Minnie Mouse ears and a T-shirt and handed them to me. Then he extracted a print of Mulan with a signature scrawled across it.

"This is so cool. Thank you!"

"You can wear all this next time when you come with us. Okay, now that the presents have been distributed, real talk," Andy said. "How was Thanksgiving with your dad?"

I shrugged. "It was wonderful. He's doing well, which is a massive relief. He was telling stories and playing cribbage and he loved the pie I made. I can't believe it almost didn't happen."

"What?" Andy asked.

"My car wouldn't start."

"Shit. If the MG were drivable, you totally could've taken it. What did you do, take the bus?"

"Jonas drove me."

Revi scrunched up his face. "Sorry, I just hallucinated. Did you just say Jonas drove you? Our roommate Jonas? As in thirty percent runway supermodel, seventy percent crotchety-retiree-next-door Jonas?"

"That's a little harsh, don't you think? He sent us to Disney. At least we should say he's the crotchety retiree who befriends the waitstaff at the restaurant where he orders the same thing every day and secretly puts them in his will. Start at the beginning and don't leave anything out," Andy said.

I was trying to decide whether I wanted to dodge or if I was aching to confess everything when Astrid called. "I'll explain it all later," I whispered to the boys as Astrid launched into her greeting.

"How's my Sophie-bear doing?"

"I'm doing okay. How about you? Are you the queen of the north yet?"

"If frozen asses were crowns, then I'd be an empress. It's so cold here. I'm in the Arctic. And I know that sounds exotic and sexy, like Bianca and I are just lying around in tents with fireplaces and animal pelts, but it's actually pocket warmers and trying to control my shivering to get through every take. I may never regain the feeling in my nipples."

I snorted. "Astrid, I love you, but I'm not sure I ever need to know the status of sensation in your nipples."

"Did I just find the line in our friendship? I knew this would happen someday. But I feel like having to hear me talk about things that make you uncomfortable is a small price to pay, considering I bailed you out of jail and used bikini photos to ensure your freedom."

I couldn't argue with that. "Couldn't you or Bianca shove some of those pocket warmers in your bra?"

"How do you think the damage occurred in the first place? This isn't my first rodeo."

It was a valid point. Astrid had definitely dealt with a range of experiences that I could barely begin to fathom. She was more experienced in life and relationships than I was. I went to the window and looked out toward the quad, where evening was falling. The lamps that lit the intersecting pathways were flickering on. I traced a line between them with my finger.

"How was the time with your dad?"

"Really nice. But I found out that he skipped his last checkup with his neurologist."

"He must've had a reason. Gerry's like the most responsible person I know."

I nodded. "You're right. I was going to ask him about it, but he seemed to be doing pretty well. I'm probably overreacting."

"Is that the only thing on your mind, Soph? You don't sound like yourself."

I let out a sigh. "Can I ask you something?"

"I live and breathe to answer your questions, Bear. Go for it."

"What does it mean when someone says that they find it hard to breathe when they're around you?"

"It means they've got it bad."

I'd never found it hard to breathe around anyone, so I had no evidence to contradict Astrid's theory. I found it hard to reconcile, though, given that I was sure Jonas did not have it bad for me. He didn't even have "*it*" . . . unless "it" was moderate dislike. *We are* not *friends* echoed in my head. I pressed my hand to my chest. At least it was a step up from pure loathing.

"I kissed Jonas in a bar. It was an accident, but then it sort of stopped being an accident." The words tumbled out of my mouth before I had the wherewithal to stop them. "Are you judging me? I am. I mean, who kisses their prick roommate who hates them?"

"I would never judge you."

"Then what? Say something."

"Nothing. I'm just wondering if you're having a few breathing problems of your own, that's all."

Chapter 19

The kids returned to school, filling the halls with their (mostly) joyful noise. Life became busy. The weather turned frigid and winter sports started. We fell into a routine.

In the mornings I called Jonas to make sure he was up for our run. This seemed a safer option than having another underwear incident. I tried to keep it light and professional. On the phone, while we were jogging, during yoga . . . when I took him through some of his hand therapy exercises, my fingers exploring his, every nerve ending awake. I *tried*. I found myself looking forward to our workouts, waking up before my alarm, taking a little extra time with my ponytail, adding lip gloss instead of Carmex.

It was Astrid's fault. She's an angel, but she's also a potstirrer, and she had stirred my proverbial pot of *do I have feelings for my roommate* soup. It's not that Jonas was less of a grump. He still angrily straightened up the apartment, practically growled at me every time I was within ten feet of Tyson, and refused to use my first name. Still, every time I touched his hand, the energy between us surged. Its quality transformed from animosity and irritation to a different kind of tension, a delicious kind that coiled in my core, begging to be released. Every moment seemed to unfurl before us, and suddenly I'd find myself hyperaware of the sound of my breathing, the sensation of my heart thundering in my chest.

I find it hard to breathe around you.

Despite any lingering confusion caused by the Thanksgiving kiss, I was certain that the statement didn't mean what Astrid thought. Maybe for some people, but not for Jonas, not with me. No, he was a tortured artist who pined for an exquisitely beautiful musician from Shanghai—I wasn't proud of it, but I had googled her. A sporty, freckled Bostonian with a bad temper who couldn't play "Heart and Soul" was not going to take his breath away, I was certain.

Despite Jonas's protestations, I started working with Tyson once a week. I gave him a set of bands to use to strengthen his arms and shoulders. We worked on mechanics. I explained that pitching too much is a risk factor for later needing surgery. Because Tyson didn't play baseball formally, he'd been lucky. His shoulders and elbow were healthy, whereas a lot of young pitchers who played year-round ball had accumulated damage. Surprisingly, he also didn't seem to have some of the overuse issues that came from the repetitive motion of playing a stringed instrument. We met on Sundays at the field house and he threw. Long throws to help his velocity and thirty pitches, ten with full intensity. He got better and better, but more than that, his smile grew.

"You really love this," I said one day as we sat on a bench drinking water after a workout.

He nodded. "Same for you, Coach Doyle. When we're playing baseball, you get all shiny."

"Ha." I laughed. "That's just sweat."

"No, it's not. I think it's baseball that lights you up." He stood up and went through the cooldown routine I'd given him for his arm. "Do you miss being a team trainer? Mr. Voss said you worked with the Red Sox."

I didn't allow myself to reflect on the fact that Jonas had talked to Tyson about me. "Sometimes. We wouldn't be playing baseball now though. It's actually really important to take breaks. Doing the same thing over and over might make you good at something, but it can break down your body."

"Is that what working here is? A break before you go back?"

"Not exactly. I don't really want to get into it, but rest assured, I like being here. Working with all of you kids is actually a pretty great job."

Tyson grinned. "I gotta run to my other practice. Mr. Voss doesn't like it when I'm late."

I laughed. "He's one to judge. Mr. Voss can barely drag himself out of bed on time for our morning runs."

Tyson raised his eyebrows playfully the way teenagers do when they think they've caught you in something.

"I have to call him on the phone," I deadpanned.

"Cozy," Tyson said. He picked up his duffel bag and his violin case. "Thanks for today."

"Awesome work, Tyson, as always." And I meant it. Not only was he blessed with talent, but he had the best work ethic I'd ever witnessed. I felt like I was doing something important in teaching him how to maximize his gift and protect it. That had always been my favorite part of my job. Sure, there was the adrenaline rush when an emergency happened and I was needed, but what I really lived for was keeping those emergencies from happening. I'd prefer a game where I wasn't needed, one where I could sit and watch the play unfold and no one got injured.

"Same time next weekend?" he asked.

I shook my head. "Sorry. I'll be at the Winter Sports Jamboree at Stowe and won't be back until really late on Sunday. But we can find a day during the week, if you have time. I'll walk with you."

"Are you going to the music building?"

"No, but I wanted to go downtown, so it's on my way."

"Cool."

As we walked, Tyson told me about the competition piece he was working on. "It's so hard. It has all this down-bow staccato and the ricochet bowing . . . I love it."

"You have such a good attitude," I observed. "A lot of people might be frustrated or worried about that."

He shrugged. "When I'm playing something really challenging, it feels like a game to see what I'm capable of. I guess I just have faith that if I keep working at it, it'll come. And when it does . . . that feeling, I don't know, Coach, it's like magic."

I nodded. "I get it." I imagined what it must be like for Jonas to experience the reverse, of not being able to do the things he was once capable of. I'd watched my dad struggle with routine tasks. Not being able to drink his coffee without spilling, struggling to button his shirts. He'd grown quiet. Though my mom was practically a human sunbeam, I'd also gotten plenty of the sunny parts of my personality from him. But when he'd started having problems, he'd grown sullen. Suddenly, Jonas's irritation, his low mood, were more understandable.

I left Tyson at the front door. He waved exuberantly before disappearing inside. I shoved my hands into my pockets to keep them warm and headed down the hill. There was a sweet little craft store at the base of the hill called Everything Ewe Need. The day of my formal dinner shopping spree, I'd seen the baskets of beautiful hand-dyed yarn in the window. I had a project I wanted to do, including making something special for Andy and Revi before the Jamboree, that required several skeins.

The Jamboree was one of the biggest athletic events of the school year. All of the New England prep schools gathered near a host school and competed in shortened versions of all the competitions with each school. The kids had been counting down to it with excitement—mostly because it meant they got to go to a resort with hot chocolate and hot tubs—but the concurrent scheduling of all the events meant that I couldn't be at all of them, and that I'd need to be extremely efficient prepping my athletes. When the events ended, we'd have Saturday night and part of Sunday to enjoy the ski mountain and the resort town before heading back. Because of the sheer number of athletes at this event, extra staff had to come along to chaperone. Andy would be there since he was the assistant basketball coach, and Revi's name was on the list. Some of the girls' sports teams had female coaches—Penny Wilkerson and Ivy Hayes for ice hockey both seemed nice. I was looking forward to getting to know them better. Rebecca, the biology teacher I was friendly with, ran the entire ski program and had invited me to go night snowboarding. I was rooming with Cynthia Jones, who I'd gotten to know a bit during soccer season and during our night out at Pumpelly's Pub. She'd already made plans for a sleigh ride and massages for us. I had been fully on board. For one thing, the mattress in my room sucked and my back had been complaining for the last couple of weeks. Plus, who doesn't want to go on a sleigh ride? They had actual Clydesdales there. Sure, it was the kind of activity that most people did as a date. But as Cynthia put it, that didn't mean we singles had to miss out on the fun.

Jonas's name was notably absent from the faculty list for the trip. Not surprising, since he hated sports—and having fun, apparently.

After wandering the knitting store aisles for a few minutes, I found some soft yarn in Monadnock colors and some crochet hooks.

"Looks like you've got plans for a project," the woman said as she packed my items in a small brown bag with a sheep stamped on it.

"Yeah. Is this enough for three adult hats?"

"Depends on whether or not you're doing pom-poms."

"Oh, definitely pom-poms."

She picked up another skein, a bright buttery yellow, and tossed it in the bag. "I ordered too much of that one, and it will look great with the other colors."

"I love it! Thank you."

When we weren't at meals, classes, or practices, Andy, Revi, and I spent the week of the trip going to organizational meetings and packing our things. I dedicated the rest of my free time to crocheting the hats. Thursday night after dinner, I put on an episode of *Brooklyn Nine-Nine* and sat down to make pom-poms.

"You've been crocheting all week," Jonas said. "Are you trying to turn into my gran?"

"Haha." I didn't look up.

He sat down in the chair and looked at the television. "What are you making?"

"Hats."

"Plural? Is this a community service project?"

"They're for Andy and Revi, for the jamboree."

Jonas pressed his lips together, and a deep crease appeared in his left cheek.

"Are you three planning to match?" he said, barely maintaining his composure. "Will you wear matching jumpers as well?" His shoulders shook as he laughed.

"Oh no, I wish I'd thought of that. I don't have enough yarn for sweaters, and it'd be so cute for the three of us roommates to match!" I gave him a sugary smile and batted my eyelashes.

"More like the Three Stooges. Besides, there are four roommates," he said. He stood abruptly. "This show is stupid."

Was he sulking? I looked down at the pom-pom I was working on. The hats were for the trip, and Jonas wasn't going. I wasn't purposely leaving him out. Besides, Andy and Revi had gotten the Minnie Mouse ears and the Mulan autograph for me. They'd been so welcoming and kind—I adored those guys. Jonas and I were tolerating each other, and the therapy sessions were going okay, but I wasn't sure our relationship constituted friendship. In fact, Jonas had assured me that we were not friends. What were we, exactly? I sighed and peeked inside my supply bag. I had about a third of a skein left. Not enough for another hat.

Chapter 20

I dragged my suitcase over to the side of the large tour bus and got in line. Rebecca was checking off names as students boarded the buses.

"Hey, Sophie! You're going to be in bus two with the basketball teams. Here's your checklist."

"Great. Have you seen Cynthia?"

She looked up from her clipboard. "You didn't hear? Cynthia has norovirus. Apparently the whole debate team is down after the meet they had Wednesday. The infirmary is completely full."

"Oh, that's awful!" I said. "I guess it's a blessing that she found out before the trip. I wouldn't want to have a stomach bug on a three-hour bus ride. Do you have to redo the assignments?"

"We had another teacher volunteer to go. He'll be covering some of the activities you and Cynthia were going to oversee. The snowman contest judging and the toboggan derby."

"Sounds good. Who is it?"

She glanced at her list. "Someone you know," she said. "Hi, Jonas. Thanks for stepping in for Cynthia."

"Happy to help, Becks." He turned and looked down at me, giving me a curt nod. "Doyle."

Becks. She got Becks. I narrowed my eyes at him.

"Voss." I yanked my suitcase behind me and trudged off to the second bus. The driver took my suitcase and stowed it in the cargo hold. I glanced back at Jonas and Rebecca. They were talking about something; she was laughing, and he was beaming. *Beaming.* I went and found my seat in the front. As the bus began to fill, I checked names off the list. Andy and Revi arrived, wearing their matching hats and identical grins. They hugged me.

"This is going to be so fun," Andy said.

"We love the hats, Sophie! You are the sweetest," Revi said.

"Don't they look fabulous?" Andy pointed to his hat, and I nodded emphatically. I extracted my own matching hat from my parka pocket.

"Did you know the hotel has a gourmet hot chocolate bar?" Revi asked. "I'm stopping there before I even go to our room."

"Aren't you adorable," Andy said. Then he winked at me. "We'll sit in the back so there's no shenanigans."

"I thought shenanigans only happened on the hockey bus," I said.

"He's adorable and you're innocent," Andy said, shaking his head. "What a pair."

Revi tossed me a baggie filled with peanuts, M&M's, and raisins. "It's GORP, for the bus ride. Just make sure to leave some room for hot chocolate."

I saluted them and checked their names off on the list. They made their way to their seats, their identical pom-poms bobbing as they walked. Any annoyance I'd felt about Jonas and Rebecca and the fact that he was being so friendly toward her when he still insisted on being rude and on a fully last-name basis with me dissipated. I picked an M&M out of the mix and ate it.

Jonas was on a different bus, I surmised. He never got on. I leaned my head against the window and fell asleep for the entire ride to the Von Trapp Family Lodge, where we would be staying through Sunday. Andy, Revi, and I hit the hot chocolate bar, then we had dinner in the lounge. The sweet potato mac and cheese was transcendent. The kids donned their outerwear and had a huge snowball fight after dinner. Since the tournament started at ten a.m., meaning the kids had to get dressed, eat breakfast, get taped and wrapped if needed, and then drive to the host prep school or Stowe Mountain (for the ski team), curfew was early, and nobody argued. I didn't see Jonas all evening.

The teams did surprisingly well. Both boys' and girls' basketball had an even split for wins and losses—a huge improvement over last year's blowout. A junior from our ski team took third in giant slalom. The ice hockey teams didn't fare as well, but they managed to eke out a couple of ties. There was one mildly sprained knee and a bad contusion, but otherwise, Saturday was a complete success. We set the kids free after the events were over, and most went to explore the town and find pizza.

"Don't forget to be back by eight for the snowman contest," I hollered after them.

"You don't want to go to town?" a deep voice said. I swiveled to find Jonas standing shoulder to shoulder with me.

"I booked a sleigh ride. Well, Cynthia and I did, but I'm still going to go. I can't say no to Clydesdales."

Thick snow was starting to fall. I pulled my scarf a little

tighter and yanked my hat down farther over my ears. Jonas's head was bare. Flakes settled on his short hair. I wondered if he was cold.

"You should get a hat before we do the judging. The temperature is dropping."

He turned to look down at me. "If only someone had made one for me."

"I ran out of yarn."

The corner of his mouth twitched. He pulled up the hood of his jacket. "Should we align on the judging before the contest?"

"All right. What are you doing until then?"

He shrugged. "I don't even know what there is to do. I only had enough time to basically throw my clothes in a bag."

I hesitated for a moment. "Do you want to come on the sleigh ride with me?"

"Are you inviting me on your romantic wintertime outing, Doyle?"

"No!" I yelped. "I just thought we could talk about the judging. Since you know it will probably take us two hours to agree. And I feel bad about the hat."

He looked straight at me with such a searching look that I felt completely exposed. I wanted to pull my scarf over my entire face. But also I wanted to grab on to the faux fur surrounding the hood of his jacket and reel him into me again, like that night in the bar. I could feel each snowflake touch down on my skin; the ones that fluttered against my lips were the promise of his lips against mine. "Wow, it's really coming down," I said, changing the subject.

Jonas surveyed the sky before he looked at me. He met my eyes for a moment, and then his gaze dropped to my mouth, where a snowflake had come to rest on my bottom lip. "I'm in," he said.

"Really?"

"What can I say, I guess I can't resist"—he paused, and I held my breath—"Clydesdales."

We made our way through the driving snow toward the barn, where an older gentleman was waiting with two large horses hitched to a genuine sleigh. He extended a hand to help me up. I climbed in and pulled a wool blanket over myself. Jonas sat next to me. I lifted the edge of the blanket.

"I'm good. This is nothing compared to winters in Fürstenberg." We headed off into the evening, over the shimmering snow. It was so peaceful. There was just the sound of the horses as they made their way through the fresh powder. The temperature seemed to be dropping by the minute. I glanced over at Jonas. In the wind, his hood had fallen back. Even in the dim light of the lanterns that marked the path we were taking, I could see his ears were turning red. I considered taking my hat off and putting it on his head, but I knew he'd never abide that. Instead, I reached over and pulled his hood back over his head. Then I scooted a bit closer and flipped the blanket over his legs.

"What are you doing?"

"Preventing hypothermia. You may be tough, but I'd be shirking my professional responsibilities if I let you get frostbite."

"Is there anyone you don't take care of?" he asked, half smiling.

I shrugged. "About the contest, we definitely need to have points for the key snow-person-defining elements," I said.

"What about creativity?"

"That too."

"And size?"

"Does it matter?" I said, and when Jonas raised an eyebrow, I thought the heat coming off of my face might be sufficient to melt all the snow around us.

The sleigh lurched around a curve and I lost my balance and teetered over to the right so that my body pressed against Jonas, sending another wave of shimmering heat through me. He turned to look down at me.

"Okay?" he asked. A snowflake landed on his eyelashes.

"Mm-hmm," I managed.

We spent the rest of the ride in silence, our thighs just touching beneath the wool blanket.

When we got back to the resort, some of the teams were already working on their snow creations. Jonas and I walked slowly through the rows of snow creatures as they morphed from giant balls of snow into recognizable characters. There was an Olaf replica, a scary snowman with maraschino cherry eyes, a Yeti, a Frosty look-alike, and a very intricate snow person by Cory O'Rourke that was nude—Jonas and I both agreed that on artistic merit it probably should've won, but it felt a little inappropriate given the age group (and a little bit reminiscent of Rebecca), so we gave it an honorable mention. In the end, after much deliberation, Jonas and I awarded first place to the Yeti. Some of the kids who weren't happy with their standings chucked snowballs at the winners, and a full-fledged snowball battle broke out.

I was happy to join the fray. After all, I'd grown up with baseball, which meant that with a perfectly made snowball in my hand, I was practically a mercenary. I could hit a person in the ear from fifty feet nine times out of ten. Jonas hunkered down behind a snow-covered hedgerow with me while I picked off three guys from the hockey team.

"I don't know whether I should be impressed or terrified. You're like some kind of sniper. I'm getting murdered by these kids."

I shook my head at him. "It's because you're doing it wrong. This is why only playing music hasn't done you any favors. Much better to be an all-arounder." I packed a snowball and placed it into his gloved hand. I held my snowball, took a single step back, and lifted my lead leg knee almost to my chest. As my front leg started to come down, I brought my hands apart. My foot hit the ground and my front hand whipped forward and up, while my throwing hand cocked back. In one fluid motion, my hips, torso, and shoulders rotated back toward my target, and I threw, leading with my elbow, then rocketing my forearm and hand forward toward release. Jonas watched as I demonstrated in slow motion. "Got it?" I asked.

He nodded. I ducked as a snowball sailed by us. "Retaliate," I yelled. "They're exposed!"

He twisted his body and launched the snowball. It had more speed than I had expected and struck the captain of the ski team in the center of his chest. He mimed a very dramatic death and then the rest of the kids came out and surrendered. There was a fireside entertainment activity that was happening at ten before lights-out, so most of the kids headed in to get out of the cold and attend.

"Nice shot," I told Jonas.

"You're a pretty good teacher," he said, an honest-to-goodness compliment. "No wonder Tyson likes working with you so much."

I shook off my surprise that he had brought my work with Tyson up in a positive light. "He's a little more advanced than you."

"Very sweet," he said. "That's what I get for being nice."

"Sorry," I said. "I'm not used to you being nice to me. I have no idea how to act."

"I can go back to being mean, if you prefer." He looked down at the snow and pushed it with the toe of his boot. "I know I haven't always treated you . . . the way I should."

"Wait, you mean being a prick isn't your only setting?" I teased.

He reached over and put a handful of snow down the back of my jacket. "You cretin!" I screeched, my muscles contracting at the cold. I stuck my leg out and tripped him. He fell into a soft snowbank, grabbing my arm on his way down. I landed on top of him, my chest heaving. I froze for a moment, not sure how to gracefully move off of him. Tiny snow crystals collected on his lashes.

His lips parted slightly. I thought he was about to say something about how my body had jeopardized his hands yet again, but instead, he reached up and tucked a strand of my hair, which had come loose from my hat, back behind my ear. "What now, Doyle?"

I gulped. My heart felt like it might somersault out of my chest.

"We should get out of this blizzard."

Chapter 21

The snowfall intensified. It was a full-blown nor'easter-style blizzard by the time the fireside chat was over. Rebecca stood next to the fireplace and clapped to get everyone's attention.

"Quick announcement. I've just been informed that the roads have been closed due to the snowfall. We probably won't be able to leave on time tomorrow. So sit tight. Many of the activities on the morning schedule may not take place as planned. Please stay at the resort until breakfast, when we'll be sharing updates about the storm. Right now the forecast has snow and ice for all of tomorrow, so we will have to evaluate when we will be able to safely return home."

"I don't mind staying," Andy said. "Is there a better place to get trapped? I don't think so."

"That's because you have all the comforts of home here. Sophie's hat, your amazing boyfriend, the hot chocolate bar—it's basically paradise," Revi said.

"I'll have to miss practice with Tyson," Jonas grumbled. "It's such a critical time."

"I think one day will be okay," Revi said.

"Spoken like someone who is not trying to be a world-famous musician."

"True. I aspire for mediocrity and a life of anonymity. Those are the keys to happiness, I'm told."

My phone buzzed and I pulled it out from my pocket and answered. "Hello?"

"Sophie? It's Maureen." My stomach twisted. Maureen wouldn't call after ten on a Saturday night unless something was wrong.

"What's going on, Maureen?" The fear in my voice was palpable. Jonas looked over, and Revi put a hand on my arm.

"I know it's late, honey," she said. "Your dad had a fall. He hit his head and is a little disoriented. We think he might have broken his arm. We're taking him over to Mass General."

My hand went to my mouth and tears flooded my eyes, hot and plentiful. "He's disoriented? Did he lose consciousness?"

"No, no. He's awake. He didn't pass out, but he's a bit confused. It could be the pain from his arm. I think he'd feel better if you were here."

"But I'm in Vermont," I said, my voice tight and high. "And there's a blizzard here. They've closed the roads." The tears spilled and rolled down my cheeks. I swiped them away, suddenly embarrassed that I was crying in front of everyone. I stood up and stepped away from the group. "Is he there? Can I talk to him?"

"Sure, Sophie. They said the ambulance would be here in a few minutes. I'll put you on speaker for him."

"Dad," I said, trying to smooth the quaver out of my voice. "Daddy, are you there?"

"Sunny," he groaned. My face contorted. He didn't sound like Dad. He sounded like someone else.

"Maureen said you had a fall."

"My arm hurts, Sunny."

"I know, Dad. I'm so sorry. I wish I could be there with you."

"Will you take me home? I want to go home."

I sucked in a jagged breath. Our home was gone. He *was* home. "I can't come, Dad. It's snowing here and I can't get there. But Maureen called an ambulance and they'll make your arm feel better and get you checked out. Okay? And as soon as I can, I'll come. The moment I can, I'm coming. I love you."

"They're here, Sophie," Maureen said. "I'll call you again with an update."

I put the phone away. I yanked my hat off and threw it on the ground in frustration. Then I squatted down and ran my hands over my damp hair. The guys approached me. "What's going on?" Revi asked, squatting down next to me.

I looked at them. "My dad fell. He's out of it, and he probably broke his arm."

"Oh no," Andy said, and wrapped his arms around me.

"Scheiße," Jonas muttered.

"He needs me, and I'm stuck here." I needed to move. I needed to *do* something. I twisted out of Andy and Revi's comforting embrace. "I'm sorry, I just, I have to get out of here."

But I couldn't, so I took off toward my room. I could feel the three of them watching me, their sympathetic faces, and I needed to flee. Inside, I flung myself down on the bed and buried my face in my pillow. I should've been there for my dad. Instead, I was unable to comfort him or help in any way. I couldn't make sure he was calm or talk to the doctors. And I trusted Maureen, but I also should've been the person who was with him. She wasn't family. Sobs wracked my body. I cried until my throat hurt, until I was too exhausted to move.

There was a knock on my door. I ignored it. I heard the beep of the lock and I sat up, swiping at my tear-soaked cheeks. Jonas stood in the doorway.

"Hey, sorry, I tried to see if there was a way to get you out of here," he said. "The resort has a van, but there was an avalanche nearby and the road's blocked until morning. We'll figure something out."

I buried my face in my hands.

"I didn't mean to intrude; I mean, I *did* intrude. You dropped your extra room key card and I didn't want . . . I just wanted to tell you that and I'm really sorry about Gerry. I'll go. I know you probably want to be alone."

I looked up at him. I sucked in a ragged breath and shook my head. "I don't want to be alone," I said.

He nodded. For a moment, he didn't move, didn't speak, just looked at me. I was falling to pieces in front of him, unable to say anything. But there was understanding in his expression. He'd met my dad. He'd laughed with him and learned cribbage from him. He knew how important Dad was to me. Wordlessly, Jonas stepped toward where I was frozen, curled into myself on the bed. He sat on the edge of the mattress near my feet, untied his boots, and set them on the floor beside the bed. I laid down on my side, my hands tucked beneath my chin, my knees pulled up, and he lay beside me. He didn't touch me, he just lay there, quietly, beside me. I listened to the gentle rhythm of his breath while I cried. Then, he moved a fraction closer. His hand, the one that sometimes couldn't play the right notes, slid around my waist, so tenderly—he brought his face beside mine.

"This okay?" he asked in a low voice.

I nodded. His touch wasn't hungry or pushy. There was nothing presumptuous about it. It was simple—somehow, he knew I needed to be held, so he did. The weight of his hand, its warmth against me, soothed me. I felt safe and supported.

I felt like I wasn't alone in this world.

Like the weight wasn't on me.

The snowstorm raged on outside the window, and the icy wind whistled in the eaves, but not in here.

In this room, in this bed, with Jonas, I was safe.

"Everything's going to be okay," Jonas whispered in my ear. I don't know why, but I believed him.

And then, only then, with his words taking the last of my worry away, did I fall asleep.

Chapter 22

I took a short leave of absence from school to visit Dad in the hospital, where they were keeping him under observation for a few days because of his concussion. His arm was in a cast, and he'd have to use a wheelchair for a while until his arm healed, since the doctor said he'd need to use a walker from now on. I slept on the recliner in his room and we played cards and reminisced over our favorite baseball memories. I showed him some footage I'd taken of Tyson pitching.

"He's a phenom, no getting around it—the smooth action, that command. Even his breakers are crisp," Dad said. "You've got an eye, Sunny."

"I know, right? He's incredible. You should see how easily he picks up the adjustments I've given him. He never complains. He's studied all the tapes I've shared with him and everything."

"And he's never played?"

I shook my head. "His family is convinced his calling is playing the violin."

"Is that what he wants?"

"I think he loves playing the violin but he loves baseball too. He's torn."

"You ever think about showing this to anyone?"

I shrugged. "I don't want to push things. Besides, Jonas and I have finally called a truce. I don't want to ruin it."

Dad laughed, then winced. My body contracted at his pain.

"A truce," he said. "Is that what you're calling it?"

"What's that supposed to mean?" I held out his water for him and he took a sip from the straw.

"I've seen you through every crush, breakup, breakdown. I know what each of those looks like, same way I could tell you a pitcher just by seeing their windup. You like him."

"I don't detest him."

He shook his head slowly. "You *like* him."

I thought back to Jonas lying beside me during the snowstorm. Even now, I could almost feel the warmth of his hand on my hip, his breath on my skin as he whispered that everything would be okay. There was two feet of snow on the ground outside, but inside my chest something bloomed.

"Oh no," I said. "No. No. This is terrible."

"What?"

"I'm not saying it's true, but just the thought. It's terrible, Dad. We have nothing in common, we can't get along, we live together. I cannot like Jonas."

"The things you listed aren't important. So what's the real reason why you say you can't like him?"

"Well, for one thing, he doesn't like me at all. He told me."

"I don't buy that for a minute. Do you know that boy missed two bingos in a row during Thanksgiving because he was too busy staring at you? Even the nurses were talking about your new boyfriend and how he was so smitten."

I shook my head. "That's bonkers. He was not watching me. He was probably thinking about music. That's all he does. Scribble arrangements of songs in his notebook. And even if he did have some sort of feeling toward me that wasn't pure loathing, we live together . . . at our job . . . can you imagine how wrong that could go?"

"But that's only temporary. When you go back to the Sox in the spring, you won't have that issue. And the commute wouldn't be all that bad between the city and Monadnock."

My shoulders tensed. "About that," I began. "I don't think that I'll be able to—"

Dad bumped his cast against the bed rail. "Damn," he said, wincing.

"Are you okay?" I asked, helping him settle his injured arm on a pillow.

"Fine. Just took me by surprise, that's all."

The moment for my full confession had passed. I wasn't the only person keeping secrets, and right now, what was going on with him was way more important than the epic demise of my career. "I need to ask you something."

"That sounds ominous, kid."

"Why did you cancel your checkup with Dr. Vurgun?"

"You heard about that?"

I nodded.

"I took a couple of minor diggers a few weeks back. Everybody says falls are a bad sign, so I was pretty sure it wouldn't be a good appointment. Sometimes a man just wants to live his life and not have to think about what's coming down the road." He sighed. "I didn't feel like hearing the bad news. I guess I couldn't avoid it. She already stopped by. She wants to adjust my medication dosage and you already know she recommended I use a walker once I'm out of the wheelchair."

"I didn't realize you were worried. You should've told me, Dad."

"I'm the father. I don't want my kid worrying about me. It's supposed to be the other way around. You know you could tell me anything, right, Sunny? If you've ever got a problem, your old man is here for you, cast or no cast."

I gave his good arm a gentle squeeze. He let out a sigh. "Anyway, all this aside, I'm okay. I don't need you nagging me about my checkups. Maureen does enough of that for both of you."

"You and Maureen seem close. She sounded really worried when she called." I waggled my eyebrows at him. "Aren't you the same age?"

"That's old news," he said. "I seize opportunities, Sunny. I suggest you do the same."

When I returned to campus, I steered clear of Jonas. Both Dad and Astrid thought I liked him, and while I couldn't argue that I wasn't affected by him, I knew he didn't feel the same way. There had been moments of chemistry between us and a couple of glimmers of genuine connection, but none of that was enough to overcome the fact that Jonas clearly wasn't seriously interested in me. Instead of ruminating about the mismatch between my feelings and the impression the two most important people in my life had of my feelings, I focused on being productive. I worked on my plan to develop a training program for the musicians based on conditioning that would help prevent injuries. At its core, it consisted of a combination of strengthening exercises and stretching, planned breaks, and musical cross-training. I felt like this could turn into a publication that would demonstrate the kind of thought leadership that might get me back into professional sports.

The only trouble was that when you live with someone, it's very difficult to avoid him. I ran into Jonas coming out of the shower, at meals, in our living room, in the middle of the night when I couldn't sleep and got up for water. And every time I was in his proximity, my focus shifted to unproductive thoughts. How was he doing? Why did he smell so good? Were Astrid and Dad right? The questions and the fluttering sensation in my stomach left me wanting to moonwalk away whenever he came into view.

"Listen, Doyle, did I do something wrong?" he asked a few days after I returned from Boston. I'd just gotten back from a hockey tournament and had run into him on my way to my bedroom, where I planned to take a well-earned nap. "Is this about Stowe? I'm sorry if I was too forward. I thought maybe you needed to be comforted. I didn't mean to overstep."

I pulled off my shoes. "It's not about Stowe. You were there when I needed you. I'm not mad. You didn't do anything wrong."

He shook his head. "I knew I shouldn't have gotten in your bed."

"Jonas. Seriously. It's not like we had sex and I'm having regrets. You were a perfect gentleman. What you did . . . it was exactly what I needed."

"Then why have you been avoiding me since you got back? I know I'm a pain in the ass. I can be moody and arrogant, and I haven't treated you very well since you came here. But I thought we were working together. You were helping me with my hand, and I've gotten up every morning this week for running and yoga and you haven't."

I hung my head. He wasn't wrong. I'd stopped. After Dad

had revealed that I apparently had the hots for my roommate, it seemed extremely dangerous to go off into the woods with him. The threat of fisher cats was nothing compared to the potential emotional upheaval. Then there was the danger of yoga, alone, dripping with sweat. Or me taking his hand into mine for therapy. Those were the kinds of moments where I got confused and my heart and my stomach swirled, when electricity sparked between us and I thought about how good it would feel to have him kiss me again.

"I'm sorry," I told him. "I've been off my game since I saw my dad. We can start the therapy again tomorrow."

Jonas looked at me. "You don't have to do anything you don't want to."

"I want to help you," I said. "I just don't want to get confused."

His brow furrowed. "Confused? Sorry, I don't understand what you mean."

"Like I don't want to spend all this time together, just us, and to start thinking that it's more than just therapy."

His eyebrows lifted for an instant. He lowered his voice to a deep whisper that somehow reverberated in my bones. "That does sound confusing. Just so I'm clear . . . confusing is bad?"

I nodded. The energy radiating off of him was like a magnet pulling me in. I grabbed on to the dresser to ground myself.

"I have a quandary," he said. "What about when you kissed me in the bar? Does that fall into this bad, confusing category?"

I cleared my throat. I could barely breathe. "It wasn't bad."

He stepped toward me. "But it left you . . . flummoxed?"

I nodded again, pressing my teeth into the soft flesh of my bottom lip.

"See, Doyle, I'm of the opinion that when I kiss someone, she shouldn't be left perplexed."

He was killing me. The tenor of his voice. The heat in his deep hazel eyes. Avoiding him had been torment, I realized. Every moment spent *not* kissing Jonas Voss felt wrong. He tucked a finger beneath my chin, and I raised my gaze to meet his.

"I have a proposal I'd like to submit," he said.

And my whole body, each cell, every nerve fiber, seemed to shout, *Yes*. The question didn't matter. "Uh-huh . . ."

"I think we should just clear up the confusion."

I sucked in a shallow breath. "How do you propose we do that?"

"Simple," he said. He slid a hand around my waist to the small of my back and pulled me tight to him. A breath escaped my lips. I was entranced, supple and practically scintillating against his touch. He used his thumb to angle my face the slightest bit more until we were perfectly aligned. And then he dipped his head and I watched as his eyes fluttered closed and his mouth drew near to me. My lips parted in anticipation and I let my eyelids drift shut. This wasn't an accidental face-smashing kiss in a bar to avoid a brawl-induced broken hand. This was one of those epic kisses, the kind that deserved a soundtrack and a wind machine. And I was going to let it happen. Because I wasn't confused. Not even a little. Astrid and my dad were right. I *was* finding it hard to breathe around him. I *did* like him. And right now, I needed him. I needed him close, his hands in my hair, on the small of my back. His lips on mine.

"Hey, guys," Andy shouted. "We got chicken finger grinders! Get 'em while they're hot!"

Jonas froze and straightened up. His hand fell away from my face.

I jumped back. Over Jonas's shoulder, Revi's eyes were wide. *Oh my god*, he mouthed. My skin was on fire.

"I . . . should probably change before I eat," I said.

Jonas ran a hand over his hair, as if pondering the whereabouts of something he'd lost, then turned and walked over to the table where the grinders were waiting. "Fantastic," he said, picking one up. He turned to look straight at me. "I'm absolutely ravenous." He took a bite. I widened my eyes at him, in complete disbelief of his brazen disregard for our nosy roommates, but I had never wanted to be a sandwich so bad in my entire life.

"I need to talk to you!" Revi shouted and chased me into my room.

Door closed, he spun around on me. "Holy shit, Sophie! What did Andy and I just barge in on? Were you guys making out?!" he whisper-shouted.

I pulled a clean sweatshirt out of my dresser. "Don't be ridiculous."

"You are such a bad liar!"

"I'm not lying." I pulled off my fleece, which carried the faint aroma of boys' hockey equipment, thanks to the long bus ride from Phillips Exeter, and put on the clean one. "We hadn't started yet."

"I knew it." He pointed at me. "I knew there was something brewing between you two. All those morning jogs. Is 'therapy' your code word for"—he lowered his voice—"*sex*?"

"No," I said, too loudly. "We're not sleeping together. We kissed once, accidentally. Therapy is therapy. Jonas has a problem with his hand. That's why he quit the piano. I'm trying to help him."

"Oh, this is so cute."

"It's not cute. It's a bad idea."

"Why?"

"Um, we're coworkers, we live together—it's bound to blow up in our faces."

"Andy and I are coworkers who live together, and it works for us. It's perfect practice for after we're married."

I stopped brushing my ponytail and eyed Revi in the mirror. "Wait, you and Andy are engaged? How did I not know this?"

"Looks like you're as oblivious to other people's relationship status as you are to your own, girl. It was an impromptu proposal though. We had the perfect last day in Disney and were riding the Barnstormer during the fireworks and we just looked at each other and were like, 'Let's get married.' We'd both been thinking the same thing. We spent the rest of our trip planning our wedding for next year."

I dropped the brush and threw my arms around him. "That's amazing! I am so happy for you both. Honestly, I'm so glad you have each other. I know I haven't known you for long, but I make a kick-ass bridesmaid."

"Maybe we can have a double wedding." He waggled his eyebrows.

"You're out of control," I said, shaking my head. "Not that I would be opposed to being princess for a day, but I'm pretty sure I have a better chance of marrying Keanu Reeves than our roommate."

"Maybe this apartment is magic. Andy and I fell in love here—why not you and Jonas?"

I might have been confused about whether or not I had a bit of a crush, but I was sure that I didn't love him. I was more interested in lapping him up like a bowl of melted ice cream. Very different beasts. "You guys are different from me and Jonas," I said. "You're such a great match . . . you both are the most caring, warm people I've ever met. You love teaching and wearing mouse ears. You finish each other's sentences. Jonas and I can't even get along."

He waved a hand. "That's just the sexual tension."

I shook my head. "I wish. No. We're just total opposites. Anyway, he's probably messing with me. He told me that night in the library before Thanksgiving that he doesn't like me."

"You say that, but it didn't seem that way at Stowe. When you got that call about your dad, he was wrecked. He was all over the place trying to figure out how to get you to Boston. That is not the MO of a man who doesn't care. In fact, it was quite curious that he came to Stowe at all. Jonas hates the cold. He even insisted on borrowing the hat that you made Andy and then didn't give it back to him."

What? No. Revi was exaggerating.

"I'm sure those events all seem like they mean something, but in reality? I highly doubt it. I think Jonas was mad that I didn't make him a hat. That's all. And he did hit it off with my dad. It's only normal that he'd be concerned. But me and him? That's never going to work."

"Okay. I'll stop pestering you. But if I catch you in one of those movie moments again, I'm warning you that I'm one hundred percent revisiting this topic."

"Well, that's not going to happen, so it's a deal. I'm so glad you guys came in when you did. Crisis averted. I'll keep helping Jonas with his hand, but otherwise, I'll keep it strictly professional, which means no double nuptials at Cinderella Castle."

"You're no fun."

"I'm loads of fun. Let's go eat. You and Andy can tell me all about your matrimonial plans, and then we can prank the seniors."

Chapter 23

On my morning run with Jonas the next day, I ran top speed the entire time to make sure that he and I didn't have enough air to actually discuss the almost kiss. It took every ounce of energy I had, since I'd barely slept the night before. When we finished, I started back toward the dorm.

"Wait? We're not going to the training room? No more dry needling?" he asked.

"You say it like you enjoyed that part. I know you aren't fond of needles."

"I don't enjoy it, but *you* seem to. You know, I think you fancy poking me with sharp objects."

I furrowed my brow at him. "Give me a break. I think I've released the triggers in your hand and arm, so we don't need to keep doing that. This phase is going to be about retraining your technique."

"Is this because—"

"No. You're ready. The contraction in your fourth finger is nowhere near as bad as it was. You're so much stronger."

"You think I'm strong?" He raised an eyebrow.

"I was talking about your hand."

He eyed his hand for a moment, opening and closing it, testing it. "So, what then?"

"I had a specialist who helps retrain pianists make videos for you. I'll record you practicing, and we'll send her the video for feedback."

I opened the apartment door.

"I'm not following," Jonas said.

We removed our shoes and headed inside. "Come on," I told him, "you'll see." I led him to my room, where I closed the door behind us. There was barely enough space to squeeze by him; when I tried, he caught my arm gently in his hand.

"Doyle," he said, voice strained, face close to mine. "What are we doing here?"

If he wanted to kiss me again, to finish what we'd started the night before, he could—he was just a fraction of an instant away from me. I rested my hand on his chest. I'd meant the gesture to calm him, but maybe I was maintaining a safe distance. Still, I couldn't help but wonder if his heart was pounding too. "You're going to play the piano."

He closed his eyes, shook his head. "I'm not ready."

"You are."

He swallowed. "What if I can't?"

"I think you can. Besides, we never use the word 'can't' in training. We use 'can't yet.' If you can't do it yet, then we try again tomorrow. And the day after that. Until you can. We keep it simple."

Jonas took a step toward the piano. Then another. He lowered himself to the bench and positioned his hands over the keys. He turned to me.

"I don't think—"

"You remember when we started this, I told you that you needed to trust me? Well, now you need to trust yourself."

I put the iPad with the video in front of him and hit play. "These are the exercises you can try. She said it's not about speed. It's about flow and relaxation."

"Full disclosure? I don't feel very relaxed."

Instinctively, I reached out and brushed my fingertips over his hand in what I hoped was a reassuring touch. His skin was cool beneath my fingertips; his hand flexed, and then the tension seemed to melt away.

"Better?" I asked.

He blinked slowly as if coming out of a daze. He nodded, bemused. "Suprisingly."

He watched the video twice and then he re-created the activity. Perched on the edge of my bed, I watched, transfixed, as his hands moved over the keys, tentatively at first.

"How did that feel?" I asked.

"Terrifying."

"Well, you know what they say about things that matter."

He shook his head.

"If you aren't afraid, you're doing it wrong."

Jonas worked for an hour, repeating the exercises. With each iteration, his body relaxed further, and a light seemed to come back in his expression. His technique became more confident, more fluid. I watched him, mesmerized, while I recorded the videos.

At the end of the hour, we left my room. "You did really well," I told him.

"Thank you." He leaned a little toward me but seemed to think better of it. Then he shoved his hands into his pockets.

"You're welcome." There was so much more I wanted to

say. I was desperate to ask him if he'd meant what he'd said the other night or if that had been a moment of madness that we were both relieved had been interrupted. I needed to know if he still didn't like me or if he also hadn't been able to sleep last night because he'd been thinking of all of our almosts—the moment in the stacks, the kiss in the bar, the night at the hotel, the near miss in the living room. Mostly I wondered if I was the only one feeling the overwhelming pull toward him. But I couldn't bring myself to ask any of those things. Sure, I was a positive person. I was generally confident that if there were an injury, I could help. I believed that if I tried hard enough, pushed hard enough, I could get back to major-league baseball and my former career. But I was also the woman who found her luggage in the hallway and lost a whole team of people she cared about in one day, and I wondered a little if I was broken when it came to relationships.

"Sophie, darling, can you come into the living room?" Andy called.

Jonas stepped aside so I could walk past him.

"Hi, guys, what's going on?" I asked.

"So, we talked to Astrid last night," Revi said.

"You called Astrid?"

"Unimportant. We're friends now. Anyway, she informed us that not only did you not go to your prom, but you never went to a single high school dance," said Andy.

"So tragic," Revi said.

"I don't know if I'd call it tragic," I said—only it was. In the months leading up to prom, my mom had been in and out of the hospital. A boy named Carlos who was the starting catcher for our varsity baseball team had asked me, but I'd been too afraid to leave my mom for the night. I shook off the memory. "Is there a point here, other than making me feel a bit pathetic about my high school experience?"

"Of course," Revi said.

"Here's the deal," Andy began, "Revi and I know that you've been going through it . . . with your job and your dad and your heartless ex." I tensed. Had they been reading my mind? "We were thinking that since you never got to experience prom, we could make the winter formal into your dance. What do you think?"

"It's really sweet, guys," I said, "but it's not for me, it's for the kids. And how would you even go about doing that?"

"Um, we chair the winter formal planning committee. And these kids will be just fine. Whatever we come up with will be fabulous. So, what do you want—under the sea, medieval masquerade?"

I'd never thought that much about it, but it came to me instantly. The year before, Marciano Velasquez had gotten married and the entire team had been invited to his wedding. They had this winter magic forest theme—I'd been sick with a horrible case of the flu, but Patrick had showed me his pictures when he got home. It was the most beautiful thing I'd ever seen.

"Could you do an enchanted forest?" I asked. "The more twinkle lights the better."

"Can we do twinkle lights and some trees? What are we, amateurs?" Andy said. "We have to adjust your expectations out of the basement, Sophie. Clearly you haven't seen pictures of last year's production of *Charlie and the Chocolate Factory*."

"No Oompa Loompas. They freak me out."

"We need to talk about more important things, guys," Revi interjected. "We've got two weeks to find you the most beautiful dress of all time. I'm thinking this calls for a road trip."

I considered this plan. It was slightly ridiculous, the idea of giving me a prom, but the notion of Andy and Revi taking me shopping for a beautiful dress sounded fun.

"All right," I said. "I'm in."

I sent Astrid a text message that read, What are you up to? Call me.

Chapter 24

The mall trip culminated in finding a dress that made me feel like a Hollywood starlet and eating two slices of Sbarro pizza the size of my head that tasted awesome and gave me a stomachache. Afterward Andy and Revi dropped me off at the field house, where I was meeting up with Tyson and a few other kids from the orchestra. Riley, the girl who played viola, had invited some other musicians who were struggling with a litany of issues ranging from blisters to what sounded like tendinitis. I was calling it "musical fitness," and my goal was to treat and prevent injuries and improve their physical resilience. We were going to meet once a week, and afterward Tyson and I would work on his pitching.

The kids worked hard, but it was obvious that they'd been using their bodies in only one way. Basic calisthenics were a struggle for several of them, but by the end of it, I noticed improvement in every student—even if the progress was marginal, it was something—and no one hated it so much that they didn't want to return.

"Thanks, Coach!" Riley said, waving from the doorway.

"See you next week," I told her. I turned to Tyson. "Do you have time to throw, or do you need to get over to the music hall for Mr. Voss?"

"I can play," Tyson said. "Mr. Voss said he had something he needed to do out of town and changed our practice session to after dinner."

I wondered what or who Jonas needed to take care of out of town. My concern about the "who" bothered me.

I got out my glove and threw Tyson the ball. "Just today?" I asked.

"Nah. He went last Sunday, and he said it's going to be an ongoing thing."

"Huh."

Tyson wound up and threw me an easy pitch. "Maybe he's in a band," he said.

"A band?" I laughed. "I have a hard time picturing that."

"He was kind of a rock star, you know. I mean, not like the tattoos and piercings kind of rock star. But in the classical world, he was awesome, revered. I saw one of his concerts once—that's why I wanted to work with him. Then he just showed up here to teach and I couldn't believe my luck."

"I didn't know."

"It was so weird when he just stopped playing. No one knew why—there were rumors that something happened during a concert, but that's it. All I know is that I'd never stop playing the violin."

I thought about Jonas's confession. He'd given the impression that he was telling me everything, but I couldn't shake the feeling that the story had only skated the surface. I didn't think Jonas was that different from Tyson. Before the incident, he probably would've said the same thing. I knew this because I'd seen the way he lit up when he was playing; even something as simple as the exercises the retraining teacher had given him brought out a lightness in him. He must've felt so awful to give that up. Thinking about it made my joints ache. I didn't share this with Tyson. Jonas had been vulnerable with me, and I would never divulge his story, especially not to his students.

"So what's in the bag?" Tyson filled in the space left by my silence.

"A dress. I'm chaperoning winter formal in a few weeks, and Mr. Chen and Mr. Malek decided I needed a glow-up."

"Cool. Winter formal's a big thing around here."

"Really? I was never much into dances when I was in high school, so I don't know much about it."

"It's intense now. We have to come up with these super creative ideas to ask people."

"Are you going to ask someone?" I threw the ball back. "Try a three-quarter-speed one," I said.

He shook his head, wound up, and hurled a perfect fastball. "Probably not. It's too much pressure."

"I get it. It sounds like a lot. Was there someone you wanted to ask?"

He squinted at me. "Riley. But it's not for me. Everyone watching, feeling all on display. That's not my thing."

"When you play the violin, aren't all eyes on you then? And if you decide you want to be a pitcher or a solo violinist on tour, thousands of people will be watching your every move. How does asking a question scare you?"

"Are you training my brain right now, Coach Doyle?"

I shrugged. "I'm going to get my catching gear on. Let's do a few full speed."

"Are you going to ask someone, Coach?"

"Ha! Yeah right."

"If you're not brave enough, why should I be?"

"Touché," I said, lowering my face mask. I squatted down and flapped my mitt at him. "I'll just go on my own. I'm really just there to supervise."

"But why the fancy dress then?"

"A fancy dress can just be for me. I don't need to wear it for someone else."

"Okay. Still. You could ask Mr. Chen. You guys do all the sports stuff together."

"He's taken."

"Okay, Mr. Voss, then. I bet he's single, unless his out-of-town commitment is a secret girlfriend."

I blanched. "Why are we talking about this still? Is it because you don't want to talk about your crush on Riley?" I teased.

"How about this—if you ask Mr. Voss, I'll ask Riley. Unless you're too chicken."

He launched a perfect pitch. It practically exploded in the palm of my hand. "Your form's getting better," I said.

"Bock bock," he said.

"Throw the ball, child!"

It wasn't the fact that a seventeen-year-old had called me poultry and proceeded to do a full rendition of the chicken dance that made me ask Jonas to the winter formal. In fact, I did not ask him. Not exactly.

"We're short a chaperone," Andy told me after dinner. "Cynthia is going to be at New England Broadway Revolution, and Rebecca and Juan are leading the sophomore wilderness expedition."

"What about Wilson?" I asked.

"Freshman class trip to New York City."

"That doesn't leave a lot of choices. Mr. Obuwe has his wife's surgery that week, so he's out too."

The apartment door opened and Jonas walked in. Andy and I both turned to look at him. He dropped his car keys in the bowl beside the door, removed his shoes, and hung up his jacket on the coat tree.

"What are you two staring at? Have I got Cinnabon on my face or something?"

"Ask him," Andy whispered. "He's not on the list."

I shook my head. Tyson danced across my brain, opening and closing his hands and flapping his arms. Bock bock, bock bock.

"Sophie. We need eight; we have seven. Ask him."

"Seriously, you guys are acting bizarre."

"Where were you today?" I asked, avoiding the question that Andy was currently glaring at me about.

Jonas shrugged. "Had to run an errand."

"Where? California? You've been gone for hours."

He leaned over the table, heat in his eyes. "Did you miss me, Doyle? You seem to be keeping very close watch on my whereabouts."

Andy pressed his lips together. "Your energy is making me uncomfortable, so I'm going to play some video games in my room."

"Cheers, mate," Jonas said, and dropped into Andy's vacant seat across from me. He glanced down at the dance planning list on the table. "What's all this? Twenty boxes of twinkly lights?"

"It's for winter formal, which might not even happen, because we don't have enough chaperones."

"Are you going?" he asked.

I nodded. "I bought a dress."

"What color is it?"

The seriousness of his tone threw me. "Okay, like you're interested in that. *Sure.*"

Jonas's eyes locked on mine. His voice was low. "I'm interested."

A shiver coursed its way down my spine and I looked away. He was messing with me again, and my body was betraying me.

"Is it green, like the one you wore to the first formal dinner?"

He remembered that? He hadn't even registered a response when the guys asked him what he thought. I'd been mortified by his silence and then I was stuck sitting with him all evening, knowing that he didn't care enough to even say, *You look nice.* The worst part, I realized now, was how badly I craved those words.

"I'm not going to tell you what color it is," I said, making eye contact this time. "If you want to know, you can sign up to chaperone with me."

Jonas eyed me. "Are you asking me to go to the dance with you, Doyle?"

I tipped my head to the side. Daring him.

He picked up the clipboard and signed his name on the chaperone list. "I'm knackered. I'm going to turn in."

I glanced down at the list, looking for the spot where he'd signed his name. But he hadn't written *Voss* or *Jonas.* Next to my name, he'd written, *Doyle's date.*

I bit my lip.

"So do I get a dress preview now or do I have to wait?" Jonas asked.

"Spoken like someone who isn't very good at waiting."

"You'd be amazed by my patience."

Chapter 25

The day of the winter formal coincided with both boys' and girls' varsity hockey home games. The girls crushed it, beating Brewster Academy 2–1, which made the day practically historic, since in the entire history of the school they'd never beaten Brewster. The guys' team was in a battle with New Hampton, and for a few moments there, I actually thought we might end the day with two hockey wins and no injuries. We'd go to the dance that night and celebrate an epic day for Monadnock sports. That's always the way it goes, isn't it? When everything is going great and you have that perfect thing in your grasp, it slips through your fingers.

Jamie Graham was flying down the ice with the puck when a massive defenseman from the opposing team blindsided him. It was a bad hit, but what made it devastating was that their center struck him at the exact same time. He was caught between the opposing impacts, helpless to escape. His leg took the brunt of the trauma. The unnatural angle, the expression on his face through the clear mask were unmistakable. I was over the boards and on the ice in an instant, my feet touching down the moment the whistle blared. I hit my knees and slid toward him, and a hush fell over the crowd until the only sound was his anguished groans as he writhed on the ice.

"We're so sorry, man," the center said. His cheeks were blotched red. "We never meant for that to happen."

Jamie covered his face with his arms to hide his tears.

By the time I'd finished splinting his leg, the ambulance arrived. I rode with him to the hospital, holding his trembling hand while the paramedics administered fluids and pushed pain medication.

"You're doing great, Jamie. We'll be there soon and get you all fixed up."

"He's a little shocky," the EMT said.

"They're doing *Singin' in the Rain* in the spring," Jamie said, swiping tears from his cheeks with the back of his free hand.

"Are you going to be in it?" I asked.

"Not anymore," he said. His entire jaw was trembling, and I was overwhelmed with the urge to smooth his sweat-soaked hair away from his face like my mother used to when I was a kid and had been hurt. He cast a glance down to his leg, and I understood. Like all of the athletes at Monadnock, he had another passion, one that was likely more important to him than hockey.

"You dance?" I asked.

"Will I? I don't know."

"You will. You're going to need some time to heal, but you're young and strong, and you *will* heal. This is scary, I know. But I promise you, Jamie. I'm going to be there every single step of the way, okay? You are not on your own here."

He nodded and tipped his face away from me. "Can you do me a favor?" he asked.

"Of course." I'd already asked the coach to reach out to Jamie's parents, who lived in Concord. They were on their way.

"Can you call Vanessa? I was supposed to take her to winter formal, and I guess that's not happening either."

"Sure. Once I get you settled, she'll be my first call."

The ambulance pulled up in front of the emergency entrance. The paramedics wheeled Jamie in through the automatic doors to the emergency department. I stood for a moment, outside looking in. There's nothing like the sense of dread going to a hospital produces when you've lost someone there. That dread had been building in the pit of my stomach while we drove. It'd been half my lifetime, but I could still remember the smell of the industrial cleaning products; one whiff and I was instantly transported to the days and nights in that chair at my mom's bedside, holding on to her hands, trying to be careful not to disturb the tangles of tubes and wires, willing her to open her eyes and come back to me. The nurses had finally turned the alarms on the monitors off, but I still heard them.

I tried to focus on the present instead of the hard memories that were pulling me below the surface. I blew out a long breath. There was a teenager in there who was scared and on his own, and he needed me. I headed inside.

It was a clean break, which was great news because it meant that Jamie wouldn't need surgery. He'd be in a cast for a while, but the doctor felt that with physical therapy, Jamie would have no problem returning to dance or hockey. He wouldn't be ready for *Singin' in the Rain*, but a fall production was definitely realistic. I watched Jamie's hospital gown–clad shoulders settle with relief when he heard that. His mom and dad arrived after they'd stopped by the school to get Vanessa, who already had her hair done, but was still wearing warm-up pants and a varsity hockey sweatshirt with Jamie's name and number on it.

"I was so scared," she said, and flung herself at him. "Sorry I was at the stupid salon and wasn't there when it happened."

He wrapped a dark ringlet around his finger. "You look really pretty," he said.

The Grahams agreed that they'd bring Vanessa back to school later that evening, and Jamie too, if the doctor thought it was okay. Otherwise, they'd bring him back to Concord to recover for a bit.

I left the hospital, trying to figure out how exactly I was going to get back to the school. A quick glance at the clock in the waiting room told me I was already late for the dance, and everyone who was not out of town was chaperoning. I was wearing sneakers, so I could run, but it was starting to flurry outside and was very dark—not an ideal road running combination. And it'd taken us a solid ten minutes to get to the hospital, so I figured I was in for at least forty minutes of running in the snow without sidewalks. I stuck my tongue out and caught a large flake. I'd sent a message to Jonas earlier after I'd called Vanessa, letting him know that I was at the hospital with Jamie and probably wouldn't make the dance. He'd asked about Jamie, but he didn't seem too sad about missing our plans. *It's probably for the best*, I told myself. Another bullet dodged.

I sat down on one of the benches to think. The dance ended at eleven—Andy and Revi would be able to come pick me up afterward. Maybe I could go inside and read a magazine until then. There was a vending machine for sustenance. I would just need to manage my emotions for a couple of hours. Not

ideal, but totally doable. Except it wasn't. I felt awful for Jamie. I was sadder than I expected to miss the dance that Revi
and Andy had worked on so hard for me. Seeing Jamie with
his mom had made me acutely aware of how much I missed
mine. I was worried for Dad. All the emotions I'd been holding
in—fear, sadness, guilt—rushed out. My face crumpled and
tears flooded my eyes.

I wiped my face with my sweater sleeve.

"Bad news, Doyle?"

I swiveled around to find Jonas sitting on the bench next
to me. He was clad in the nicest suit I'd ever seen, looking like
a blond James Bond. His forearms rested on his thighs, his
fingers pressed against each other. He was looking straight
ahead.

"I thought you were at the dance?"

"I don't actually care for dances," he said. I laughed at
that one.

"Why am I not surprised?"

"Especially if my date's stranded at the ER." He turned
and looked at me. Then, without a word, he reached over and
swept the back of his index finger gently over my damp cheek.
"How was it, then?"

I lifted my shoulders a fraction and let them fall. "Jamie's
going to be fine. I just really don't like hospitals."

"What do you say I take you home?"

"If you say you left your car running with the seat heaters
on, I might fall in love with you."

"Dear god, yes. It's bloody freezing out here."

We drove back to the dorm, climbed the stairs, and entered
the apartment in silence. "You look nice, by the way," I said.

"Thanks. I wish I could say the same, but honestly, it's
almost as if you didn't even try."

I gave his arm a gentle whack. "I had an amazing dress, I'll have you know."

He raised an eyebrow. "Had? Did you sell it or something?"

"No, it's hanging in my closet."

Jonas took a step toward me, surprising me with the intensity of his expression and the gentle, deep tone of his voice when he spoke. "Why don't you go put it on? I'd hate to have your shopping trip go to waste. And I know you won't want to miss seeing what Andy and Revi made you. It'll help distract you from the other things that are bothering you."

I smiled and made a beeline for my room. I flung the door shut, yanked my dirty training clothes off, and pulled the dress from the hanger and over my head. I'd planned on doing my hair and makeup, but there wasn't time for that. My hair had started to dry from the snow and fell in slightly damp, gentle waves over my shoulders. I put on some lip gloss and a coat of mascara. It wasn't exactly what I'd envisioned, but it would work. The dress was off the shoulder with a fitted bodice and an A-line skirt that skimmed over my hips and moved when I walked. The silver contrasted nicely with my red hair, and I felt . . . lovely, which was new to me. I wondered what Jonas would think. I wondered why I cared so much about his reaction.

After a quick final glance at myself in the mirror, I stepped out into the living room. Jonas was looking at his composition book, but after a moment of me standing awkwardly in front of him, shifting my weight from foot to foot with nervous energy, he looked up. I watched his Adam's apple slide down his throat and up, and a strange surge of anticipation coursed through me.

He cleared his throat. "Wow," he said, his voice raspy. "You were spot-on when you said you had an amazing dress."

I beamed. I reached down and grabbed the skirt, stretching it out to the sides. "You think so?"

"You're stunning."

I stood still for a moment, replaying the phrase. "What?" Jonas asked.

"Jonas Voss, did you just pay me a compliment?"

"Try not to faint from shock, Doyle. I've been told I'm actually quite debonair."

I resisted the urge to snap something back about us having very different definitions of "debonair." He smiled at me again, a lopsided, intimate grin, and the last lingering cold from the snowy night dissipated; my entire body radiated with warmth. "Should we go?" I asked.

Jonas looked around. "Hang on," he said, and disappeared into his bedroom. For a moment, I got worried that maybe he'd changed his mind or all of this had been some sort of roommate-hazing ritual. But then he reappeared holding a plastic box with a flower inside. "It's ridiculous," he said. "It's a wrist corsage. A gardenia. The guys said you'd missed dances in high school, so I thought I could give you the full experience."

I stood as still as possible, a challenge because my entire body was trembling, as he slid the band over my hand and around my wrist. The white flower smelled heavenly. "It's not ridiculous," I said, pulling in the sweet scent in a deep breath and marveling at his thoughtfulness. "It's perfect."

Chapter 26

We crossed the quad in the darkness. I walked close to Jonas, acutely aware of his proximity. Occasionally, we'd drift toward each other and his knuckles would brush against mine. Each instance of contact sent a thrill shivering its way up my spine. Finally, we reached the music building, where the dance was being held in the ballroom. Jonas pulled the door open for me. He was grinning. I'd never seen him smile like that. The happiness carved a deep crease in his cheek and etched fine lines at the corner of his eyes. My heart squeezed.

And then I saw the room.

Calling it the most beautiful thing I'd ever seen would be an understatement. My hand went to my mouth as I took it all in. There were clouds, lit from within. Twinkling stars on the ceiling. Northern lights projected in the distance. And everywhere I looked, there were birch trees, twinkling in the darkness. A slow song came on and Jonas reached down and laced his fingers through mine.

"What do you say, Doyle? Do you want to dance with me?"

I nodded, blinking slowly at him. It was almost too wonderful to believe, but I trusted Jonas's hand around mine. I'd held that hand so many times in the last few weeks. I knew its secrets and its strengths. I knew the history it held. Maybe this had been a dare, and we fought more than we got along, but right now, he was leading me to the dance floor, and I would've followed him anywhere.

We passed by Tyson, who was dancing with Riley. He grinned at me. "Looking good, Coach," he said.

The music played and students swayed, rested heads on shoulders, wrapped hands around necks and waists. Moved dangerously close. I probably should've said something. I didn't. I was too busy anticipating the moment when Jonas and I reached the center of the dance floor and he swept those hands around the sides of my waist and settled them into the space on the small of my back.

"So, what do you think?" he asked, letting me turn slowly and then reeling me back to him. "Was it what you expected?"

I shook my head. "It's so much better." I rested my cheek against his chest and we moved in unison.

"Even I have to confess, they did an amazing job."

"I didn't just mean the design," I admitted.

"So you're not disappointed by your date?"

"Is this a date?"

"It's not?"

"I'm not disappointed. I sometimes don't know what to make of you. That night in the stacks you said you didn't like me."

"I always say what I mean. I meant that."

I was grateful for the low light in the room, because I was sure that my blazing cheeks were bright red. I started to pull away, but Jonas trapped my hand against his chest, gently. He leaned close to me. I held my breath. "'Like' doesn't accurately describe my feelings, not when it comes to you . . ." he said.

I wanted to ask him how I should interpret that. My heart was soaring with the implications, but the rest of me worried. What if I was misinterpreting this moment and setting myself up for disappointment?

Andy and Revi stopped by. Andy was dressed in a charcoal gray suit and Revi in plaid, and they were both glowing. Jonas's hand fell away from my back and I flung my arms around the guys. "This is the most amazing thing I've ever seen."

"We can't take all of the credit," Andy said. "Astrid had the set designer of *Moon Gazers* draw some plans for us. We just executed."

"I don't deserve you," I said.

"Yes, you do," Revi said, giving me a squeeze. "You deserve all of this." He tilted his head in Jonas's direction, and I bit my lip. "Do everything I wouldn't do," he added. Andy gave me a wink and then they waltzed away.

"I love them," I said. "They're like the brothers I never had."

"Annoying brothers," Jonas said. "But I get what you mean. From one only child to another. It's a lot of pressure, isn't it?"

I'd never thought of it that way, but it made sense to me now as I reflected. Jonas had all of his parents' hopes on his shoulders. No wonder he'd retreated from them when he couldn't play his best anymore. And then there was me. I'd wanted to tell Dad the whole truth so many times. But I couldn't bear to let him down. "It is," I said.

"Do you think that's why we push so hard?"

"Speak for yourself. I don't push; I'm a human sunbeam."

"With a serious competitive streak and a repressed rage issue. Imagine what life would be like if you didn't think you were responsible for everyone's happiness all the time."

"I never tried to make you happy," I said.

"And yet . . ." His voice trailed off.

The slow-song set ended and the DJ announced he was going to take it to the next level before the night was over. A high-energy banger with a deep bass beat came on and Jonas frowned. This was not his kind of music. "Come with me," he said over the music. "I want to show you something."

I followed Jonas through the crowd of teenagers dancing to the beat, bounding up and down to the music, out the way we'd come. Jonas led me down the corridor, past the orchestra practice room. Finally, at the end of the hall, Jonas guided me into the auditorium. He settled me in a chair in the center of the room.

"Wait here," he said cryptically before he walked away.

I sat in the dim space, waiting, curious. A single stage light came on, illuminating a shining black grand piano in the center of the stage. Then Jonas walked out and sat down at the piano. My heart thundered in my chest. He lifted his hands above the keys and I pulled in a breath. He began to play. It wasn't something by Mozart or Gershwin. It was "Tessie" by the Dropkick Murphys, but it was different. Gentler, happier. He'd arranged it. Kept the soul of it, but made it into something novel, something beautiful that I felt in my bones and the tips of my fingers. It was like every wonderful moment, every home run, every Cracker Jack, every time Dad and I leapt to our feet to cheer. My childhood and my future wrapped into one melody. He'd taken something I knew and transformed it into the song of my heart. I watched his hands move masterfully over the keys, his shoulders dip and rise, the concentration on his face. It ended too soon. I could've listened to it forever.

When he finished, he sat still in the light for a long moment.

Then he turned and faced me. We rose at the same time. I rushed between the seats to the aisle, and he strode to the edge of the stage and hopped down. We met in the middle of the theater, our chests heaving.

"You wrote that?"

"It's something I've been working on"—he looked down for a moment, and then raised his gaze to meet mine again—"for you."

I thought of him, all these days, with his earbuds in, his head down, scribbling away in that notebook. This whole time, I had thought he was avoiding me. But he had been writing the perfect song . . . for me.

"You played. You played so well," I said. Tears blurred my vision, splintering the stage lights into a starburst, but I didn't care. "You said you wouldn't again."

"You made me feel brave."

I was quiet for several seconds, trying to work up the courage to speak. "So when you said 'like' didn't accurately reflect your feelings . . ."

He took my face gently between his hands, those talented hands that had played a song that made me feel like I was flying, and looked into my eyes. I didn't know what he was going to say, but I knew what I wanted to hear. When he said it, I thought it was a wish I'd whispered to myself.

"It wasn't enough." He ran his thumb over my bottom lip, and I thought I might perish there in that theater. "For weeks I've been trying to find the right way to tell you that I've fallen for you. Even before you taught me how to throw a snowball. Before that kiss in Boston, before I knew what it was like to hold your hand and have you hold mine and make you laugh and keep you safe. I've never been that good at saying the right things. I say a lot of the wrong things. You probably know that better than anyone at this point. I hope . . . I wanted to express how much I care about you. The best way I know how to do this is through music. Thanks to you, I was able to play the right notes . . ."

I nodded. "They were really good notes," I said. My whole body buzzed with a mix of emotion and anticipation.

I took one shallow breath, and then Jonas leaned down and pressed his lips to mine. Since the night in the stacks, the near miss bar fight, the close call in the living room, I'd been anticipating this kiss. But nothing my imagination could've created came close to it. If the song he'd played had made my heart soar, his kiss rocketed me through the galaxy. Around us, stars spun, planets sped by. Jonas curled his arms around me; I felt the heat of his body through our clothes. My fingers traced along his jaw down to his throat, where his pulse raced beneath my fingertips. His mouth was made for mine, firm, tender. Soft and languid, then hungry. When my legs went weak, he held me in place. After a time, we separated, breathless.

Jonas grasped my hand and led me toward the stage.

"Sophie," he whispered against my skin.

He never called me by my first name. What did it mean that he'd used it now? And why did it sound so perfect on his lips, in my ears, deep in my chest? My heart beat like hummingbird's wings, light and rapid.

"Sophie." He'd only said it twice, but already I was addicted. My name would never sound as good as this if spoken by someone else. Jonas walked backward as I followed him.

When we reached the edge of the stage, Jonas spun me in one quick movement and lifted me onto it. His muscles flexed and stretched beneath his skin, evidence of our hours of training. In one fluid motion, he bounded up beside me and pulled me to my feet. It was so powerful and sexy that I forgot to breathe for a moment.

I knew where we were headed.

I bit my lip as he swept me up and settled me gently on the lid of the grand piano. We were still for a moment, reveling in each other. I wanted to learn the rhythm of his breathing, the feel of every line of his body. I'd never been looked at like that before, like he was coming home to a place he knew in some dream, something new and something ancient, someone he could lose himself in. I took his hands, his left, and then his right, and kissed each fingerprint, until I got to his fourth finger. The one that had caused him so much heartache and shame. He'd hated that finger, thought it was his fatal flaw. But I loved it. I took my time, dusting that finger with soft kisses. Because the thing he saw as his downfall had brought him here, to Monadnock, to this moment, to me.

We wove our fingers together and he brushed his lips over each connection point between us.

"Sophie," he said, one last time, raising his eyes to meet mine. I'd never felt so entirely seen.

And I knew in that moment, with my name on Jonas's lips and the stage lights twinkling in his eyes, things between me and him would never be the same.

Chapter 27

Jonas pressed his forehead to mine. "I didn't expect this," he said.

"Me neither." I waited for him to respond, but he didn't. "Do you want to stop?" I said finally, concern creeping into my voice.

He shook his head slowly. "That's the last thing that I want, but we probably should. It's not very private here, and to be honest, I'm not exactly prepared."

Prepared? Every inch of me was ready. Every inch of him . . .

He lifted his eyebrows. *Oh.*

"It's fine," I said. "After all, we are molding young minds here . . . we should be responsible." Heat was creeping its way up the back of my neck. I suddenly felt incredibly exposed, my pale skin splotchy with desire. "I mean, how would it look if we—"

Jonas cut me off with a searing kiss on my lips. When it ended, he gently helped me down. Every nerve ending crackled with electricity as he skimmed the fabric of my dress with a torturously slow caress. "You're so beautiful," he rasped.

I felt the truth in his words.

We headed toward the exit. My head spun with a million thoughts and questions, but I couldn't say them.

We both reached for the door handle at the same time, and our hands met.

Jonas cleared his throat. "We should get back."

I meant to say, *Yes, we should.* But instead, I threw my arms around his neck and kissed him again. I couldn't help myself. There was a strange longing within me now that seemed like it could only be relieved by the touch of Jonas Voss, and I was powerless to resist it.

Finally, when I knew I was only prolonging the inevitable, I pulled back. Jonas opened the door for me, and as I passed by him out into the hallway I wondered if this would be the last time we'd be like this with each other. Was this just the magic of a good dress and clouds lit from within? But he took my hand, as if reading my mind, and smiled reassuringly. We walked back to the dance together.

There was a slow song playing when we arrived, and Jonas led me to a quiet spot where we stood watching over the kids as they swayed to the music. I could feel his hand near mine; I ached to have his fingers brush against my palm. The song that played was pretty, but I barely noticed. I could only hear the song he'd played for me earlier, when everything between us had shifted.

A few yards away, Tyson and Riley rocked to the beat, beaming at each other. A few of the hockey players stood huddled together.

"Tyson looks so happy, but I feel terrible for Jamie," I told Jonas. "He was having such a good season, and now it's over."

"Will he recover?"

"Sure, but it will take a while. If he was hoping to play in college, it might not be possible next year. And I didn't realize he was a dancer. He's going to miss the spring musical."

"You must see injuries like that a lot."

I shrugged. "I guess. I've seen some bad ones."

"Does it bother you?"

"It bothers me that I couldn't keep him safe. And I can't fix it. It just has to heal on its own. Once it does, I can do my part, but most of this is out of my hands. It can feel sort of helpless."

"I've never met anyone less helpless than you," he said.

"Really?"

"Yeah. You find that hard to believe? You saved me from a brawl, defeated a pack of wild teens in a snow battle, and took out a giant with a pastry . . . I've heard."

I bit my lip.

"You're a really strong person. But I wonder if it ever occurred to you that expecting yourself to be responsible for everyone is a bit of an unrealistic expectation?"

I looked over at him. No one had ever said something like that to me. "You mean like expecting yourself to never make a mistake?" I said gently.

"Touché, Doyle. Touché." He reached out and replaced a strand of my hair that had gone rogue and then rested his hand on the small of my back, and just like that, I was spellbound again.

I almost didn't notice the audience until someone cleared their throat.

"Hey, Coach." The assistant captain of the hockey team, Mike Beauvous, shifted nervously in front of us. "How's Jamie? Did his folks come?"

"Yeah, they're with him now. He's going to be okay. The doctors didn't think he'd need surgery, but he'll be in a cast and on crutches for a while."

There was a commotion somewhere in the crowd. Jonas shifted to get a better view.

"What's going on over there?" I asked.

Mike looked down.

"We'll figure it out, you know," Jonas said. "There's no point trying to keep quiet."

"Summer Trawick and Cassidy Cooley brought vodka. Couple of the theater kids have been passing around a flask," Mike confessed. I scrutinized him. "Not me, Coach. We all listened when you gave that talk at the beginning of the season about watching what we put in our bodies, as athletes."

"We better get over there," I said to Jonas.

"I got it. I'll find Josephine, the theater teacher. If it's her kids who started this mess, she'll want to handle it."

"Okay."

He leaned in. "I'll be back. Save me the last dance?"

I smiled.

The event ended a few minutes later when the chaperones realized the extent of the alcohol that had infiltrated the dance and shut the whole thing down. Jonas and I supervised the procession as everyone filtered back to their dorms, and then we started cleaning up.

"It's always those theater kids," Andy said. "They're wild."

"Weren't you a theater kid?" Revi asked.

"Ha, not me. I was too nerdy for theater."

"Is that a thing?" I asked. Andy feigned being offended.

"They won't be laughing when they realize how many hours of campus service they'll have to do, but it'll be a funny story when they're on Broadway," Revi said.

"Someone puked on one of the handmade birch trees!"

"This sucks," I said. "You both worked so hard making

tonight beautiful. Why don't you go home and put your feet up?" I caught Jonas's eye. "We've got this."

"Right, we'll take cleanup duty," he added.

They protested for a few moments, but finally gave in. "You just want to be alone, right?" Andy said, giving me a squeeze before they headed out. "Don't think we didn't see the way you guys were devouring each other with your eyes."

My cheeks flushed. "'Devouring' is a bit of a strong word, don't you think, friend?"

"Please, you were looking at him like those waffles at your first brunch."

"I was not."

"Hungry, Sophie. You looked hungry."

"You are a monster," I said, trying to suppress my laughter.

After they'd gone, I turned to Jonas. He'd taken off his suit jacket and rolled up his sleeves. I watched him for a moment as he took out a garbage bag and began collecting trash. My pulse quickened. Who was I kidding? I wasn't hungry; I was ravenous.

"I feel awful," I said, stacking the cups that were on a table. "We were off, well, *you know*, and those kids—"

"They do it every year. I'm only telling you this because I know you're going to beat yourself up over it, and I don't want you to have any regrets about earlier. They're teenagers—it's pretty much inevitable that they're going to mess things up from time to time. We could've been standing right there and they would've found a way."

"Seriously?"

"Absolutely." He picked up some paper plates that had been left on one of the tables and put them into the bag I was holding. Then he took out his phone and started some music.

"Will they get in trouble?"

"Come dance with me, Doyle. You promised to save me the last one."

The clock tower chimed midnight as Jonas and I made our way across the dark quad in silence. If someone had been able to make out our figures, they wouldn't have known the earthshaking transformation that had occurred beneath the stage lights, where we'd gone from a tentative truce to something entirely different.

We walked with space between us, a safety measure that felt physically painful to endure, part of an unspoken agreement in which we recognized that if we got any closer than a foot apart, we wouldn't be able to stay separate. The only sign of what had transpired was the fact that I was wearing Jonas's jacket over my bare shoulders. It kept out the harsh cold and smelled like him. And for the hundred yards where we didn't touch or speak or look at each other for more than an instant, that had to be enough.

We crept up the stairs, then entered the apartment without turning on the lights. There was a moment in the living room where we stood at the crossroads between my room and his. He put his hands into his trouser pockets.

"What did you think of your first formal?" he said, his voice almost a whisper. "Was it everything you imagined?"

I flashed back to Jonas sliding his hands beneath me, lifting me up and settling me down on the lid of the piano where he'd played my heart song only minutes earlier. My skin still tingled where he'd touched me. I hadn't imagined the depth of my attraction to him, or the intense connection that had forged between us.

I tilted my head up at him and smiled.

"It was more," I said.

"Good night," he said.

"Good night."

We stood there, both unable to leave and go to our own rooms. I glanced at the living room. Jonas followed my gaze and then, in one quick motion, he reeled me in to him for one last, epic kiss.

Chapter 28

I rolled over in bed, emerging from the very realistic fantasy I was having about a certain moody and musically inclined roommate whom I could not stop thinking about, to paw at my ringing phone.

"Hello?" I grumbled.

"I was promised pictures and I did not receive pictures." Astrid. "You are going to need to be extremely detailed. Think sights, sounds, smells."

"Smells?" I glanced at the wrist corsage Jonas had gotten me. I'd left it on top of the piano. Its fragrant gardenia scent had perfumed my room. "It was great," I said.

"*Great?* You're not giving me anything to work with here, babe. A playlist. Something?"

I pulled at the edge of the comforter. I didn't know how to talk about the previous night. It seemed ridiculous to call it what it had been . . . magical, like some kind of fabulous fever dream. I was an adult. And Astrid would've never let me hear the end of it.

"Something happened, didn't it?" she prodded. "You're never this tight-lipped about anything."

I glanced at the wall that separated me and Jonas and wondered what he was thinking over there. "Um . . ."

"How's your breathing?" Astrid said. I could hear the smile in her tone.

I smiled too. "It was pretty fast when he lifted me up onto a piano last night," I squeaked out.

"This. This is what I was talking about. Start from the beginning, and don't leave anything out."

"He's a really good kisser."

"Is that all? Given the amount of bickering between you, I would've thought you'd have less self-control."

"My self-control is wicked good, okay." It wasn't my self-control as much as it was the fact that we were down the hall from a bunch of students and we were molding young minds. If not for that and our sense of duty, I'd probably have been perched on the piano in my underwear. I tried to sound nonchalant. "Who knows—we probably just got caught up in the moment. He can really wear a suit and I had on the push-up bra you recommended that seems to be enchanted with some kind of spell."

"Right? There's a reason I won best bust at the Slime Awards last year. Sucks to be objectified for sure, but I'm pretty proud of my boobs. They never fail to perform."

"Speaking of performance, how's the shoot going?"

"We're getting ready to wrap in a week or so, which is a good thing, because I'm exhausted. I'm going to sleep for ten days when I get home. Then it's off to the Caribbean."

"Oh, beach vacation?"

"No, I got another movie, actually. The script was incredible. I cried, and you know me—I'm not a crier."

"You are the world's biggest crier!" I said, which was true. Astrid cried at commercials. It was part of what made her such a great actress. Her emotions were close to the surface. I think that's also why she'd struggled in high school. Astrid had big feelings, and those were hard to manage, especially for teenagers.

"One of my kids broke his leg yesterday at the hockey tournament," I said.

"Shit."

"He's really good too. The hockey team's actually pretty decent, but this one is also a dancer. He was going to be the lead in *Singin' in the Rain*."

"And you're beating yourself up about it."

"I'm trying not to. Jonas says that thinking I can take care of everyone isn't a fair expectation."

"He's right. It's possible I'm turning a corner about this guy. Maybe he's more than convenient hookup material." Astrid was quiet for a beat. "You know, Soph, you couldn't have helped what happened on an ice rink anymore than you could've prevented your dad's fall. Some things are beyond our control."

"I know. I just wish I could help him more. I've been so busy on the weekends I've barely gone down there. Every time I think about him being in Sommerset Meadows, hours away from me, instead of our house, I feel horrible."

"He was the one who said you should sell the house. I don't love this narrative you've got going. Your dad is a grown man. He chose to cancel his checkup. He chose to sell the house."

"But he chose the assisted living facility because of me."

"Really? Aren't some of his friends there, like Dennis? And so what if it was because of you? You are a valid reason to choose something."

I drew my knees into my chest. "All right, Astrid. I give up. You win."

"Good. Something we agree on. Now tell me more about Jonas Voss. You didn't sleep together—did you at least dance?"

"We did. He smells really good. Like Irish Spring soap and . . ."

"I'm trying hard not to make a joke about that."

"Very generous."

"'Magnanimous' is my middle name."

"Okay, Astrid *Lavinia* Tyler. Do you want to tease me, or do you want to know the best part?"

"There was a part that was better than you getting it on on top of a piano?"

"He played me a song."

"I thought you said that he doesn't play anymore."

"I did. He hasn't been playing at all until recently. We've been working together trying to heal his hand injury and re-train his fingers—"

"Are you doing this on purpose? The material you are giving me today, it's too much," she said, and laughed.

"Get your mind out of the gutter, Astrid. He played me 'Tessie,' only it was this beautiful arrangement I've never heard before. He wrote it himself."

"Seriously?"

"He did."

"When's the wedding?"

I ignored her. "I've never heard anything so perfect," I said. "It was like he was playing directly to my soul. I got chills. Instantly, I was transported back to those games with Dad. No one's ever done something like that for me. And seri-ously, Astrid, he's so talented. I can see why he was a profes-sional with an orchestra."

I was about to delve into the many ways in which he was talented, but a knock on my bedroom door saved me from myself. "Hang on, Astrid, someone's knocking." I crawled out of bed, adjusting my oversized Red Sox T-shirt. On my way to the door, I traced my fingers across the smooth piano keys. Not that long ago, Jonas's hands had glided over those same keys. I smiled reflexively as I remembered those same skillful fingers skimming along my spine until my body was singing. When I pulled the door open a moment later, he was standing there in his workout clothes.

"Oh," I said.

"Oh." He eyed my sleepwear. "Are we not working out today?"

"Just give me a second," I said. I pressed my phone to my ear. "Astrid? I've got to go. I'll call you later."

"Is he there?"

"Bye." I pressed end and set the phone on the piano next to the corsage that Jonas had given me.

Jonas shifted his weight on his feet. I suddenly wished I were wearing something other than this particular giant T-shirt. Last time I'd worn it, he'd called me an obsessive fan.

"You want to go running?" I asked, confused. Maybe my thought that last night had been a fleeting moment of madness wasn't so off base. Sometimes worries are legitimate.

"Yeah, well, I believe my trainer said consistency was key."

"She sounds boring."

His gaze flicked up from the floor. "She's not boring."

The corners of my mouth tugged up, so I covered my burgeoning grin with my fist. "I suppose I could go for a run."

"Just a short one."

A bubble rose in my chest. Did he have other plans for our time? A quick run and then more of what we'd started last night?

"I've got to head out of town by ten."

Chapter 29

I spent the rest of the day in a state of distraction. I thought about Jonas while I ate waffles across from his empty seat at the table. I wondered where he was, what was so important that it took him away for half the day every Sunday. I missed a catch when I was working with Tyson and ended up with massive welt smarting on my chest—thankfully, he'd still been warming up.

"Sorry! You okay, Coach?" he said as I stuffed an ice pack into my sweatshirt.

"Yeah, I'm fine. It was a bit of a stinger, that's all. I should've been more on my game."

"Are you sure?"

"You weren't bringing that much heat, kid. That's why in sports we always have to be paying attention. It's on me."

"Why weren't you paying attention?"

"Just thinking about things."

He nodded. Tossed a ball up in the air and snatched it into his glove.

"Did you and Riley have fun at the dance last night?"

He grinned and poked at the artificial turf with the toe of his shoe.

"That good, huh?"

"Yeah, it was pretty good. I asked her to be my girlfriend."

I handed him a training band so he could start some of the strengthening exercises I'd added to his program, and he turned away to set it up. "Oh really? How'd that go over?"

"Must've gone pretty well, because she's my girlfriend now." He beamed over his shoulder. "Did you know that she took second last year at the Primrose Viola Competition? She's a badass. She's funny too."

"That's great, Tyson."

"How was the dance for you? Before everyone got caught drinking and ruined it?"

My face warmed.

"I saw you and Mr. Voss dancing."

"And?"

"Looks like you're into each other. That's all."

"We're not into each other, trust me."

"He was smiling. I never see him smiling. He always seems like he's sad or something but trying not to show it, even during orchestra. Riley thinks he's depressed; I think he just misses playing. But you made him smile, Coach."

I lifted the ice pack away to peek at the damage. The skin was mottled from the ice, but I could still make out the beginning of a sick bruise.

"Did he ask you to be his girlfriend?"

"No, he didn't." I imagined for a moment what that would've been like and then reminded myself that I was an adult . . . who needed to stop letting all these teenagers and their juvenile relationship status ideas rub off on me. "We had a nice time. It was fun to get dressed up and listen to music and see all of you students enjoying yourselves. Fix your scapula, Tyson. Like we practiced."

He made an adjustment and corrected the issue.

"Have you thought any more about what you're going to do?" I asked. "Baseball season isn't far off."

"I want to play, but I don't think I can convince my parents. In their eyes, it's not a legitimate pursuit and I should be focusing totally on my music. I have this big competition coming up, and when I call home it's the only thing we talk about."

"Sounds hard."

His shoulders lifted a fraction and dropped. "I never minded the pressure, but there's other parts of me and my life, and those don't seem to matter that much. I just want to do music and have a girlfriend and play sports. I couldn't tell them about Riley. They'd think she was just a distraction."

"I'm sure your parents want what's best for you. But expectations can be stressful. I was never like you. I wasn't exceptional at one thing, let alone two. So I've never dealt with what you are dealing with. The only advice I can offer is that your parents won't know how you're feeling unless you tell them. Think about it."

"Okay. I'll think about it."

"When's your competition?"

"Next weekend. Mr. Voss and I will leave on Thursday and come back Sunday."

"I'm sure you'll be amazing. Let's take some tape," I said. "I want to analyze your mechanics again. I'll set up the target."

After Tyson and I were finished, I walked down to The Grind to pick up two chicken finger grinders. Jonas had planned to be back around four, so I thought he might be hungry. I wanted the time to think. We'd been quiet on our run. The overwhelming passion from the night before had faded in the light of day, but the back-and-forth, the pesky tension between us, had dissipated too. I didn't like it. I wanted Jonas to be obnoxious and hurl some sort of annoyed dig at me, or press me up against a lamppost and kiss me like the world was ending. I did not want polite quiet. It sounded too much like regret.

Back in the apartment, I set the subs on the table and took a shower. I was not immune to my feelings, so I washed my hair and put on lotion and some light makeup. I dressed in my prettiest green sweater and favorite jeans, and then I sat at the table, facing the door, and waited. At 4:04 on the dot, Jonas walked through. He seemed to see me first, and then the bag from The Grind. The corner of his mouth twitched.

"I got some food," I said. "Want some?"

"I always want grinders," he said, kicking off his shoes by the door. He sat down across from me. "Were you the thousandth customer and won an extra or was this an act of kindness just for me?"

I'd almost forgotten how handsome he was. My cheeks warmed. "I thought you might be hungry."

He smiled as he unwrapped his food. "I'm famished, actually. I didn't have lunch."

"You've been gone all day. You didn't eat?" I took a bite of my grinder.

"Nope. I was busy."

"What were you doing, anyway? You're pretty mysterious about these Sunday trips. Tyson said he thinks you have a secret girlfriend."

Jonas coughed. He took a swig of soda before he spoke. "Secret girlfriend, huh? What'd you say about that?"

"The truth. I told him I didn't know."

"I don't have a secret girlfriend." He set down his grinder and looked up at me. "And if I did, I don't think I'd need my car to go see her."

Beneath my sweater, my skin was covered in goose bumps. "Oh," I squeaked, before taking another bite. I could feel him watching me chew. I swallowed hard. "If it's not a girlfriend, what are you doing on Sundays?" Had I sounded casual? I'd meant to, but I didn't *feel* casual. I felt like some sort of spring, compressed to its maximum tension, about to unfurl across the room.

Jonas wiped his mouth with a napkin. "I'm not ready to tell you yet."

"Why? Will I be upset?"

He shook his head. "I don't think so. You might find it a bit odd. I will tell, though, I promise. Just not today."

I nodded. One of us was going to have to go there. I thought about my dad's words, about seizing opportunities. I pulled in a deep breath, mustered every bit of confidence I had, and began, "So, last night—"

"I need you to know that I meant what I said to you, every single word," he interjected, "but I understand if maybe it was just the setting and you don't feel that way. I won't make things weird."

Relief flooded over me. It hadn't been a moment of madness. Jonas had feelings for me. I set down my sandwich. "It wasn't the setting. Or the dress. It wasn't just the dance. I'm feeling it too."

"You're sure? I was a bit unnerved this morning when you didn't want to go running. I thought maybe you were feeling differently in the daylight, or regretted things."

I shook my head. "I was just nervous. I was worried about

the exact same stuff. It can be hard to tell what you're thinking sometimes."

"You're not the first person to tell me that. Maybe it would help if I just said it instead of making you try to figure it out. Truth be told, I was thinking how adorable you looked in just the oversized T-shirt, though I would've preferred if it had been one of mine."

I bit my lip. I had not been expecting that kind of disclosure or the delicious warm sensation it stirred up in my core. His eyes were locked on mine, and for a brief moment, I had the overwhelming desire to crawl across the table to get to him, even if it meant sacrificing the sandwiches.

Revi and Andy burst into the apartment just then. They were talking about some rock climbing trip they were planning, but stopped when they spotted me and Jonas. Revi dropped into the seat next to me.

"What do we have here?" he teased. "You guys got grinders without us?"

"Can't you see you're interrupting?" Andy said. "They're clearly on a date. Come watch the new *Fast and Furious* with me."

"It's a late lunch," I said. "Not a date."

"You know," Revi said, whispering in my ear as he rose from his seat to follow Andy, "chicken finger grinders means it's serious."

I flushed. When I looked up, I recognized the same pink tinge in Jonas's cheeks.

Andy and Revi settled in on the couch and soon the room was filled with the sounds of Vin Diesel's baritone and the roar of engines.

"Do you want to take a walk?" Jonas asked.

I nodded. I adored Revi and Andy, but more than anything,

I wanted to be alone with Jonas, even if that meant braving the New Hampshire winter. We grabbed our coats and headed in the direction of the lake. The December air was sharp and burned my cheeks. We left our hands buried in our pockets, out of the cold.

"Tyson told me he has a big competition on Friday," I said.

"The Yehudi Menuhin International Violin Competition, yeah. It's the biggest competition in England, if not the globe, for violinists under the age of twenty-two. He's been working on his piece for it all year. It could open every door for him, honestly, if it goes well."

"You're going to England? Are you going to see your mom?"

He frowned and shook his head. "Not likely. We haven't talked in some time."

"Maybe you should. I was telling Tyson he ought to talk to his family—maybe it will help."

"So you're still doing the pitching training with him?"

"I know you don't approve."

He shook his head. "It's not that. I just don't want him to lose his chance. It's kind of like how you wanted to protect Jamie. I want Tyson's dreams to be a reality, and part of that is making sure that he doesn't sustain an injury or lose focus."

"To be honest, I'm not sure he knows what his dream is. Did you know at his age? I didn't."

"You mean you haven't always wanted to be a trainer?"

I shrugged. "I love sports. I knew I wanted to help people. There was a point when I thought about being a teacher or a doctor. A trainer kind of seemed like the best of both worlds. And it meant I wouldn't graduate with hundreds of thousands of dollars in debt. Good thing. The place where my dad lives is pretty expensive. But I sometimes wish I had gone to medical school. Then maybe I would've noticed something was wrong earlier and could've helped him before it got this bad. But then I wouldn't have gotten to work with the Red Sox."

The lake drew out before us, glistening silver where a thin layer of ice had formed on the surface.

"You really loved working for the Red Sox," Jonas said.

"I did. I miss it. The players. Fenway. The cheering and the crack of the bat. It felt like home to me. You know, I practically grew up there. That's life, though, right? I really like it here too. I've been enjoying working with the athletes, and I'm especially excited about this program I'm working on with the musicians. It's kind of wild to think about the stress that playing an instrument the amount they do puts on their bodies, and yet no one teaches them how to take care of themselves or gives them the tools they need to ensure their physical health."

I glanced over and found him looking at me. "What?" I said, failing to suppress a smile.

"You light up when you talk about the kids and your work. It's like you're one of those clouds from the dance with twinkle lights."

"That's how it is when you play the piano," I admitted. "The way you looked last night when you were playing for me . . . I'd never seen you look like that before."

"I was a tad petrified, if I'm being completely honest."

"Why?"

"Because I was playing for you."

"Surely my opinion is nothing compared to an opera house full of people."

He turned to me, smoothed my hair away from me face. "I wouldn't say that."

I swallowed. "What would you say, then?"

Jonas was quiet for a moment. "I really want to kiss you right now. If that's okay."

My body trembled, a little from the cold, but mostly with anticipation. This thing with us, it was real, it was happening. I nodded. As Jonas leaned down to close the remaining distance between us, I let my eyes flutter shut and rose onto the tips of my toes. The warmth of his lips was a welcome sensation against my own cool skin. He circled his arms around my waist and held me tight to him. The wind whipped at my hair and the back of my neck; instinctively, Jonas moved his right hand, smoothing back my hair and covering the bare skin at the nape of my neck to block the cold as he deepened the kiss. I pulled back for a moment, searching his eyes. "I have to tell you something," I said.

His brow furrowed almost imperceptibly, but I knew his expressions by now.

"That song you played was the most incredible thing I've ever heard."

He grinned at me, sliding his fingers into my hair, and then he kissed me again. This kiss started slow, but the heat built.

"I can't stop thinking about last night," he whispered against my neck. "When you were on the piano . . . I've never wanted anything or anyone the way I want you. But I don't want to rush this. I want to do it right."

"And preferably not in the snow. I've noticed you're a bit temperature sensitive."

He tucked a thumb under my chin. "You're very astute, Doyle."

"But you're right. I'm at Monadnock until spring. So we can take our time."

"What do you suggest, then?"

"The couch?"

"I don't think Revi and Andy would be psyched if we

christened the couch. Otherwise, I'm enjoying your line of thinking."

"I meant for a movie. What are you insinuating?"

"Oh. Yeah, I'm down for a movie with you. Did you have something in mind?"

"I'm one hundred percent making you watch *The Rookie*."

"It's about baseball, isn't it?"

"You bet your ass it is. And it's going to make you cry, Jonas Voss."

Chapter 30

Jonas and I watched a movie on the couch each night until the day he left for the competition with Tyson. He did tear up during *The Rookie*—I knew he would; I've never met anyone who is immune to the trope of a person's lifelong dream coming true during a second chance—I could see it when I glanced over at him sitting next to me. On Monday night, he picked *Pride and Prejudice*. I teased him about the choice, but he said it was for the score. He watched half of it with his eyes closed, taking in the music, but I made sure that he witnessed the hand flex. If this thing between us was going to work, he needed to know. Tuesday was my pick, and I chose *Field of Dreams*. We watched it with my feet over his thighs. He rubbed them and said he enjoyed the movie, but I'd barely been able to focus. I know we wanted to take things slow, but the amount of lust I was feeling was practically unbearable.

When we watched *Amélie* on Wednesday night, I laid my head on his chest and he draped his arm over my shoulders, letting his hand rest on my waist so naturally, as if we'd always been like this.

"I haven't seen this one—did you pick it for the music, too?" I asked.

"The whole movie's phenomenal, but the score is amazing," he admitted. "'Comptine D'un Autre Été: L'Après-Midi' by Yann Tiersen is a work of genius. It's not even that hard to play; I could teach you."

"Really? I actually would love to learn to play. You'd really teach me?"

"Why are you surprised? You've done so much for me. Look at how far I've come. I never thought I would play again at all. And now, almost all of it's come back, except for certain glissandos. I feel optimistic for the first time in a long while. There's a piece of me that thinks maybe I could play professionally again."

"Do you want to?" I asked.

He hesitated for a moment before he spoke. "I do. Before, admitting it seemed like getting my hopes up, and I wasn't prepared for that kind of loss again. I've learned to appreciate the life that I carved out from the remnants of my previous one. It's smaller and quieter, but good. I like working with the kids and conducting. It's rewarding."

"I know what you mean. I miss my old world, but there's definitely things about this one that I love. And I didn't expect that. I never really had a chance to think about pursuing something different before . . . or maybe I have, but I haven't taken those chances."

"Exactly. I'd only ever let myself want one thing. And then when it was gone, my life seemed sort of pointless. I guess I had this feeling of grief over losing piano. But I'd made peace with this new version. I was doing okay."

I nodded.

"I told myself that I'd had everything I wanted for a while, and that had to be enough." He brushed his thumb over my lip. I held my breath in expectation of what he would say next. "And then I walked into that room over there and found you messing with my piano, and it was like being woken up. You made me want it back, and you helped me believe that I could get it back."

"I did that? My hand exercise game must be more potent than I thought."

He grinned. "Seriously, you made me want to be great again, for you. You deserve someone great."

My whole existence changed on that couch. I died and went to heaven through the space between the seat cushions. For most of the semester, I would've settled for civility from him, and then later, as I saw the other layers of Jonas and realized that my hot roommate was more than just a grump, I'd started hoping he'd give me the time of day. To think we'd actually be falling for each other was beyond my wildest imaginings. The sincerity in his expression was enough to do me in.

"Should we start the movie?" I asked, listening to the sound of his heartbeat.

While we watched, Jonas drew slow circles on my hip bone; sensation rippled through my body. His chest rose and fell beneath me. The film was beautiful—striking images and moments pieced together and supported by the music. I wondered if that was what life was like for Jonas. A piece of art. I wasn't sure, but I did know that I wanted to be a part of it.

When the movie ended, we folded the blankets and switched off the living room lights. In the hallway in front of our rooms, I turned to him. "I can't believe you're going away to England for four days in the morning. It probably sounds silly, but I wish you didn't have to go."

He glanced at his watch. "We still have a few hours. We could spend them together. If you want to."

I nodded. "Do you?"

"You have no idea," he said.

I blinked slowly, taking in his words, asking myself what this would mean and what tomorrow might look like if I followed him into his room. He brushed the edge of his thumb over my cheek and pressed his forehead to mine.

I reached up and slid my hand over his, drawing it away from my cheek and then using it to lead him to his room. I had my answer. It didn't matter what it meant, or what tomorrow could be. Tonight, it was just us. Me and him. That beautiful melody still playing in my ears. We'd been on a collision course since the day I broke through the walls of protection he'd built up around himself and touched his piano.

Inside his room, he closed the door behind us and waited there, back against the door. I was suddenly very nervous. Even so, I reached down, crossing my arms and pulling my T-shirt over my head. He still hadn't moved. I wondered for a moment if he'd changed his mind or if the inertia kept him fixed there. Then he pulled his sweatshirt over his head in one fluid motion. I walked back over to him, pressing one hand to his chest, and looked up at him.

He leaned down until his lips were only a whisper away from mine. "This feels . . ."

Monumental, I thought.

". . . right," he said.

He touched the bruise the baseball had left on my breastbone with painstaking gentility. "How did this happen?" he asked.

"Just an accident," I said.

"As long as no one hurt you."

I thought back to how he hadn't hesitated to put himself in harm's way with that barbarian back in Boston. I cupped my hand to his cheek. "No one hurt me, Jonas. You don't have to worry."

"It was sports related, wasn't it? You told me that baseball isn't dangerous."

"It's dangerous if I'm daydreaming about you instead of focusing on catching Tyson's pitches."

He traced lines lower with his fingertips, trailing over my ribs down to the spot where the top of my jeans met my hip bones. "You were fantasizing about me?"

I bit my lip.

"I've been thinking about you, about this, nonstop. You have no idea."

Jonas walked over to his stereo and turned on some John Legend, though it wasn't any mix I'd heard; this one had piano and violins and the singer's raspy voice. Then Jonas drew me back into him. His mouth met mine again; he pressed his fingers into the flesh at the base of my spine, sinking his hands deeper into the waistband of my jeans while his lips moved on to graze the line of my neck. I sighed deeply. I explored him with my hands. The breadth of his back, the sinew of his strong arms, the chest that definitely *had* been doing push-ups since the day I'd teased him in the bathroom. I knew his body. I knew it from the training, the yoga, the runs together. But not like this. I wanted to know him better. The places I could touch to make him groan or smile, the ones that would make his breath hitch. I wanted to learn the tender spots, the feel of his skin beneath my fingertips. He was magnetic, pulling me to him. I couldn't get enough.

Jonas helped me lower myself to the bed. Then he reached down and unbuttoned my jeans with what seemed like an expert flick of his thumb. As he lowered them, he kissed a trail from my hip bone to my knee all the way down to my ankles, leaving my skin tingling in the wake of his touch. He discarded the jeans beside the bed, and then traced the same path, slowly returning to the crest of my hip and then with torturously slow speed, he followed the curve of my body all the way up to my collarbone. I looked up at him, so full of desire and recklessness and feelings that I trembled. He stilled. "Sophie, you're shaking. Is this okay, or should we stop?"

I touched his cheek. "Don't stop, Jonas. Whatever you do, don't stop."

"You do enjoy bossing me around, don't you?"

"I love it," I said. Every time he touched me, every instant his lips met mine, or he fit himself to a new curve or space I hadn't realized needed his touch, something substantial and new bloomed in my chest. I clung to him. Every ounce of tension that I'd been holding uncoiled.

"I love this," I said, breathless, as Jonas's hands grazed over my navel.

He paused for a moment. "I could listen to you talk about what you love all night."

"Then you better keep doing exactly what you're doing."

"Sweetheart, that is exactly what I intend to do."

Chapter 31

I watched Jonas as he walked to his dresser in the dim dawn light and pulled out a pair of joggers for himself and a T-shirt. God, he was beautiful. His lean muscles rippled while he stooped to put on the pants. He returned with the shirt, giving me a soft kiss on my forehead as he handed it to me.

I held it out, examining it. "Your old orchestra?" I asked.

He nodded. "That's my favorite shirt, Doyle. You better take care of it."

I pulled it over my head.

He settled down on the bed next to me. "See, now I feel like I've made a mistake."

My body tensed. "You don't trust me with the shirt?" I hoped that was all, because a deeper worry was swirling around my stomach now—did he regret last night? Or was he thinking about what had happened when he was with the orchestra . . . the mistake, his father's awful reaction.

He tucked a thumb under my chin and lifted it gently.

"It's not that. It's just that you're clothed now, and I pre-ferred you without clothes."

I beamed at him. "That's very good to know. I thought that you might be having some thoughts about the history of the shirt since you're going back to England. But you're okay, then?"

"I'm fine. It's all ancient history. If anything, I'm just wishing I could catch a later flight. I can't believe I have to leave in ten minutes."

"A lot can be done in ten minutes," I said. "Some people can run two miles in that time."

"Are you running a five-minute mile?"

"No. But I have something else I can accomplish in that time, and given your questionable running mechanics, I'm sure you'd prefer my plan." I swept my hair up into a ponytail.

"Listen, we'll discuss my questionable running mechanics when I get back. Now that I know how important those kinds of things are to staying injury-free, I'll want to address it. Perhaps I'll need some extra training." He ran a hand over my ponytail and trailed his fingers down my neck. "But like I told you at the lake, I don't want to rush anything with us. Ten minutes won't be enough . . . not with you, anyway, and I can't be late today. International flight and all. So we'll revisit bio-mechanics and all the wonderful and wicked things we want to do to each other when I get back on Sunday."

I bit my lip.

He groaned. "You have no idea how cute you look right now."

After Jonas left, I stayed in his bed for a few minutes. I pressed my face to his pillow, inhaling deeply—there was the faint scent of Irish Spring soap and something else, something clean and warm, and completely Jonas. Last night had been this kind of epic, beautiful conclusion to what we'd started the night of dance, but it had also felt like the beginning of something important and real. I climbed out of bed, collected my clothes, and tiptoed out into the hallway.

"Good morning, Sleeping Beauty," Revi said.

"Cute nickname," Andy chimed in, "but we all know that Sophie wasn't doing any sleeping last night."

I hid my face in my clothes.

"Don't be embarrassed, Sophie. You guys weren't that loud. Besides, we're happy for you. Come have a celebratory doughnut."

I shuffled over and dropped down into a seat at the table. Embarrassment wasn't enough to keep me away from a doughnut, especially when there was a French cruller that had my name on it. And I was too happy to hide in my room. I picked up a doughnut and took a bite.

"Andy," Revi said in a tone normally reserved for someone cooing over a box full of puppies, "she's wearing his T-shirt."

"Berlin Philharmonic?" Andy translated.

"He used to work there. He didn't tell you?"

Andy and Revi shook their heads. Andy said, "You know how Jonas can be; he's a man of few words."

I couldn't argue with that—Jonas *was* always holding back a bit, but I knew that when he let go, he had a lot to say. That had definitely been true last night. "I don't think it's something he likes to discuss. There's a hard history there. Kind of like me and the Red Sox situation. It's not a fun topic to talk about, if that makes sense."

They nodded.

"A favorite T-shirt makes it seem like this isn't just a one-time thing. Should we be purchasing earplugs?"

Heat flashed in my cheeks.

Revi raised his eyebrows. "That's a yes if I've ever seen one. Astrid's going to love this." He typed something on his phone and then there was the whoosh of a message sending.

"Did you just text her?" I asked.

"Yeah. Why not? We've been talking daily since we came up with the idea of the winter formal. We love her. And you."

I snatched Revi's phone from the table and scanned the screen. "Is this a group chat? Concerned friends of SoJo?"

Revi took a bite of his doughnut. "I came up with that. Sophie plus Jonas. SoJo." He looked quite proud of himself.

"You all are too much," I said, shaking my head. "What do you have on for the day?"

"I'm feeling like it's a good day for a pop quiz," Revi said.

"You're clearly still mad about the formal. Don't you have a bunch of the troublemakers in your class?" asked Andy.

"A few. I'm just tired of supervising their service detentions. I've never heard anyone grumble as much as they do about easy tasks like mopping the hallways. They're worse than peak moody Jonas."

Andy broke first, hiding his chuckles with his fist. Revi followed next, and soon we were all laughing.

I planned to work on the article about my musical fitness program before teaching a class on kinesiology to Rebecca's biology students. After doughnuts, I headed out toward the training room. I glanced briefly up at the clear sky. Soon Jonas would be boarding a plane, passing over the ocean. I missed him already.

Chapter 32

Jonas made it home from the competition just in time for Sunday night study hall duty with me at the library.

"Hi there, Doyle," he said, smiling at me. He let his overnight bag slip off his shoulder and drop on the floor next to his feet.

"I thought I was going to have to do study hall by myself," I said, grinning back.

"I wouldn't have let that happen," he said, taking a step toward me and brushing his thumb over my cheek. "Who would patrol the stacks for lusty teenagers?" He took my coat off the hall tree and helped me put it on. "Ready?"

I nodded. Despite the long nighttime phone calls we'd had while he was gone, I was a bit nervous to be near him again. I wondered if things would be different between us after these days apart. We walked down the dorm hallway in silence.

"It's bloody freezing outside," Jonas said, as we neared the front door.

"You want to take the tunnel?" I said.

"I thought you'd never ask."

We descended the stairs to the tunnel. It was a dimly lit space with a damp smell, and had Jonas not been there, I would've found it creepy. Rebecca had warned me that sometimes students would come down here to make out, and I'd found it hard to believe—the atmosphere wasn't exactly romantic—until now. Jonas laced his fingers through mine.

"You haven't told me about how everything went. How did Tyson do?"

He stopped and pulled me toward him. The stone walls rose up beside us, arcing low over Jonas's head. With one swift turn, Jonas spun me up against the cool stone. He lowered his face to mine. "I'll tell you everything," he said. "I just have to do this one thing first." The touch of his lips on mine made my fears dissipate. This was not the move of someone who had changed his mind over a few days apart. I could practically taste the yearning on his tongue. The sound of voices echoed down the stone corridor, and Jonas and I broke apart. He took my hand and led me at a jog farther down the tunnel and then took a branch off to the right. It was one of the parts of the tunnel that needed repair and was closed with a piece of construction fencing. Out of sight, Jonas pulled me to him. "I've been thinking about kissing you since the second I left you in my T-shirt on Thursday morning," he whispered.

"I think I'm claiming it as mine."

"Oh yeah?"

"I slept in it every night."

He looked thoughtful for a moment. "I'm not sure I gave it to you. It was more of a borrowing situation. After all, it is my favorite T-shirt."

"I really like it though."

"You make a very compelling case. Perhaps we can reach

an arrangement. How about this—I'll give you full custody of the shirt if you'll agree to be with me."

"I thought I had," I said, flashing him a playful look.

His face was open and earnest. He tucked a strand of hair behind my ear. "Fair," he said. "But I mean officially. I want us to be together."

I swallowed.

"What do you think?"

What did I think? My heart had practically turned into a symphony, with a thrumming percussion section and wood-winds twittering joyously. Here came the strings. Was I going to cry? Possibly. I was that happy.

I nodded.

"Since that's settled, we probably should try testing your five-minute-mile pace on our way to the library. We're late."

It was final exam week before the students went home for the winter holidays, so the library was silent during study hall. Jonas and I sat at the desk, smiling about our new status. I'd texted the "Concerned friends of SoJo" to tell them it was of-ficial, and I had to silence my phone so the flurry of excited messages from Astrid, Revi, and Andy wouldn't disturb the kids.

"I want to hear about the competition," I said. "Was Tyson amazing?"

Jonas nodded. "He's so mature. Those things are really nerve-racking even for me, but he's always composed. Quite a few conservatories approached him, but he has interest from several major symphonies as well. You should have seen the audience listening to him. They were completely captivated. It's no wonder he took first place."

"That's fantastic," I said. "He must've been so pleased."

"He was, I think. But you know Tyson—he's so humble. He's not one to make a huge deal out of that sort of thing."

I thought back to the time that Tyson had thrown a perfect 101-mile-per-hour pitch. He'd leapt in the air and whooped. He'd run in a circle with his arms out like an airplane about to take off fueled by sheer elation. "I'm the king of the mountain," he'd hollered. And I laughed and told him not to get too carried away. But then I'd pretended to be a jet and zoomed around myself.

"What was it like being there for you?" I asked, changing the subject.

"You mean back in the music world, or back in England?"

I lifted my shoulders. "Both?"

"I have mixed feelings about England. I grew up there, and obviously, I love it. It's a fantastic place. But I've got some shite memories from those times too, so I wasn't keen on being reminded of all that. Fortunately, I was so busy, I didn't have too much time to reflect on the past, except at night, and then I had a cheery, gingery conversationalist who kept my mind occupied with more pleasant thoughts."

I smiled at that. "Interesting. And the music part—was that okay?"

"I was nervous to see some of the people who know me from before, but I was focused on Tyson, so that helped. Actually, it wasn't as hard as I thought. I saw Boris Vesteppan, first violinist from my old orchestra in Berlin, and that was great. We had dinner on Friday. And then I ended up sitting next to Roy Sampson from the London Philharmonic."

"How was that?"

He outlined my hand with his fingertip. "Great, actually. I told him about the training you've been helping me with and how I've been recovering and regaining my abilities. He mentioned that they were thinking of adding a permanent pianist for next season." Jonas paused and looked up at me. "He wants me to come and audition in the new year."

"That's huge!"

He shrugged. "I don't know. He was probably just being generous, and anyway, I'm not sure if I'm ready. That last thing I want to do is make a fool out of myself and waste everyone's time."

"Why would you think that? You've made such amazing progress in a short time."

"Well, that was mostly you," he said, rolling my chair toward him.

"No it wasn't. You did the hard part; I was just there to push you and cringe at your running form."

"Is that what you were doing behind me? All this time, I thought you were admiring my arse."

I laughed. "You're hilarious. We both know you spent ninety percent of our runs trying to keep up with me."

"Well, yes, you have a very admirable backside."

"I knew you were secretly a perv. You probably orchestrated that bathroom run-in when I first moved in."

"Okay, I'm offended. I'm a gentleman. That was fully an accident. A happy accident maybe, but an accident nonetheless."

"You're thinking about it right now."

"Maybe. Fancy a trip to the stacks, Doyle?" There was an impish twinkle in his hazel eyes.

"I thought you'd never ask."

I'd never fantasized about coiling myself around a man in between library shelves, but within moments, in the depths of the Greek classics section, that exact event was quickly elevated to my highlight reel. *So this is what being with Jonas Voss is like*, I thought, smoothing my tousled hair and reshelving the editions of Homer's *Odyssey* that had ended up on the floor. I hadn't been this happy since I'd gotten the job offer from the Red Sox. But that's the thing about getting what you want: the moment it's in your hands, you have to make sure you don't lose it.

Chapter 33

On Monday morning I rolled over and snuggled into Jonas's warmth. I still greeted the sight of him near me and the heart-squeezing sensation it brought with a bit of disbelief. It seemed utterly surreal that we were here after all of the weeks of bickering. I'd believed we were so different from each other, but I'd come to realize that we were more alike than we were disparate.

"Good morning," he said, and smiled at me sleepily before he wrapped his arms around me and pulled me into him.

"This is nice," I told him. "It's different."

"Different than what? Your ex?"

I shook my head. "Patrick was a very busy person. Most mornings I was alone. I worked out by myself. Ate breakfast on my own, unless I'd hit the bakery on my way into work. Honestly, it wasn't until I got to the training room that I found myself surrounded by people."

It seemed odd to me now, that I'd been so lonely and hadn't even realized. No wonder I'd mentally positioned the team as my family and it had been so painful when I was forced to walk away from them. But I wasn't alone anymore. I had Andy and Revi, who were the kind of good friends who felt like brothers. The students, my athletes and musicians, who worked tirelessly to reach their goals, even if they stumbled along the way. And then there was Jonas. Jonas, who was only cranky part of the time. Who made me feel at home in myself and in his arms. Who made my heart do a roundoff back handspring in my chest when I spotted him across the crowded dining hall.

"I can't imagine not wanting to be near you all the time," he said.

The ease with which he said it surprised me, but it rang true, because that was how I felt about him, I realized. In such a short time, I'd become completely comfortable with him. But it was more than that; I craved him. The way he smiled, just a little, as if only one corner of his mouth could overcome his stoicism. Everyone knew he was good with the kids, but according to Cynthia, most of the other staff thought he was a full-fledged curmudgeon. They hadn't broken through his icy defenses, but apparently, I'd melted them and been rewarded with the real Jonas. Beneath the pride, the crankiness, under all that arrogance he used to shield his shame, he was sweet and thoughtful. I sensed there was a deeper hurt there than just the problem with his hand—he'd hinted at it after the trip to England and with other comments here and there—but I wasn't sure if it was safe to probe yet.

"Want to go for a run?" I asked him.

"Want to? Not really. It looks like *Game of Thrones* out there. I half expect a White Walker to emerge from the woods and chase us."

"Okay." It's not like I needed him to go.

"But if it means we get to spend more time together before the day starts, then I'll risk hypothermia."

"What about frostbite?" I teased, rising out of bed. "You wouldn't want to lose any important appendages."

"I'll wear an extra layer of drawers."

"I meant your fingertips and that super cute nose of yours. Get your mind out of the gutter, Voss," I said.

Minutes later at the door of the dorm, watching the wind toss around the glittering snow that had fallen overnight, Jonas shook his head. "I don't think two layers of drawers were enough."

"Me neither. Let's just skip the run and hit the showers instead."

"I thought you had a strict rule about me not being in the bathroom when you were showering, Doyle. 'No barging in,' I seem to recall you saying."

"It's not barging if you're invited."

Afterward, Jonas stood in the steam-filled room and helped me dry my hair. "I can't believe the semester's almost over," I said. "It's gone so fast."

"I should warn you, the students get a little intense during exams. Most of them are not sleeping enough, and the mood is—"

"I think I can handle it," I said over the hum of the blow-dryer. "I managed to deal with you."

He clicked it off. "Was I that awful?"

"No." I held my arms out wide. "You were *this* awful."

He clutched at his chest dramatically and then blasted the blow-dryer on high.

In the dining hall at breakfast, I saw what Jonas had meant. Normally, the morning crowd was buzzing with energy and animated conversation. Not today. Instead, there were extra carafes of coffee at the beverage station and barely anyone talked. "This is creepy," I told Jonas when he set the Belgian waffle he'd made down in front of me.

"They're stressed."

"How do they think I feel?" Andy asked, dropping into his seat with a mug of coffee in each hand. "I have to set up an anatomy and physiology practical exam and grade twenty-two AP Genetics term papers by the end of the week. These kids, the less they know, the more they write. It's been brutal."

"Yikes," I said. "Do you want help setting up the practical? I'm just working on a paper I'm submitting to the *American Journal of Sports Medicine*, so I have time."

"You're such a rock star. And yes, that would be a massive help, if you don't mind."

Revi said, "I had to add four extra office hour sessions today and tomorrow for calculus."

"How about you, Jonas?"

Jonas took a bite of his waffle and swallowed. "I love exam week."

"You really are evil," Revi said. "Andy thought I was mean for a few pop quizzes. You enjoy watching everyone around you suffer?"

Jonas shook his head. "That's not what I meant. My final is not like yours. There are no all-nighters, no extra office hours. Each of the kids had to write an original piece, then they submit the sheet music and play it for the whole group. It's honestly my favorite part of the year, because most of the time, I have no idea what they've been working on, and then they walk up there and blow everyone away. Last year, Riley Santos wrote this lullaby for viola that was so beautiful some of the students cried."

Andy eyed him. "Translation: you cried."

Jonas gave a half smile. "Yeah, maybe I did shed a few tears. I'm in touch with my emotions."

"Sure," Revi said. "It's just that usually your emotions are sullen and cantankerous. Not since you and Sophie have gotten together, though. She's been a good influence on you."

Jonas looked over at me. I took a sip of my coffee. I wondered now if blabbing to the group text that we were officially together maybe hadn't been the best plan of action. Jonas got along with Andy and Revi, but he was a private person; that much I'd learned over our time together.

"She didn't have to tell us, by the way—we knew. Who do you think orchestrated the world's best first date, also known as winter formal?" Revi added.

Jonas said, "That wasn't our first date."

I sputtered on my coffee.

"Our first date was to a lovely little dive bar in Boston, where the very good influence that you speak of kissed me out of the blue and nearly got into a brawl."

I pressed my lips together to stifle a laugh. "I was trying to save you."

"Did I mention that after that we shared a hotel room, and that she introduced me to her father?"

Andy and Revi's eyes widened and then they gave each other a look before turning their attention on me. "Seems that someone has been holding back on us, *Sophie*."

"Please. You two were riding a Disney high. I didn't want to make things weird."

"Have you met us? We love weird," Revi said.

"Well, it all worked out. No harm, no foul," I said. "Andy, what time should I meet you in the bio lab?"

Andy swallowed the bite of bagel sandwich he'd been chewing. "Maybe ten? The exam starts at one."

"Great. I'm going to my office to see if I can finish up my musical fitness paper. I'll find you in a bit."

"I'll walk with you," Jonas said, rising from his seat. Outside, he extracted a hat and put it on.

"Is that one of the hats I made for Stowe?" I asked.

"Andy doesn't need it. He has super thick hair!"

I reached up and snugged the hat down over his ears. "I would've made you one too, you know, if you'd asked."

"Will you make me my own now? I suppose I should give this pilfered one back to Andy before he and Revi go to Sugarloaf for the holidays."

"Sure! I'm actually going to make some more hats for the staff and residents at Sommerset Meadows as Christmas presents, so I can buy yarn for yours when I go to the store this afternoon. What's your favorite color?"

He eyed me in the warm morning sunlight. I could smell the faint aroma of maple mingling on our breath. "Green, I think. Like your formal dinner dress."

"Green it is then," I told him. We started across the frozen quad. I held on to his arm as we made our way over an icy spot on the walkway.

"Speaking of the holiday," Jonas started. "I've been meaning to ask what your plans are. Are you going to spend the whole time in Boston?"

"I thought I'd spend Christmas Eve and Day with my dad, but then I was going to come back. Astrid said she might have a break, and since her apartment is sublet, she was going to stay here. Revi said she could use his room since they're practically best friends now."

Jonas nodded. "I'd like to meet the famous Astrid."

"She's incredible—hilarious and strong. Everyone who meets her falls in love with her."

"Not that I don't believe in the captivating power of your friend, but I don't think I'm likely to do that. Hopefully we'll be fast friends though, since she's so important to you."

My heart ran a little victory lap in my chest at his words. I'd learned that Jonas didn't find making friends easy. His life as a virtuoso had meant he was mostly surrounded by adults and under enormous pressure to be perfect during his formative years. To survive, he'd armored himself against vulnerability. It made him less susceptible to pain, but it also meant he had a hard time forming real connections with people his own age. The fact that he wanted to befriend Astrid because he cared about me was significant. And admittedly, I couldn't help but feel gleeful that he had answered so quickly and with such conviction that he wouldn't fall in love with someone else.

"Do you want company when you go visit your dad?" he asked. "I don't want to intrude on your family time, but I have something for him."

I stopped mid-step. "You got my dad a present?"

"I got you something too," he said, and patted me on the head. "Don't worry that gingery little head of yours."

"Seriously? I haven't had a chance to get presents for anyone yet."

"You don't have to buy me anything," he said. "If you want to give me something, you can help me get ready for my audition."

"You're going to do it?" I asked. He'd seemed ambivalent when we'd talked about it the night before.

"I thought about what you said. I feel like I owe it to myself to try."

"That's great." I squeezed his arm.

He lifted his shoulders. "What can I say? You make me feel like anything is possible . . . with the right cross-training, of course."

"I'm glad you see the importance of cross-training." I stood on my tiptoes and pulled him down to me to press my lips to his.

A couple of guys from the hockey team who were headed toward the dining hall with Jamie whooped at us. "Get it, Coach Doyle," one of them hollered.

"Watch the ice on those crutches, Jamie!" I yelled back.

"And your manners, gentlemen," Jonas added.

"See you at practice, Coach!" the boys yelled back.

"They have practice, even during exams?"

I nodded. "It's the last practice before the holiday. They need to stay sharp for playoffs."

"I'll pick you up at the rink then," he said, and then he lifted me off my feet and kissed me again on the mouth. "Text me when you're almost done."

Even when he set me down and walked off toward the music building, my feet still felt like they weren't touching the ground. The world had shifted so completely, I almost couldn't believe that I wasn't in the midst of an extremely realistic dream. Somehow, Jonas had evolved from a bickering almost-bully to someone who made butterflies flit around in my core.

I took out my phone and called my dad.

"Hey, Dad," I said when he answered. "How do you feel about having an extra person for Christmas?"

"As long as it's Astrid or Jonas, I'm game."

"I didn't realize he'd made such an impression on you."

"Oh yeah. He made quite an impression. Nice fella. And

like I always say, the more the merrier. Besides, being a Brit and all, it's not like he's got family here."

"No, he doesn't. Our other roommates are headed to Maine to ski, and he hates the cold, so he'd be alone on the holidays."

And I really wanted him to come along.

Chapter 34

As promised, Jonas was waiting at the rink when hockey practice ended. He was leaning against the doorway, looking like a very tall cup of tea, wearing a black peacoat and the Stowe hat.

"Still holding Andy's hat hostage, I see!" I called. "I just need to finish picking up the water bottles and do a few other tasks before I head out."

He left his post in the doorway and walked around the edge of the rink toward the bench where I was cleaning up balls of tape and other things the players had missed when they'd headed to the locker room.

"I'll help you."

I eyed him. "You know, I have a better idea. We have this whole place to ourselves. We could skate for a little bit."

"You skate too? Is there anything you don't do, Doyle?"

"I don't play an instrument, as you well know." I tossed a water bottle and watched it land upright in the drink carrier.

"You really are Sporty Spice."

"Perhaps I am more athletically inclined than most, but I'm not talking about wind sprints here. Just a lap around the ice. Doesn't everyone skate?"

Jonas lifted his shoulders a fraction.

"You don't know how?" I asked.

"I've never tried. I wasn't allowed. Too dangerous, you know. Everyone seems to have a story about falling back and breaking a wrist. If there's a cautionary tale, I took it to heart."

"You roughhoused in the snow with me."

"That's different. It was my only opportunity to be close to you . . . and snow is soft. This ice? Not so much."

"I won't let you fall."

"When you say that, I actually believe you. Too bad I don't have skates."

I laughed. "You know the great thing about ice rinks? There's always a bunch of skates lying around."

He followed me over to the bins where we stored the skates for sharpening. I found a pair his size and handed them to him. Without protest, he put them on. I laced up a pair quickly, and together, we penguin-walked to the ice.

"This seems very ill-advised," he said.

I took his hand. "I'm not about to let all of my hard work fixing you go to waste. If you feel like you're going to fall back, just throw your arms out in front of you, bend your knees, and sit back. That isn't going to happen, by the way."

He gripped my hand tighter and we stepped out onto the ice. After a couple of tentative steps, Jonas picked it up right away. "You're a natural," I told him.

"Look at you," he said. "You're practically ready for the Olympics."

"Well, I grew up in Boston. I was always skating in winters.

Dad loved going to the rink. When I was really small, the three of us would go and he and my mom would whip around on the ice."

It was so long ago, but I could still see tiny snippets of them in my memory, flying around the ice, hand in hand, her red hair flying out behind her like crimson flames licking the wind. She was so beautiful. "They loved each other so much—you know, like those people who meet their soulmate when they're young . . . that was my parents. And she was really good. Not just at skating, but at everything."

"Sounds like you took after her."

I twisted a section of my hair around my finger. It wasn't as bright as hers was, at least as I remembered it. "Not really. My cooking is terrible. She was a wonderful baker, and she was always in a good mood. I try very hard to be as optimistic and sunny as she was, but it's hard. I've got a bit of a temper."

"Hadn't noticed," he snarked.

I bumped him with my hip, and he stumbled a little, but regained his footing.

"You just demonstrated my point! One tiny provocation and you turn into a terminator," he said, but he couldn't keep the grin from his face.

"You're having fun, aren't you?" I asked him.

"Yeah. I'll admit it. Perhaps some of your sporty endeavors aren't all bad. Plus, I'm enjoying hearing you talk about your family. Mine wasn't like yours. We didn't do things together, not really, other than competitions and concerts and taking me to my lessons. My mom was lovely; she didn't bake, but she was kind and funny. She used to make up stories to keep me from being nervous when I was little, and she made signs she'd hold up at recitals. Super embarrassing, but I loved them."

"She sounds amazing."

He nodded. "They fought all the time, though. He thought she was too soft. They argued about me, about work and bills, my dad's moods. She sort of disappeared into her work, and he took over managing my music as I started to win competitions and got invitations to play with different orchestras. And then one day—I think it was right around my fourteenth birthday— they just gave up. Dad took me back to Germany and that was that."

I stopped and spun in front of him. "He took you away from your mom?"

"He wasn't like your dad, Doyle. He made a lot of sacrifices for my career, but he wasn't a nice person."

I sensed that there was more to this story, given the way Jonas closed in on himself when he said those words. His grip on my hand loosened. Then there was what he'd told me about his last concert and the cold, cruel way his father had re- sponded to his mistake. My heart ached thinking about the indelible mark that painful rejection had left on Jonas. He was prickly and tough at times, but he was also someone who was thoughtful and sensitive. It made me furious that he'd been treated like that. I could only imagine that it was like what I'd felt when the entire city of Boston had turned on me, except that it would be a deeper and more acute pain coming from someone who's supposed to love you. I hated feeling like there was nothing I could do.

"I'm sorry," I said.

"There's nothing to be sorry for. It is what it is. I suppose without my father being the way he was, I might not have had the career I had. Even if it was only for a short time. It was something amazing while it lasted."

I wanted to ask what "the way he was" meant, but I didn't. I clung to his arm and focused on the rhythmic glide of our skates on the ice and the way we fit together.

"I wouldn't change this," I said. "But I wish things hadn't been so hard for you."

"You haven't had it easy either. That's just life. It's complicated and painful, but it's beautiful too."

I nodded.

"Doyle, I've got to say something and I'm not sure you'll like it."

"That's never stopped you before," I said.

"You really need to tell your dad the truth about what happened," Jonas said. I shook my head. "I know you planned to return to the team and thought that knowing you were fired might upset him, but I'm not sure those things are true. He's tougher than you think, and he'll support you."

"I'm supposed to support him. There's still a chance that I'll get my job back and he'll never have to know."

"I'm not sure anything good ever comes from keeping things from the people we care about. It's been months. Have you heard from the Red Sox? Has anyone there reached out to you? And if they were to come calling, would you still want to go back, after everything that's happened?" His words seemed to hang in the air between us for a moment. "In my opinion, they don't deserve you."

When I first came to Monadnock, I'd thought about it all the time. I pictured what it would be like when they asked me to come back and exactly what they'd say. In those fantasies I could smell the Cracker Jack, hear the way the people around us would fall silent the way they do in movies. But I hadn't thought about it in a while, not since I'd started working with the kids on the new program. Now my days were consumed with reading journal articles about the strain of different types of arts-related activities on the human body, writing up my research, working with the athletes and musicians, filling ice bags, doing ultrasound therapy, and setting up e-stim. On the weekends, I worked the games, ran my musical fitness class, and then trained Tyson. I ran and meditated and marveled at the mountains and the woods and the freshness of the air. I stretched and climbed the wall in the gym and crocheted hats. I talked to Dad and Astrid and goofed off with Andy and Revi. And everything else, the other moments, the nights . . . those I spent with Jonas. I hadn't thought much about the Red Sox since I'd fallen for him. I couldn't deny that a piece of me wanted that life back, but I had a new life now, or I was starting one here, with Jonas.

"I don't know what I'd do," I confessed. "I had the ultimate job for a few years—I'm not sure I could walk away if I got a second chance." And that was true; I was extremely ambivalent. I wanted to ask him if he would mind if I went back, but it felt too soon and a bit like pressure, given that we'd only been something for a short time and he'd just decided to do the audition.

"Well, it's a big decision."

"And hypothetical. Those are the hardest choices to make," I said. I blew out a long breath. "What about you? If the audition goes well . . . would you leave Monadnock?"

"I haven't really let myself consider it. Best not to get anyone's hopes up, especially since it's unlikely anything will come of it. If I fail, which I probably will, given my track record, I'd rather not feel like I lost anything."

There was so much I wanted to say to him. That I believed in him with every fiber of my being. That if he played in his audition like he had the night of the formal, no one would tell him no. He had to learn to trust his hands again. I could help with that. I knew about visualization and sports psychology. But I wasn't sure how to put the magnitude and depth of my emotion into words. And then there was the tiny, inconvenient fact that the orchestra was in London, and I was tied to New England. If Jonas chose a new beginning with the orchestra, it would probably mean the end of whatever we'd started. Sometimes you can't prepare for the things that come next, so you lean into the edge you're skating on and just try to enjoy the moment. I rested my head on his shoulder.

"You won't lose," I said.

Chapter 35

Finals ended and the campus and all its inhabitants seemed to breathe a collective sigh of relief. The students and faculty who had trips planned raced to leave the campus.

"Have a fantastic break," I told Revi and Andy as I hugged them both tight.

"We're planning on it," Andy said. "They just got three feet of fresh powder. It's going to be sick. The black diamonds are calling my name."

"Sounds amazing," I said. "Wear a helmet."

"Wear a condom," Revi shot back, eyes gleaming. "A SoJo baby would be adorable, but Christmastime doesn't seem like good timing for a not-so-immaculate conception."

Jonas, who was standing next to the sink drinking a coffee, sputtered.

I whacked Revi on the arm. "Ouch. You're like the Incredible Hulk, Soph."

"We're going to spend the holiday with my dad, so no, there will be none of that."

Revi raised his eyebrows. "Whatever you say."

Andy picked up his skis. "Happiest of holidays, you two. C'mon, babe, if I don't get a large coffee from Dunkin's and a bagel in my system soon, I'm going to turn into a monster."

When they'd left, Jonas handed me a mug of coffee. "Are you all packed?"

A shaft of winter morning light sliced between us. I stepped forward into it, nodding up at him. He slid a hand around my waist. I still wasn't completely used to this, but the feeling of his touch on my lower back was simultaneously comfortable and intoxicating and new. He set his coffee cup down and smoothed my hair as he placed a gentle kiss on the top of my head.

"We should probably hit the road then."

Outside, it had started to flurry. Giant, soft flakes floated down around us as we made our way out to the nearly empty parking lot.

"Too bad my Subaru is still out of commission," I said. "The Tesla doesn't seem like the best choice for a snowstorm."

"Maybe we should try your car?" Jonas said. "It's got all-wheel drive, right?"

"And a shot alternator. It's a no-go."

"Just try it, Doyle."

I gave him a look but complied. I unlocked the door and climbed in. I hadn't been in the car since Thanksgiving. Had it really only been a month since Jonas and I had gone to Boston and things had changed so much between us? I put the key in the ignition and turned. The car started up instantly. I turned to eye Jonas. "I don't get it."

"I thought you should have a working car."

"Wait, you got it fixed?"

He shrugged and put on his seat belt. "It wasn't a big deal."

"It is an expensive deal," I said, pulling out of the parking space. "The place I called said it would be eight hundred and fifty dollars." I hit the gas and turned onto the main road.

"Oi, that was a stop sign. At the very least, I'd like to keep my investment in one piece," he teased.

"You really have to stop being so nice to me," I told him. "It's unsettling."

"You're just going to have to get used to it."

I was getting maybe a little too used to it. I didn't want to get dependent on Jonas and his generosity. Last time I'd depended on someone, it'd ended with suitcases in a hallway and me with no place to go. That was history.

"So, have you picked a piece for your audition? Or do they give you an assignment?"

"No, it's my choice. I was thinking about playing 'Winter Wind' by Chopin."

"What's that like?" I asked.

Jonas fiddled with his phone for a moment and then music began to pour out of the car speakers. I didn't know much about classical music, but it started out slow and low and then all of a sudden it burst alive into something dynamic and fast, flitting from super high to low in an instant. "That sounds really hard," I said.

"It's considered a particularly challenging piece, one of Chopin's most difficult etudes, but I've done it before. It requires dexterity and strength, so I thought it would be a good selection to demonstrate that I've overcome my problem, in case there was any doubt."

I nodded. It made sense, but I worried. The health and function of Jonas's hand had improved dramatically since we'd started working together and also during the time that he'd been collaborating with the retraining expert. But the piece sounded impossible to my ears. I reminded myself that he was a world-famous pianist, and if he felt he could do it, then he could. I didn't have the musical knowledge to know what he was undertaking or capable of, but I had faith in him. And that was almost the worse possibility, because it meant he'd go to London and we both knew that long-distance relationships rarely worked out. It had been hard enough for us to come together when we lived in the same apartment. What would hundreds of miles and an entire ocean do?

"It's going to be incredible," I said.

"We'll see. It'll be a lot of work. Hours of daily practice until the audition in March—I'll probably need to participate in your musical fitness class."

"It's pretty hard to get into," I said. "Very full. But I know the coach, so I'll put in a good word."

He lifted my hand, which was intertwined with his, and kissed it. "I've heard this coach is pretty hot."

I raised an eyebrow. "She's not available, sadly. Dating a musician, from what I've heard."

He laughed.

"So, what'd you get my dad for Christmas?" I asked.

He shook his head. "Don't try to change the subject. I want to hear more about the coach's musician. Is he handsome?"

I glanced over at Jonas. In the sunlight, his eyes were a rich maple. There was the beginning of a playful smile at the corner of his mouth and the shadow on his cheek where the crease would form when he smiled fully.

"Very," I said. It was true. His attractiveness was undeniable, but that wasn't what drew me to him. It was the way I felt when he looked at me, the way he took care of things, of me, it was how amazing it was when his defenses lowered and he smiled or laughed. It was the way he felt like home.

. . .

Sommerset Meadows was all decked out for the holidays. There were wreaths on the door, with bright red ornaments and berries on them. Inside, they had beautiful decorations for Kwanzaa and Hanukkah as well. A fire burned in the stone fireplace in the lobby; candles and bows abounded. There were red and green as well as black, blue, and silver everywhere I looked. The place smelled like Fraser fir and gingerbread.

I found Dad sitting in a recliner near a large gold-themed Christmas tree in the library. His arm was still encased in a cast. He was leaning back, eyes closed; my throat tightened at the sight of him. "Dad," I said. He didn't move.

"He can't hear you," Jonas said.

"Dad."

"He's got earbuds in, love," Jonas said, taking my hand and gesturing toward them.

I'd totally missed them and panicked. Jonas squatted down and touched Dad's arm.

"Hey there, Gerry. Merry Christmas."

Dad's eyes opened and he pulled at the earbuds. "You two made it," he said. "Sorry, I was listening to music. The noise cancellation on these puppies is something."

"Glad you're enjoying them," Jonas said.

I flashed Jonas a quizzical look and he shrugged. Dad eyed the bags of gifts we were holding. "You can put those in my room," he said. "I think the festivities should be starting soon."

We headed down the hall toward Dad's room. "Glad you're enjoying them?" I said.

"My gift—well, part of it. I got the delivery notice yesterday."

I stopped in front of the door to Dad's room and eyed Jonas.

"What?" he said. "Your dad really likes music. I got him a subscription to a streaming service and made him some playlists. He's terribly fond of Ed Sheeran."

The stinging feeling in my nose snuck up on me. "Who *are* you?" I asked. "Wait, my dad likes Ed Sheeran?"

"Maybe it's because he's an adorable little ginger like you."

"If you call me a leprechaun again, Voss, I'll hurt you."

"There's only one way you could hurt me, Doyle, and it's not with a cannoli or these tiny little fists of yours." He set the bag of gifts down on a trunk and glanced over at me.

I extracted a package wrapped in penguin-covered paper and set it by the window. "I didn't know my dad was into music. What's the other part of his gift? Is it this?" I asked, holding up a rectangle with a red bow. It felt like a magazine, only thicker. "I know I didn't wrap this one. What is it?"

"You'll see. First, festivities. Then presents. Patience." I wrinkled my nose at him and set the gift down next to the others. Jonas took my hand. "Let's not keep your dad waiting."

I wasn't sure what the facility had planned, but it turned out to be a nice lunch, followed by cookie decorating and music in the activity room. Dad struggled with the frosting; he just didn't have the control anymore, and with his broken arm, he couldn't manage. I bit my lip and tried to hide the fact that I'd noticed. I wanted to reach out and help him, but that would only make it worse. He grew frustrated until he discovered that cookie decorating was Jonas's secret skill and started serving as creative director. "A thin line of black would add some dimension there," he said, gesturing to the baseball player snowman Jonas was creating. "Don't forget the carrot nose." Jonas reached for the small bag of orange-colored frosting.

"Sure thing, Gerry. You've got a great eye."

Dad beamed. "I was known for my eye," he said. "Sophie's probably told you that I used to have quite a reputation for spotting baseball talent."

"He was better than any scout I've seen," I said. "And I've seen plenty. He could've been one of the greats."

"Don't you do that. I try not to think about what might have been. I don't wish things were different. I might've been great, or I might have ruined something I loved with pressure and stress. Instead, I got to enjoy it. I provided for my family. We had those times together. If I'd been a scout I would've been on the road all the time and I would've missed precious time with your mother and you. Besides, I loved my job."

Jonas nodded as he piped a hat that bore a remarkable resemblance to the one that I'd made for Vermont onto a gingerbread man.

"See, Jonas understands. He made a career out of the thing that he loves, so he knows just how miserable it can make you."

"Dad!"

"It's fine," Jonas said. "He's right. There were times when I was quite miserable, but there were moments when I felt happier than I thought possible. The pain was the price I paid for those times."

Maureen came in then. "Everyone ready for some music?" she asked.

Dad gestured to Jonas. "What do you say? You up for it?"

"Dad, no. He doesn't—"

Jonas put his hand on my arm gently and stood up. "You got it, Gerry. I'm not playing 'Little Drummer Boy,' though. I refuse. No matter how many times I'm asked."

Dad laughed, a full, hearty laugh. I hadn't heard him laugh like that in such a long time. "'Little Drummer Boy,' absolute shit. Good call."

"I like that song. Rum tum tum tum," Dennis said.

"I don't think that's how it goes," I said, still wrangling with my confusion over the turn of events. It couldn't hurt, playing in front of this audience; they were extremely supportive. Last year, a local Irish dancing school had put on a performance that did not go well. The space wasn't optimal for them—too small and too slippery—and there were quite a few near misses. One girl slipped on the linoleum and her wig flew off and hit Mrs. Williams in the head, and a high kick came dangerously close to Dennis's face. *I just saw my life flash before my eyes!* he'd shrieked. *It was invigorating.* After that, everyone wanted a turn. *Hey wig-girl, come kick me in the face!*

Jonas sat at the piano, hands poised above the keys. Even though we were just in the activity room of a nursing home, beneath fluorescent lights that reflected off of the linoleum floor, there was an air of drama in the room. The feeling was practically electric. I watched him take a deep breath, and then he began to play. He started off with a few classics—"O Holy Night," "It Came Upon a Midnight Clear"—but then he launched into elaborate versions of popular tunes and classics. I turned my gaze from Jonas to watch the residents. They were enraptured. The thing that surprised me most was how into the music my dad was. He'd never shown a big interest in music before, but there was a spark in his expression that I hadn't seen in a very long time. I reached over and squeezed his hand.

When Jonas finished, everyone clapped. Maureen and some of the other staff brought out eggnog and hot chocolate and everyone was smiling and laughing. I excused myself and headed back to Dad's room. I picked up the largest bag and brought it back to the activity room. Jonas held the bag while I distributed the—okay—badly wrapped packages to the patrons.

"Now what's this?" Dennis asked.

"Nothing much," I said.

He unwrapped the gift—a red beanie with a blue and white pom-pom—almost tenderly. "Nah, that's something, kiddo." He pulled it onto his head and did a little strut in front of everyone. "How do I look?" he asked.

"Gassy," a woman with light purple hair called out.

Dad snorted out a laugh and then tore into his package. He had the same hat plus a matching scarf. Each of the other residents had a different color beanie. In the past few weeks, I'd spent most of my free time, when I wasn't writing my paper or working with the students or Jonas, crocheting. I'd fallen behind schedule, though, so I'd also enlisted the help of Rebecca and some of the student athletes and the kids in my musical fitness class. It was a win-win: they helped me finish enough hats for all of the residents and staff, while the motion of crocheting would help with their dexterity and was also a form of meditation.

"What a sweet girl," Maureen said. "Look, Gerry, we match."

Dad leaned over and kissed my cheek. "This has been the best Christmas I've had in a long time. Great presents, fantastic music, and wonderful company." He beamed. Seeing him so happy was worth more than any present someone could have bought for me. Though it was hard not to have our own tree in the house we'd shared, this was nice. I was glad he'd found a community, that he laughed and smiled here, and had people who looked out for him. That people yelled things about gas. Dad had even found new interests—like music. I couldn't help but think back to the residents' reactions to Jonas playing.

"How long did you practice those songs?" I whispered to Jonas.

"You think I needed to practice some carols?" he said. "I'm hurt, Doyle. I was a world-renowned pianist."

I fixed him with a look. "You are a pianist. A great pianist. But a shit liar."

He sighed dramatically. "Fine, busted. Are you happy? I spent two weeks cramming. My memorizing game is not what it once was." He went to collect the wrapping that now littered the activity room.

"He's a keeper," Dennis said.

"That depends. He's got the looks, but how's he in the sack?" the purple-haired woman, who turned out to be called Doris, said, much louder than I'd have preferred. I choked on my hot chocolate.

Dennis pressed his lips together and raised his eyebrows. "Well, that answers that."

"Jesus, that's my kid you're talking about," Dad said.

Jonas arrived at the table. "Did I miss something? You lot look like you've robbed a bank." He sat next to me.

"Apparently, Dad's friends think you're a catch," I said.

"Just your dad's friends?" he asked and nudged my shoulder with his.

"Not just them," I whispered, leaning close. The corner of his lip hitched up. "Gassy Doris too," I added.

I liked teasing him. But the simple truth was this: Jonas might've been the catch, but I was the one who was caught.

"I better go talk to Doris then," he said. He flashed a smile and headed over to where Doris and some of her friends were starting a poker game.

When Jonas was out of earshot, Dad turned to me. "I didn't

get a chance to give you your present, Sunny. It doesn't exactly fit in a box."

"You didn't have to get me anything, Dad. This time together is more than enough. It's wonderful to see you happy and getting healthy." I gestured to his arm.

"Yup, another four weeks and the doc says this can come off. I never thought I'd be glad to use a walker, but I'm not very good at this wheelchair thing."

"Did you make a follow-up appointment with Dr. Vurgun?"

He nodded. "I went in last week. The new dose seems to be working for now. I'm holding steady. Well, not steady, but you know what I mean. That's off topic. I wanted to tell you about the surprise."

"Okay, let's hear it." I already felt like he'd given me a gift. He'd seen the doctor and was doing okay. That was all I wanted. It was everything.

"I talked to Barry Marsalas—don't know if you know him, but he was a scout for the Sox years ago when I was still working there. He's retired now but he still knows most of the big names in the industry. Anyway, I shared the video you'd shown me in the hospital, the one of Tyson, and he got real excited. He sees what I do—the smooth action, the command and speed. Then some of the other guys he knows got excited too. Anyway, there's interest there. They were also pretty impressed with the work you'd been doing with him and they wanted to come up and see the two of you together."

My cup of hot chocolate trembled in my hands. I set it down.

"You're not serious."

He nodded. "Since when have I ever yanked your chain, Sunny?"

Chapter 36

We picked Astrid up from Logan Airport on our way back to New Hampshire the following day. She was waiting outside the terminal in a full-length fuchsia faux fur over a black jumpsuit and a black aviator cap.

"There she is!" I cried.

"Where?" Jonas said. He searched the crowd as he tried to find a spot to pull the Subaru over.

"She's the Barbie look-alike in pink fur."

"Are those moon boots?"

"Be nice."

"I am nice. But nice goes both ways. Your best friend has assaulted my eyes with her ensemble. I can't be blamed for that."

"Not everyone dresses in gray scale, Jonas."

"I do n—" He glanced down at his charcoal sweater and seemed to think better of finishing his sentence.

"Pull over here."

As Jonas eased over to the curb, I waved to Astrid. She waved back, and before the car had even come to a complete stop, I flung the door open and hurled myself at her.

"I missed you!" she yelled in my ear.

"Me too. I'm so glad that you were able to get away for a little bit so we could have this time together."

"You're letting Jonas drive the Subaru? You never even let me drive the Subaru."

I opened the trunk and put her suitcase inside. "That's because your driving is in line with your fashion sense. How do you get away with these outfits? Is it the general hotness or the fame?"

"This?" She pulled the fur around her and flashed a demure look. "I threw this number together to mess with your new flame." She opened the door to the back seat and sat down.

"The singular Astrid," Jonas said.

"Guilty as charged," Astrid said. "Here for inspection."

"I wouldn't dare."

"Of course not. I'm here to inspect you."

"Astrid!" I cried.

"It's fine, Doyle," Jonas said, "I'm man enough to handle whatever someone wearing moon boots and the pelts of a thousand slaughtered pink Furbys has to say about me."

Astrid broke into a grin. "What are your intentions with my Sophie?"

I turned toward Jonas just in time to see a red flush rise up his neck. My knee bounced with nervous energy. "So, tell us about the next film. What's the script like?" I interjected. I'd been expecting Astrid to be interested in getting to know Jonas better—I had not expected an inquisition.

Jonas reached over and rested his hand reassuringly on my thigh. "Entirely honorable, I assure you."

She was quiet for a long time. Then she said, "You seem like a safe driver. I'll accept that."

We stopped at the state liquor store on the border and

picked up a few bottles of wine. Astrid had the idea for an outdoor movie and we all agreed that it might be fun. On campus, Jonas went out and collected some wood for a bonfire, while Astrid and I assembled the fixings for s'mores. Together, we set up camp chairs, a projector, and a sheet on the side of the dorm near the fire.

Jonas handed me and Astrid glasses of wine. "You're the guest," Jonas said, "so you get to do the honors, Astrid."

"How exciting. What to pick, what to pick—I know. *Titanic*. It will help me get into the mindset for the tragic love story I'm doing that starts production in a few weeks." It was a cold, clear night, but the warmth of the fire and Jonas's hand around mine beneath the quilt and the gooey sweetness of the s'mores made it perfect. I took a sip of wine, enjoying the way it loosened my body and created heat in my cheeks.

Jonas watched the icy water on-screen. He leaned over and whispered into my ear, "I feel like I'm in that water right now. Whose idea was this again?"

"I always have the best ideas," Astrid, who had better hearing than a bat, said. "Did you know that it was my idea for Sophie to come work here?"

"Then I suppose I should be thanking you," Jonas said. "My freezing cold body feels a bit less gratitude about the outdoor movie concept at the moment."

"You know, when Sophie was about eleven, she developed a massive crush on Leonardo DiCaprio. I'm not even sure if 'crush' is the right word. Obsession? Anyway, on Christmas Eve she decides that she needs a giant cutout of Leo. Her mom had no chance of making this happen, of course. But because our darling Sophie bear is such an optimist, she was convinced that Santa—she was like the last kid in our class to still believe in Santa—"

"There's no way! I was eleven!" I interjected. "I was very savvy. I knew the ways of the world. I did not believe in Santa."

"You absolutely did. In fact, you convinced me to write a letter to him, and even though I knew better, I went along with it."

"I don't recall this."

"I still have the letter. I'd be happy to have my assistant dig it out of my storage unit and send a picture. May I continue?"

"I think it's sweet," Jonas said, giving my hand a little squeeze.

"Anyway," Astrid continued, "Sophie has it in her head that this last-minute letter is going to reach the North Pole magically. She tells us all at Christmas Eve dinner—this is before my parents got divorced, so we all had dinner together before midnight mass. She declares, resolutely, that in the morning, she will have her very own life-sized Leonardo DiCaprio. He's going to live in her room and they're going to be happy until the end of time. You can imagine that the parents are struggling. My dad, who was a real piece of work, can't stop laughing, but Sophie's parents look like deer in the headlights, no lie, their faces are just like, shit, how are we going to make this happen."

I hid my face in my hands.

"I get a phone call at six a.m. On Christmas morning. It's Sophie, and she's squealing unintelligibly. I thought something was wrong. Finally, I say, 'Soph, calm down and talk like a human.' She goes, 'Santa brought Leonardo.' I nearly died. Died, I tell you. For a second, I was wondering, 'Does Santa exist? Has every kid at school except Soph got it wrong?' It's a freaking Southie miracle. Sophie's off the wall. She's planning the wedding at this point, Jonas. But I cannot figure out how this happened. It took me three years before I finally discovered the truth."

I smile, because this is the best part of the story, and I know it by heart. But my throat tightens too.

Jonas leaned forward. "What was it?"

Astrid looks at me before she continues. "Her mom stayed up all night cutting cardboard boxes, and then she painted him by hand. She was a really talented artist."

"Seriously?" Jonas asked.

"I always wondered why her hands were covered with paint when we were opening the gifts, but I never put it together," I admitted. "She told me when she got sick. I was really scared, and she said she thought it was going to all turn out fine. I wanted to believe that too, but I couldn't. And she said, 'You always believed in miracles before,' and mentioned Leonardo. She confessed that she'd pulled an all-nighter to make him. Of course, I was like, 'That sort of proves my point, Mom,' and she said, 'No it doesn't. It was a miracle that I finished in time.' And that having a daughter you loved so much"—my voice broke—"that you wanted to stay up all night making a life-sized cutout of her celebrity crush for was a miracle in itself."

Jonas reached out and squeezed my hand. I wiped my cheeks. Astrid got up out of her chair and came and hugged me from behind.

"She was the best," I said.

"She was. You're just like her—the best."

"It's getting pretty late," I said. Jonas and I dumped snow on the fire and we all headed inside.

"You okay?" he asked, pulling the door open for me.

I nodded. "It's nice to remember. Really hard, but nice."

"I can imagine. Your mom sounds like a very special person.

Your whole family, wow—it's shocking, honestly, how utterly wonderful you all are."

I stood on my tiptoes and pressed my lips to his cheek. "You know, you're pretty wonderful. So much so that I would've let you have the door," I said.

"If you really care about me, you'll let me have the shower first. I desperately need to thaw."

"You both are so sweet, I can't handle it," Astrid said. "I mean it. I'm recovering from the inevitable end of an on-set romance with my costar. All this adorableness is too much." She took a swig directly from the wine bottle. "Let's go inside."

"Agreed," Jonas said. "I think my feet are frozen solid."

"See, Mr. Voss," Astrid cooed, "that's what you get for mocking my moon boots. What they lack in aesthetics, they make up for in warmth."

Chapter 37

Astrid left two days before New Year's, and then the phone calls started. Dad had not been kidding about the interest from scouts—at least four were eager to see Tyson pitch and to talk to me. There was mention of inviting him to a showcase.

"They really think I can play, like for real?" Tyson asked as he wound up. He let the ball fly. The sound of the ball thwacking into the glove was thunderous. I resisted the urge to pull my hand from the mitt to shake it. Even after months of working together, I still wasn't accustomed to the shocking sting of the first pitch.

"You can play," I told him. "There's no question about that. What you should be asking is if that's something you want. I know this isn't what your family thinks you should be focused on."

"Do you think they're right?"

I shook my head. "I don't know. I believe in your ability and raw talent as a pitcher, but I also don't want to pressure you."

"Honestly, I can't even envision what that kind of life would be like. Since I was three, I've been playing violin. It's all I've ever known. Sure, I liked to throw, but it just seemed like a party trick, not something legitimate that I could actually turn into a college scholarship or a job or whatever. And playing pro—that isn't even something that exists in my universe."

"Sure, it can be those things—school, pro, endorsements . . . But it can also be brutal and grueling and full of heartbreak. There are no guarantees in sports, just like there aren't in music."

"I guess I wish I had a better idea of what that life is like and what I'd face if I chose something that my family didn't want for me, you know? Before I can even think about it."

I considered Tyson's words. Even though I'd been working with him for months and he was your typical teen in a lot of ways—really stupid humor, obsession with crushes, knowledge of weird social media trends, occasionally questionable fashion sense—he also constantly surprised me with his maturity and pragmatism. It was a good idea, actually. I'd done my best to train Tyson, but ultimately, I didn't know what it would be like to abandon a path that my family had chosen. I'd walked that path until I'd messed it all up. But I knew someone who had experienced that, and he'd come close to having all of the sacrifice be in vain when he'd been cleared to pitch in the World Series with a serious elbow injury— Iwasaki.

"You know," I told Tyson, "I just might be able to make that happen for you. I have a friend, he's pretty busy so he might not be available, but he had a similar situation . . ."

"He's a musician too?"

"No, but his family definitely had other plans for him, and he chose baseball. He's also faced the dramatic polarizations that can happen as a major-league pitcher."

As soon as I said "major-league pitcher," Tyson's eyes widened. "Pro? No shit!"

I flashed him an I'm-still-a-teacher-dude look, so he corrected to a "No way!"

"Like I said, no guarantees, but I'll try."

"What do you think Mr. Voss will think about this?" Tyson asked. Good question. I'd avoided the topic over all of winter break. Dad hadn't said anyone would call for sure; he'd only mentioned significant interest. I'd thought either it would turn out to be nothing or I'd have time to find the right way to broach the subject with Jonas before anyone reached out. I'd been wrong on both counts. I still hadn't figured out how best to tell my dad exactly what had happened with the Red Sox, and now withholding the truth was starting to feel like a nasty habit. What I needed to do was either suck it up and tell Jonas what was going on with Tyson or halt the plans altogether. The only thing holding me back was that this felt like such a critical opportunity for Tyson, if he wanted it—I didn't want to jeopardize it.

After we finished practice, I looked up Iwasaki's number in my phone. It took me a minute to work up the courage. Since the article, I'd worried that he blamed me too, but I took a deep breath, summoned my strength, and made the call.

"Sophie, it's been a long time. How have you been?" There was no trace of animosity in his voice. Relief washed over me.

"I've been in New Hampshire," I said, less glumly than I'd intended.

"New Hampshire's nice. I went to Lake Winnipesaukee once. Are you working with the New Hampshire Fisher Cats?"

"I'm working at a boarding school."

Iwasaki was quiet. "It's because of me."

"No. I would've done what I did for any of the players. I

thought I was making the right call. I know you probably don't agree—"

"You don't understand, Sophie. I meant, it's my fault about your job. But I don't think you were wrong. I wanted to pitch, but I couldn't. I would've lost everything—the game, the series, my arm. I went to a different specialist after the game. They agreed with you. They said that Dr. Pat did something very serious when he said I could play."

"Malpractice?"

"Yeah, that was the word. He's not our doctor anymore, so are you coming back?"

"Oh. I didn't know any of that." I'd thought that the moment when I realized my vindication, I'd feel some sense of elation, but I didn't. "That's probably for the best," I said. "I haven't heard from the team management, so probably not. But actually, that's not why I called you. I've been working with a student here who is an amazing pitcher—a couple of scouts are interested in seeing him. This kid is also a really talented violinist, and his family has a whole plan for him in music. I was hoping that you two could talk. Maybe you could share a little bit about what it was like leaving Japan and not going into finance when your parents wanted you to do that."

"I can talk with him," he said. "I have time before spring training. Then maybe I can go back to that lake."

"It's probably a little cold for the lake," I said.

"It's not as bad as that whirlpool you used to make us sit in."

"It worked, didn't it?"

I remembered the way the athletes would breathe fast and lower themselves into the icy whirlpool. It was a rather unpleasant experience—I never subjected my athletes to things that I hadn't tested myself—but it did the trick. I was going to have to tell Jonas, so I figured it was time to slide into the cold water, even if it stung.

I practiced the conversation in my head several times before I brought up Iwasaki's visit to Jonas. In my visualizations, Jonas saw that I was simply trying to ensure that Tyson had every possible opportunity to have a meaningful life. I'd been preaching the benefits of this kind of mental exercise to the athletes I worked with for years.

Visualizations are bullshit. They certainly don't account for unpredictable, stubborn musicians who have a tendency toward extreme grumpiness.

"I don't understand you," Jonas said.

"It's not confusing. This could be a big career opportunity."

"He just had a big career opportunity. He took first in Menuhin, for chrissakes. Do you have any idea what that means? It will open every door for him. It's what he and his family have wanted and sacrificed for. Do you have any idea how much it costs to get the kind of lessons and training that Tyson has had? How many hours of missed work and school are needed to go to competitions and recitals? To go here? The Browns aren't rich people. His mom works two jobs, and even then, he still needed a scholarship. Travel to that competition? I paid for that. Over the summer, I tutored him for free. I do these things because I believe in him and want the best opportunities for him. You should have heard him, the way he played to win that competition . . . it was some of the most sensitive, brilliant playing I've heard in my lifetime. It was a triumph."

"Okay, but you said he was calm."

"He's a calm kid. He was happy."

"What if Tyson was calm about the contest because it's not what he loves?" I said. "I've seen him truly excited about baseball. I've seen him shout and jump and celebrate. If he doesn't do that with the violin, then maybe he's not doing what *he* wants. Maybe he's doing what's expected of him."

"Being serious doesn't mean that you aren't happy. Maybe he's just demonstrative about baseball because that's what people do in sports, they run around and showboat, acting ridiculous."

"So sports are ridiculous to you?"

"That's not what I meant."

"You know, sometimes I think this thing with Tyson is more about you than it is about him."

Jonas narrowed his eyes. "What does that even mean? I could say the same thing to you. You've basically turned him into a project. I can't believe that you showed the tape of Tyson pitching to a scout."

"It wasn't a scout," I said. "You're overreacting when you don't even have the facts."

"What are the facts? A scout saw his tape."

"My father did. I showed him a video I took on my phone. I thought it would be a good distraction to cheer him up when he was in the hospital after his fall. Tyson is the kind of pitcher that coaches see once in a lifetime, and you know how obsessed my dad is with pitchers. He knew them all. I thought he'd enjoy it and maybe have some pointers. That's all. I didn't know he was going to call his buddies."

"Fine. But it didn't end there. Maybe Gerry made those calls and you didn't intend for those scouts to start calling, but now you want to bring some pro player here to meet him? Can't you see how over-the-top that is?"

"Well, you're obsessed with making sure that this child

prodigy becomes the best, even if it comes at the expense of his happiness. Sound like anyone you know?" As soon as I said the words, I regretted them.

Jonas stopped walking. "You think I'm like my father?"

"No, I don't. You're not. I didn't mean for it to come out like that. I just, sometimes when I get angry, I don't think, I react. I'm so sorry. I shouldn't have said that."

When Jonas looked at me, all of the fire had gone out of his expression. "How did you mean it then? You don't know the first thing about my father, Sophie. I am *nothing* like him. The only thing I ever wanted for Tyson, for any of those kids, is to ensure that they have every opportunity to pursue their passion and that they are safe. This industry—bad things can happen . . . it can break you. I'm trying to keep them whole."

"We want the same thing—I only wanted to help Tyson . . . and you. I—"

"I don't need your help. You push and push, and maybe that's helpful in your job, but I'm not one of your athletes. I'm not some broken thing for you to pity—"

"I don't—"

"And I would never be like him." The hard edge seemed to falter when he said this and something inside of me cracked. He turned and started to walk away from me.

I reached out and grabbed the sleeve of his shirt. "Jonas, wait. What do you mean?"

He stared at the ground. I reached out and gently put my hands on the sides of his face, lifting it just enough so he met my eyes. The deep hurt in them, the tears that welled there, knocked the wind out of me. I had never seen Jonas look like that, not once in the entire time I'd known him. I thought I'd seen his full range—exasperation, elation, anger, annoyance, arousal, joy, fear—but this . . . it was pure, deep pain. It was

shame. Witnessing it, knowing that I'd brought it to the surface with my thoughtless comment, was heart-wrenching.

"It wasn't enough that he took me away from my mom and
everything I'd known or cared about. He forced me to play
from dawn until late in the evening, until my body ached and
I could barely sit up." He closed his eyes. "You know, even now,
most of the time I can hear his voice thundering in my head
when I play and I can't get it quite right or make a mistake."
His expression twisted. "Nichtsnutzig. Good-for-nothing.
Maybe he was right."

A sick twisting sensation in my stomach kept me from
speaking.

"I know I'm not like him, Sophie. But that doesn't mean he
was wrong about me."

"Yes, he was," I said, pressing my forehead to his. "He *was*
wrong, Jonas. Wrong in every single way. He was supposed to
love you no matter what. That's what family is about. It's not
conditional."

He closed his eyes.

"You are so much more than your shortcomings. You're
more than the piano or your talent or your hands."

"I don't know. Without them, who am I, Sophie? I'm not
anything. No matter what I do, I'll never be more than my
failure; I'll never be enough."

I wondered what he felt he wasn't enough for—his family,
Tyson . . . me?

"Jonas, I wouldn't be better off without you. I know what
it feels like to define yourself by one thing and then not to
have it anymore. My situation doesn't come close to yours, but
I realize it's devastating. But none of us is just our job or our
team or music or any single thing. We're more than that.
We're a million dreams and possibilities. You are."

"You only think that because you don't really know me."

"I might not know everything that's happened to you or your entire history, but I am ready to listen to whatever you're willing to share. And I know exactly who you are now. You are the man who has inspired those kids, you've helped them believe in themselves, helped them grow. You've given them a safe place to figure out what they can be and who they are. You've done that for me too, whether you know it or not." I pressed my lips to his cheek. "I didn't really get it before. Now I see why you've been trying so hard to protect Tyson from everything, including losing what you lost. But, Jonas, don't you think he deserves to be free? He should have the chance to find out what brings him to life. Maybe it's the violin and maybe it's baseball, or maybe it's something else entirely. We owe it to him to let him find out."

I bit the inside of my lip to keep it from trembling. "And you aren't good-for-nothing. You're just good." I had to stop to take a breath before my emotions spilled over. I lightened my tone a bit. "Mistakes are part of living. They're what make us human and unique. They're why chocolate chip cookies exist."

Jonas was silent for a few moments. Finally, he said in a low voice, "I don't know if I can do the audition."

"That's okay," I told him. "You don't have to do anything anymore. Whether you audition or don't . . . it doesn't matter. You should do what you want. And know that it changes nothing for me. I'll still feel the same way about you." I raised his hand to my lips and kissed it.

The sun was dipping low behind me; it caught the flecks of mossy green in Jonas's eyes and made them look almost golden. I'd waited for my whole life to see the kind of look they held, inquisitive and full of promise, to see myself reflected in them. "Really?" he asked.

He looked so hopeful and vulnerable. I thought about how my words had wounded him, and how his father had hurt him and split him and his mother apart, and about my own dad who had given me my love of sports, let me dance on his feet when I was small, and always supported me, even when we'd both lost Mom and he was drowning in grief, and how much they'd loved each other. I loved Jonas, I realized in that moment. And I wanted to tell him, but it felt like too big of a risk. I didn't want to say it and have the memory linked to his painful past. And then there was a possibility that if I uttered those words, the ones I hoped he wanted to hear, that he might not audition at all, since success would mean we'd have to go our separate ways. Even if only one sliver of him wanted to reclaim his life as a concert pianist, I couldn't hold him back.

Really? he'd asked.

I nodded, pressed my hand to his chest, and said in a soft voice, "Really."

Chapter 38

After the argument and my revelation about my feelings, I wanted to believe we were fine. Sometimes being optimistic is great; other times, you're just wrong.

He'd said he understood that I hadn't meant for things to get out of hand with Tyson and the scouts. He seemed to appreciate that neither of us should impose our own values on Tyson—ultimately, no one, not even Tyson's family, would be able to make the choice for him. He had options, and we should support him, but the decisions that would impact his life were his alone. He also said he knew I never would've made that thoughtless comment about his father if I had known the complete truth, that not knowing wasn't my fault. But still, I blamed myself.

Jonas retracted from me, into himself, into the music building. He morphed back into that sullen, nearly silent guy whom I'd met back in the fall. He ate less. When he got back from practicing, he didn't come to my room and slide under the covers beside me to drape his arm over my hip.

I thought we were okay, but we were not. And worse than

that, he was not. I didn't know what to do. I'd helped him re-cover from his physical problem, but I had no idea how to help him with the emotional pain he was suffering. The world seemed to have shifted off of its axis. Spring was coming and my time at Monadnock was ending and I worried that this amazing thing between us might come to a close too.

This seemed like another time when I'd wanted to help and it all fell apart, like the World Series, and I didn't want it to end like that had.

I couldn't talk to Andy and Revi; I wasn't sure they would understand. But Astrid might. I told her what I'd said and what Jonas had told me about his father.

"I don't know, Astrid, I'm pretty sure that I really messed things up. This feels like before. Do you think it's because that conversation he and I had opened up too many memories about his dad, and he's not in a good place, or maybe his feel-ings have changed . . . ?"

"The little he's shared about his dad sounds like abuse, honestly, Soph. It can re-traumatize a person if they're not in the right state to process it. Our minds have these amazing defense mechanisms built in to protect us from things that are too much to handle. If Jonas had buried those memories deep and then your argument forced them to the surface, he could really be struggling. I guess we never really know what some-one else is thinking."

"He's clearly suffering and he's closed himself off . . . what have I done?"

"You didn't do anything. Sophie, you are the last person who would ever cause someone harm. It's like your mission in life is to prevent anyone from getting hurt. But you can't save everyone, especially if they don't want to be saved. If he's pulling away, you may need to just let him."

"Is this one of those rubber band, cave things from *Men Are from Mars*, where the guy needs the space to work through stuff and then he comes back even closer to you? Or are you suggesting that we break up?"

"I'm not suggesting anything. And it might not be about the conversations. He has the audition coming up, right? Could be this is just how he gets before a performance. The stakes are pretty high."

"They are. But, Astrid, I don't want to lose him."

"I'm sorry. I don't have any good advice for that situation. I can tell you what I do when I feel like the person I'm with is pulling away from me, but I would like to offer the disclaimer that it isn't recommended or healthy, according to my therapist."

"Let's have it," I said. "At this point, I'd try anything to not feel so helpless."

"I'm not proud, but I spy on them," she said. "I'm going to blame that one on my dad. When he thought my mom was cheating, he actually took me with him to the private investigator's office."

"Okay, I know I said I was willing to try anything," I said. "But I thought you were going to describe some sort of mind-bending joint meditation or intensive striptease routine."

"Sounds like you've got lots of alternatives. You'll sort it out. I honestly think you two have something special. So put your Boston pants on and fight for it, and if it doesn't work out, I'm just one plane ride away."

Later I thought about what Astrid had said about her special approach to relationship problems and wondered if standing in the very back of the recital hall loft in the darkness while Jonas practiced constituted spying. I was looking for a sign, or something to make me feel like what we'd had together wasn't about to slip through my fingertips while his glided over the piano keys. I closed my eyes and let the music wash over me as it drifted through the concert hall. I recognized the melody as the one he'd played in the car—the Chopin piece he was planning for his audition. Except he was playing a single passage over and over, as if he was stuck. I didn't remember fully how the piece was supposed to sound, but there was a strange dissonance that happened right before he started over each time. Finally, he stopped. He was still for a time, three slow breaths in and out, and then he sprang to his feet, snatching his music up and hurling it into the seats. The papers floated down like giant flakes of confetti, and he dropped down to the bench. His elbows pressed the piano keys, making a horrible sound as he put his head into his hands. My throat got full, and my hands ached. Something was wrong. Playing for therapy or at the holiday party had made Jonas feel good— I could tell by the way his eyes twinkled, how tall he became with his chest and shoulders lifted. Afterward, a smile or laugh came easily. This was nothing like that. I snuck back out the way I'd come in and returned to the apartment.

Up until now, I hadn't watched any video footage of Jonas. I'd been tempted, of course, to see what his career had been like, but it also felt like something private that he wouldn't have wanted me to see. Like watching replays of the worst baseball injuries or horrible Formula One crashes, it wasn't something I wanted to view. After seeing him on that stage looking so desolate and dejected, I looked. I consumed video after video, as if seeing him in concert was food after a long hunger strike. Then I found the one. There was something tense about the way he carried himself even when he walked out onstage and sat at the piano. The camera had been zoomed in tight on him, so when he made the mistake, I actually saw his face contort. He flinched. It was so obvious that his body anticipated some kind of punishment. It didn't come, of course—he was on a public stage—but he didn't recover after that. His play became tentative, careful, without the same kind of energy and passion as before. He was terrified.

I looked at the title of the video.

Piano phenom broken by Chopin's Etude Op. 25, No. 11, "Winter Wind."

The exact piece that he'd selected for his audition and had been playing nonstop for days.

Oh, Jonas, what are you doing? I thought.

The door to my bedroom opened, and I swiveled around. The look on Jonas's face cut straight through me. His wide eyes, the deep parallel lines between his brows. I closed my laptop.

"You've seen it then," he said.

"I'm sorry. It's not what you think."

When he spoke, his voice was taut. "It's exactly what I was afraid of."

I shook my head. "No, it isn't. I promise. I was worr—"

"It is, Sophie. I can't fucking do it," he said. He sat on the edge of my bed and I moved to sit beside him. He closed his eyes. "I thought I was better but I'm not. I've played it a thousand times and the mistake keeps happening. I can't do the final climax . . . not at speed anyway. My hand's too fatigued."

"Are you sure you're not pushing yourself too hard? You just regained your dexterity—the amount you've been practicing, it's too—"

"Four hours is nothing compared to what I did as a child," he said. I winced. "It's not that. It's me. I don't have it in me. I'm just going to call Roy Sampson and tell him that I'm not coming. I knew this was a mistake."

I took a deep breath. "Jonas, why are you trying to play *that* song? You could choose anything else. Why?"

"I feel like Sisyphus rolling that stone up a mountain. 'Winter Wind' is my mountain."

"So you're punishing yourself?"

He shook his head. "It's not that . . . I don't think. I just—I have to get to the top to believe in myself again. I need to know that I am capable of beating it. It's the only way that I'll know for sure, that I'll be able to prove to myself and everyone that I'm back. Otherwise, I'll always wonder if another night like that is waiting for me."

"But it's the hardest piece, right? No one would expect that you had to play it."

He frowned. "It's not the hardest. It's the hardest for me."

"Okay, then don't play it."

"It's not that simple."

I rotated to face him.

He took a breath before he went on. "Every single night after it happened, I heard those notes—my biggest mistake— ringing in my ears. My father taunting me; his footsteps as he walked away without uttering a word. The only times since it happened that I didn't hear them are the nights I've spent with you. I need them to stop, Sophie. I want to be free from this torment on my own terms. You can't be the thing that keeps the memories away. What if you're not there?" He looked at me, pleading. "I can't need you the way I do. Every moment it's there in the back of my mind."

I reached for his hand, but he withdrew it. "What's there?"

"I'm not good enough." He swallowed. "If I can't be what I was, I'm nothing." He looked at me then, his eyes shining with tears, and my hands ached for him. "You deserve more than nothing. You deserve everything."

"So do you."

He shook his head. "This was a bad idea. I've been wasting your time and distracting you from the work you need to do to get your job back. Honestly, you'd probably be better off without me."

The air rushed out of my lungs, but I managed to collect myself. "I don't think that. I think being with you has made my life better and so much happier than I knew I could be. It doesn't matter what happens—I'll still think that I'm better off with you."

He twisted his hands together but didn't say anything.

"Do you know how many times the Red Sox have won the World Series?" I asked him. "Eight times. They won in 1915, 1916, and 1918, and then they didn't win again until 2004. Almost ninety years without another World Series win. And this year, they lost . . . because of me. But the city, their fans . . . never gave up on them. We loved them when they won, rushed into the streets, dancing and singing and going wild, celebrating them until morning, and we cried with them when they lost. They are the best, Jonas, and even they fail more than they triumph when it comes to proving it. We all do. That's the nature of things. When we lost the series this year and everyone blamed me, I was crushed. My heart was broken. But I told myself the same thing I do every time I encounter something devastating: there's always next year, next game, next time." I reached out and pressed the palm of my hand to his cheek. "There's always another chance."

"You really believe that?"

I nodded. "I do. I believe that you're going to play beautifully again and I think that next year, the Red Sox are going to win the World Series. Maybe I won't be working with them when they do, but I'll have my chance to get back into the

MLB. And you'll have your chance to play packed houses and move people with your beautiful music again. I'm sure of it." I wrapped my arms around him. "Honestly though, what I think doesn't matter, because this isn't about me at all. It's about you. *You* have to believe it too."

He lifted his head to meet my eyes. "What if I can't?"

"Keep trying. And until you do, I'll believe for both of us."

Chapter 39

Iwasaki arrived to meet Tyson at the beginning of February, right before the Red Sox pitchers were due to leave for spring training in Fort Myers. A heavy quiet had settled between me and Jonas after the day I'd seen him rehearse, and I was eager for the distraction. Iwasaki pulled up in front of the field house in a bright red McLaren just after noon on a Sunday. I derived an extreme amount of glee from how Tyson's jaw dropped; he failed to hide his mouth with his fist. "Coach! What kind of car is that? I've never seen one like that before."

I'd seen every kind of car imaginable back when I was with the team. Ferraris, Lamborghinis, custom Corvettes and Range Rovers, Bentleys—if it was a luxury vehicle, chances were a player owned it. When you made twenty million dollars or more per year, you could afford it. Most players had more money sitting in their garages than Dad and I had sold our house for.

Iwasaki looked good. His black hair was a bit longer, but he otherwise hadn't changed in the off-season, except for the absence of that tight, pained expression that he'd worn after his injury. He seemed unburdened, moving with ease as he climbed out of the car and jogged over to us. He hugged me, and then shook Tyson's hand.

"This is incredible," Tyson said. "Kenta Iwasaki, holy shit. Sorry. Just, this is unreal."

"It's nice to meet you, too," Iwasaki said. "Sophie told me that you are a pretty good pitcher. You want to throw?"

Tyson beamed. "Really? Yes!" He ran to get his glove, and Iwasaki pulled his Red Sox duffel out of his trunk. "So, you all ready for the Grapefruit League?" I asked.

Iwasaki nodded. "I'm feeling good." He straightened and flexed his elbow a few times. "Pain free. I had a plasma injection before the holidays, and the new doctor said my last MRI looked good."

I held the door open for him. "I'm so happy you're doing well."

Inside, Tyson was warming up with the routine I'd taught him. "That looks familiar," Iwasaki said. "You taught him well." He pulled his own glove and a ball out of his bag and jogged over to Tyson. I sat on a bench while they tossed the ball to each other, gradually increasing the speed and force of their throws, chatting as they hurled the ball at each other.

After a while, Jonas came and sat beside me.

"Hi, Doyle," he said. "I thought I'd see how the meeting was going?"

I lifted my chin a little toward them. "What do you think?"

Across the way, Tyson was grinning and talking animatedly about something.

"Tyson looks happy," Jonas said. "They throw almost the same."

"It's uncanny, actually. Iwasaki is probably the best pitcher in the league when he's healthy, and Tyson's matching him. I don't know how he does it—it's like he was born for this."

"That's how it seems when he plays the violin."

I nodded. I'd heard Tyson play, seen the dreamlike expression, the absolute command he had over the instrument, over the listeners. I had to agree. "I suppose sometimes lightning does strike twice."

Jonas reached over and tucked a strand of my hair behind my ear. "Sophie, listen—"

"Coach Doyle," Tyson hollered, "we're starving. Time for a late lunch?"

"Sure."

We walked down the hill to The Grind and ordered food. A couple of people who were having coffee at a table by the window recognized Iwasaki and started snapping pictures with their phones. He gave them a little wave but saved his attention for us. Tyson had worked up the courage to ask about what it had been like for Iwasaki to leave his family and the future they'd planned for him.

"It was very hard. They were sad and angry about my decision, and they didn't want me to leave. I was very lonely here when I first came. I wanted them to be proud. They were not in the beginning. They wanted me to take over the family business since I am the only child. It took them some time. But now they are my fans." He took out his phone and showed a picture of his parents in matching Red Sox jerseys and smiles.

"So it got easier?"

Iwasaki nodded. "This sandwich is delicious. It is still very hard sometimes, if I am being honest, but I love what I do. I love baseball, so I can get through the hard things."

"You don't regret your choice?"

"No. I miss my family, but I feel honored that I get to do what I was meant to do."

Tyson's head bobbed as he processed the information. I noticed Jonas picking at his food. He was listening to Iwasaki.

"Can I ask you something?" Jonas said.

"Of course," Iwasaki said.

"What if you couldn't pitch like you once could? What would you do then? Would you still feel the same?"

Iwasaki looked thoughtful. "I wouldn't regret this. I wouldn't stop. I would keep going with what I *could* do. That is my only choice. I hope I don't have to deal with that for a long time. I know I came close to it, but that didn't happen because of Sophie. She knew I shouldn't pitch, and she didn't let me do something that would have ruined my chance to keep playing."

Jonas turned to me. "She's pretty special."

Iwasaki grinned. "Yes."

Tyson took a slurp of his orange soda.

The woman who owned the café stopped by and asked Iwasaki if she could take a picture with him in front of the restaurant for their social media pages. Iwasaki agreed, and Tyson offered to take it. They strode off toward the front of the restaurant, and I realized they were the exact same height. Uncanny.

When we were alone, Jonas turned to me.

"Are you still mad at me about inviting him to talk to Tyson?" I asked. "I know that—"

"You're sort of amazing, Doyle."

"How's that?"

"You were right about this—Tyson needed this opportunity,

and honestly, it seems like I did too. I've been stuck in the past. It follows me around like some kind of rainstorm I just can't escape. I've been fixated on getting back what I lost—the ability to play the hardest things, the songs only a handful of people in the world can play flawlessly—but really I think I *was* punishing myself, as you said. I love to play. It never mattered what I played. It was the act of making music, of doing the thing that I felt I was meant to do, that made me happy. It was the one thing that made me happy. Until I met you."

He twined his fingers through mine, and I squeezed my eyes shut for a second to keep the tears from spilling. I lifted my shoulders. "What does that mean?"

"I'm going to do the audition. I'll play something else, not 'Winter Wind.'"

"Are you sure?"

"I never cared much for the bloody cold anyway."

I leaned over and kissed his cheek. "Very good point," I said.

"Besides, I'm feeling lucky."

"Oh yeah?"

"I mean, I ended up with you as a roommate and now we're . . ." He pressed his lips to my hand. "A bloke doesn't get much luckier than that."

Chapter 40

In February, I submitted my article to the *American Journal of Sports Medicine*. The Red Sox headed to Florida for spring training. Jonas went deep into practice mode on Chopin's Nocturne Number 3 in B Major (Op. 9 No. 3) and "Pern" by Yann Tiersen. I watched the games and practices as the winter sports seasons came to a close. I continued my efforts with the musician athletes and Jonas started working with the school orchestra on preparing their spring concert. We waited for the campus to thaw. News of college acceptances started to trickle in. The date of Jonas's audition—March 14—drew near. I planned to drive him to Boston and then take him to the airport for his flight to England. Andy and Revi were taking a group of students on a service trip to San Salvador, where they would be helping rebuild after a devastating hurricane and putting on arts performances for the local children.

"Hey, Jonas, we got you a little something for luck," Andy said. "It's in the kitchen."

"Are we supposed to say 'luck'?" Revi asked. "Maybe we say the gift's for leg breaking? You know, like 'break a leg'?"

"Not in front of Sophie," Andy said. "She's still traumatized after the hockey incident."

Jonas set the sweater he'd been folding on top of his suitcase. "You didn't have to do anything. But I'll take all the luck or legs I can." He followed Andy and Revi to the kitchen.

"I don't see anything," he said.

They sang a little fanfare and then parted, revealing a small red appliance shaped like a circle.

"That's great, guys," Jonas said. "What is it?"

"It's a Mickey waffle maker," Revi said. "Best waffles in the universe, and you can take it anywhere you go. We all know your favorite breakfast."

Jonas reached over and opened the lid to see the design inside. His expression brightened. "Breakfast *is* the most important meal of the day. Thank you."

He hugged Revi and then Andy in turn, clapping them each on the back. "We'll be cheering you on," Andy said.

"And if you decide not to go through with it, we've got extra spots in Puerto Rico and no judgment."

I hugged the guys too and then they left, dragging their suitcases behind them. I eyed the waffle maker. "What do you think? A lucky waffle breakfast before we head south?"

Jonas grinned. "I thought you'd never ask."

We ate our waffles drenched in real maple syrup silently. Jonas had told me that quiet was best before performances, so I tried to honor that and contain the hundreds of thoughts that swirled around in my mind. I wondered who was more nervous, me or him. We washed the dishes, a slow dance of soap bubbles and sponges, fingers meeting on a damp plate, drying with a towel, until all signs of our meal were erased from the kitchen.

"You ready?" I asked him.

He picked up his keys from the counter. "Not quite. I'm

prepared, but I'm not sure I'll ever feel ready to be up there again on the stage."

I nodded and squeezed his hand. He pressed the keys into them. "You feel like driving? I slept like shite last night."

O ur itinerary in Boston was simple: visit with Dad; dress rehearsal with Elliot Moore, Jonas's acquaintance who'd just been appointed the new conductor for the Boston Symphony; and then the airport.

Dad looked good. He was clean shaven and wearing a light blue polo shirt that brought out his eyes. I wondered if Maureen had helped him with the buttons.

"My two favorite people," he said when he saw us. He held his arm up. "Look, no cast."

"That's great, Dad. You seem well."

"I am. I'm doing a new kind of therapy that seems to be helping me recover after my broken arm. The PT gave me some kind of stretchy tubing that I'm using to get my strength back. Dennis and Maureen helped me get all polished up for your visit."

"You clean up well," I told him.

"And what about you? You feeling okay about your big adventure?" he asked Jonas.

Jonas pressed his lips together and gave an unconvincing bob of his head.

"Sunny," Dad said, "can you give me and Jonas a few minutes?"

"Sure." I rose from the couch. "Maybe I'll go to the dining room. Want anything?"

"You know, I thought I heard Maureen say something about bringing in her famous soda bread. If there's some of that, I'd love a slice."

I looked at Jonas. "None for me," he said.

"You're making a mistake, son," Dad said. "Best soda bread you've ever had. Authentic Irish."

"I do like Irish things." He winked at me, and I left the room with a bounce in my step. I paused outside the door to tie my shoe.

"Sunny tells me that you're going to play for the Boston Symphony director."

"Just casually. Elliot's a friend of a friend. He said he'd listen to me before my London audition to see if he could provide anything helpful. It's kind of a chance for me to get my nerves out, I guess."

"Are you nervous?"

"More than I could possibly say."

"Well, if it gets really bad, just—"

"Picture the audience in their underwear? I've tried that, and I can't say that I recommend it."

"No, son, I was going to say pretend like you're in the rec room playing for us. You've got a whole bunch of fans who love your music. You think we care if you make a mistake? Safe to bet none of us would even know."

"Thanks, Gerry."

"Just don't picture us in our skivvies, okay? That might have a less than calming effect."

Jonas laughed. "I solemnly swear not to picture any of you in your underwear, even Doris," he pledged.

"Great. Now that that's settled, I want to talk about you and my Sophie."

I finished the double knot and continued on my way down the hall. I wasn't sure what my dad or Jonas was going to say, but I was past my spying phase.

Chapter 41

I'd planned to visit the planetarium while Jonas was per-forming a mock audition and catching up with his friend, but at the last moment, Elliot Moore called my name.

"Sophie, you're welcome to stay and watch," he said.

I glanced at Jonas to see if he would mind, but he dipped his chin, and I followed them into the concert hall. "I have to confess, I've never been here before. It's beautiful."

"The best view is from the balcony," Elliot Moore said. He gestured toward the route to the stairs, and I smiled as I made my way in that direction. I gave Jonas a little wave. He headed toward the stage as I settled into a seat in the front row of the balcony. I wanted to be able to see him, his hands moving over the keys, the dreamlike expression he exhibited when he was really playing, not just thinking about the technique. There was a warm spotlight on him, and my heart squeezed in my chest as he lifted his hands just above the keys and then began to play. I'd thought the pinnacle of achievement was hitting a home run, pitching a perfect game, winning the pennant. I'd been wrong. I realized those things were incredible, and rare.

But what Jonas was doing? It moved me; it changed something inside me. I felt it in the goose bumps that raised on my skin; in the thundering of my heart, which seemed to change pace with the rhythm of the music; in the elation that made me feel as if I were soaring above the clouds one moment; and in the shift and sinking of sorrow the next moment as the mood of the music changed. I wasn't sure I took a breath the entire time. I'd been so completely immersed in the music, the world had ceased to exist. It was a double play, a line drive that just keeps going when the game is tied in the final inning, at turns painful and then sublime, the entire depth and breadth of what we're capable of experiencing in a game or a piece of music or a life-changing moment.

Even when it was over, the notes still resonated on my skin and rang in my memory. I descended the stairs in a slow-motion haze. When I reached him, I was still processing what I'd experienced. I pressed my hand to my cheek to bring myself back to the present and found my skin wet—I hadn't realized I'd been crying. Jonas turned to greet me, and I watched his face. It had been wonderful, brilliant even, hadn't it? To me, it had been perfect.

"What did you think?" Elliot asked.

"I can barely find the words," I said.

"Masterful," he volunteered. He gave Jonas's upper arm a squeeze. "You know, most people don't come back. They share their gift with us for a certain amount of time, and then when it ends, it's over. Not you, my friend. If you play like that for London, they'd be fools not to ask you to join them on the spot."

I slipped my hand into Jonas's. He thanked his friend, who excused himself to make a call, and then turned to me. "Did you hear what I did? Did Elliot just say what I think he did?"

I smiled. "You must know how brilliant you were. That was the most beautiful music I've ever heard in my life."

"I was so nervous, I thought I was going to black out."

"I would've never known. You looked at peace while you were playing," I told him. "How did you calm yourself? Did you use the underwear trick or something? Was it the lucky waffles?"

He shook his head. "Not a trick, not waffles—though they were delicious. I simply glanced up at you in the balcony, took a deep breath, and told myself that today, at that moment, I was only playing for you, Sophie."

I wrapped my arms around Jonas and rested my head against his chest. "We should celebrate. How about an early dinner?"

He nodded. "Yes, Elliot was telling me about this place, you might know it—Giovanni's—he said it's really nice. Should we try it?"

I did know it, and for a long time I hadn't wanted to go back, but I thought of the bravery that Jonas had just shown. I told myself that maybe I could be brave too and face that place. It was time to make a new memory there.

Dinner service had just started, so we were able to get a table. We ordered a bottle of Italian wine and house-made pasta dishes. We toasted and then dove into the warm bread, dipping it in rich olive oil swirled with balsamic vinegar. "This place hasn't changed a bit," I said.

Jonas's brow furrowed. "You've been here before?"

I nodded, then took a sip of wine. "I took my dad here to celebrate when the Red Sox offered me a spot on their training team. We were eating tiramisu and laughing about something, I can't remember what exactly, when I first saw the tremor in his hand."

I took a piece of bread, sopped up a bit of the oil with it, and let it melt in my mouth. "To be honest, I haven't been here since. I guess I never wanted to come back after that because it felt like a place where I made a critical error. He hid his hand in his lap and I didn't press the issue. It must've been so scary and lonely for him to keep that secret to himself. To go to the doctors' visits alone. I suppose he had his reasons." I tried to smile.

"I didn't tell anyone when my hand stopped cooperating. Even the people I trusted."

I nodded slowly, thinking about his admission. "Why?"

"At first, I was hoping it would go away. I thought maybe it was just a fluke or something. And then later, I felt a bit like saying it would make it real. I didn't want it to be true. Maybe that was why Gerry didn't tell you."

"What about after that?"

He lifted his shoulders a fraction. "I hadn't been able to fix it. I practiced more and more and it didn't help. I was ashamed . . . and scared. I had no one in my life to turn to, so even though I knew I shouldn't play that concert, I did it. I couldn't think of another option. I walked out onstage practically petrified."

"And now look where you are. You were so fantastic today on that stage, and now you're so close." I smiled at him. "Have you thought about what it will be like?"

"I've been trying not to. I'm not an optimist like you, Doyle. I didn't want to get excited about something when there's no guarantee, but today, I did. I like teaching the kids, but playing is what I was meant to do. I want that life again so badly."

"Did they say when they might want you to start?"

"The season starts in September, so I'd need to go as soon as the school year ends."

I nodded. I'd been hoping for this for him, but as excited as I was, I also felt a sense of dread. The school year's end was less than three months away and then he'd move back to England and I'd . . . I'd what exactly? The Monadnock trainer would be back from her leave soon and I'd be without a job. Again. I consoled myself with the fact that Astrid would be home, her apartment wouldn't be sublet anymore, and I could stay with her until I sorted things out. At least I'd be close to Dad again.

"You're awfully quiet," Jonas said.

"I was just—"

"Here we are, one gnocchi with sausage and wild mushrooms and one pappardelle with chicken, lemon, and parmesan crisps." The server set hot dishes in front of us. He grated fresh cheese on our meals, topped off our wineglasses and our waters, and then departed.

I dove into my food before Jonas could ask me to finish. We were celebrating and I was going to smile and be happy for him, even if it hurt.

"Sophie Doyle? It *is* you. Ralph said it was, but I couldn't believe him—sure didn't expect to see you here. I heard you were living in New Hampshire."

I looked up to face my former boss at the Red Sox, Jim Drake. I dabbed my mouth with my napkin. "Nice to see you, Jim," I said. I wanted to mean it, but it was hard to see him, to make nice, when he'd questioned my ability to do my job and had taken everything from me in a single afternoon. "I *am* living in New Hampshire, actually. I'm just here for a visit."

He stuck his hand out toward Jonas. "Jim Drake. Sophie used to work for my team. Pleasure to meet you."

Jonas met my eyes for a moment. "Jonas Voss. Wish I could say the same."

Jim laughed awkwardly. "Well, this is serendipity, running into you, Sophie. I've just come up from Florida for a couple of days. Spent a bit of time watching Iwasaki. He's doing great."

"That's wonderful." I turned my attention back to my food, but Jim was undeterred. He signaled the waiter, who brought over a chair.

Jonas looked at me again. His expression was questioning, and I imagined he was asking if I wanted him to get rid of Jim. I smiled tightly.

"I saw Iwasaki not that long ago, so I'm glad to hear he's well, but I don't really need an update," I said. I turned my attention back to impaling my pasta with my fork. "I don't work for you anymore."

"Now, that's what I wanted to talk to you about. We made a grievous error letting you go. You were clearly in the right, and we never should've trusted Patrick. I'm not a man who doesn't try to correct my mistakes. So what do you say, Sophie? Will you come back and work for us? We've got an interim head trainer at the moment—Billy Haas, you know him—but he's not you. With a healthy Iwasaki, we've got a real chance at another run at the series, and we want you there for it."

My fork stilled. I looked up at him and blinked, but I didn't say anything. It wasn't that I didn't have anything to say. I had plenty. I simply couldn't make the words come out. Jim seemed to take my silence to mean that I was playing hardball.

"We'd offer you a much higher salary than previously, of course, plus back pay."

I set my fork down. "I'm glad to hear that you realized I was doing my job, and I appreciate the offer. I'm going to have to think it over."

He pulled a card out of his pocket and scrawled a number

on the back. "That's my personal cell. You let me know what you decide. Call anytime. I'm headed back down to Fort Myers in a few days—I'd like to let everyone know if you'll be back in time for the regular season." He stood and returned the chair to a nearby table, then buttoned his suit coat and left the restaurant. I turned to Jonas. "Did that actually just happen?"

"It certainly did. Was it a good thing or a bad thing, though?"

I shrugged. "I don't know. It was surreal, that's for sure."

"Maybe it's good. Like you told me when you were sharing your optimism with me. You said that I'd be playing again and you'd be back in the MLB. We both could get what we want."

"Yeah. That was the plan the whole time, right? Both of us getting our jobs back. That's what we've been working toward."

Jonas nodded slowly, just once. I took a very long sip of my wine. He excused himself to make a phone call, and I sent Dad a text.

See you tomorrow for bingo after the airport.

He texted back.

Can't wait. And share this with Jonas, please. Just in case he actually does need to picture us in our underwear.

I waited for the image to load. It was all of the residents— fully clothed, thank goodness—lined up with signs that had letters painted on them. *Go Get 'Em Jonas!*

I laughed and swiped a tear away.

Chapter 42

I never park at Logan Airport, but I parked the car for Jonas and walked him to security. I savored those last moments together, the feel of my hand in his as we neared the TSA checkpoint line. He paused at the entrance to the queue and turned to me.

"Have you decided about the job?" he asked.

"No. I love the team, and the players, and it would be great to be closer to Dad." *But they're not you. And if tomorrow goes like yesterday did, you'll be in London.*

I closed my eyes. "I didn't expect this," I said. "I mean, I believed it could happen, but I never thought we'd be standing in an airport about to get everything we thought we'd lost." But was the price losing what we'd gained?

"Are you all right, Doyle? You seem sad," Jonas said.

I shook my head and forced myself to smile. "I'm not. I just wish I were going with you."

"Me too," he said, sliding his hands around me. "You're my little lucky charm."

I laughed. "Was that your idea of a subtle leprechaun joke?"

"It made you laugh, didn't it? Then I'd say it was very effective." He brushed his lips over the top of my head. "In all seriousness, I don't want to leave you here, even for just a few days. I love being with you. I love living with you and waking up beside you. I even love your messes and your rotten temper."

"I thought you enjoyed my sunny disposition."

"Yes, you're like a little sun, shining brightly and then incinerating a poor sod who gets on your bad side."

"I've never incinerated you."

"Slightly singed then."

I shook my head, grinning at him. "What am I going to do without you eating all of my waffles and being crabby and sullen and forcing me to clean? I'll be living in a maple syrup squalor."

"Good thing it's only a few days. More than that would be too much to endure."

But we'd have to endure more than that if things went to plan. I'd stayed up late the night before, thinking about Jim's offer and what it meant. If I took it, things would go back to the way they had been. Jonas would return to being a world-famous pianist, and I'd rejoin the Red Sox, and it would be like we'd never lived together. Except for the six-foot-tall hole gaping in my heart. *Could I follow him?* I wondered. The United Kingdom wasn't like Japan or Taiwan or Latin America. They were into soccer, not baseball, and Dad was here. I took a slow breath. I didn't even let myself think that maybe Jonas wouldn't succeed.

Jonas leaned down and kissed me gently. I crushed the fabric of his shirt in my fists until my hands hurt. The airport seemed to slow and swirl around us, people coming and going, reuniting and separating from their loved ones, and I had no choice but to meld myself to him or be torn into two.

"I've got to go," Jonas said finally. "I'll see you soon."

I nodded.

I watched him get in line. He glanced back at me, and I wiped a tear from my face quickly and smiled. I hoped he hadn't noticed. It was easy to track him even in the crowd, thanks to his height and his distinctive hair, the way he moved. The farther away from me he was the more my chest tightened. He waved just as he stepped up to show his passport, and I blew him a kiss and fled the airport before I fell apart.

D ad took one look at me when I showed up for bingo and knew; he'd always been able to read my emotions the same way he could spot pitching talent. "Sunny, what's wrong?" he asked.

"I don't even know where to start," I said, and burst into tears. Dennis looked around uncomfortably and then got out of his seat and scooted off. Maureen set a box of tissues near us wordlessly and retreated. Through jagged breaths, I started at the beginning. "I wasn't taking a break at Monadnock. I got fired after the last game of the World Series. I had to take a job at the school because Patrick thought I'd betrayed him by going against his medical opinion, and he left all my stuff in the hallway with a note. For months, all I've thought about is getting the Red Sox to see that they were wrong and to ask me to come back, and last night I ran into Jim Drake at dinner and he practically begged me to come back. He offered me back pay and a higher salary. I've been dreaming of that exact moment, but all I felt was . . . panic. Jonas is going to get that job in

London. I know it. He's so talented, they'd be crazy not to make him an offer. I was only supposed to be at the school for a few months, just room and board until I figured something out. I was not supposed to end up in a closet room with a piano, a few steps away from a moody musician who would change me and what I wanted from life. I wasn't supposed"—I sniffed—"I wasn't supposed to fall for him. We're both going to get what we want, only now I don't know if I want it anymore. What's a dream job if you can't be with the person . . ." My voice cracked.

"The person you love," Dad filled in. "You love Jonas."

I took a very big breath before I nodded. "I do. I love him."

"Big-time," Dennis said from the table he'd moved to.

"Have you told him?" Dad asked.

"I wasn't sure I should."

"You need to tell him. No good comes from holding back. Did you get anything out of keeping the truth from me, other than a headache and a guilty conscience?"

I shook my head.

"I may be an old man who doesn't know much, but he loves you too, Sunny. I'm sure of it. You've got to tell him."

"How do you know?"

"I've got three reasons. One, he's not a fool. And a person would have to be a complete fool to not love you. Second, you don't teach a gal's old man how to play the piano unless you love her something awful. And third, I used to look at your mom like that, like how he looks at you. That's major."

I'd been reaching for a tissue, but I froze. "Really?"

Dad reached down and plucked one from the box. His hand trembled, but he was able to grasp the tissue and use it to dab my cheeks.

"He looks at you like he's never seen a blue sky before. That's how I felt when I saw her. Before her, my life was gray.

Drab city gray. And then there was your mom, Technicolor, like my very own bit of gold at the end of a glorious rainbow. Magic. I've seen it in his eyes. The way he watches you when you're occupied and you don't notice. The expression on his face when you're not around and he's talking about you."

"What did you mean about teaching you piano?"

"That was my Christmas present. Jonas said he read this article when you were researching his injury; it was about a man with Parkinson's who learned how to play the piano and it helped him. It's not a cure, nothing like that. It didn't give him back anything—and I'm not deluding myself into thinking that I'll get better—but for this guy, it held it off for a little while. Jonas gave me a primer lesson book and he's been teaching me. Do you know I can even play your mother's favorite song, 'Galway Bay,' sort of. Jonas made a simple arrangement and I play the top part, the right-hand part. He plays the left-hand bit. I play it at a snail's pace and get the notes wrong most of the time, but Jonas said it's not half bad. He says my showmanship makes up for my lack of accuracy. Flair. Your mother would have said I have flair."

"I didn't know that."

"He didn't want to trouble you with it. In case it came to nothing. Probably a bit like how you didn't want to burden me with all of the details of your job situation and the incident over in the North End."

"You don't seem surprised."

"Kid, I've lived in Boston my whole life. I may not run around town anymore, but I still know everything that happens here. You think you could get forced out of the Sox and arrested for assault with a cannoli and I wouldn't know? I figured you would tell me when you were ready."

I closed my eyes. "Astrid has a big mouth."

Dad shook his head and laughed. "Just so you don't go after your best friend with a baked good, I knew well before she filled in the details. I know you. Of course you did the right thing looking out for Iwasaki. And it's no surprise that those pricks made you a scapegoat and pushed you out. I didn't have to have a confidential celebrity informant or watch ESPN to know exactly what happened."

"I was on ESPN?" I groaned. "No, you know what—don't tell me. I like to think I've moved past this."

"My point is, you could've told me, Sunny."

"Getting fired and flirting with felony assault with a pastry isn't exactly the kind of thing that screams 'proud parental moment,' Dad."

"If the higher-ups over there didn't recognize how lucky they were to have you, then they didn't deserve you. That's their problem. In fact, I've got a few choice words for them. As for the other part of it, I'm told you saved a renowned musician from getting creamed in a Boston-style bar brawl, so it seems like you're breaking close to even."

"Geez, how often do you and Astrid talk?" I asked, smiling and shaking my head. "She's spilling all my secrets, but the things I could tell you about her . . . you wouldn't believe all the scrapes she's gotten into over the years."

"I know about her scrapes too. That girl really needs to stop getting involved with her costars. She calls me all the time."

"Seriously, are you omniscient?"

"Well, think of me as a father duck. You seem to be surrounded by ducklings who had crappy dads. We know Astrid's was a real piece of work, and I don't know the whole story about Jonas's father, but I'd venture to say that he did some pretty serious damage there too. Least I can do is take them under my wing."

"I had no idea about this."

"It's no trouble. It's nice to be needed. You spend most of your time worrying about me, and I love you for it, but it's humbling too. I'm supposed to be taking care of you. At least this way I feel useful."

"You are useful, Dad. We take care of each other . . . I just didn't want to disappoint you."

Dad squeezed my chin between his thumb and forefinger. It wasn't the same way he used to do it when I was little. He struggled with the tender gesture, but it had the same comforting effect. I smiled. "Nothing you could do would make me less proud of you. Maybe if you'd gouged that fella's eye out with the cannoli, but that's about it. Nothing else you could do would ever disappoint me."

"I don't know how to choose. Do you think I should go back to the Red Sox?"

"I'm not going to tell you, Sunny. Do you want to go back?"

"You're here," I said.

"That's not what I asked you. I know losing your mom was hard on you, and you worry and want to stay close to me because of it. But you can't let that make your decisions for you. I'm not going anywhere anytime soon, and anyway, it's time for you to live for yourself. You should be choosing for you, not for me, not for anybody. So I'll ask you again: is working with the Red Sox again what *you* really want?"

"I thought it was, but now I'm not so sure."

"You'll work it out. And when you do figure it out, which you always do, you'll do what's right . . . and if not, then you'll try again. Like your mom used to say, there's always a next time."

Chapter 43

Two days later, I waited for Jonas at Logan Airport. The day he'd left there'd been a cold snap, making March feel like January. I stood at arrivals with the hat and scarf I'd made him for Christmas and his wool peacoat in my arms. While I scanned the crowd for him, I shifted nervously from foot to foot, equal parts hope and dread filling my core. I'd visualized this—old habits die hard—down to the look on his face when he saw me, the feel of his arms as he embraced me, the sound of our declarations over the cacophony of the airport, but that didn't stop the nervous energy from coursing through me. I'd made my decision; had he made his? I wasn't sure what was going to happen; an emotional home run or heartbreak, both seemed entirely plausible.

And then there he was—tall and elegant and smiling the second he saw me.

He reached down, wrapping me in his arms and hugging me tight. "I missed you," he said. "I have so much to tell you."

"Me first." I pressed my cheek to his chest. "I didn't take the Red Sox job."

"You didn't? Why?" He took a step back and looked at me.

"I love you," I said. "Actually, that's not why, but I do. I had to tell you now—I wanted to tell you weeks ago. I've wanted to tell you every day since, but I didn't want to hold you back."

Jonas was quiet for what felt like a long time. I reminded myself that I was my parents' daughter, a die-hard Red Sox fan, and that meant that I *believed*.

"Would you do me a favor?" Jonas asked finally, his eyes locked on mine. "Would you say that again? The first part? I want to remember exactly the way you sounded when you said it."

I gifted him a slow smile. "I love you."

He leaned down and wrapped his arms around my waist then lifted me up against him. "You have no idea how long I've been waiting for you to say that."

I shook my head. "Seriously?"

"Was that not totally apparent to you? I thought you were astute."

"No," I laughed. "It was not apparent. I'm still getting used to you not hating me."

"I never hated you. Not for a single moment."

"But you didn't like me at first, remember? When did your feelings change?"

"They didn't."

A pang of anxiety made me want to drop to the ground and run, but there was something so gentle in his expression as he looked at me, in addition to the comforting warmth of his arms circling my waist. I had faith—in him and in us. "I've felt the exact way I do now since the moment I met you."

"And how is that?" I asked, trying to keep the nerves out of my voice.

"Utterly besotted." I closed my eyes and shook my head.

"'Like' would've been such an understatement. You really had no idea? I thought I made it clear the night of Winter Formal."

I shook my head. "Did you? I was too overwhelmed by the way you played for me and you setting me on that piano . . . I guess it didn't compute. I can't believe it—you were a total dick to me."

"You don't seem to mind when we're in my bed." His lips curled into a cocky, crooked grin; he looked so pleased with himself.

"Put me down," I grumbled, failing to suppress the smile playing on my lips.

I glared down at him until he set me gently back on the ground and I turned my back to him. "That's not what I meant, you punk. I'm referring to how you wanted me to move out of the apartment, or when you ate all the waffles, and when you saw me in my green dress that first time and said nothing, or how about the fact that you disappeared every Sunday for the past few months and made it seem like you were seeing someone—Oh god, you weren't seeing someone, were you?"

"That's quite a list, love. Where should I begin?" He slid his hands around my waist and tucked his chin over my shoulder. "Okay, you want answers. I'll give you answers. Shall I go in reverse order all the way back to the beginning? No, I wasn't seeing anyone. On Sundays, I've been driving to Boston. Once I was confident enough to play, I thought about how your dad and his friends had asked for music and I'd said no. I'd been too afraid then to embarrass myself. I've been going to play for them. I will not comment on how many times I've been asked to play 'Piano Man.' At least I have something new to listen to in my nightmares."

I wrapped my arms over his and made him squeeze me tighter. "Dad told me that you've been teaching him to play."

"Just a bit after Christmas once his orthopedist cleared him; his neurologist said it was okay."

"And the other things?" Hope was flooding within me like helium; I thought if we didn't cling to each other, I might float away.

"The dress? I couldn't put my thoughts into words. Not in front of the guys—I would've never heard the end of it. But I thought you looked gorgeous. Why do you think I wore a tie to match you?"

"You did?"

"You didn't even notice, Doyle? I'm devastated."

"You're not off the hook yet. You still owe me two explanations. Waffles?"

"You look so cute when you're angry. Plus, I had to stuff my face so I wouldn't have the chance to say all the things that were running through my head."

I rotated my body so I could face him and ran my hands over his hair. "What kind of things?"

"Are you sure you're an athletic trainer and not a detective?"

"Okay, tell me about why you didn't want me here, then."

He closed his eyes and tilted his head back. "You are such a ballbuster. You're really going to make me say it, aren't you?"

"That's me, the ball-busting Boston bitch."

"All right then." He lowered his voice to a near whisper. "I didn't want you to live in the room next to mine because the moment I saw you, I knew that if I wasn't careful, I might fall for you, and I would be done for, completely and devastatingly gone. You can't live next to someone you have no power to resist."

I pulled back a little. "That can't be true."

"I thought that very thing when I discovered you manhandling my piano that day."

I couldn't speak.

"Is it hard to believe someone could fall for you like that?" he asked gently. "I didn't stand a chance."

I swallowed. "So that means . . ."

"It means I'm in love with you, Sophie Doyle, and I have been for quite some time."

The cognitive dissonance of this situation did not escape me, but I felt like I'd won the World Series. I turned around and stood on my tiptoes, grabbing on to Jonas's jacket and bringing my lips to his.

Jonas cupped my cheek in his hand. "You are like a song that my heart has been waiting for. I recognized your melody the moment we met."

"I thought music required pain," I said.

"Not always. Sometimes it's a celebration, and sometimes it's letting go of pain from the past."

I waited for a moment before speaking. "And what about your past?" I asked, tentatively. "How did things go in London?"

He shook his head. "So much happened there, but the most important thing is, I'm not going to be the pianist for the London Symphony Orchestra."

I searched his expression. "Why? Did something go wrong? Is your hand okay?"

"It's fine. It wasn't a hand issue, it was a heart problem. I don't want an ocean between us; I don't even want a wall. I got there, had dinner with Roy, the conductor, and everything was great. He's a nice guy, and the orchestra is wonderful, but it's not the right place for me."

"It's not?"

"You're here. Your dad is here. And I would never ask you to choose. I didn't even do the audition."

I bit my lip, but it did little to suppress the grin that was forming.

"Wait," I said, "you've been gone for days. Why didn't you just come back?"

"Ah, actually, I went to see my mom. It was . . . a bit hard at first, but it's good. There's a lot of things I didn't know. She tried to get me back after my dad took me away, but I was a German citizen and she was not and it was really tough for her. There were legal issues and she just couldn't do it. She tried reaching out to me for years, but my father kept that from me. She didn't know about how he was treating me, but I guess it was a pattern for him. She has a lot of regrets and I think it was really difficult for her to talk about it, but she was so happy to see me."

I nodded. "Of course she was. It's amazing that you visited her. I'm really glad you got to connect with each other again."

"Me too. It will be a long road, I think, but it's good. It's a start. We're going to see a family therapist through televisits to work some things out. She said she'd like to come to the States to visit me sometime. She wants to meet you."

I bit my lip. "That's wonderful. My news isn't big like yours, but I finally told my dad everything."

"I'm really proud of you for that."

"He already knew. I should've known better. I never was able to get anything past him, even when I was a teenager. He had everything figured out. He even knew about our first kiss."

Jonas grinned, tucking a strand of hair behind my ear. "Oh yeah? Did he have spies at the bar?"

"Nope. He doesn't need spies. He has an Astrid."

"I told you that you can't trust a woman in moon boots and a hot pink faux fur jacket."

"Ha," I said. "You love her."

"Well, she is your best friend; I'm willing to overlook a few things."

I grinned at him, and he tucked my hair behind my ear. "So what do we do, now that both of us have turned down our big job opportunities?" I said.

"Actually, I didn't. You know the night in the restaurant? When I had to make a call?"

"Yeah."

"I phoned Elliot. Essentially, I told him that I was desperate to stay in the area and asked if he knew of any other orchestras that might be interested."

I sucked in a breath. I was practically levitating.

"Turns out *he* was."

I stared at Jonas, watching his handsome features transform into splotches of my favorite colors as tears pooled in my eyes.

"I'm going to be in Boston," he said. "But what about you? Can you call the Red Sox back, tell them your situation changed?"

I shook my head, smiling, and used my sleeve to dab my wet cheeks. "It didn't. I know what I want to do, and it's not being a trainer in professional baseball. Honestly, I loved it once upon a time, but I found something I love more. I think I was meant to work with kids. These past months, the athletes, the musicians, Tyson . . . they've been the most rewarding thing I've ever been involved with. I want to start a training center focused on injury prevention for young people involved in sports or music, and I want it to be in Boston, where I'm from, so I can give something back to the community where I grew up, and the people who raised me."

"That's beautiful," Jonas said. "Can I be your first investor?"

I nodded.

"You know what this means," I told him. "We need to start apartment hunting."

Jonas grinned. "I only have two rules."

"Please tell me you're not about to break out poster board and a Sharpie."

"Not unless you push me. Are you pushing me, Doyle?"

I shook my head. We loved to push each other. "All right, go ahead," I said. "What's the first one?"

"No walls between us, ever again."

"I'm okay with that. What's the other one?"

"You can touch my piano anytime you want."

Epilogue

The air is electric tonight. There's a full house at Fenway and it smells like popcorn and cotton candy and magic. It's the night that the Red Sox might win the World Series. In the dugout, Iwasaki is preparing to pitch a perfect game, with a healthy arm this time. My dad's seated to my left, and Tyson, who is decked out in a commemorative jersey and an obnoxious foam finger, flanks my other side. He's back for a brief visit from Indiana, where he's a sophomore studying violin performance and was a starting pitcher on their division one baseball team last spring. I never ask him what his plans are—he's keeping his options open—and tonight, he's just like everyone else here, hopeful.

"We have a very special treat, baseball fans," the announcer says. "Our very own Boston Symphony is taking care of the music on this momentous evening, featuring award-winning pianist, Jonas Voss!"

How Jonas managed to keep this a surprise, I have no idea, but that's him, always surprising me. The whole orchestra is there in their Red Sox baseball jerseys, and within a measure,

I know what they're playing—the version of "Tessie" that Jonas wrote and played for me. But the music appears to come from everywhere. I look at the Jumbotron, which is zoomed in on Jonas, who is smiling so brightly as his fingers dance over the keys. I glance over at Tyson, expecting to find him waving his foam finger, but he's standing on his seat, playing his violin. And then, suddenly, I realize that they are everywhere—Jonas's orchestra from two years ago. The students who were with us when we fell in love working at Monadnock, they're all here. I see Riley on the first baseline, a few rows below us standing on the stairs beside Jamie, who is dancing. I've thought of these students every day since the year ended. Wondered how they were, if Jamie had recovered from his broken leg and been able to dance again, if Riley and Tyson were still smitten with each other, if they were going to form a violin and viola duo and go on tour. To my left I see Andy and Revi in Boston Red Sox–themed Mickey Mouse ears shaking tambourines. Astrid is next to them, sporting a ponytail, a beat-up Red Sox hat, and a plain navy blue fleece jacket that makes her nearly unrecognizable—or it would have except for the moon boots . . . she just couldn't resist. I am so filled with joy, I feel like I might explode into glittering confetti.

I look over at my dad, who is swaying back and forth to the music. "Did you know about this?" I ask him.

"Who, me? I'm just an old man, what do I know?"

As if I'd believe that.

"Man, he can really play, can't he?" Dad says.

I beam. "Yeah, he really can."

"Your mother would've loved this," he says, and we both get a little more than misty-eyed, because it's true—she would have stood on her stadium seat and danced and sung along, and later she would've talked about this magic night for months.

When the music ends, the crowd goes wild. The players race out to the field. I watch for Jonas, waiting for the next song he'll play, but he's not there. Instead, he's making his way to me, a box of Cracker Jack in his hand.

"I seem to remember you having a thing for this particular snack," he says, settling down in the seat that Tyson has abandoned to join Riley below. They're watching us. I peek up at the Jumbotron, just for an instant, where Iwasaki is swinging his arm, doing his ritual final warm-up.

"Oh good," I say. "I'm starving." I rip the box top open and take a mouthful. "The song was incredible, honey," I tell him. "Just as special as the first time you played it for me the night of Winter Formal."

"So what do you reckon, you think it's going to be a good night for Red Sox fans?"

I nod, unable to contain my enthusiasm. "I am feeling incredibly optimistic," I say.

"You know, I'm feeling strangely optimistic myself," he says. "They tell me there's usually a prize in those—is that true?" Jonas asks, nodding toward the Cracker Jack box.

"I can't remember," I admit. "They used to, when I was a kid."

"Maybe you should check?"

"I'm eating my snacks, they're about to start," I say, and pop another mouthful of popcorn.

"Look in the box," my dad says. Did he just wink at Jonas? I turn to Jonas, who is grinning, one of those bright, beautiful, I'm-up-to-something grins. I narrow my eyes at him for a moment before I stick my hand in the box and dig around.

The moment I touch the smooth surface, I freeze.

It's a ring.

I glance up at the Jumbotron, which now displays the batter

who is striding up to the plate, and breathe out a sigh of relief. It wasn't so long ago that I was notorious; I'm not eager to have my face broadcast in front of a stadium-ful of fans.

I pull the ring out of the box, pressing my teeth to my lower lip to stifle a delighted squeal.

Jonas is facing the field, but he leans over a little so his lips are near my ear. I can just hear him over the jubilant crowd. "Sophie Doyle. You are the most exasperating, adorable, optimistic, giving, hot-tempered woman I've ever met. You healed my hand, but what you did for me beyond that was so much more. You brought music back into my life. You restored my faith in myself. From the moment I saw you messing with my piano, I knew, I *knew*, I was done for. You're my symphony, my World Series, my everything. So now, there's one last thing I hope you'll be for me."

I suck in a shaky breath and turn to smile at him, already nodding.

"My waffle supplier."

"Are you freaking kidding me right now, Voss?" I say. "You are so lucky I don't have a cannoli."

He wraps his arm around me and pulls me onto his lap. Those talented hands of his take the ring from my grasp and bring it just to the end of my finger, and I can't help but think of all those times we sat in the training room and entrusted each other with our painful pasts and our hopes for the future with our hands close just like this. He fixes his eyes on mine— his irises look extra green tonight, just like the emerald grass in the outfield. "All right then, Doyle. If not my waffle supplier, then will you be my wife?"

Ahead of us, beneath the shining lights, Iwasaki winds up and lets the first pitch fly. A flawless fastball, strike one.

"Yes," I say.

Acknowledgments

The summer before tenth grade, I moved to a new state. I passed two of the loneliest months waiting and dreading fall, when I'd start as a scholarship day student at a nearby boarding school. What started as a low point ended up being an amazing experience I will always treasure. I made lifelong friends, roamed the tunnel, learned lessons, played sports, and was in a musical, and I'm so grateful. To Kate and the other Tilton kids, thank you for three amazing years and for giving me so much material to work with.

Every day I am filled with gratitude for my husband, Tom, who never ceases to blow my mind with how great a partner and father he is. I love you and our life together so much. To my little darlings, oh how I adore you. I've learned so much getting to be your mom.

I continue to count my lucky stars that I get to work with my brilliant editor, Kerry Donovan. It was so fun to connect over our mutual love of Boston on this one! Thank you also to Mary Baker. I'm so grateful to Bridget O'Toole and Chelsea Pascoe, as well as the talented artists and creative team, who create the most beautiful covers and art for my books.

Sharon Pelletier, my wonderful agent, thank you for everything you do to support my career and my mental stability. None of this would be possible without your guidance and calm emails. Thank you also to the rest of the Dystel, Goderich & Bourret team for your continued support, especially Michaela Whatnall and Lauren Abramo. Thank you to Lucy Stille.

To Elizabeth, Ali, and Mazey, I honestly don't know what I would do without you. You bring so much joy to my life. Toxic Affairs forever. Lynn, Nekesa, Freya, Sarah, Denise, Jen, Jesse, Olivia, Tracy—I'm so glad the writing journey connected us. To anyone I forgot, it's just the exhaustion, I promise. I appreciate you too.

Most of all, I want to thank the faithful and fabulous readers who entrust their hearts to me and the pages of my books. I hope you find the hope and happily ever afters you all deserve.

Play for Me

Libby Hubscher

READERS GUIDE

Discussion Questions

1. When Sophie arrives at Monadnock, she has a rude run-in with Jonas in her new room. How would you have reacted in that situation?

2. Both Sophie and Jonas experienced significant losses before meeting each other. Do you think this contributed to their bond?

3. At times, it seems like Jonas and Sophie are total opposites—she's a sunshine; he's a grump. She likes sports; he thinks they're a waste of time. How are they similar? Can relationships with big differences work out?

4. Sophie discovers that Tyson is both a violin and baseball phenom. If you could be amazing at two things, what would they be?

5. Sophie tries to keep her firing and brush with the law from her dad. Have you ever kept a secret from someone you love?

6. Jonas plays Sophie her favorite song on the piano the night of the winter formal to show his feelings for her. What's the most romantic gesture you've ever been on the receiving end of?

7. Do you think Jonas and Sophie would have fallen for each other if they had met in a different way? Why or why not?

8. Jonas reveals that he thought he might fall for Sophie the moment he found her touching his piano. What moment do you think was the one where Sophie developed feelings for Jonas?

9. The themes of shame and rejection are explored through Jonas's injury, his memory of the performance and aftermath, his refusal to play, and his fixation on playing "Winter Wind." How did Sophie help him move past his shame?

10. Though Sophie and Jonas both gain opportunities to reclaim the dream careers they lost, they choose differently. How much of their decisions do you think were based on their relationship? If you had to choose between the job or person of your dreams, what would you decide?

**Keep reading for
a special preview of
Libby Hubscher's next romance!**

I've made a life out of searching for lost things. Not tonight, though. After nearly two weeks of trekking around the wilds of Iceland in the hopes of unearthing the fabled Skallagrímsson gold and coming up empty, my best friends were forcing me into a laid-back evening in a bar in Selfoss. I'd protested at first, but then Zoey had presented her blistered feet; Gus had muttered something about how this trip was supposed to be a vacation; and Teddy had fixed his deep blue eyes on mine, his expression half pleading, half dare. I caved like a bridge made of tissue paper.

Gus parks the camper van at the edge of a small gravel lot, and we pull on our coats and head into the damp cold toward the bar Teddy heard about from a local while picking up groceries at Bónus. Hlýjar Nætur—Warm Nights, according to Zoey's pocket phrase book—is housed in a squat metal building next to an outdoor outfitter. The interior lives up to its name, with rich wood accents, fireplaces, and a variety of subdued eclectic lights ranging from chandeliers to bare bulbs hanging from the ceilings. It's cozy. We find a nook and plunk down on soft vintage couches.

"Aren't you glad you listened to us, Stella?" Teddy asks, pulling off his hat and leaving his sandy blond hair in disarray. He tousles it back into submission. "This place is perfect."

A small group of women standing nearby eye him. "I'll say," one with a distinctly Australian accent says before clapping a hand over her own mouth. Her companions giggle and then migrate out of earshot.

Zoey scrunches her face. Over the years, we've grown accustomed to having an audience when Teddy is around. The amalgamation of his James Dean looks and charming charisma often proves magnetic. He enjoys the attention, and it means he never has to be lonely, but no one ever sticks around for long.

"What's everyone drinking?" I ask. "My treat."

"Beer," Gus says.

"Vodka on the rocks," Zoey says. She tips her head toward her feet. "For the pain."

"I'm sorry," I say. "I did warn you to break in your boots."

"She feels no remorse," Zoey says, a smile playing on her lips.

"If she's buying drinks, she must feel pretty bad," Gus says. "When was the last time she took us out?"

"Key West," Teddy says.

"Oh yeah," Zoey says. "It was so rough that day, and we were in that tiny boat." She turns to me. "You refused to go in because the metal detector we were towing had turned up something. Gus and I were both so sick. He threw up in the cooler."

The something had turned out to be nothing exciting, just some chain, and I'd spent the rest of the trip trying to atone for the bad call.

"Stella's very focused," Teddy says, draping an arm around me. "And we love her for it. Without her leadership, we'd all have soft hands and no stories. C'mon, vicious leader. Let's fetch the refreshments."

"I do feel bad about Zoey's feet, and Gus having to throw up in a cooler," I confess to Teddy once we're clear of our friends. Once again, I'd been so fixated on the treasure, I'd forgotten that we were also here to have a good time. Ever since the four of us had met in the Outer Banks of North Carolina ten years ago and found a piece of eight that we were convinced was part of Blackbeard's treasure, we'd often come together for two weeks, just the four of us in a new place, hunting down some legend, enjoying each other until we had to go back to the real world. The enjoying part was especially important, since so far our trips had yielded plenty of memories but only a few antique coins, the infamous chain, and a lot of rusted-out trash. But I can feel that we're close to finally finding something big . . . the aching sensation in my hands that started the moment we'd entered southern Iceland is still there.

"How about tomorrow we do something fun and relaxing, and I can make it up to them. Maybe we could head north and visit the Secret Lagoon in Flúðir?"

"Sounds great. And then afterward we can check out Hjálparfoss and see if the gold's hidden behind it. How long have we been friends? You still think you can fool me?" He laughs. "We all know what we're signing up for when we take these trips. I support you. Especially since I've invested half my trust fund in you by now. Honestly, at this point I'm sticking around for my payday."

I bump Teddy with my shoulder. "I'm not sure which part of that is more ridiculous—the idea that you've spent half your money or that you're only here to cash in once we finally find our treasure."

"It's lucky for you that I am so loyal," he says. "Those two would leave you for an all-inclusive spa in the Bahamas first chance they get. They're nowhere near as hard-core as us."

I glance back to where Zoe and Gus are nestled on a love seat. "I don't know about that," I mumble. "They were pretty hard-core last night."

"I think it's nice that they're taking it to the next level after all the years of pining."

"You wouldn't be saying that if you were the one they were bumping into during their sleeping bag gymnastic routine."

I want to be happy for my friends, but I do not think this is nice. I think it is dangerous. Sure, it seems lovely now, two old friends taking it to the next level, but the higher you go, the harder you fall. What if it doesn't work out, and our friend group, this little family of ours, doesn't survive the impact?

"Stop overthinking, Stella," Teddy says, using his thumb to flatten my furrowed brow. "The only trouble with this situation is that we should've gotten two camper vans so neither of us had to be subjected to their amorous activities." He hands me his credit card. "I'm going to hit the bathroom. Can you order me an Einstök white ale? I'll help you carry everything back."

I flag down a woman with pale hair behind the bar. "Can I get a vodka on the rocks and three white ales?"

"Have you tried the Icelandic Doppelbock?" I turn to face the owner of the deep voice, who is slouching on a barstool next to me, picking at the label of his beer. His dark hair is blocking the top half of his face from view, but his unsmiling mouth seems nice enough.

"What's so great about the Doppelbock other than the fun

name and the"—I lean a bit closer to eye the label—"Rudolph the Reindeer gracing the bottle?"

He turns slowly, lifting his face, using one hand to push his hair back and the other to slide the beer toward me. "See for yourself."

His irises are glacial blue, his hair the jet black of a volcanic sand beach. He'd be one beautiful man if it weren't for the defeated expression and shadowy half-moons beneath his eyes that scream of sleeplessness. It's odd, though—he looks like someone I've seen before; I just can't think where. I spend enough time trying to place him that the bartender clears her throat. I pick up the bottle and lift it to my lips. It's malty and chocolaty with a smooth, rich finish . . . and I'm not even a beer drinker.

"You're good," I say to the guy. "That is delicious."

He scoffs, taking the beer back from me. "My editor doesn't seem to think so."

"Can I get two Doppelbocks as well?" I ask the bartender. I hand the extra beer to the man. "You look like you could use a refill. What's this about an editor?"

"I'm a novelist," he admits.

"Really?"

"Is that so unbelievable?" he asks.

I shrug. "It just seems like the kind of career that everyone has in books or movies, but no one actually really does. What do you write?"

"Adventure fiction, mostly, but currently I'm doing everything *but* writing."

"Anything I might know?"

"The Casablanca Chronicles." He says the series title so nonchalantly that I almost miss it. Do I *know* it? I only stayed up for three days straight this fall rereading the whole series.

When Teddy and I found out that the series was over and we'd never learn the fate of the main character, Clark Casablanca, we'd spent an evening drinking Negroni Sbagliatos—Clark's drink of choice—and contemplating ways to compel the author to write one more book. That's why he looked familiar—his author photo on the back of his book jackets.

"I've heard of it," I say. Then, playing it cool, I add, "What's your name again?"

"Huck Sullivan." Frenetic energy fills me. I glance around for Teddy—he would absolutely die. I am sharing a beer with Huck freaking Sullivan . . . I plan to wave Ted over, casually introduce him to my new friend, and let him charm his way into an epilogue, but he's currently engaged in a conversation with one of the women who were ogling him earlier. I suddenly have the sinking feeling that he's on his own mission, and it's more finding himself a solution for the whole only-one-camper-van situation and not convincing our favorite author to revive the series.

I stretch out my hand. "I'm Stella Moore," I say. Huck wraps his fingers around mine, and that strange longing I'd been feeling in my fingertips dissipates in an instant and is replaced by a light tingle on my skin.

"So, Stella who thinks being an author is unbelievable, what do you do for work?"

I lift my shoulders a fraction. "This and that," I say, which is true. To support my summers at sea, I spend the off-season doing property maintenance and moonlighting on fishing boats.

"Very mysterious. What brings you to Iceland, then?"

"You first," I say.

"I guess you could say I'm searching for inspiration," he says. "I have a deadline looming for an outline and chapters for my next series, and I've been dealing with false starts for months, ever since my last Casablanca book came out and the critics tore me apart. Everything I've written since then is awful, trite bullshit. I can barely even look at my laptop, let alone open it. I guess I thought a change of scene to someplace wild and completely different would shake me out of my funk."

"How's that going?"

"Super. So far all this trip has done is make me contemplate switching my profession to sheep farming."

"The sheep are pretty cute."

That elicits a smile from him, and it's just as warm and inviting as I suspected. "Right? I went over to Westman Islands, and I was standing in a field near this cliff, high above the ocean contemplating my place in the world, and one waddled over to me and booped me on the leg with his nose."

"Sounds life-changing."

"Oh, it was. It just didn't cure my writer's block. So that's my story about why I'm here. Now it's your turn."

I wonder if I should tell him. What the four of us do on our expeditions is something that we keep to ourselves. But something about Huck Sullivan makes me want to spill my soul to him. Maybe it's because I've read his books, and that makes me feel like I know the kind of man he must be. Someone brave and trustworthy and authentic. Someone who would find my focus on treasure-searching compelling instead of thinking I was wasting all of our time.

"Believe it or not, I am also searching for something."

The corner of his mouth quirks. "Oh yeah? What's that?"

I press my lips together for a moment, preparing to be laughed at. "I'm searching for treasure."

Something flashes in his eyes, an instant of lightning in

the glacial pool, and it's as if my body has forgotten how to breathe; I have to force myself to take in air. He turns toward me on his stool; his knee glances my thigh. "And how's *that* going?" he asks, his voice full of intrigue. "Are you also contemplating a life of sheep farming, or have you found it?"

I take a slow sip of my beer, a smile playing on my lips as I lower the bottle. I wave him toward me until our faces are only a whisper apart. I make my voice quiet. "So far the only thing I've found is you."

PHOTO BY THOMAS HUBSCHER

Libby Hubscher is an author and scientist. She studied biology at Bowdoin College in Brunswick, Maine, and holds a doctor of philosophy in molecular toxicology from North Carolina State University. Her work has appeared online and in text-books, scientific journals, and literary journals. Her short story "The Unwelcome Guest" was long-listed for the Wigleaf Top 50 in 2018. She lives in North Carolina with her husband, two young children, and a menagerie of pets.

CONNECT ONLINE

LibbyHubscher.com

🐦 EMHubscher

📷 LibbyHubscher

📘 LibbyHubscher

Ready to find
your next great read?

Let us help.

Visit prh.com/nextread

Penguin
Random
House